A DETECTIVE INSPE

BEHIND THE WIRE

JACK GATLAND

Hooded Man MEDIA

INFORMATION & PRODUCTION & PUBLICATION

Published by Hooded Man Media.
Cover photo by Paul Thomas Gooney

First Edition: December 2021

PRAISE FOR JACK GATLAND

'This is one of those books that will keep you up past your bedtime, as each chapter lures you into reading just one more.'

'This book was excellent! A great plot which kept you guessing until the end.'

'Couldn't put it down, fast paced with twists and turns.'

'The story was captivating, good plot, twists you never saw and really likeable characters. Can't wait for the next one!'

'I got sucked into this book from the very first page, thoroughly enjoyed it, can't wait for the next one.'

'Totally addictive. Thoroughly recommend.'

'Moves at a fast pace and carries you along with it.'

'Just couldn't put this book down, from the first page to the last one it kept you wondering what would happen next.'

Before LETTER FROM THE DEAD...
There was

LIQUIDATE
THE PROFITS

Learn the story of what *really* happened to DI Declan Walsh, while at Mile End!

An EXCLUSIVE PREQUEL, completely free to anyone who joins the Declan Walsh Reader's Club!

Also by Jack Gatland

STANDALONE BOOKS

THE BOARDROOM

AS TONY LEE

DODGE & TWIST

For Mum, who inspired me to write.

For Tracy, who inspires me to write.

CONTENTS

PROLOGUE

Declan Walsh sat in the Land Rover, fidgeting slightly with nerves as he stared out at the abandoned building rising up in front of him through the dawn light.

'You sure about this, Eddie?' he muttered, distracted by sunlight appearing from behind the peaks to the east. One peak was known as Mam Tor, but he didn't know which of the imposing mountainous rises took the name. Turning from it, he glanced across to his left where, in an army uniform and Red Cap beret, the red and black 'MP' patch prominent on his right arm sat Lance-Corporal Eddie Moses.

'It's where the guy at the pub said they'd seen someone mucking around late at night,' Eddie replied cautiously, still as uncertain about this as Declan was.

'Being here isn't a crime,' Declan shifted in his seat.

'It is when it's out of bounds for all military personnel,' Eddie nodded at the building. 'They decommissioned the warehouse a good few years back, and the Quartermaster's Stores said they turned the power off at the same time.'

In case Declan hadn't truly grasped what he was nodding

at, Eddie now pointed at a lower window across the car park, facing them from the darkened brick of the warehouse, and through which the faint glow of a lamp could be seen.

'So, someone's either re-wired it, brought their own generator in, or they're paying a load of cash for a shit-ton of lamps,' Eddie finished with the slightest hint of a smile, mainly because he knew that his lead and hunch had been correct.

Someone was indeed in the building.

'Could be kids,' Declan argued. 'Look, I just want to be sure here. I'm aware we've made a few screw ups in the past and I need this to go well.'

'Yeah, we all know about your Sergeants' exam,' Eddie chuckled. 'Can't for the life of me understand why you'd want to dump this awesome headgear for a sensible suit.'

Declan took off his red beret, staring at it. The distinctive scarlet colouring was what named the Military Police the *Red Caps.*

'It's personal,' Declan admitted awkwardly. 'I promised Liz.'

'Liz?' Eddie bellowed with laughter. 'Christ, Dec, you're telling me that your bloody *wife* wants the promotion more than you?'

'Sergeants have a better pension,' Declan muttered.

'Well, of course they do,' Eddie sneered. 'They leave all the work to us Corporals, that's what they bloody do. Makes sense they'd have a better payout too.'

He shook his head.

'Bloody pension.'

Declan pulled out his pistol; in a chest-holster, it was a Glock 17, standard army issue; but not the usual weapon of the *Royal Military Police.* Officers, especially non-coms like

Declan, would normally only use an extendable baton, but Declan and Eddie had recently returned from a tour in Eastern Europe, and guns were required in all overseas territories. Major Yates should have ordered them straight to the armoury, but in the time between arrival in Portsmouth and travelling north, they simply hadn't the time to do it. Besides, in all the years Declan had been in the Military Police, he'd never once fired a gun at a suspect. Granted, he'd pulled it out a lot when on exercises, or if he was on any kind of operational deployment or service, and sometimes waved it around to gain attention, but he'd never fired it at a suspect. Ceilings, cars, even armoured transports—

But *never a suspect.*

'Probably should have handed that in,' Eddie chided, pulling out his own gun, checking it before re-holstering. 'Probably should have done it myself.'

'Probably should have left this to the suits,' Declan muttered. 'This one feels off. For a start, we shouldn't be here.'

'He's not expecting us. We'll be in and out without the little bugger realising,' Eddie opened the passenger door of the Land Rover, climbing out onto the hard tarmac. 'Besides, if he didn't want us checking into it, Yates shouldn't have mentioned Harper was back here.'

Sighing audibly, Declan holstered the pistol and placed the red beret back onto his head, following out of the driver side door, joining his partner.

Declan and Eddie had been partners pretty much from the start; both training at Pirbright in the same class, they quickly learnt they were two of the more capable members of the battalion.

Because of this, as the postings arrived after training, they found this belief was held by the staff and examiners too, as they were sent to the same unit in Germany, and then into Northern Ireland together. And, although they weren't partners in the same way that a US cop show would have them, they often found themselves paired up, the MP squaddies sent to fix the broken non-coms of *Her Majesty's Armed Forces*.

Non-coms were the *non-commissioned officers*; the soldiers who never went to fancy officer school. From Privates, fresh from the camp, all the way to Corporal, uniforms usually policed the 'uniforms'. Only when you became Sergeant, Staff Sergeant or even Sergeant Major in the *Special Investigation Bureau* did you get to lose the khakis. And then, in civvy suits and ties, you more often than not dealt with the *juicier* cases. The murders, the traitors, the full-on criminals. Eddie and Declan? They were just Lance Corporal and Corporal between them. Their average day included hunting stolen regimental pets, breaking up drunk squaddie fights and closing down black market suppliers—although with that one, they often made sure a little of the product stayed in their pockets.

A kind of 'finders' fee' for what they did.

It was simple work, sometimes brutal, when you wore the uniform rather than the suit. Accidental deaths on the firing range, squaddies beating the crap out of each other over the same woman, even drug overdoses, these often fell under their remit. Declan had lost count, over the last ten years, how many times he'd walked through open wastelands or forests, searching for missing bodies, or faced the carbine of an assault rifle, a screaming, terrified soldier on the other end.

Because to have the *Red Caps* hunting you never meant

anything good. And, more importantly, it usually meant your army career was over, in one form or another.

In the beginning, Declan had enjoyed the work; it wasn't combat, and he felt he was doing good, following in the footsteps of his father, although in a different uniform. But, as the years went on, Declan had seen the *other* side of being an MP; you weren't a soldier in many squaddie's eyes, just someone who wasn't welcome at a party, in case something illegal happened. You weren't someone a troop wanted in combat, because you weren't backing your brothers and sisters up, you were working out which of them you'd gut first, arresting for whatever tawdry crime they'd committed.

None of this was true; Declan couldn't give a shit what anyone did, as long as it didn't hurt others. And, it was this attitude, one that was also held by Eddie Moses, that had probably cost them both a couple of field promotions over the years. There was loyalty to the army, and there was loyalty to the *cap*.

Walking towards the abandoned Quartermasters Stores, a two-storey warehouse that rose out of the dawn in front of them like an abandoned fun house, colourful graffiti sprayed over the frontage, a variety of letters and symbols that were most likely tags by bored locals, Declan pulled out his baton, feeling more comfortable with this in his hand than the gun.

'Liz made you weak,' Eddie chuckled. 'You're playing with your toddler when you should be catching bastards.'

'You're just bitter because you don't have a toddler to play with,' Declan laughed. 'Although you're always welcome to babysit Jessica. Just don't let her near paints and crayons.'

'Destroys the walls?'

'Eats them,' Declan smiled at the memory, grim as it was.

'Nothing so terrifying as when your daughter shits out fluorescent green poo.'

They stopped at the door to the warehouse, their tones changing now, more nervous before they entered. It wasn't locked, and the glass in the middle was broken, although still barring entry with a mesh of criss-cross metal wires. Someone had thrown stones at it, more likely than breaking in. The door was ajar.

'Why do you wanna be a Sergeant, anyway?' Eddie muttered. 'You'd be splitting up the team. And you've got years ahead of you to get it.'

'Not that many,' Declan shook his head. 'I made a promise. I leave at twelve years, whatever rank I am. That's almost two years away, so I need to hurry.'

'You're leaving?' Eddie stood straight, lowering the gun. 'This is new.'

'Not for a couple of years, you idiot,' Declan shook his head. 'Decided right before we came back from Hamburg last week. And don't give me the 'what will I do without you' shite, as we both know we'll probably be kicked out after this.'

'We tried to tell them, but they ignored us,' Eddie shifted grip on his gun, preparing to enter. 'Bloody Postie and his rules.'

'Major Yates has them for a reason,' Declan listened against the door, using their superior officer's real name, rather than the nickname Eddie had muttered. Major Yates was a stickler for the rules, and Eddie had once mentioned he was 'as stiff as a post', a comment on Yates' unbending personality. Ever since then, *Postie* had been their codename, something useful when complaining about him, when near people who could inform of this. 'Especially after Tooley got murdered. And I didn't see Yates stopping us.'

'You weren't there for the conversation,' Eddie stared up at the windows of the warehouse in silence, and Declan knew he was remembering Private Jo Tooley, only in the Red Caps for a year before she went off alone after a suspect one night, and was found dead the following morning, her throat slashed beside a Hamburg airfield.

It had only been four months ago.

Jo and Eddie had been an item.

'You're right, I wasn't,' Declan admitted. When they'd arrived back a couple of days earlier, Declan had called Liz to tell her he'd landed, while Eddie reported to Yates. At the time, Yates didn't know Eddie had any kind of personal connection to Tooley, but when Eddie explained they'd been seeing each other before her death, there'd been a distinct change in tone, and Yates had *accidentally* mentioned where Eddie should look, forgetting to order them to the armoury.

It was almost as if he wanted them to come here.

And the suspect was now believed to be in this building.

'This is an arrest, not a revenge mission,' Declan reminded. Eddie snorted at this.

'Bastard raises any kind of weapon, I'm shooting,' he muttered. 'And Postie knows I will, that's why he left us these.'

He waggled the Glock in his hand.

'You sure we shouldn't be calling this one in?' Declan looked back at the Land Rover. 'This feels wrong. Personal.'

'Because it is,' Eddie snarled. 'It's wrong because they let that prick return home. And it's personal because he killed one of ours.'

'We don't have proof of that.'

Eddie stroked the barrel of his Glock.

'Give me time,' he said, his voice ice cold.

And with that chilling warning given, he led Declan into the warehouse.

THEY'D BEEN WATCHING SERGEANT PADDY HARPER FOR A while now. He'd been accused in Basra a few years earlier of stealing flash bangs and throwing them at Iraqi cars while driving, but nobody could prove it. There'd been more rumours, ones of locals going missing, found dead the following morning, and although in the same area, nobody could prove the other side didn't take them. He'd then been accused also of assaulting women in Hamburg a couple of years later, but Harper was lucky enough to have 'one of those faces'; average in looks, height and build, and an expression that, when lined up with others, simply didn't step out of the crowd. And, when he'd escaped those pointed fingers, they transferred him back to the UK, back to his wife and children, pressing the 'good parent' button as many times as he could. He'd been shipped back four months earlier, but not before Jo, sweet innocent Jo had found something on him, something that caused her to confront him immediately before he left Germany, a confrontation that Harper denied ever happened, but left Private Jo Tooley dead.

They didn't know what it was she'd found out; she never told them, and they found nothing on her body. Her beret insignia, however, had been torn off and taken, maybe as a trophy.

After that, Eddie and Declan had started their own investigation, from their Hamburg barracks. The suits at SIB, having missed out twice on Harper, were happy to keep their distance and wait for him to screw up again, but Eddie was impatient. And, when he heard rumours from the UK, stories that women were going missing in the Peak District near where Harper was deployed, Eddie and Declan had arranged with Yates, now back in Portsmouth, to transfer back to the UK themselves, and, after Yates had 'accidentally' confirmed the stories when speaking to Eddie on arrival, the two of them immediately went hunting Sergeant Harper once more.

The story they'd been told was simple; a Private in the Light Infantry who'd been passing through four months earlier had been convinced he saw someone matching Harper's description in a Castleton bar, briefly chatting to one of the women who went missing, Susan Jenkins; but when the SIB had checked into this, it was debunked and classed as a simple mistake. At the time of her disappearance, Harper was still on paper as deployed in Hamburg, and wouldn't be booked to fly back for another three days.

At this point, Jo Tooley was also still alive.

Susan Jenkins was found dead two days later, in a ditch near the Castleton base. There were no clues who her killer had been.

But Declan and Eddie knew who it was. They didn't know *how*, but they knew it was Harper. And, when they'd arrived back into Portsmouth two days ago, Declan and Eddie had heard the most recent news; four months after Jenkins' murder, and four months after Tooley's death in Hamburg, another woman had gone missing in the Peaks, a Private in the Logistics Unit named Malik. This had been another thing Yates had mentioned accidentally, having only just heard of it himself. And although they couldn't prove she'd been taken by him, Eddie had been utterly convinced it had to be Harper as, in his mind, nobody else could do such a thing, especially when Declan learned that Harper and Malik had known each other briefly a year earlier, before he'd been deployed in Hamburg.

And now, creeping softly through the warehouse, they were looking to end Sergeant Harper's terror once and for all.

Declan, however, was looking for a less *final* way than Eddie.

'You'll miss this,' Eddie said softly as they moved from room to room. They'd found the source of the light; a battery lantern, placed beside a pile of books. There was no chair, but someone had thrown a rug on the concrete floor. Declan grinned, but it faded quickly as he looked around.

'Bastard made himself a library,' Eddie shook his head. 'Means he won't be too far.'

'Battery powered,' Declan examined the lamp. 'That means he's close. He wouldn't leave it on if he went out. Unless this was a message for someone.'

'What, a light in the window means *come in?*' Eddie considered this. 'Nah. He's not that bright.'

Carefully, they continued through the room, stopping as they reached a pile of metal sheets and overturned metal shelving.

'This is welded,' Declan noted, pulling at the sheeting. 'It's fallen over, but someone's welded it all together while it laid there.'

'Who'd do that?'

Declan shook his head.

'Nobody. And not like this, unless you're hiding something.'

Eddie nodded understanding at this, and slowly they pulled the sheeting away from the corner of the room. It scraped across the ground, making a dull *screech* noise, and

Declan winced at this; if Harper didn't know they were there, he did now.

Eventually, they'd cleared a small space in the corner, revealing a small door embedded into the back wall. Opening it, they found it led down a set of narrow stairs.

'Basement,' Eddie muttered. 'Of course it's a bloody basement.'

'*Hidden* basement,' Declan muttered. 'That's even worse.'

Moving slowly down the stairs, Declan saw that here, there were no lights on, probably because the power was still turned off. If Harper, or whomever had hidden the basement wanted to come down, they probably used the battery lantern.

'You should have brought the lantern,' Eddie muttered, coming to the same conclusion as Declan had. Reaching into his pocket, Declan pulled his torch out, turning it on and shining it into the enormous expanse they were entering. Eddie had done the same, now holding the torch along the side of his gun in a two-handed grip as he scanned the basement, looking for any signs of Sergeant Harper.

'There's a bed,' he said, aiming the torch at a makeshift cot to the right, a small sleeping bag crumpled up on top. 'Why would he have a bed here? He's not on the run.'

'Maybe he's expecting to be on the run?' Declan suggested. 'Maybe he needed somewhere he could spend the night that wasn't in dorms or at home.'

'But why would you—' Eddie stopped, his words choking in his throat as he shone his torch into a side room on the right-hand side of the open space in front of them.

There were bodies in it.

At least three of them.

The closest, chained by the wrist and laying on the floor,

possibly unconscious but maybe dead, was the prone form of Private Malik, blood clotted on her temple.

'Malik!' Eddie ran into the room, gagging at the stench. 'Jesus, Declan, they're rotten! There's no way they're new!'

As Eddie tended to Malik, now opening her eyes, staring blankly up at him, wincing slightly from the torchlight, Declan examined the other bodies. There were two more, one half-hidden in the corner. Both were long dead; easily a few weeks, if not more. Young women, injured or bruised, and both with a hole, likely from a bullet, in their forehead.

'She's drugged,' Eddie was pulling at the chain. 'We need to call this in.'

'We need to get her out first,' Declan held his phone up. 'There's no signal here. I'll—'

'You'll do nothing,' a familiar, slurring voice said and, as Eddie and Declan turned to the door, they saw Sergeant Paddy Harper slowly making his way down the stairs, his Heckler & Koch SA80 A2 Assault Rifle already aimed at them. Stocky and bald, he looked like a fighter, and Declan knew this wasn't a man who could be talked down. And, to be honest, Declan knew Eddie didn't want to do that.

Eddie wanted blood.

'Bloody hell, Harper!' Eddie shouted. 'She needs medical help!'

'I've got what she needs right here,' Harper said, but because he didn't show anything, Declan assumed he meant the rifle, rather than medical supplies. He gripped the baton tightly, wishing he'd pulled the Glock from his holster when he had a chance, very aware that any movement would likely bring a bullet.

'What is this?' he asked softly. 'Please, explain these

bodies. Explain Jo Tooley. You played with grenades, slapped women around. When did it progress to full-on murder?'

Harper paced back and forth, rifle still aimed at Declan and Eddie.

'You should have just left me alone,' he hissed. 'I was having fun in Germany. Doing my job, following orders. But no, you had to come after me. That bitch MP should have been more careful about who she was screwing, so she didn't have to—'

Eddie's pistol, constantly aimed at Harper since he arrived fired; a flash of violent sound and light in the darkness. Instinctively Harper's finger tightened on the trigger of his rifle, but the snap back of his shoulder as the bullet hit him square in the chest threw the angle upwards, and the bullets flew wildly into the air as Eddie and Declan dived to the side, Eddie shielding the still drugged Malik as he did so.

Harper fell to the floor, spluttering blood. Declan, kicking the rifle aside and kneeling down, leaned in close, examining the wound.

'Stay with us, Harper,' he commanded. 'Don't you dare die on me right now.'

'He'll see you...' Harper whispered, the words coming out more like a gurgle than as a sentence. 'He sees everything. Tells us what to do... gives us orders...'

'Who does?' Declan looked back at Eddie as he tried to staunch the flow of blood. 'God? Are you talking about God?'

'God ain't seeing you,' Eddie hissed. 'You're going the other way.'

'Wasn't me...' Harper breathed. 'Sentry... for...'

He reached up, as if trying to grab the sky.

'High... all...'

And before he could finish, Sergeant Harper's eyes glazed over, and his words turned into the hiss of a death rattle.

'*Sentry for who?*' Declan screamed at the body. 'What do you mean, it wasn't you? What wasn't? What was high?'

'Leave him,' Eddie pulled Declan to the side. 'We have an injured woman to attend to.'

'We have a murdered Sergeant to attend to!' Declan snapped. 'What were you thinking, firing? He could have killed us! He could have killed *her!*'

'It was self-defence,' Eddie claimed calmly. 'He fired first, I took the shot.'

'But he didn't—'

'I said *he fired first*,' Eddie repeated. 'Dec, we have two choices here. We come out of this as two uniforms who brought guns to a rifle fight when we shouldn't have and almost died, or we're two uniforms who stumbled onto a serial killer, ending his streak.'

'And what if he wasn't the serial killer?' Declan looked back at the bodies.

'Dec, he killed Jo,' Eddie insisted. 'He wasn't working for anyone. He was a nut job. And I'm not losing any sleep that he's dead.'

He looked at the dazed Private Malik, now dabbing at her forehead, realising finally that it was bleeding.

'And she won't either,' he finished. 'She won't be dying today. And you've just got a little closer to your Sergeant stripe.'

Declan stared down at Sergeant Harper and knew that what Eddie said made sense, and there was every chance that his action, that of firing first, saved both of their lives. Because of that one act, Declan would see his baby girl that night.

So why did he feel he was getting away with *murder?*

1

SUMMER HOLIDAY

IT WAS HOT FOR JULY BUT THE WATER WAS *FREEZING*.

Declan stared across at Wayne, early twenties and full of life as he sat on his own surfboard with the ease of a man who'd done this since childhood; straddling the board like one rode a horse, legs dipped into the water as he watched the waves building behind him with a relaxed ease. He wore a trendy *Riptide* wetsuit with short arms and legs, his feet and shins bare as he dangled them in the sea.

Declan currently hated him.

He too was straddled, if that was the word that could explain the constant shifting and scrambling he was doing on his board, apparently called a 'mini mal', whatever that was, while trying not to let any piece of exposed skin hit the freezing water. He also had a five millimetre wetsuit on, but his one covered up to the ends of the ankles and arms. And, unlike Wayne, Declan wore wetsuit booties and gloves to fight back the numbness from the water. He'd seen he could hire headwear too, little neoprene balaclavas that covered the skull, but felt this was a little overkill.

Now, he wasn't sure.

'This isn't that bad,' Wayne carried on with his surf lesson. 'It's warming up. Best time to surf is October, as then the sea's had all summer to heat up. It's actually quite refreshing right now.'

'It's freezing, right now.'

'Only because you've just got in,' Wayne chided. 'Let your body heat the trapped sea water. Then you'll be nice and toasty.'

Once more, Wayne looked behind him.

'There's a swell coming. You ready? Paddle to match it and then jump up—no, it's passed. Wait for the next one.'

Declan nodded at this. He'd spent the entire morning on the beach at Whitesands Bay, laying on a surfboard placed on the sands, and pushing himself up with his arms as he jumped into a crouch, his left foot forward. By the end of the morning, he felt like he could *totally surf the sands, dude,* or whatever they said.

Then Wayne had taken him into the water, and the day got far worse.

It was Declan's fault; he'd accidentally started up a conversation with Wayne the previous night in the *Farmer's Arms,* and had mentioned he'd always wanted to try surfing. It was said in the same way someone says 'I always wanted to try skydiving', in that *I don't really want to do it right now, but sure, maybe way down the line* kind of way, but Declan hadn't considered the enthusiasm of the millennial mind, and at nine in the morning the following day he'd found himself slid into a wetsuit and dumped on the sands with a way-too-enthusiastic-for-the-time -of-day Wayne explaining the basics of surfing.

He'd only gone in the pub because he was investigating

*Francine Pearce's holiday home explosion. He hadn't even intended
to have a drink.*

'So, what made you decide to try something like this?'
Wayne smiled, completely at ease in the water. 'I mean,
you're not the usual—wait, here we go, start paddling, no
wait, that's fading too—type of student we get. Midlife crisis?'

Declan shrugged.

'I don't think so,' he replied, almost sliding off the board as
he did so. 'I came to investigate the explosion at Bryn Road.'

'Ah, man, that was awesome,' Wayne laughed out loud.
'We thought it was the end of the world! Right scared the shit
out of us!'

'A woman died in that blast,' Declan's tone darkened.
Francine Pearce might have been a gigantic thorn in his side,
but nobody deserved to die like that, especially if killed as a
sick serial killer's apology to Declan.

'No, of course,' Wayne replied, sobering a little. 'So is this
connected to the Government? Was she part of the plot?' he
tapped the side of his nose and quietly, Declan groaned. One
reason he'd come to St Davids, apart from the investigation,
was because he wanted to escape to a place where people
didn't know who he was. When he was *the copper who punched
that priest on TV,* it was a quick moment on *ITV News*; bar
YouTube, the occasional gif and a question on *The Big Quiz Of
The Year*, it'd been quickly forgotten.

But a month earlier, Declan had run into the middle of a
Government State Dinner, in front of the Queen herself, with
a *BBC News* camera crew following, and single-handedly
taken down a potential mass murderer before they could kill
multiple targets. Not only had this been broadcast live, but
it'd been picked up globally; by the end of the day Declan

was trending on *Twitter*, and wannabe Prime Minister candidate Charles Baker had milked him for all he could get—until he realised Declan had made an *error*.

It was that error that had brought Declan here, in a roundabout way, after handing in his resignation a month earlier.

Because Declan, as far as he was concerned, had *failed*. He'd arrived too late to stop what needed to be stopped, and it was only by the actions of another that the murders had been thwarted.

All he did was arrest the suspect.

This time people had survived, but the list of victims he couldn't save, the ones he didn't know the names of, and more importantly, the ones that he did, and had even loved—well, they had mounted up.

Declan had failed them all.

'Hey! Supercop!' Wayne's voice cut through Declan's thoughts. 'You gonna surf or not?'

'Sorry,' Declan repositioned himself on the board. 'It's been a tough month.'

'I'll bet,' Wayne sat back on his board. 'But investigating an explosion doesn't lead to deciding you really want to sit on a surfboard. Still sounds like a midlife crisis to me.'

Declan smiled.

'Thought it could be fun,' he said. 'I don't seem to have done many fun things lately.'

No, that's not correct, the voice in his head muttered. *You do fun things all the time. This isn't it and you know it.*

'I'm running away,' Declan sighed. 'That's the honest truth. I'm running away because I don't want to be used by anyone right now.'

'Sounds like you have a job issue,' Wayne suggested. 'You hate it, maybe?'

'I don't hate my job at all,' Declan shrugged. 'But I think it hates me.'

'So you're—quick start paddling, no wait it's not worth it —thinking of quitting?'

'Already have,' Declan nodded. 'Handed the letter in a month back. I have to work my three-month notice, but Bullman, that's my boss, understood the reasons behind it all and told me to take time off. I spent a couple of weeks at home and my partner—work partner that is, although I suppose she's just a housemate now—got sick of me moping around, so I came here, see if I could find anything out.'

'And did you?' Wayne asked.

'Not what I was considering, anyway,' Declan admitted, shaking his head. 'I found I was happy being somewhere nobody really knew me.'

'So go somewhere in the middle of nowhere and be a copper then,' Wayne laughed, as if this was the easiest answer in the world. 'Don't just walk away from it all.'

Declan slipped off the board as Wayne spoke, floundering in the water for a moment before pulling himself back up, spluttering as he slicked back his hair, spitting out sea water before continuing.

'I considered it,' he eventually replied. 'Saw an opportunity to go to a small village in Yorkshire named after cheese or something, but the DCI there was a grim bastard. And then there was a chance to go to the middle of nowhere in Scotland, but that seemed to be covered by some DCI near Fort William, and I got the impression they didn't need me either.'

'So what now?' Wayne asked. 'Run away to be a surf instructor?'

Declan laughed out loud at this.

'I think I need to actually be able to do it before I instruct,' he replied. 'Is that what you did? Run away? Your accent doesn't tie you in as a local. I get more of a Manchester twang.'

'Spot on, Sherlock,' Wayne grinned. 'I was an accountant in the city. Manchester, that is. I worked for a company that dealt with media types. So actors, directors, all that sort of thing. Thought I was one step from Hollywood, but I hated it. Came here for a stag weekend, loved it, decided to stay.'

'So you did the same, then?'

'Nope, because I'm still an accountant,' Wayne replied. 'I just surf as well. You need to be a detective, Declan. You're a bloody good one. Saved the Queen and all that. You just need to believe in yourself again.'

'I haven't believed in myself since I—' Declan stopped as, on the shore, two military Land Rovers drove through the car park, continuing down the ramp to the left of it as Declan was facing, pulling to a halt at the edge of the tide.

'Friends of yours?' Wayne asked as from the lead vehicle, a familiar-looking Army Officer emerged, waving out to Declan, indicating for him to return to shore.

'That depends,' Declan sighed. 'Sorry mate, I'll have to go in.'

'At least go in on a wave,' Wayne grinned.

Declan looked behind, saw a moderate swell building and, as it approached, he paddled hard with his gloved hands, aiming towards the shore as the wave came up behind him, rising him up slightly as the board balanced on the swell. Declan took this moment to grab the board, pushing up with his arms as he leaped up onto the board, rising—

'It looked painful,' Colonel Yates said as he sipped at a small cup of tea.

'It wasn't painful, it was just embarrassing,' Declan muttered as he drank from his flat white coffee. 'And then when you fall off, the wave goes above you and it's disorientating and you rise up—'

'And get smacked in the face with the surfboard,' Yates continued. 'Painful.'

Declan rubbed at his cheek. After his less than dignified return to the beach, he'd returned the wetsuit and board to Wayne, quickly changing back into jeans and a t-shirt before taking the Colonel, with his soldiers waiting outside, to the nearby café for a drink. Now, leaning back, he took in the man in front of him.

'The pips suit you, sir,' he admitted.

Yates smiled.

'Came as a shock,' he admitted. 'But I can't complain.'

Declan nodded at this. The last time he'd seen 'Postie' Yates, he'd just been promoted from Major to Lieutenant Colonel.

'So, what's this about?' he asked. 'I mean, I can't believe you just happened to see me on the sea and came to say hi.'

'Always to the point, Walsh, even now,' Yates sighed, placing his cup down. 'I was told where you were from the guesthouse you're staying at. And your Unit commander, Detective Superintendent Bullman, informed me of its location.'

Declan didn't like where this was going.

'A lot of trouble for a catch up,' he replied cautiously, looking out of the windows of the café at the two vehicles outside. 'I'm guessing this is work related, and if you're here, it's connected somehow to me or Eddie?'

'When was the last time you saw Staff Sergeant Moses?' Yates asked.

Declan chuckled.

'Before he became a Staff Sergeant, I can tell you,' he said. 'Must have been eighteen months, more likely a couple of years back. I'd just separated from Liz, and he pretty much turned up to give me the 'I told you so' speech he'd been writing since they met.'

Declan thought back to the night.

'He was like some kind of born-again zealot, maybe doing the twelve steps? A bit pious and condescending, to be honest. Anyway, we had a row, I told him to piss off and not come back, and he took it personally,' he continued. 'Didn't even come to my dad's funeral.'

'Yes, sorry about Patrick's passing,' Yates seemed uncomfortable, and Declan couldn't work out if it was because of Eddie or because he, too, hadn't made the funeral. 'They deployed me. You got my flowers, though?'

'I did,' Declan nodded. 'You didn't know him well, I didn't expect you to attend. Eddie, however, he spent years chatting to dad. Sometimes he'd joke that Eddie was his real son to people.'

'There's a reason Eddie didn't make your father's funeral,' Yate's tone had become sombre, measured as he replied.

Declan leaned back, laughing.

'Christ, did he go AWOL?' he exclaimed. 'I heard he'd done that a while back. That'd be about right, that prick—'

'No, Corporal Walsh, he didn't go AWOL,' Yates interrupted, and Declan couldn't help but note the military rank being added. 'He's dead.'

Declan felt all the colour drain out of the room, the vibrant sky greying out, as if someone were sliding the saturation filter down.

'How?' he asked. He knew it wouldn't be something normal, like a *heart attack* or even *cancer*; your old commanding officer didn't appear with bodyguards when it was that simple.

'We don't know,' Yates admitted, shifting in his chair. 'Dog walker found him in the Peak District a week ago. Probably came as a bit of a shock, to be honest. Apparently her terrier got into a small cave or something near Blue John's Cavern, just outside of Castleton, and when the fire brigade came to get it out, they found Eddie.'

'Accident?' Declan asked. Yates shook his head.

'He was in a body bag,' he replied. 'Wedged into a shelf at the back of a small hollow. Unless you looked for him, you wouldn't see it. And it was airtight, as the bags are supposed to be, so...'

'What about smell?' Declan shook his head, unable to accept this. 'There would have been a hell of a stink—'

'There was a sheep carcass nearby, probably got trapped,' Yates shrugged. 'The smell of that would have masked anything to do with Eddie.'

'How long?' Declan continued. 'How long was he left there?'

Yates looked at the table for a moment before replying.

'Around twelve months,' he whispered. 'We're still waiting for an exact date, but we think Summer last year. The body bag allowed nothing in, so the usual dating things; maggots, larvae etc aren't there.'

'How did he die?'

'Again, don't know,' Yates looked back at Declan. 'The body, well, it—'

Declan raised a hand to stop Yates; he knew from experience what a body sealed up looked like after a while. *Bear Studios* in Hayes had held one such body, although that had been hidden for decades.

'He'd been gone a year, and you didn't bother looking for him?' Declan was angry now, almost spitting the words.

'No, Declan,' Yates snapped back. 'We had a similar farewell chat as you did, and to be frank, I didn't see *you* trying to find him either.'

Declan nodded, abashed. He had no right to accuse Yates of anything, as he'd been just as bad. People went AWOL all the time. He just never expected Eddie to be like that.

'What did Eddie say when he last saw you?' Yates continued. 'Apart from the 'I told you so' part in relation to your ex-wife?'

Declan thought back to the moment.

'He was *holier than thou,* as I said,' he replied. 'Never acclimatised to the suit and tie aspect of SIB; he liked the red cap. I knew that from his comments when I moved up. But this Eddie, he was at peace. Kept saying he'd finally shed his guilt and weaknesses. Unlike me.'

'Ouch.'

'Yeah,' Declan sighed. 'As I said, we had a row. He was being a prick, acting like he was better than me, that I was the nobody. I might have taken that personally.'

'Did he mention any cases he worked on?'

'No, sir.'

'And would he have had a reason to contact you before he died a year back?'

Declan shifted in the chair, watching Yates carefully.

'Look, sir,' he replied cautiously. 'You've arrived with armed MPs who have been waiting outside while we talk, but anyone can see they've secured all exits. You arrived like the devil himself was after you, and you're asking me about my dead partner as if I know more than I'm letting on. So how about telling me what's happening here?'

'You're right,' Yates nodded. 'You're a person of interest.'

'In the murder?' Declan was surprised at this, half-rising as he spoke, but stopping himself.

The men outside might think he was about to run.

'When we found Eddie, the body was decomposed,' Yates continued. 'The, well, the *juices* were everywhere, having soaked into the clothes. And the acids in them didn't help with evidence much.'

He pulled out his phone, opening it up and, after a few swipes, turned it to show Declan. On it was a photo of a piece of paper, torn from a sheet, with quickly scrawled hand-writing in black marker, as if written in a hurry. However, the card had been soaked in something unmentionable, and the words were faded out, except for the first two on the top line;

DECLAN KNOWS

'Declan knows what?' Declan didn't like the direction this was going. Yates placed the phone down now, staring at him.

'That's what we want to know,' he replied. 'Don't worry, you're not a suspect for the moment. But we need your help in understanding what happened.'

Declan nodded, relaxing a little.

'How can I help?'

'Well, first off, you can investigate this case for us,' Yates forced a smile. 'The body bag was ordered and quartered by the Castleton SIB, which meant that only the Military Police or Ministry of Defence Police could acquisition it.'

'Both of whom would investigate this murder,' Declan was catching up now. 'And, because of this, a potential murderer could make sure they weren't checked. You need an outsider.'

'I need an outsider who knows how the SIB works,' Yates rose from the table. 'I've spoken to your superiors, and they said they can requisition you to us for as long as it takes to solve this. We're not police, so we don't care about any police issues or crybaby emotions you might have right now.'

Declan rose as well, ignoring the jibe. Postie had never been known for his bedside manner. There was a reason he had the nickname.

'When do you need me to start?' he asked.

'You already have,' Yates nodded to the two Land Rovers. 'One of these will take you wherever you need to go today to pack up. Tomorrow, you begin the investigation.'

Declan thought for a moment.

'You said you're not police, so don't care about any police issues, sir,' he said with a smile. 'Can I bring someone with me?'

'Bring whomever and whatever you need, I'll sign off on it,' Yates was already walking to the door of the café. 'Just find out what the hell was going on.'

2

MEET THE NEW BOSS

Chief Superintendent Bradbury was waiting for Bullman as she arrived at the gates.

He was in his uniform, crisp and crease-less, his short grey hair now whiter on the temples than before, wiping his black-rimmed glasses before placing them back on, staring hard at Bullman as he did so. She was in her usual grey suit, a salmon blouse underneath and, even though it was freshly dry-cleaned, she still felt underdressed compared to her superior.

'Thought you'd be in uniform,' Bradbury said as they nodded to the guards who opened the gates, holding back the tourists and the protesters as Bullman and Bradbury entered the street, the gate closing behind them. 'I mean, the world's press are about to take your photo.'

'With all respect, sir, the world's press couldn't give a damn who I am,' Bullman replied and, to prove the point, waved to the row of cameras that lined the other side of Downing Street.

Not one of them flashed.

Bullman smiled ruefully at this.

'I was never Baker's buddy, remember?' she continued. 'I was just a suit in the background. Wearing the uniform would actively make me more interesting. This? I'm just an advisor, or a lobbyer. And that's boring.'

'I guess we can be thankful for some small mercies then,' Bradbury nodded to the policeman on guard at Number Ten Downing Street, and passing through the now opening door. 'Showboating detectives never do well. Talking of which, how's your one?'

'Which one?' Bullman frowned as they walked into the lobby, an aide immediately moving in to take Bradbury's offered cap before escorting them up stairs. 'Monroe or Walsh?'

'Christ, I'd forgotten Monroe was yours too,' Bradbury gave a rueful smile. 'It's been blissfully quiet with him not around to cause me hassle.'

'Any idea when the hearing will be?' Bullman sat on one of the indicated chairs in the waiting room they now stood in. 'With Walsh on leave and Monroe on—well, whatever, I'm a little short staffed.'

'We'll discuss it after we learn what the new Prime Minister wants with us,' Bradbury stayed standing, with the coiled energy of a man who desperately wanted to pace, but didn't want to be seen doing so. 'You wouldn't know why we've been called in, would you?'

Bullman shook her head and was about to reply as the door opened, and a junior aide emerged, nodding to them to come closer.

'The Prime Minister is very busy,' he said, 'But we've made time for you.'

'Considering we were ordered here, that's very nice of

you,' Bradbury forced a smile. At this, the aide looked confused for a moment.

'You're not the inner city rejuvenation project?' he asked, paling a little as Bullman and Bradbury shook their heads. 'Then I don't have you on the list—'

'I put them on the list,' a voice shouted out from inside the Prime Minister's office. 'So stop bloody dawdling and let them in.'

The aide, stepping meekly to the side, allowed Bullman and Bradbury to enter the Office of the Prime Minister of the United Kingdom. Standing behind the desk, rising to meet them with a smile, was the country's new leader, having won the Conservative Party's Leadership Election the previous week.

'Chief Superintendent Bradbury, Detective Superintendent Bullman,' Michelle Rose said, walking around her desk to shake them both by the hand. 'Thank you for taking the time to speak with me.'

She waved away the aide, who left the office, shutting the door behind him.

'Congratulations on your win, Prime Minister,' Bullman said. 'I voted for you.'

'I don't know what's more surprising,' Michelle laughed as she moved back to her side of the desk. That you're a Conservative party member, or that you didn't vote for your buddy Charles Baker?'

'DI Walsh is the 'buddy' of Baker,' Bullman replied calmly. 'As far as we were concerned, he was simply a person of interest in several cases.'

'Fair point,' Michelle sat in her chair. 'Pretty much what cost him the election, too. But at the moment, call me *Ma'am* rather than Prime Minister, as I'm still not sworn in, or whatever the hell I do. Haven't been to see the Queen yet as she's been unwell, and after that's when it gets scarily real.'

'Can I ask why we're here, Ma'am?' ever to the point, Bradbury cleaned his glasses once more before placing them on, and Bullman wondered whether this was a nervous reaction.

'Indeed,' Michelle Rose steepled her fingers together as she considered her next move. 'The Government and the Temple Inn Unit seem to be indelibly linked to each other, either by costing our party valuable members, or by saving our lives.'

Bullman knew immediately what the Prime Minister was insinuating; in the last year alone, the *Last Chance Saloon* had saved Charles Baker's life, arrested Malcolm Gladwell, the Conservative Party's troubleshooter for murder, and saved the entire Cabinet during a State Dinner.

'We do our best to follow the rule of law,' she said carefully.

'But are you loyal to me, or to Charles?' Michelle asked, almost impishly. Bradbury went to speak, but noted Bullman straighten, bristling, and sat back.

'With all respect, *Ma'am*, we have no loyalty to any one *person*,' Bullman said icily. 'Charles Baker utilised our expertise for his own uses, and tried to use us for political and press capital, which hideously backfired on him, with you sitting here as proof. We are loyal only to the *Crown*, of which we are its servants.'

Michelle Rose considered this for a long moment. Bullman glanced at Bradbury, only to find him staring back at her, equally confused by what was going on here.

'Chief Superintendent Bradbury,' Michelle finally spoke. 'I have need of your Unit for an investigation. It's secretive, and I know they've signed the *Official Secrets Act*, while you, unfortunately, have not.'

'No Ma'am, I haven't,' Bradbury replied stiffly.

'In that case, may I have your permission to utilise the skills and staff of the Temple Inn Unit, whilst at all times guaranteeing that they will act in accordance with their duties as City of Police officers, while not informing you of why I need them, where they'll be, and for how long they'll be used?'

Bradbury looked uncomfortable here.

'An entire Unit taken off duties is no small matter,' he started. 'We have—'

'I didn't explain myself, and for that I apologise,' Michelle interrupted, picking up a piece of paper and reading from it. 'I only need the use of D Supt Bullman, DC Fitzwarren, DS Kapoor, DC Davey, PC De'Geer and Doctor Marcos. I believe these officers are known as the *Last Chance Saloon?*'

There was an awkward moment as Bradbury glanced at Bullman, unsure whether or not to agree to this. And Bullman couldn't help but notice that both Declan Walsh and Alex Monroe had been omitted.

'It'll be fine, sir,' Bullman said with a smile. 'I promise not to get us into an international incident. Those all happened before I arrived.'

She could see that Bradbury didn't want to leave, but he was in a situation he couldn't rightly argue; you didn't tell the new Prime Minister they couldn't have what they wanted, if you ever wanted to rise higher in the ranks. With a curt acknowledgement, Bradbury rose and nodded to Michelle.

'I'll be outside, Prime Minister,' he said, forgetting to use the *Ma'am* honorific.

'Please stay though,' Michelle insisted. 'When I'm done

here, I do need to talk about regional crime figures in the City.'

There was a quiet, drawn out pause as Bradbury left, and then, as if relieved, Michelle Rose seemed to relax.

'PC De'Geer hasn't signed the Act, Ma'am,' Bullman commented.

'Then get him to do it,' Michelle replied. 'Today would be good. I'll arrange it.'

'In that case, Chief Superintendent Bradbury could also sign—'

'Bradbury is old guard,' Michelle shook her head. 'Part of the old regime, the ex-Prime Minister's picks. I'd rather keep him out of this until I know his ambitions, thanks.'

Bullman accepted this. She'd noticed a few times recently that when people reached the higher levels of police, politics became more important than beliefs.

'Okay, so what's the problem then?' Bullman asked.

'What I'm about to say goes no further,' Michelle continued. 'Apart from the immediate team I've mentioned. Agreed?'

'With reservations,' Bullman replied.

'Reservations?'

'You named most of my core team, but neglected DI Walsh and DCI Monroe.'

'I was under the assumption that Walsh and Monroe were no longer a part of your team?' Michelle said, waving a hand to stop a reply. 'Don't worry, I'll get to them in a moment.'

With this ominous statement made, Michelle Rose passed over a file. As Bullman opened it, she saw TOP SECRET in large, red letters on the inside.

'You can read it,' Michelle insisted. 'I have a delicate problem, something that stems from my days in the Cabinet.'

'A rifle?' Bullman looked up from the image on the first page. 'I'm not a weapons expert, Ma'am.'

'It's not the rifle you're here about,' Michelle motioned for Bullman to keep going. Turning the page, Bullman now read a crime scene report.

'Dead scientist,' she said. 'Soldier, too. I'm guessing this is it? Wait, what?'

She looked up from the sheet.

'His pacemaker *melted?*'

Michelle Rose nodded.

'If you understood the first part, this might become easier to grasp,' she said. 'Lieutenant Colonel Falconer was the lead scientist in a research and development department liaised to the Derbyshire Regiment, near Castleton.'

'Any reason for the Derbyshires being used?' Bullman enquired. 'Surely this would have been more along the lines of the Defence Science and Technology Laboratory?'

Michelle leaned back, watching Bullman.

'You know your departments,' she said, visibly impressed.

'I Federation Repped DI Walsh when he was accused of terrorism a few months back,' Bullman shrugged. 'I learned a lot of things then. Also, we have mates who are spies.'

'Well, the DSTL are involved, but in an advisory capacity,' Michelle replied, but Bullman thought she sounded a little *too* rehearsed here. As if she'd been expecting the question, maybe even before. 'Apart from his long term connection, the Derbyshire Regiment have been involved in the application of long range firearms for years, and because of this, his team had been tasked , in conjunction with the DSTL, with creating a British rival to the Chinese ZKZM-500 hand-held laser assault rifle,'

'Laser assault rifles,' Bullman shook her head as she started reading through the notes. 'I'm living in *Star Wars,* or one of those other films Billy Fitzwarren loves. *'Unlike ordinary sleek assault rifles, this rifle is a rectangular shape with a pistol grip, fore grip, and telescopic sight. It's powered by a lithium battery capable of supplying power for up to a thousand two-second shots...'*

She trailed off as she read the next line, looking up in horror at Michelle Rose.

'This says the ZKZM-500 can reportedly inflict pain 'beyond human endurance', and is so powerful it can set clothes on fire or burn through a gas tank. It's silent, with no gunshot, and the beam is invisible. Is this real?'

'Probably not,' Michelle shrugged. 'It is the Chinese, after all. And, more importantly, *Protocol IV* of the *Geneva Convention on Certain Conventional Weapons* states that laser weapons can't be used with the intention of permanently blinding human beings. And any weapon that can burn one? Can blind one, and is damn sure not going to conform with international human rights laws, in particular the *Convention on Certain Conventional Weapons.'*

'But we're making one as well.'

'No, we're researching into it,' Michelle corrected. 'We have created no weapon. That I know of.'

'That I know of,' Bullman echoed the ominous sounding phrase. 'Let me guess, Ma'am. The melted pacemaker was thanks to something like this?'

'It seems coincidental, don't you think?'

Bullman leaned back, concerned.

'Prime Minister, you have intelligence sections more

tasked to this than us,' she said. 'Also, this is a military matter, so Special Investigations and Military Police should be investigating. At the least, the Military of Defence Police—'

'Could all be compromised,' Michelle interrupted. 'I'm taking a leaf out of their own books here.'

She leaned forward, resting her arms on the desk as she did so.

'I need a team to examine this while *not* looking to examine this,' she explained. 'I need people to find out what happened without alerting anyone.'

'Going to be hard, if we all rock up—' Bullman stopped. '—this is why you didn't mention Walsh, isn't it?'

'DI Walsh has been seconded by SIB Castleton,' Michelle explained. 'Murder victim with a connection to Walsh, from what I was told by my Security Advisor. He was allowed a partner and, as it's not a City police matter, he asked for DCI Monroe.'

'Castleton being the same place that we're going to,' Bullman flicked through the file some more. 'We're going to help Declan, but actually look into this?'

She placed the file back onto the desk, looking the new Prime Minister in the eye.

'We're not Section D or Rattlestone,' she said carefully. "We don't play favourites and we don't moonlight as security forces. If we do this, we play to our strengths and we follow the rule of law. If we find anyone guilty who you don't want to be guilty? Then that's tough luck, Ma'am.'

'Wouldn't have it any other way,' Michelle Rose smiled, but Bullman distrusted the woman.

'The Chinese rifle press release is dated 2018,' she said.
'Indeed.'

'Malcolm Gladwell was *Minister of State for the Armed*

Forces until 2018,' Bullman continued. 'Charles Baker was an Under Secretary there until the Balkans problem occurred in 2015, and was moved when Theresa May became Prime Minister in 2016. I believe you were his replacement?'

Michelle Rose didn't reply. Bullman nodded, accepting this as confirmation.

'So you were there at this point.'

Again, no reply.

Bullman considered this.

'What do we get out of this?' she eventually enquired.

'What do you mean?' the new Prime Minister now leaned back, as if realising she'd underestimated her opponent here. Bullman shrugged.

'This is something so secretive that you couldn't tell Bradbury about. That you brought to us because you knew we'd all signed the *Official Secrets Act*, but also because Declan is on his way there now, and you can use us. The same team that always worked with DI Walsh, and wouldn't raise any eyebrows if we all turned up. The Last Chance Saloon, as predictable as ever.'

'Go on.'

'The body of Falconer was found a week back, so this isn't recent news. You've sat on this until you can find an excuse to get someone in, and the start date of this project was during the time you were the Minister rubber-stamping these things,' Bullman shifted in her seat. 'If I was a cynical person, and believe me, Ma'am, I am, I'd say that you were worried that something very dangerous had been used or even stolen from a military base, something you personally agreed research on, and something that, if it came out would show the British Government, and in particular you, were wilfully ignoring *Protocol IV* of the *Geneva Convention on Certain*

Conventional Weapons back then, the reveal happening a week or two into your Prime Ministership, and before the Queen signs off on you and your new Cabinet. How am I doing so far?'

The temperature in the room dropped as Michelle Rose stared icily at Bullman.

'You're pretty much spot on, so far,' she said. 'So what do you want out of this?'

'If we sort this for you, solve this case, you get the police commission to drop the case against DCI Monroe,' Bullman straightened as she spoke. 'He's made mistakes, but he's a good copper. We scratch your back? You lose the files.'

Michelle nodded.

'I can do that,' she said. 'The Home Secretary owes me a favour.'

Bullman was actually surprised at this; she'd expected to have to work harder and now wondered what else she could have got away with.

'I want it in writing,' Bullman continued. 'Before I leave this building and signed by your hand as the current Prime Minister. I want it to state once we locate the rifle, if it even exists, and identify the killer, all current investigations into DCI Monroe are not only dropped, but removed from his permanent record.'

Michelle Rose clicked her tongue as she contemplated this.

'Wait outside, and I'll get this done before I bring your boss back in,' Michelle rose, offering her hand. 'In the meantime, start sending texts, or WhatsApp's, or whatever you use to get your people ready. You're going on manoeuvres.'

Bullman rose, shaking the Prime Minister's offered hand.

'I really did vote for you,' she said as, taking the file from the desk once more, she turned and left the room. 'I didn't want another Charles Baker in that chair. Don't prove me wrong.'

The door closed behind her.

Michelle Rose stood alone for a moment, drinking in the silence.

Then, tapping on the intercom, she spoke into it.

'Maisie, get Colonel Yates on the line,' she said. 'Tell him I'm adding a few more people to his shopping list, whether he likes it or not. Then get me a meeting with the Brigadier, so I can get him up to speed. And finally, bring me the notes from our source in Castleton before I aim coppers at the place.'

This done, she sat back down in the chair, looking up at the ceiling, realising that every Prime Minister had probably done the same thing at some point of their tenure.

That piece of plaster had probably had more Prime Ministerial scrutiny than the Leader of the opposition.

For a moment, Michelle Rose wondered if she'd made the right decision pushing for the role. And then, stretching her arms, she laughed.

'Damn right I did,' she muttered. 'If only to stop bloody Baker.'

Buzzing the intercom again, she spoke.

'Oh, and send someone in right now with a pad and pen,' she said commandingly. 'I need to draft and sign a quick letter right now before it gives me a bloody headache.'

3

REUNITED

AFTER ALLOWING HIM A QUICK FAREWELL WITH HIS RECENTLY gained surfing buddy, the Military Police had taken Declan back to his St Davids guesthouse before heading off to the Peak District, where the Colonel had stated he'd meet Declan the next day. Which was surprising, as Yates was based in Portsmouth, and as far as Declan knew, had never really spent time around Castleton, apart from clearing up Declan and Eddie's mess a good decade ago. Now alone, Declan had taken a moment to breathe, sit down and briefly grieve for his friend before he packed, paid his bill and clambered reluctantly into his Audi to make his way back home. He'd intended to go to Hurley by the weekend anyway, and although the news of Eddie's death had moved aside most other emotions, there was a little piece of resentment at Yates and his arrival in the back of his mind, one that was unhappy at having his break curtailed early.

Of course, it did get him out of more surfing lessons.

The drive from St Davids to Hurley was a good four and a half hours but he resisted the urge to turn on the flashing blue lights, and instead took the time to mull over the last conversation he'd had with Eddie, stopping at a service station after the Severn Bridge and sipping at a coffee as he stared out of the window over the estuary, remembering his onetime partner.

Eddie had been cold when Declan left the RMP, damn-right rude if he was honest. Declan understood this, as he could see the pain in Eddie's own expression; but Eddie was a bachelor with an army career path ahead of him, and Declan was married, with a kid, and looking at safer jobs to have.

Declan had chuckled at this; that 'safer' job had cost him his marriage, eventually.

Over the years that followed, Eddie and Declan had drifted apart, in the way people often do. Eddie had gone from the guy Declan spoke to every day, to a phone call a week, to once a month catch ups, to the eventual one a year Christmas cards finality of a close friendship. In the end, Eddie had kept better contact with Patrick Walsh, Declan's dad than with Declan himself. Which had hurt, but Declan understood fully why Eddie did this.

But Eddie had been odd when they last met, and Declan even asked his dad whether he'd heard any stories about Eddie finding God; he seemed at peace for the first time in his life, as if finally making a decision that he could live with, something that would shape the rest of his life. It almost felt as if Eddie had some kind of terminal diagnosis, and had come to terms with the inevitable end, but when Declan not-so-subtly enquired about this, Eddie had shot the idea down. Of course, after they had the row two years back, Eddie never replied to an email or returned a call again, and Declan just assumed that, like many others, this was a friendship that had run its course.

Declan couldn't remember what his last words to Eddie were. He hoped they'd been kind, but he doubted it very much.

By the time he arrived at the house in Hurley, he'd been driving for most of the afternoon and evening, it was almost eight pm, and he wasn't surprised to see Anjli Kapoor's far newer police-issue car in the driveway. His housemate for the last couple of months, Anjli was still a part of the Temple Inn Command Unit, and before he'd left for his St Davids break, Declan had found the workload wasn't busy enough to keep him late at the office, so unless something major had occurred in the last few days, the same would have been true for her.

Besides, with Declan being away, she probably enjoyed the house all the more.

Entering through the front door, dumping his leather overnight duffel to the floor as he closed it behind him, he saw Anjli walking out of the kitchen, a mug of tea in her hand.

'Thought you weren't coming back this week?' she asked, walking over to the coffee table and placing the mug down, picking up an iPad and placing it in a messenger bag.

'Things caught up with me,' Declan replied as he glanced at the messenger bag, not missing the fact that she'd immediately hidden the tablet within it. 'I texted you. I've been seconded on another case.'

'That's nice,' Anjli said, grabbing the bag and mug as she started for the stairs. Declan, however, moved quickly to block her way. 'Must have missed it. Been a bit busy—'

'Anj, do we have a problem?' he asked. 'I didn't think we'd ended on an unpleasant note?'

'We ended?' Anjli laughed, and it was a bitter bark of a

laugh. 'Yeah, you need to *start,* to end, Declan. And you've pretty much shown you don't like doing that.'

There was a pregnant pause in the room, as Anjli backed away a little, realising she shouldn't have replied so harshly. Declan wasn't angry, though; he would have been the same way, and he knew she was in the right.

'Look, my decision wasn't anything to do with you,' Declan shook his head, 'I swear. This is about me—'

'And now you're using break up lines to make me feel better?' Anjli pushed past Declan. '*It's not you, it's me.* What a crock of shit. Let me end that line for you. *It's not you, it's me, being a coward and a martyr and deciding to stick my head in the sand.*'

'That's fair,' Declan nodded. 'But I still stand by what I said. I felt I'd failed, and if it hadn't been for other circumstances, I'd have let dozens of Government Ministers and possibly the Prime Minister and the Queen die on my watch. If that happened, I'd have been crucified live on TV.'

'And you weren't, because it *didn't*,' Anjli shook her head, the anger now being replaced by sadness. 'You're the only one blaming yourself, Declan. And you're killing your career because of it. You remember when Billy tried to quit? You made him stay, and he's far happier now. I was going to quit when you found out about Johnny and Jackie Lucas holding my mum's cancer treatment for ransom, forcing me to spy for them, and you made me stay. When Monroe was going to quit after Birmingham, you had Trix delete the resignation letter he was writing when Frost attacked him.'

Declan went to reply, but stopped as Anjli punched the wall in anger, the sound of the fist hitting plaster echoing around the house.

'*Why do we all have to stay and you get to piss off?*' she snapped, looking down at her hand. 'Ow.'

'Bullman could have denied the resignation,' Declan muttered. 'She showed me the door.'

'She was doing reverse psychology, you muppet,' Anjli sighed. 'By the time she realised it'd gone wrong, you'd walked.'

Declan turned away from the stairs, giving up on blocking Anjli. Instead, he walked to the sofa and slumped down on it.

'It's not just the Houses of Parliament,' he whispered. 'It's a long list of dead people who I couldn't save. An ex-wife and daughter who constantly have to hide or get police protection because I'm connected to them.'

'What, and you think that going to work for ASDA as a security guard will stop that?' Anjli followed him, placing the messenger bag on the side as she sat in the armchair facing him. 'They'll still gun for you. But now you won't have your warrant card to help you arrest them.'

'No, I'll have you for that,' Declan forced a smile, but it felt wrong. 'Look, I know. And I'm still unsure if I've made the right decision, but I need to go with my gut. And right now, I think I'm toxic to the people I care about. To Liz, to Jess, to the team... to *you*.'

Declan could have misread it, but it looked like Anjli flushed a little at this line; he'd probably took it a little too far, and she was uncomfortable at the comment.

'As a partner, and a housemate, of course,' he added awkwardly.

'Of course,' Anjli nodded, answering a little too quickly. 'So, changing the subject from your resignation idiocy, what did you find on your little holiday jaunt?'

'Francine Pearce kept to herself,' Declan leaned back on the sofa. 'She'd buy food every couple of days and bought a saveloy and chips every night from the chippy rather than eating in the pub.'

'So nothing then?'

'I didn't say that,' Declan nodded at the mug of tea, now on the table. 'Is that for me?'

'Go on, I'll make another,' Anjli rose from the chair and walked off into the kitchen. 'Keep talking. I can hear.'

'The day we found her and took her to Haverfordwest, Trix sent some Section D operatives to wire up her house with cameras,' Declan continued. 'The idea was to scare her and Tricia, and flush out where she hid things, to see if we could gain information without her realising we knew.'

'And then she blew up,' Anjli replied from the kitchen.

'Well, someone blew up,' Declan said as Anjli walked back into the living room with another mug of tea. 'You see, whatever Section D did, they forgot that St Davids is a village, and the infrastructure isn't that great for Wi-Fi. They blew a fuse or something, took out the block of houses and cottages around Francine's.'

'Power cut?'

'No, just a broadband and phone signal outage,' Declan sipped at the tea. 'Urgh. It's got sugar in it.'

'Make your own, then,' Anjli replied. Declan sipped again with a smile.

'Anyway, the outage meant the cameras didn't work,' he explained. 'Apparently they would have gone onto some kind of hard-wired *super secret squirrel spy backup mode* and recorded everything, but they lost those in the explosion.'

'Okay, so why the 'someone' line?' Anjli asked. 'We saw

the results of the postmortem. The DNA matched. So did the fingerprints.'

'I know,' Declan nodded. 'But then we also know that people can change these, if enough money passes hands. You need to look at the facts on the ground rather than the more visible options.'

'Thanks for the detective tip, boss,' Anjli mocked. 'I'd never have worked that out.'

'Francine Pearce died in the explosion,' Declan nodded. 'But an hour before it happened, she bought her evening meal from the chippy. Cod and chips.'

'So?'

'So, I checked, and Francine was allergic to seafood,' Declan placed the mug down. 'She *never* ordered cod. She had saveloys, pies, sausages, never fish of any kind.'

'Maybe she wanted a change?'

'Or someone else was eating the food,' Declan shrugged. 'She was picked up and swapped with another, maybe thinking the police were watching and needing to have a quiet council of war, not realising that Karl had left her a farewell gift.'

'And the DNA?'

'Someone tried to blow her up,' Declan smiled. 'Maybe after the dust settled, she realised this was an opportunity to get out.'

'So the double goes to the cottage and you can't see this because of the outage,' Anjli considered this. 'And then she buys fish and chips, and boom.'

'That's as far as I'd got before I was brought back,' Declan rubbed at his neck, feeling the tightness there. 'I think she's gone, and with luck she's gone for good, whether dead or not.'

He looked at the messenger bag.

'You off somewhere?' he asked.

Anjli smiled.

'New case,' she said. 'Given to us from the Prime Minister herself.'

'Oh aye?' Declan raised an eyebrow. 'Now Baker's gone, you've become the next go to?'

'Bullman, actually,' Anjli patted the messenger bag. 'We're to go up north, work a case in the Peak District.'

Declan felt a chill wind move down his spine.

'What part of the Peak District?' he asked.

'Castleton,' Anjli rose, picking up the bag. 'Same place as you. Apparently, we're to assist you and DCI Monroe. Bullman said she'd explain everything tomorrow.'

'Wait,' Declan rose. 'Why would Michelle Rose command that? This isn't a major case. It's a dead soldier, nothing more.'

'Wouldn't know, as Bullman hasn't explained it yet,' Anjli replied, watching Declan. 'So why don't you? Unless you have something better to do?'

There was a long, unspoken moment before Declan nodded, motioning for Anjli to sit back down.

'I was a Corporal in the Special Investigations Bureau before I was a copper, you know that already,' he said. 'But I don't think I ever said why I left.'

'Jess told me once,' Anjli replied. 'Her mum was badgering you for a more stable life, and after your twelve years, your dad got you in with his team in Tottenham under DS Salmon.'

'That was the official reason,' Declan admitted. 'And it was a lot of why I did it, but it wasn't the actual reason I left.'

Declan walked to the cabinet by the front window,

opening it up and pulling out a bottle of whisky. Pouring a generous measure into a tumbler, he replaced the bottle and, glass in hand, walked back to the sofa.

'Sergeant Paddy Harper,' Declan said, staring at the glass. 'Mean bastard, wife beater, racist homophobe, general all-over prick of the highest degree. Eddie—that's my partner at the time, Lance Corporal Eddie Moses, we'd been hunting him for ages. Eddie was seeing a Private, Jo Tooley, while we were in Hamburg. She was a junior engineer in the RMP, and one night, while we were on patrol, we think she found something on Harper and tried to find us. But we were out hunting down our own leads. Rather than waiting, she confronted him on her own. When we found her, she was dead.'

He took a mouthful, feeling the warmth of the spirit slide down his throat as he tried to numb the memory.

'Her throat was slit with a serrated knife, and her Red Cap insignia had been removed, cut away like a sick trophy.'

'Was it Harper?' Anjli's eyes had widened, and she sat on the edge of the armchair seat, cradling her mug with both hands. Declan shrugged.

'Evidence pointed at him. She'd left a message saying she was off to confront him, and we never found what she had, or even why she did this. But there was no proof, his superiors didn't need the shite, and as far as they were concerned, on paper he'd already been shipped off home, as there was some kind of flight manifest discrepancy that had him in the UK before she found him. A few months later, we followed after hearing worrying rumours from the UK. They billeted us in Portsmouth under Postie—I mean *Major* Yates, who'd been our CO for a couple of years by then, and had arrived in the UK a month or so before us, learning that Harper went to

Castleton, up north, where Harper's regiment, the *Derbyshires,* were based. Didn't take Eddie long to find him.'

'This was personal.'

'More for Eddie than me, but yeah,' Declan nodded. 'Shortly before we left, Yates heard that a female Private in the Logistics Unit was now missing, too. We decided no smoke without fire, had already pre-judged Harper and drove up there. We asked around, followed a lead from a pub, and found her through this hidden door to a basement in an abandoned warehouse.'

He took another mouthful; this time he finished the whole glass.

'There were two other bodies with her, both women,' he explained, rising and walking back to the cabinet. 'She was only just alive. Harper caught us. He had a rifle.'

'I know this bit,' Anjli nodded. 'I had to read your record back when DI Frost was claiming you were a terrorist. He came in and shot at you, but Lance Corporal Moses fired his pistol in self defence, killing Harper. You saved the victim.'

'That's the official report,' Declan shook his head, his eyes haunted. 'The truth is that Harper was more surprised to see us than we were him. I think he was drunk, too. Or at least on something. And before he could do anything, Eddie shot him first.'

Declan walked back to the table, this time taking the bottle with him.

'The official report claimed we were heroes. We found Malik. We stopped a killer. Sure, we were bollocked for going off script to do it, we had weaponry on us we should have handed in the previous day, and it pretty much scuppered any chance I had of making Sergeant anytime soon, but they couldn't really punish the guys who solved a serial killer case.'

'But you didn't think he was the killer?' Anjli read Declan's expression. Declan shrugged.

'I don't know,' he said. 'I mean, sure, at the start I did, but there were other things that turned up after the case. There was another woman, killed the same way Jo Tooley was.'

He mimed a knife across the throat.

'A journalist named Susan Jenkins. Found dead near the camp, dumped in a ditch. Eddie was convinced it was Harper, but the dates didn't match up. She died two, maybe three days before he returned from Hamburg.'

'He had help? Maybe there was more than just him doing this?'

Declan rubbed at his eyes, as if trying to push back a headache.

'I have nightmares. Always have. After Kendis died, before we took on the Red Reaper case, I started seeing Jo Tooley in them. Never understood why; now I wonder if it was Jo, telling me to find her real killer.'

He took another mouthful.

'Harper spoke to me that day,' he whispered. 'He said we should have just left him alone, that he was having fun in Germany. Then he said *that bitch MP should have kept her mouth shut, so she didn't have to—*'

'Have to what?'

'No idea, because Eddie shot him,' Declan replied. 'As he was dying, Harper spoke one last time. I'll always remember it. *He'll see you... He sees everything. Tells us what to do... gives us orders... wasn't me... Sentry... for... high... all...*'

Declan stared at the glass.

'He was a sentry. He was guarding for someone else.

Someone who ordered him on what to do, maybe someone high up. After he died, we checked his house, everywhere, but we didn't find the trophy he took from Jo.'

'What happened?'

'Nothing,' Declan shook his head. 'Army likes straightforward answers. Killer *killed people*, killer *dead*. End of. I wanted to carry on, see if there was more, but Yates spoke with Eddie, pointed out what would happen if we opened it back up. The wife and kids were already getting flack from the press, from the locals. I think the mum took to drink. I never checked. In the end, once my twelve years were up, I was gone.'

'And how does this link to a dead soldier?'

'Because the dead soldier is Eddie Moses,' Declan replied. 'Yates, now a Colonel came and found me in Wales. Eddie's body was discovered in the Peak District, only three miles from the location we killed Harper in all those years ago, which apparently has been bulldozed down and turned into a research complex for the Ministry of Defence. He'd been dead for a year at least, taped up in a body bag and hidden.'

Anjli leaned over, grabbing the whisky bottle and filling her empty mug with it.

'Yeah, I can see why this is going to be hard for you,' she said. 'So what's the plan?'

'The plan is you stay in London,' Declan suggested. 'Temple Inn shouldn't get involved in this mess, no matter what Whitehall says.'

'Yeah, that's not gonna happen,' Anjli leaned closer, punching Declan on the arm. 'We'll help you find who killed your friend. After all, what are partners for?'

She stopped.

'Who told you about the warehouse?' she asked.

Declan frowned.

'What do you mean?'

'I mean, you drive up to Castleton, ask around and then some bloke in a pub sends you to the exact place you needed to be? Sounds convenient.'

Declan considered this. Anjli was right. If it happened now, he would have been suspicious, but back then they'd wanted blood, and they appreciated any answer. But for the life of him, he couldn't remember who told them. It wasn't even in the report. He just remembered it was a local. *Maybe with a beard?* It was a decade ago and was five minutes of Declan's time.

Declan stared at the glass in his hand, but he wasn't looking at the tumbler. He was a hundred miles and a decade away, staring at a dead Sergeant in a warehouse basement.

A Sergeant he didn't believe was as guilty as everyone had stated.

A moment that had defined his life from that point on.

And now he was returning; to the same place once more. His last case for the police, a murder enquiry that was too coincidental to not be connected. He'd checked the file while packing; they had stationed Eddie in Portsmouth before he disappeared.

So why was he back in the Peak District?

4

BASE RULES

THE ARMY BASE WHERE DECLAN AND HIS TEAM WERE TO WORK from was a small military installation run in part by soldiers of the *Derbyshire Regiment*; a unit that had been decommissioned almost twenty years earlier.

Now, it amalgamated the *Bedfordshire Light Infantry,* the *remnants of the infamous Cardigan Regiment* and the *Cumberland Fusiliers,* returning to where it once held court around a decade after its death, to the west of Castleton and east of Chapel-en-le-Frith, held just within the Peak District National Park, with the high slopes of Mam Tor watching down on them.

Actually, this wasn't quite true; Declan and his team weren't going to be on the base, but in a building just outside, currently occupied by the Derbyshire branch of the Ministry of Defence Police. And 'building' was a little grand, Declan decided, as he pulled up outside what looked to be a dozen modular, one-storey mobile buildings, in the style of the Portakabin 'mobile classrooms' his school had during his teens, all linked by corridors and pathways like some mad inventor's Lego design.

As Declan and Anjli emerged from the Audi, Anjli having decided that car sharing would be a more logical solution than the two of them driving separately from and to the same locations, Colonel Yates, in his army fatigues appeared in the main entrance to meet them.

'Detective Inspector Walsh,' he smiled, shaking Declan's hand. 'See? I'm trying not to use Corporal.'

'That's appreciated, sir,' Declan replied, nodding at Anjli. 'This is Detective Sergeant Anjli Kapoor. Anjli, this is Colonel Barry Yates, my old commanding officer.'

Yates nodded, glancing at Anjli, taking in her grey suit, her pulled back hair. She'd dressed as she did for every case, but Declan had noted while driving that she'd worn a minimum of makeup this day. When asked, she'd explained this was to match the female soldiers she'd be meeting, even quoting Chapter 5, Part 9, Paragraph 5.366 b of *The Queen's Regulations for the Army*, something that even Declan hadn't read in a very long time, explaining that make up, if worn, was to be inconspicuous.

Declan had wondered whether Anjli had a secret desire to be in the military, but had kept quiet on this.

'I thought DCI Monroe seemed to have changed,' Yates smiled. 'Last time I saw him was at your wedding, but even that wouldn't have altered him so...' he left the point hanging, the joke made. 'Call me Barry. It's less military.'

'I believe DCI Monroe is on his way,' Declan replied. He went to speak again, but Yates, his tone clipped, interrupted.

'I guessed that, Walsh,' he said. 'However, I seem to find myself a little confused here. I brought you in to do this alone. I agreed to your request and gave you one assistant in

Monroe, but here you are with a Detective Sergeant, and already we have on site a new Divisional Surgeon and her assistant, a Detective Constable connecting a wealth of computer equipment to our server and a beast of a Police Constable who I'm seriously considering recruiting.'

He leaned closer.

'Not really the 'one advisor' you mentioned. And this is a circus that's definitely *not* what I wanted, or even expected, Walsh.'

'I seem to recall your actual order was to *bring whomever and whatever you need*,' Declan replied icily, preparing for a fight. Colonel Yates might not be the simple Major he once was, but he also wasn't Declan's *boss anymore*.

'DI Walsh isn't to blame here, sir,' Anjli moved in now, realising that an argument was about to spill over into a full-blown row. 'We were brought into the case to assist him by orders of the new Prime Minister herself. Our boss, Detective Superintendent Bullman, will arrive shortly.'

She looked back at Declan.

'Personally, I thought we'd be first,' she said morosely. 'Billy will have grabbed the best spot.'

Declan nodded for Anjli to rejoin her colleagues, and as she left, looked back at Yates.

'I only found out last night,' he explained. 'I don't think Whitehall trust me without my handlers.'

Yates looked like he was about to spit out nails.

'Bloody Whitehall did this,' he muttered, with the expression of someone who not only believed that someone had done this deliberately to spite him, but also probably knew who it was. 'Well, it's a bloody pain, and it's right royally pissed off the Ministry of Defence Police.'

'If *Mod Plod* has an issue—'

'We don't call them that here,' Yates snapped. 'You civvies might think they're not up to scratch, but we've been in the trenches with them. Literally.'

'Sorry,' Declan flushed. 'I'm just a little tired, sir.'

'You need to be on your game with the MDP,' Yates warned. 'The officer running their side of this is already waiting for you to slip and fall.'

He nodded over at the entrance, where a slim, harsh-looking woman in her twenties was now approaching them. She was in a black suit, with a-line skirt, sensible shoes, a white shirt and shoulder length hair pulled back. She looked like an agent from *The Matrix* more than a police officer, but there was something eerily familiar to her.

'I see you've all made yourself at home,' she said icily. 'No change there, then.'

'Sorry about that,' Declan held a hand out. 'I didn't know it was happening. I'm DI Walsh.'

The woman made no attempt to shake the hand; Declan let it drop.

'And you are?' he eventually asked, the warmth in his tone now gone.

'Detective Inspector Declan Walsh, City Police, meet Ministry of Defence Police Detective Sergeant Carrie Harper,' Yates introduced, emphasising the surname. 'You last saw her over a decade ago.'

Declan recognised Carrie Harper now; a woman-once-child, and the younger of the two Harper children.

Harper, who Eddie Moses shot in cold blood, in an abandoned warehouse not more than three miles away.

'You're on the case?' he asked with surprise.

'You have a problem with that?' Carrie's expression matched her voice. Declan, appealing, looked at Yates.

'Sir, her father was Sergeant Paddy Harper,' he protested. 'Eddie Moses shot him.'

'I'm aware of that, Walsh,' Yates replied icily. 'I did read the occasional report during my time over you both.'

'He shot him in self-defence,' Carrie interrupted, looking at Declan as she continued. 'I'm not my father, DI Walsh. And whether or not I believe *Lance Corporal* Moses did the right thing, I'm now investigating the murder of *Staff Sergeant Moses.*'

She moved closer; easily a foot shorter than Declan, she still intimidated him.

'A man I made peace with over two years ago, after he sought me out to speak to me,' she said. 'Something you never did, *sir.*'

Declan was speechless, caught short. Numbly, he nodded.

'Of course,' he breathed. 'Sorry.'

'Why should you be? You weren't the one that shot him. You just stood over him as he died,' Carrie snapped, nodding her head at a car now arriving. ' I've briefed your people and they're waiting for you, I believe these are the last two you're waiting for.'

And, before Declan could reply, DS Carrie Harper spun on her heels and walked off, incredibly stiffly.

'You could have warned me of that,' Declan muttered. Yates shrugged.

'Turnabout is fair play, Corporal,' he said, nodding at the approaching Monroe and Bullman. 'You could have told me the circus was coming to town.'

Yates walked towards Bullman, intercepting her before she could get any further, and Declan knew he was now complaining to her about their arrival. Which was fine, as Bullman could argue with the best of them.

'Did I miss much?' Monroe asked as Declan turned and walked in step with him towards the building.

'Pretty much everything, Guv,' Declan smiled. 'Hey, I thought you would have cadged a lift with Doctor Marcos?'

Monroe shook his head.

'Things are a little sketchy there,' he replied. 'I might have cooled things down a little after the suspension.'

'Why?' Declan stopped, facing his mentor. 'You needed her more than ever back then.'

'Because she'd only just been accepted back into the force, remember?' Monroe replied bitterly, and Declan remembered that for the first few months of his tenure at the Last Chance Saloon, Doctor Marcos had been banned from crime scenes because of her unorthodox antics, something that had helped move her to the Last Chance Saloon in the first place.

'She wouldn't have cared,' Declan said, and Monroe sniffed.

'Not on my watch,' he turned and carried on towards the door. 'I wasn't going to let her shite away her career again because she had any kind of affiliation with me.'

He stopped, looked back at Declan with a wry smile.

'I mean,' he added. 'The only other idiot keeping any kind of affiliation up right now is two months from the door anyway.'

Declan laughed at the comment.

'This was supposed to be our last hurrah,' he said, joining Monroe as they walked to the MDP entrance. 'Now it's a bloody reunion episode.'

'Could be worse,' Monroe opened the door, allowing Declan through. 'Could be hosted by that guy who's in all the movie musicals.'

Declan nodded. That, sadly, was very true.

———————

THE LAST CHANCE SALOON HAD REQUISITIONED A SMALL briefing room, with a whiteboard at the front, and rows of desks facing it, not really removing the overlaying style of 'school classroom'. At the front was Doctor Marcos, pinning images to the whiteboard with blu-tac, while DC Billy Fitzwarren sat morosely at the side, staring at his laptop. At the back, Anjli, PC Morten De'Geer and DC Joanna Davey were laughing, but that stopped as Declan and Monroe walked in.

'Rosanna,' Monroe said to Doctor Marcos, and even Declan, useless at picking up non-verbal signals, could tell that it was uncomfortable.

'Alexander,' Doctor Marcos replied. 'It's good to see you out of your house at last.'

'Aye,' Monroe mumbled, walking over to the desk behind Billy and sitting at it. Declan followed, looking down at the dejected Billy.

'You alright?' he asked. Billy, in his trademark expensive, tailored three-piece suit, shrugged.

'There's no plasma board,' he murmured, as if to himself. 'How am I supposed to show images if there's no plasma board?'

'Print them out?' Declan showed Doctor Marcos pinning pages onto the board and was amused by the look of horror that Billy gave him. 'Just think back to how it was in Hurley. At least there's better Wi-Fi here.'

There was a sudden silence, and Declan looked up to see Bullman enter the classroom—no, *briefing* room.

'Right then, sit down,' Bullman smiled, looking around. 'Looks like the lesson's about to start.'

'Ma'am, why exactly are we here?' De'Geer asked. 'It's not regulation—'

'Regulations are out of the window right now,' Bullman replied. 'Orders from on high, but we'll get to that in a moment. First, if DI Walsh can get us up to speed?'

Declan stepped forward, nodding to Bullman as he turned to the Unit.

'First off, this wasn't my idea, so don't blame me,' he said. 'I only dragged the old man with me.'

'Old man. Nice,' Monroe muttered.

Declan ignored the comment as he looked back at the images Doctor Marcos had stuck to the whiteboard; a military ID for Eddie, as well as crime scene photos of his discovery.

'Staff Sergeant Edward Moses, Special Investigations Bureau,' he started, feeling a lump in his throat. 'Over a decade ago, he was Lance Corporal Moses, and my partner in the Royal Military Police.'

There was a murmuring at this, and Declan had to remind himself that currently, apart from Anjli, nobody else really knew what was going on here.

'A couple of days ago, a dog walker, taking her Terrier for a stroll just south of the Mam Tor Bridleway, and just north of Blue John Cavern saw him run off after some sheep on the hill.'

'Staff Sergeant Moses?' DC Davey was confused at this.

'No, the terrier,' Declan replied, remembering that with these people, you couldn't be generic.

'That makes more sense. Supposed to have them on leads around there,' DC Davey muttered. 'That's bad dog owning.'

'You know the area?' Declan asked. Davey flushed at the attention, usually happier to stick to the shadows.

'Used to spend my summers here, Guv,' she replied.

'Excellent. You're the local guide now,' Declan smiled. 'Anyway, the Terrier finds his way into a small cave on the side of the hill. The landscape is littered with them, and people don't go in because of collapsing roofs. Bit of a drop into the cave, dog's now trapped, won't come out, she won't go in, calls the Fire Brigade. Some local volunteers from the army base arrive and slide into the cave—' he pointed at another image, a picture that was literally showing a slit in the ground, only a foot in height, '—and when they got in, they found it went back about ten metres where, on a shelf at the back of a small hollow, a body bag had been wedged. Unless you looked for it, you wouldn't see the bag, as it was black; and a dead sheep's carcass was hiding any smells.'

'Probably what attracted the Terrier, too,' Monroe suggested.

'Most likely. The only reason they found the bag was because they'd shone the torch around the inside, looking for the dog.'

'Was the Terrier okay?' De'Geer now asked.

'Yes, PC De'Geer, the Terrier was fine,' Declan replied.

'I kinda feel you're just saying that to keep him quiet,' Anjli grinned. 'The Terrier was fine and went to live on a farm, and wasn't—'

She made a *skrrrttccchh* noise as she ran a finger across her throat.

De'Geer looked in horror at Anjli, and Declan realised that he might have suddenly learned a terrible secret from his childhood with that one sentence. Sighing, Declan looked at Doctor Marcos.

'Have you had a chance to go over anything?' he asked.

'I've not examined the body yet, but the SIB forensics have been quite thorough,' Doctor Marcos nodded. 'The body was sealed in a body bag and they taped the zip up to make sure it was totally air tight. Now, this wasn't for decades like the one we had in the recording studio a while back, but a year still makes the body a little... unsightly.'

There was an uncomfortableness that crossed the room, and Declan understood it. Dead bodies were one thing, but ones that were, well, *juicy* weren't so nice.

'The body is estimated to be a year old, but there's no way to accurately date it, as there's not any external situation to assist. If he'd been dumped in a grave, we could have checked the maggots, the dirt itself, all sorts of things. Here, we just have an estimation. Even the temperatures would have pretty much stayed consistent in the bag. Apart from if it was freezing, that is, and we had a mild winter.'

She pointed at another A4 sheet of paper, with an image of some items upon it; placed on a table and photographed together, these comprised a single dog tag, a stainless steel watch and a stained leather wallet.

'He didn't have any personal items on him, apart from his ID tag, which are usually two circular non-reflecting stainless steel tags that go around the neck, stating the soldier's blood group, service number, surname and initials, and their religion, if they have one—'

'You said tag, and usually,' Monroe interrupted. 'Is one missing?'

Doctor Marcos nodded.

'The tags are on two chains,' she explained. 'One is around the neck, the other linked to the first by a smaller chain. It's so you can pull it off easily to identify the dead.'

She pointed back at the image.

'This one is a single tag. The chances are the other was removed as a trophy, it came off during his death, or snapped off when the killer dumped him in the bag.'

Declan stared at the image.

'Can we zoom in on the picture, maybe on Billy's laptop?'

'Here you go,' Billy tapped on his keyboard for a moment before he spun his laptop to face the others, the screen now filled with the image of the tag, eager to be of use.

'There,' Declan pointed at the edge of the tag, where three markings were visible. 'It looks like someone's punched some indents into it.'

'Looks like a Phillips, or crosshead screwdriver for the first and third ones, and a Torx screwdriver in the middle,' De'Geer peered closely. 'I use both on my bikes. But you'd have to really hammer on it to make that. This isn't an accidental scratch.'

'Okay, we can look into that,' Declan looked back to Doctor Marcos. 'What else do we have?'

'A kinetic watch, out of battery,' Doctor Marcos continued. 'As long as you move, it keeps going. We're hoping this can help with time of death, as the old ones used to stop after four days. However, this could have gone on for another six months, so it might not help. And then we have the wallet. No cards, no money, just one faded receipt that's unreadable, and a piece of filing card that's unfortunately been damaged.'

She pointed at another photo where, fading into a watered out mess on torn notepaper, were the words

DECLAN KNOWS

There was a second uncomfortable movement.

'Knows what?' Monroe asked.

'I wish I knew,' Declan sighed.

'There could have been more writing there, so we're looking into it,' Doctor Marcos interjected. 'No phone found with the body, but then we weren't expecting that. And then we come to the interesting one. I've not been able to work out cause of death as we haven't had a good rummage in the body yet, but we do have this.'

She nodded to Billy, who spun the laptop back around, showing a zoomed image of a small, silver ball.

'What the hell—is that a *musket* ball?' Declan leaned in.

Doctor Marcos clapped her hands.

'Well done, give that man a prize,' she said. 'Or, rather, a half-prize. It's not a musket ball, but the rifling marks on the side and the size estimate this was a projectile from what looks to be a .44 calibre duelling pistol.'

'Someone shot Eddie with a duelling pistol.'

It was stated as a comment rather than a question by Declan, but Doctor Marcos took it as the latter.

'More than that,' she explained. 'Duelling musket balls are usually lead. This is solid silver, although we're having it checked to see if it's all from the same source. Whoever killed Staff Sergeant Moses, there's a strong chance it was ritualistic.'

'Or he was a werewolf,' Billy spoke aloud, reddening as everyone looked at him. 'What, I can't be the only one thinking that.'

There was a long silence in the room, as if everyone there was either silently judging Billy, or silently agreeing with him.

'Okay, so we know what to do then,' Declan said. 'So. Tasks—'

'Hold on that,' Bullman stepped forward, closing the door behind her to make sure that nobody could listen in. 'Walsh, Monroe, you're on task here, as Colonel Yates called you in personally. And we *will* assist, especially as Doctor Marcos will examine the body. But, before I return to London, I need to explain to you all why the Prime Minister *really* sent us here.'

'I knew it,' De'Geer smiled. 'I knew there had to be more going on, when they made me sign the OSA.'

'Well done,' Davey mocked. 'We're all very proud of you.'

'So,' Bullman clapped her hands together, bringing the attention back to the whiteboard. 'Who here knows about *hand-held laser assault rifles?*'

5

MEMORY LANE

After Bullman had explained the Last Chance Saloon's *true* mission, she'd driven back to London, claiming that if she'd stayed, it'd have looked even more suspicious; as it was, Declan, bringing a full unit, had ruffled feathers in both the SIB and the other officers, especially DS Harper.

Everyone started working on their individual tasks; Billy had started work on examining the mysterious note about Declan, while Doctor Marcos went to see the body, conveniently in the same morgue as Lieutenant Colonel Falconer, him of the melted pacemaker. Anjli and De'Geer had gone to check into the research team, situated in a building complex the other side of Mam Tor, one built on top of a warehouse that once held a gruesome secret, while Declan and Monroe went through Eddie Moses' possessions.

The problem was, there *weren't any.*

According to the files that Yates had passed Declan on a beach in Wales, they had stationed Eddie in Portsmouth, over two hundred miles and a four-hour drive south from where his body had been found. More importantly, Eddie had told no one he was going to the Peak District, and for the first week he was missing, people simply assumed he was ill and laid up in his barracks dorm.

That he was likely already dead as they considered this was chilling.

But then again, there was a chance that Eddie *hadn't* been dead, as there was still no solid date of death. The last time Eddie was definitely seen in Portsmouth by any reliable witness was the twenty-third of June, over a year earlier, but Billy had examined the receipt found in the wallet and was convinced that he'd seen a very faint JUL on it, which could point to July, at least a week after that. He was looking into it, still; the print had faded, but the paper hadn't been as contaminated by, well, *Eddie,* as the other piece had.

Until they had some solid clues, though, Declan and Monroe had nowhere to start. They didn't even know if Eddie had even visited Castleton, regardless that the evidence they had seemed to point to it. There was no signing in sheet in the base with his name on, and if Declan really wanted to go down the conspiracy rabbit hole, there was every chance someone could have killed Staff Sergeant Edward Moses in Portsmouth around the start of July and brought the body to Castleton in a car, or van. After all, Declan had seen similar done before with Tom Marlowe and Karl Schnitter.

Billy had already spoken to a Quartermaster in Portsmouth by the time Declan arrived; Eddie's personal items had been placed into storage, only two boxes worth, and Billy had these sent up to the Peak District—but this would still take a day before they arrived. The only option they had was to ask if anyone recognised Eddie, and that started right there on the base.

It wasn't Declan's plan to start in the MDP office, but

Detective Sergeant Carrie Harper turned out to be their first port of call, mainly because she was in the office next to them, and they passed her while on the way out.

'Let me get something straight, sirs,' Carrie said as she sat at her desk, looking up at Declan and Monroe. 'You might be DI and DCI respectively, but this is *my* case. They gave it to me.'

'All I want to do is find who killed Staff Sergeant Moses,' Declan held his hands up. 'You've been working the clues since they found the body, I was hoping you might have a little more than we do right now.'

'Like why he was here, where he was staying, who he was talking to, things like that?' Carrie smiled, but it was a more mocking one. 'Yeah, that's not happening, Guv. Not that I don't want to, it's just we're coming up blank there. It's why the Colonel called you in, claiming you're the wonder copper who solves everything. Well, that and you're the prime suspect. Want to tell me where you were a year ago? On the record, perhaps, in the interview room?'

Declan bristled, but took the comment. The note in Eddie's wallet damned him, no matter what he said.

'Why the Colonel?' Monroe asked.

'What do you mean?'

'Colonel Yates is SIB but surely he doesn't run the case over MDP?'

Carrie shrugged.

'Army's really worried about this one. We usually deal with the more civilian aspects of military life, and currently, we don't know if it wasn't a civilian that killed him.'

'Do you know anything about the body bag then, lassie?' Monroe asked.

Carrie glared at him, and for a moment Declan was very glad that for once he wasn't on the other end of such a gaze.

'I ain't nobody's lassie, old man,' she muttered.

'I like her,' Monroe grinned, ignoring her expression and looking at Declan. 'And she doesn't like you, which makes it even better.'

Carrie stared at Monroe for a long moment before shaking her head, returning to Declan.

'Your dad's a bit of a character, isn't he?' she muttered.

'You should see him after last orders.'

'The body bag was taken from Quartermasters Stores on the seventh of June, so at least two weeks before Edward Moses even arrived here,' Carrie ignored the joke as she checked her notes.

'Any idea who could have requisitioned it?' Declan asked.

'Look around,' Carrie replied. 'Literally anyone here, or on the base. That's the problem.'

'Surely there's a record of the removal?'

'Only if you want it for, shall we say, *legitimate* reasons,' Carrie leaned back in her chair. 'If it's not, then you're not really going to tell people why you want it. Chances are you'd take it out with something else, and if challenged, class it as an oversight. At the end of the day, it's just a body bag. Who the hell steals one of those? The only reason we know it was taken then was because they were doing a stock check and the numbers were wrong over the space of three days.'

Declan nodded at this.

'What about the silver ball?' he enquired. 'Any thoughts on that?'

'Are you asking me because you're curious, or because you have to keep me in the loop, sir?' Carrie's voice was stiff and official. Declan went to snap back at this, finally tiring of the attitude being given to him, but stopped himself, taking a breath.

She deserved her shots here.

'Look, DS Harper,' he eventually said, lowering his voice. 'You don't like me, and to be honest, you have reasons to. I get that. But don't for one second think I'd keep you anywhere near this case if I didn't believe you were capable enough to be on it.'

Carrie Harper stared at Declan for a long moment before replying.

'I was out of line, I apologise,' she said. However, it was almost robotic, almost devoid of emotion, and Declan still couldn't tell if it was genuine or not. Considering this, he eventually shook his head.

'No, you weren't. I'm surprised you're not more hostile towards me, to be honest. It's completely justified.'

'Thank you, sir,' Carrie looked back at her monitor, as if uncomfortable looking at Declan, which was completely understandable to him. 'My father was a complex man.'

Declan looked at Monroe as he answered this.

'Look, this isn't relevant, but DCI Monroe here brought me into his unit to solve a case in Westminster. An old one, where my father accused and convicted the wrong man in a murder enquiry. I found the actual killer, and they were arrested.'

'Why are you telling me this?'

'Because for ten years, I've wondered whether your father truly did all the things we accused him of, and I did the same as my father once did—but at the same time, I've done nothing about it.'

Declan looked out of the office window, out towards the car park. He could see Anjli and De'Geer outside, talking, and more than anything wanted to be out there with them rather than having this conversation; but he knew he owed it to Carrie Harper.

He owed it to a lot of people, to be honest.

'I think I've been brought here not only to solve Eddie's murder but also to re-examine the evidence in your father's case,' he added. 'I think there has to be a connection somewhere.'

'The army won't like that,' Carrie replied, still looking away. 'Trust me on that one.'

'I leave the job in two months,' Declan smiled. 'And DCI Monroe here is technically suspended. What can they do to us?'

Carrie was silent, slowly nodding as she took this in. Declan knew she probably wouldn't have known this, so it was new information. More importantly, it was information she wouldn't usually receive, and Declan was hoping she understood he was giving her his trust.

'You should speak to my brother, Devin,' she said after clicking her tongue on the roof of her mouth for a few seconds, considering her next options. 'He's a Lieutenant in the *Derbyshire Regiment*, on the base. It's the unit that dad was in. His Major, Henry Eaton-Jones, was a Lieutenant when dad was alive. *He's* said for years it was a setup. Dad, that is. They should be here in a bit, I'm going for a late breakfast with them.'

'Probably not the best people for the guy who was involved in the attempted arrest and subsequent shooting to be chatting to, then?' Monroe winked.

'Depends why they're chatting, Guv,' Carrie seemed more relaxed now, as if realising that the two men in front of her weren't the enemy. Or, at least, were less an enemy than she'd expected.

Monroe shrugged an agreement with this.

'I'm curious about the ID tag,' he said. 'Did you spot the markings?'

'The screwdriver indents?' Carrie nodded. 'We saw those. Most likely accidental. They get battered around a lot.'

'I have a theory about those,' Monroe walked over to another desk and pulling the chair over. 'I'm wondering if they're killing markings. You know, like fighter pilots had on their cockpits, showing how many enemy planes they'd taken down.'

Declan considered this.

'Eddie never served in combat situations,' he said.

'But he has killed,' Carrie replied coldly.

'Yeah, but I don't recall him ever taking a screwdriver to his ID tags after shooting your father,' Declan shook his head, instantly regretting the cavalier way he'd spoken. 'Sorry. I didn't mean that the way it came out.'

Carrie rose.

'This is falling into the world of conspiracies and make believe,' she muttered. 'I need a cigarette.'

'We'll come with you,' Monroe smiled. 'After all, we still haven't talked about the silver ball.'

ONCE OUTSIDE THE BUILDING, DECLAN NOTICED THAT ANJLI and De'Geer had disappeared, as Carrie lit a cigarette, taking a deep drag, glancing around as she did so.

'Look, this isn't your world anymore, sir,' she said to Declan. 'Can we speak as equals? Off the record?'

'Always,' Declan replied. 'I don't want you feeling as if you can't speak to me.'

Carrie nodded, unconsciously scratching at her forearm. Declan glanced at it, and saw that there were at least three burn marks on the underside, all together, as if she'd stubbed cigarettes, or had cigarettes stubbed out by someone else on the arm, all in a line. Declan didn't comment on this; the scars looked red, so were likely from the last year or two. This wasn't a childhood trauma, this was some kind of self harm.

And currently, he wasn't anywhere near qualified enough to comment on that.

'I think you should just leave,' she said. 'You've already said you're out in a few months. Piss off back to London and work your notice out arresting City bankers or politicians. That seems to be your usual style.'

Declan raised his eyebrows, a little taken aback. When Carrie had asked to speak off the record, he hadn't expected her to be so brutal.

'My ex-partner is dead—' he started, but Carrie raised a hand.

'Who you hadn't spoken to in what, two, maybe three years?' she snapped. 'So don't give me the 'avenging my brother' bullshit. All you're doing is coming in, stepping all over the case with your DCI here and the bloody circus of other coppers you've dragged along, causing me personal trauma and playing the hero for yourself. Don't tell me you think you're here to re-examine the evidence, as you don't give a shit about it. You haven't for ten years. Don't make my dad, my *dead* dad, your mid-life crisis case before you sod off into your new security consultant role.'

She was red faced and furious as she finished. Monroe had stepped back, wisely allowing Declan to be the one that dealt with this. And Declan, in turn, wasn't sure how to. Carrie Harper was in pain, a lot, and Declan was only now realising it was his fault. He should have come back, even apologised. Eddie had managed it. He'd talked about visiting Castleton when they last spoke. Maybe it was this born-again, cleansed Eddie that had arrived and healed all wounds?

'You okay, sis?' A man's voice cut into the conversation, and Declan looked over at two officers walking towards them. One was in his late forties, a few years older than Declan and a lot greyer, tall and muscled, the insignia of a Major on his collar, while the other wore the insignia of a Lieutenant, and was only mid-twenties. He had the same hair colouring and eyes as Carrie, though, and Declan immediately knew that this was Devin Harper, the brother. Which made the other one Major Eaton-Jones, here for the late breakfast Carrie had spoken of. Declan didn't remember meeting him back when he was a Lieutenant, but that didn't mean Declan wasn't known to him.

'Yeah,' Carrie turned to her brother. 'I was just telling *Detective Inspector Walsh* here that his services weren't really needed.'

Devin looked at Declan, his eyes narrowing as he now recognised the man standing in front of him.

'You're not welcome here,' he said softly.

'I'm getting that,' Declan forced a smile. 'But I've been seconded here—'

'You should leave,' Eaton-Jones added. 'Dangerous places, army bases. Anything could happen. As well you know, Corporal Walsh.'

'*Detective Inspector*,' Declan snapped back, already tired of this. 'And we've been tasked by Colonel Yates of the SIB, so if you have a problem—' he indicated Carrie, '—take it up with her boss.'

Monroe, by now accurately reading the situation, stepped forward, offering out a hand to shake, not expecting it to be taken as he faced Eaton-Jones.

'DCI Monroe,' he said with a stiff smile. 'You're Patrick Harper's old Lieutenant, right?'

'That's right,' Eaton-Jones stared down at the offered hand with disdain. '*Derbyshires* forever.'

Undaunted, Monroe continued.

'Well then,' he said with a wider smile now. 'You have a reason, just as Harper's children do, to kill Staff Sergeant Edward Moses in some kind of revenge action. So, as you can understand, you telling us to 'piss off' is effectively the work of a suspect tampering with an investigation.'

'I'm a suspect?' this actually surprised Eaton-Jones. 'On what grounds?'

'On the grounds that you're being an obstructive, boorish prick,' Monroe finished. 'And if you don't back off right now, I'll arrest you myself.'

Eaton-Jones stared long and hard at Monroe.

'You were never in the military, were you,' he stated, more a comment than a question. Monroe, however, took it as a question.

'No,' he replied. 'But I grew up on the streets of Glasgow, and I've done my time in the trenches. And I've seen misguided loyalty more times than I'd like to admit. So, *Major*, if you don't mind, we'd like to solve this case and *then* piss off. That okay?'

Declan almost laughed as Major Eaton-Jones, obviously not used to being being spoken at like this, adjusted his beret before turning and marching off.

'No slap with the glove?' Monroe shouted after him. 'No pistols at dawn? Not the army I'm used to.'

Devin glared at both Monroe and Declan, and then followed his commanding officer. Declan looked to see where Carrie was, but in the confusion, she'd obviously finished her cigarette and left as well. Only Declan and Monroe were left.

'God, I'd love to be a wee fly on the wall when they all get together over crumpets,' Monroe chuckled.

'Pistols at dawn? Army you're used to?' Declan half laughed. 'What army does that?'

'The ones in the *Sharpe* novels I read, laddie,' Monroe smiled. 'Granted, they're set in the Napoleonic Wars, but there's a lot in there that still seems valid right now.'

'Well, just be lucky you're not being challenged to a duel,' Declan's phone beeped with a message, and he went to pull it out. 'These guys are killers.'

'You've not seen me during paintball,' Monroe protested. 'I'm a force to be recognised.'

Declan stopped, hand still in pocket.

'Duelling,' he said.

'What about it?'

'Doctor Marcos said it was a duelling pistol ball. What if duelling still happened?' Declan asked, pulling the phone out and tapping on the screen to wake it. 'Maybe that's why there's a ball in Eddie's body?'

'He was shot in a bloody duel? Surely they'd use more modern weapons?' Monroe shook his head. 'Although I suppose that'd be the best way to solve squabbles without court martial. What's the message?'

'From Billy,' Declan said, showing Monroe. 'He's scanned the note in the wallet and screwed around with the contrast on his laptop. Although the words are still unintelligible, there's something there.'

> DECLAN KNOWS
> W   I   AYING

'Declan knows what I'm saying?' Monroe suggested. 'Playing? Saying?'

'Staying,' Declan muttered, looking up from the phone. 'Declan knows where I'm staying.'

He moved across the car park, heading towards his Audi.

'Eddie was staying here,' he said. 'But he was off reservation. He couldn't grab a bunk on the base, as he wasn't officially here. So he went to the same place we went ten years ago.'

He entered the car, already turning on the engine as Monroe clambered in beside him.

'He went to the *Castle Tun Guesthouse*, in Castleton.'

6
─────────

DESIGN AND DEVELOPMENT

ANJLI AND DE'GEER HAD LEFT THE PORTAKABINS THAT doubled as the SIB offices at Castleton, and, with Declan and Monroe using the Audi, had taken Billy's Mini, driving it to a small research and development building on the other side of the Mam Tor Bridleway, an unassuming building that looked more like a sales office than a location that analysed some of the most dangerous weapons the army now employed. Indeed, if it wasn't for the high fences surrounded it and the armed guard on the gate, Anjli wouldn't have given it a second glance.

These same gate guards needed to call in Anjli's visit, but since it had been rubber stamped by Whitehall, they were quickly waved through and told to wait at the visitors car park until someone came to pick them up. This Anjli did, reversing into the offered spot so that she could stare straight ahead at the main entranceway.

'You think we'll be here long?' De'Geer asked. Anjli shrugged, settling into her seat.

'Who knows,' she replied. 'The army can be officious, after all.'

She finally looked over at De'Geer, sitting awkwardly, his seven-foot frame cramped in the Mini's passenger seat.

'You comfy?'

'Oh fine, Ma'am.'

'Need to stretch your legs?'

'I'm good, thanks,'

Anjli chuckled quietly, amused at the politeness of the obviously uncomfortable Viking beside her.

'You and Davey didn't work out, then?' she asked. 'Not prying, it just seemed that you were a good fit, and you're still getting on so well.'

'I think I liked her more than she liked me,' De'Geer reddened as he spoke. '*Like* her more than she liked me.'

'So there's no chance?' Anjli leaned back into the driver's seat, rotating her head to click out a tightness in her neck. In return, De'Geer made a cramped movement that resembled an attempt at a shrug.

'I like to hope there is,' he replied. 'Ma'am—'

'Anjli. We're not on the clock right now.'

'Yes, Ma'am. Can I ask a personal question?'

'How do I rock these suits? Pure style,' Anjli smiled, realising that De'Geer hadn't smiled at all. 'Sorry. Of course you can. Shoot. Say anything, I won't mind.'

'Why aren't you and DI Walsh together?' De'Geer asked. 'It's obvious you both have feelings for each other.'

Anjli stared silently at the officer beside her for a very long and uncomfortable moment.

'You think I like Declan?' she replied. 'Like that?'

'Oh,' De'Geer shook his head. 'I misread. I'm sorry.'

'Wait, you think Declan—DI Walsh—likes *me* that way?'

'It's just that you worked so well together—'

'Yeah, I heard the jokes,' Anjli half-snapped back. 'That we were like a married couple.'

'They weren't jokes,' De'Geer insisted. 'You had the short-hand that couples have. It's why you work so well together. And I've seen the way he looks at you.'

'Oh?' Anjli hadn't noticed Declan looking at her in any way, but she recalled a moment in Hurley, right before Declan had found Karl Schnitter waiting for him, when they'd been talking about long, luxurious baths, and the thought of Declan seeing her naked had popped into her head—and *hadn't* felt abhorrent. 'And how does he look at me?'

'Confused,' De'Geer smiled. 'Like he doesn't know what he's supposed to think when he looks at you. Which, in my experience, usually comes when someone likes someone else but doesn't know what to do next. He also looks at you with a little admiration, too.'

'That's because I'm awesome,' Anjli replied, still trying to make light of this, but just as thrown as Declan seemed to be. De'Geer, however, didn't notice this and carried on.

'Of course, Ma'am. And with respect, *Ma'am*, as I'm allowed to say anything, you've been an absolute cow in the office since DI Walsh has been away.'

'Well, yeah, sorry for that, but there are reasons,' Anjli admitted. 'Being annoyed at the situation doesn't mean I'm...'

Anjli stopped.

The situation?

The situation was that Declan was leaving and there was nothing she could do about it.

'Just shut up,' she muttered, looking back at the building. 'Someone's coming.'

The *someone* was an obviously irritated lab technician in her thirties, walking out of the building and waving at them to exit the car and join her.

'Cheerful chaps here, aren't they?' De'Geer said as they climbed out of the Mini, Anjli managing this with considerably more ease than De'Geer did, and walked over to her.

'I'm Detective Sergeant Kapoor, this is PC De'Geer,' Anjli flashed her warrant card. 'We're here because of Lieutenant Colonel Falconer.'

'I thought you were on site because of the MP that was found?' the woman, hawkish in looks and tall in stature, pinched at her nose, pushing her thin wire glasses back up her nose with her left hand.

'You knew we were here?' De'Geer asked.

The woman laughed.

'Christ, officer, *everyone* on site knows you're here,' she replied. 'I'm Second Lieutenant Cullen,' the woman replied, 'but we rarely use that rank in the army by name. Call me Doctor Cullen.'

'Thank you, Doctor,' Anjli attempted her most disarming smile. 'And yes, we are here because of the MP, but Lieutenant Colonel Falconer apparently died the same day that his body was found.'

'And you think they were connected?' Doctor Cullen, who from her expression seemed to have relented on whether or not to like Anjli, raised an eyebrow.

'His pacemaker exploded,' De'Geer shrugged. 'Doesn't really sound like an accident.'

'Lots of pacemakers have issues,' Doctor Cullen argued, opening the door to the building and ushering Anjli and De'Geer inside. 'Over two thousand implants a year malfunction.'

'Malfunction doesn't sound the same as melting inside the chest,' Anjli suggested.

Doctor Cullen stopped and nodded.

'Yeah, there is that,' she said. 'I can't talk about it because—'

'Of the *Official Secrets Act?*' Anjli pulled out a sheet of paper, folded up; a letter from Whitehall, given to them all when Bullman explained their genuine reason for being there. 'I think you'll find that this allows us to hear whatever you need to talk about. In particular, Falconer's work on invisible laser guns.'

At the reveal of the paper, though, Doctor Cullen's demeanour changed instantly.

'Whitehall's little lapdogs, all the way from on high,' she muttered, glaring at Anjli. 'Here to tear us apart and take our secrets, no doubt.'

'We don't work for Whitehall,' Anjli replied coldly.

Doctor Cullen nodded, a mocking *sure you don't* expression on her face.

'Those papers you have there? They say otherwise,' she smiled.

Anjli looked at the sheet of paper in her hand, considering her next move. She understood Doctor Cullen's anger at Whitehall; she too was sick of being used as a pawn.

'You said Second Lieutenant,' she said. 'So you're a soldier and a doctor?'

'Not really.'

'But you've done basic training?'

Doctor Cullen reluctantly nodded.

'Of course.'

'So you understand about weapons being tools to use,' Anjli tried her best disarming smile. 'You're given one, and shown what it does, but it's up to you to decide what you do with it?'

'That's not really how the army works, but I get the idea,' Doctor Cullen replied.

'This is my weapon,' Anjli said, holding the sheet of paper back up. 'It gets me where I need to go, and in to where I can't gain entry. But Whitehall? They can only hope I'll do what they ask, and only if they ask nicely, because I've had enough of their shit to last a lifetime, pardon my language.'

Doctor Cullen didn't reply, instead observing Anjli silently, as if reevaluating her opinion.

'Good to know,' she said eventually with a faint smile. By now they were walking down a white-walled corridor lined with neon lights along the ceiling, turning right into Doctor Cullen's lab; a similarly white-painted, bland space containing PCs, oscilloscopes and hot running data servers. Anjli assumed this looked like every wet dream Billy ever had, and she had to shake the memory away as she continued in.

'I heard this was once a warehouse?' Anjli asked. 'But it was torn down?'

'Yes, nothing remains,' Doctor Cullen clicked a couple of switches on the wall, lighting the room up. 'Even the basement was turned into a gun range for testing weapons.'

'Like James Bond,' De'Geer replied, and, after receiving a blank stare from Doctor Cullen, added 'you know, like Q has in the movies. Big open space with rifle ranges and all that.'

'I think you'll find the real Ministry of Defence has a far smaller budget than James Bond does,' Doctor Cullen replied. 'But we do have similar toys.'

To the left of the lab was a desk, likely Cullen's one, as it was recently sat at, the mug of hot coffee still steaming. There was a DELL laptop open on it, currently showing a Ministry of Defence screensaver, and a photo frame behind it showed Doctor Cullen and two men, all in military dress uniform. One of them, a ginger haired man, was embracing her in it, laughing.

'Nice photo,' Anjli said, nodding at it.

'Didn't realise you were here for a social visit; thought you were here for that,' Doctor Cullen replied, pointing at the table to Anjli's right. Anjli went to reply, but stopped as she turned to look.

In the middle of the room was a device that would never have been in a school lesson. If anything, it looked more in place within Tony Stark's laboratory in the *Avengers* movies. It was a large, gunmetal coloured table with what looked like a rifle butt and trigger at one end, three focus lenses along a metal track connected by metal piping and, about three feet on from the muzzle of the 'gun', a wide metal base where a target could be placed.

'That's your laser gun,' Doctor Cullen smiled, pointing at it. 'You can't really call it that, though.'

Anjli looked at De'Geer.

'We were told it was a little more compact,' she muttered.

'Oh, that's just to counter the propaganda bollocks that the Chinese were peddling,' Doctor Cullen flicked some more switches, and Anjli noticed that a low level hum that had been in the room since she entered had now stopped. 'They released information on this magic assault rifle that could blind people and blow up tankers or something back in 2018. Enough battery power to fire a thousand two-second shots. They showed photos and everything; stupid bloody monstrosity that looked like a Nerf Gun with a massive flashlight glued onto the front.'

'You don't believe it worked?' Anjli was curious as she stared at the rifle.

'Oh, I believe it works, and it probably even exists,' Doctor Cullen replied. 'But not in the style and manner the Chinese reckoned. You want something that performs how they claim it does? Then it's welded to the top of a tank or a car of some kind, purely to carry the battery. You could do it with a Tesla battery, but not something the size of a rifle butt.'

She picked up a small, flat charger, the size of an iPhone.

'This charger, right? It can power up my phone before I need to plug it into the mains,' she explained. 'I can even power up my headphones. My tablet in a pinch. But if I want to charge my laptop? Not a hope. I'll need something a lot larger. This provides five thousand milliamp hours, which is a unit that measures electric power over time. To charge the laptop, I'll need five or six times that amount and that would up the size considerably.'

'So, are you saying a rifle like this couldn't exist?'

'Pretty much,' Doctor Cullen shrugged. 'We know the Yanks have the *personnel halting and stimulation response rifle*, which is basically a name they created so the initials pretty much spelt out 'phaser', and that's a non-lethal laser dazzler developed by the Air Force, aimed at temporarily blinding people. Portable, but still stupidly large. The UK's focusing on warships mainly, with the *Dragonfire Laser Directed Energy Weapon* to be installed on our most advanced ships. That's fifty *kilowatts* of laser. And the funny thing about that is its base tech comes from Formula One racing. But it's still years from getting anywhere.'

'Then why do it?' Anjli asked. 'Surely if it's not worth looking at now—'

'Because everyone else is,' Doctor Cullen smiled. 'And

while they do it, we have to do it. And lasers are the future; they can be used discreetly, perhaps for covert ops, as the radiation doesn't generate sound, and is invisible if outside the visible spectrum.'

'Invisible laser beams just sounds like cheating,' Anjli muttered.

'It's worse than that,' Doctor Cullen smiled, happy to be talking about things she felt more comfortable on. 'The lasers aren't affected by gravity or wind, giving them an almost perfectly flat trajectory. This makes aim much more precise, and extends a rifle's range to line-of-sight, limited only by beam diffraction and spread. You can even set the laser to stop at a set distance, or at least dissipate there, and people are looking into lasers that pass through things and only detonate, so to speak, when they hit that distance. Nobody would know. The ultimate assassin's tool.'

'Would Lieutenant Colonel Falconer have been working on something like that?' Anjli asked.

'Why?' Doctor Cullen frowned. 'I mean, I think he might have added that to his *to-do* list—'

'Because you've just said that there could be a device, maybe existing in some kind of developmental form, that could line up a target, work out a distance and then effectively release an immense amount of power, or heat inside them. Perhaps even enough to slightly melt a pacemaker?'

Doctor Cullen didn't reply, her face paling.

'You'd have to stand very still,' she answered. 'The day that he died, he was giving a lecture. He stood behind a lectern for forty minutes. There would have been plenty of time to work out a distance and aim. Even a small laser, given the right circumstances before...'

She stopped, shaking her head

'No.' It was definite in the way she stood, the force of the refusal. 'There's no way. He wasn't close to building it. He wasn't even *close* to being close, and he had body armour on that day, I'm sure of it.'

'Can we see his workspace?' Anjli asked. 'Maybe even look at where he gave the lecture?'

Doctor Cullen nodded, but De'Geer spoke, halting her.

'One question, Ma'am, before we move on,' he asked. 'You mentioned pacemakers explode a lot. If this occurs, what happens to the patient? Is it instantaneous heart stoppage, or something—'

'No,' Doctor Cullen interrupted. 'I never said they explode. Most of the time, the issues are because of *implantable cardioverter defibrillators,* or ICDs. It's a device similar to a pacemaker.'

'Did Falconer have a pacemaker or an ICD?'

'Both,' Doctor Cullen explained. 'An ICD, however, sends a large electrical shock to the heart if it stops, that essentially 'reboots' it to get it pumping again. If an ICD battery 'pops', there's only minor local injury to the pocket, the artificial space created for the *pacing generator,* which is usually between the skin and the pectoral muscle.'

'You seem to know a lot about these,' De'Geer commented.

'Anything that produces a strong electromagnetic field can affect a pacemaker,' Doctor Cullen walked over to a side table, clicking off another switch. 'Guess what the batteries of big lasers can sometimes do? That's right. Falconer had to be even more careful than others when working on this. We all learned by osmosis on what he could or couldn't do.'

By now Doctor Cullen was leading them down the corridor, away from the laboratory and towards an office at the end.

'Surely Lieutenant Colonel Falconer shouldn't have been on such an assignment?' De'Geer asked. 'If such a thing was hazardous to his health?'

'It's not like we were creating them every day,' Doctor Cullen stopped at a door. There was a metal name tag on it, reading CPT. FALCONER. She pulled out a key, held on a small chain of other such keys, and after checking carefully it was the right one, inserted it into the lock. 'Oppenheimer wasn't hanging around the isotopes all the time when creating the *Manhattan Project.*'

There was a click as the door unlocked, and Doctor Cullen led them into Falconer's office.

It was small, sparse and utilitarian in style and colour. A desk was at the back wall, cabinets on either side of it. There was a window with a half-height shelving cabinet underneath, and on the back wall was the only piece of decoration, a painting of what looked to be a pierrot clown, a sword in his hand being laid on the snowy ground by his companions, as to the right, two men walked off, one dressed as a harlequin, the other a Native American Indian.

'*Suite d'un bal masqué,*' Doctor Cullen noticed De'Geer staring at it. 'Jean-Léon Gérôme, 1857. It's a print, as the original is in the Musée Condé in Chantilly, France. It was Charlie's favourite.'

Anjli looked up at this; it was the first time that Doctor Cullen had spoken about Lieutenant Colonel Falconer familiarly.

'Were you close?' she asked.

'As you could be,' Doctor Cullen muttered, looking away, and Anjli got the distinct impression that the conversation, at least about Doctor Cullen's relationship with Falconer, was over. She also wondered if the ginger haired, smiling man in the photo knew about her potential feelings.

'Did Lieutenant Colonel Falconer have any enemies?' De'Geer, now examining the desk, asked.

'No,' Doctor Cullen shook her head vehemently. 'He was well respected.'

'You can be respected and still be hated by someone,' Anjli replied. 'Professional jealousy perhaps?'

Doctor Cullen shook her head again.

'He wasn't the sort to ruffle feathers,' she said. 'He kept to himself, had a war-game club he was a member of, that was about it, really. We arrived around the same time, back in summer 2019 when this was all started. In all that time he's just... well, he's just been Charlie Falconer.'

'Did he ever meet Staff Sergeant Moses?' Anjli looked back at Doctor Cullen now.

'The man who was found?' Doctor Cullen looked confused. 'He died a year ago.'

'Yes, but you've both been here for a few years,' Anjli pressed. 'So, maybe their paths crossed?'

Doctor Cullen turned away, walking to the low shelf.

'He kept a journal,' she said. 'Day-to-day shit. Guess it doesn't matter who reads it. Maybe it has something in it?'

She pulled out a leather-bound book, passing it over to Anjli.

'If he met him, and if it was important, it'd be in there.'

De'Geer picked up a lead war-gaming figure, holding it up to the light.

'Who did he war-game with?' he asked.

'People on the base, and in Sheffield, half an hour away,' Doctor Cullen replied, and Anjli felt it was a little too quick, as if she wanted to move past it. 'Inter-regimental fighting, nothing more. Like the Olympics.'

'They war-gamed in the Olympics?' Anjli raised an eyebrow at this.

Doctor Cullen reddened.

'No, of course not,' she said. 'Boys and toys, nothing more.'

'You never got involved?'

'Not my thing,' Doctor Cullen replied. 'Anyway, I need to carry on with my research. Lieutenant Colonel Falconer might be off the clock, but I'm not.'

And before Anjli could say anything to stop her, Doctor Cullen left the room at speed, closing the door behind her.

'So what did you make of that?' Anjli asked.

'Cullen had a crush on her boss, perhaps,' De'Geer looked from the desk. 'She was definitely closer than she's making out.'

Anjli flicked through the journal.

'It'd be better if we knew when Moses died,' she said, reading the pages. 'It'd definitely cut down the date range.'

De'Geer straightened, pulling out from the drawer a sheet of paper.

'He's got an *acquire and keep* explosives certificate from Sheffield Hallam Police,' he said, showing it to Anjli.

'Falconer? Maybe he needs it for the job?'

'No, Sarge. I used to see these when I was in Maidenhead nick,' De'Geer was looking over the document again. 'Lots of people do clay pigeon shooting around Henley, and there's a few clubs in the area. Most of the people owning guns though, well they need to have a personal explosives licence for what's known as *shooter's powder,* which gives them up to ten kilos worth of black powder.'

'It's not the same as a firearms licence then?'

'No,' De'Geer placed the licence back on the desk. 'Black powder is used in cartridges...'

He stopped, looking back at the painting.

'Black powder is also used when firing reenactment rifles,' he said. 'My cousin does a lot of civil war reenactment, and he's got a similar licence.'

'Does your cousin look like you?'

'Yes. Why?'

'I just assumed he'd be more Viking reenactment,' Anjli smiled before stopping, realising where De'Geer was going with this. 'Wait. You mean he fired muskets?''

'Yes, Sarge,' De'Geer nodded at the painting. 'And according to the wiki page, *Suite d'un bal masqué* is known as *The Duel After the Masquerade*.'

'So Falconer dies the same day as Staff Sergeant Moses' body is found, has a licence to store black powder and loves a painting involving a duel,' Anjli worked through the facts. 'He was on base when Moses returned a year ago, and Moses has a silver duelling pistol or musket ball inside him.'

'I wonder if Falconer has markings on his dogtags?' De'Geer mused.

'That, constable, is a bloody good question,' Anjli opened up a folder on the desk. 'I think we need to have a look at Falconer's quarters. If he was holding gunpowder on the base, we should find out why.'

She stopped, flipping through the pages in the folder.

'He did make a rifle,' she breathed. 'Look.'

The notes were scattered on the paper, but Anjli could make a little sense of them; *Prototype created* was a giveaway for a start. *One shot, RA to fire in test range.*

'One shot, RA to fire in test range?' De'Geer looked

around the room with a smile, as if expecting to find a secret door embedded in a wall. 'Who's RA?'

'No idea,' Anjli smiled. 'But hey, buck up, sonny. Looks like we get to see Q's basement after all. Let's find Doctor Cullen. Looks like her tour isn't over yet.'

7

BREAKING FAST

'I DON'T CARE WHAT YOU THINK, THAT MAN NEEDS TO BE TAKEN somewhere quiet and shot,' Henry Eaton-Jones muttered as he dug into a plate of egg and chips.

'That's not helpful, is it,' Carrie muttered, her own table spot clear of any food, having not ordered anything, her appetite now gone. 'Look, Henry, you've always been there for us, but this is a little close to home, you know?'

'Bloody cheek, if you ask me,' Devin muttered, eating a sausage sandwich made with no sauces, with only butter used in the making. 'It's Yates, being a prick.'

'*Colonel* Yates,' Henry mumbled through a mouthful of food.

'Yeah, well, your dad's higher than him, so if Yates has a problem with me calling him a prick, I'm sure I can find a bigger person to shout him down,' Devin leaned back on the cheap, plastic chair of the officer's mess and looking back to his sister. 'You're not eating anything?'

'Lost my appetite the moment Walsh walked in,' Carrie admitted, but not before reaching over and taking a slice of toast from Devin's plate and biting in, taking a mouthful, allowing the buttery slice to drip down her chin before wiping it away. 'Christ, Dev. You drown the bloody thing in butter.'

'I need the saturated fats, don't I?' Devin muttered, chomping into his own sandwich.

'Yeah, I'm not sure it works that way,' Carrie finished the slice, wiping her mouth. 'They're looking into Falconer too.'

'Dad told me,' Eaton-Jones nodded. 'Nothing he could do about it. His new boss is trying to distance herself from everything. And I know Yates is pissed that he wasn't involved. Right royally screwed up his organisational chart, most likely.'

'Prime Minister's got the right idea to distance herself, aim people at Charles Falconer,' Carrie mused. 'We had nothing to do with that.'

She paused, noting that neither her brother nor Eaton-Jones had agreed with her.

'We didn't have anything to do with that, right?'

Eaton-Jones shifted in his seat.

'The fact of the matter is, Carrie,' he started. 'I mean to say, in the grand scale of things—'

'Oh, for God's sake, Henry, just say the bloody thing,' Carrie snapped. 'They're saying a top secret laser was stolen and someone used it to melt Charlie's heart. Are you telling me you knew?'

'No!' Eaton-Jones shook his head. 'It's not that. The rumour mill's gone wild, people reckoning a weapon must have been stolen, because there's nothing in the armoury or in Falconer's lab that fits the bill. He was killed by a laser, the laser isn't there, ergo it must have been stolen.'

'But?' Carrie observed the Major.

'But Falconer was building things off books too,' Eaton-Jones replied carefully. 'That bloody vest he made to cheat in the contests.'

Now Devin looked up at his Major.

'Contests, sir?' he asked. 'He was using lasers during the duels?'

Eaton-Jones waggled his hand in the air, fork still in it, a piece of egg, caught in the tines of the fork now falling to the plate.

'Ish,' he said eventually. 'He was working on a small laser, no bigger than a pinhead, that could be attached to a barrel. The idea was that a second before firing the pistol, he'd set the laser off, and it'd momentarily blind the opponent.'

'You're bloody kidding me!' Carrie rose from the chair before remembering they were in a public space. 'He was *cheating?*'

'Not really,' Eaton-Jones replied, now back at his food. 'There was no way to power it without a huge battery. He'd talked about making a suit for it, but he had to weigh up the practicalities. He made a vest but claimed it didn't work. And when the guy from the Royal Marines complained about it blinding him in a shoot off, Charlie kicked off and said it was a bulb playing up that had caused the glare—'

'Was he working with anyone on this?' Carrie shook her head. 'No wonder he was keeping away more. He knew I'd smack him.'

'He was working on it with Cullen, I believe. And the Colonel, I think. He was a marksman, so had been assisting off books.'

'Cullen's a nightmare, too,' Carrie muttered, staring down at the table. 'I told you to stop this. I said it'd bring you nothing but trouble.'

'I did stop it,' Eaton-Jones snapped. 'We haven't done anymore specials.'

Carrie looked up at him now, her eyes flashing.

'Yes?' she asked. 'And when exactly *did* you stop, Major Eaton-Jones?'

'The day Eddie Moses was shot,' Eaton-Jones kept Carrie's eye, as if daring her to look away. After a moment, she did.

'The same day *you* stopped,' he added triumphantly. 'The same day you ran for cover like, well, a *civilian*.'

Carrie rubbed absently at her burn marks as she considered this.

'No more honour duels since Moses,' she whispered, a statement more than a question. 'Can you believe that of Charlie?'

'He's a soldier,' Eaton-Jones finished his food, placing his cutlery down. 'He follows orders. Colonel said stop. We stopped. Sure, he might have been trying to gain an advantage in them, and he might have been preparing for when they come back, but he wouldn't have risked anything.'

'Not even with your trainees?' Carrie asked, raising a hand to halt Eaton-Jone's response. 'And don't lie to me, Henry. I know you've been indoctrinating your TA classes. You've been doing that since the *Cardigans*, from what I can see.'

Now it was Eaton-Jones' turn to rise angrily from the table, his plate scattering to the side as he towered over Carrie.

'You *what?*' he snarled in red-hot fury. 'You've been *investigating* me?'

'Of course I've been investigating you!' now not caring who heard, Carrie rose to meet Eaton-Jones. 'You're a bloody suspect! Your name was the first that came up the moment they found the body! Everyone knows you threatened Moses the moment he arrived!'

'That's because he wasn't invited to the party!' Eaton-Jones was reddening with anger. 'He turned up telling us what to do? Me? I started the bloody thing!'

'I thought the Brigadier and the Colonel did?' Devin spoke calmly, still eating his sandwich, ignoring the argument happening beside him. Carrie and Eaton-Jones looked down at him, and then, the anger dissipating, sat back down at their places.

'Dad and the Colonel created the duels,' Eaton-Jones replied sullenly. 'But I was the one who weaponised them. The contests are fine. It's the silver level shots that have to be watched.'

'And how's that going?' Carrie shook her head, sighing. 'Your little gang is getting everyone killed, Henry. If they find out you had anything to do with Moses or Falconer...'

'Well, it's a good job I have family in the room with them then, isn't it?' Eaton-Jones stared at Carrie unwaveringly, waiting for some sign, some facial twitch or change that showed she wasn't on the same team.

There wasn't one.

Eventually Carrie sighed morosely, finished her mug of tea, and stood up.

'I'll keep you in the loop,' she said, nodding to her brother and leaving the Officers' Mess.

Devin finished his sandwich finally, wiping his fingers on a disposable napkin before looking at his commanding officer.

'I know she's my sister, but we're going to have to do something about her,' he said carefully.

'I know,' Eaton-Jones nodded. 'I don't want your father's remaining legacy destroyed, either.'

'Sir,' Devin was uncomfortable, and Eaton-Jones knew this was because he had a question he didn't want to ask. 'Did you have anything to do with Lieutenant Colonel Falconer's death?'

'No, Lieutenant,' Eaton-Jones shook his head. 'Although I have a bloody good idea who did.'

'And Moses?'

Eaton-Jones looked directly at Devin now, watching his young subordinate for a long, silent moment before replying.

'Don't worry,' he said. 'She'll never know it was you.'

———

DECLAN AND MONROE HAD DRIVEN INTO CASTLETON RATHER than walk, on a route that passed by the Blue John Caves which gave the local area the beautiful blue jewellery it was known for. However, despite a warm and sunny day, there was no time for sightseeing; they both knew there were already a lot of moving parts involved in this case. So they parked near the Village centre, climbed out of the car and glanced around.

'Had you been here before?' Monroe asked. 'You know, apart from when you came and shot that fellow?'

Declan winced at the bluntness of Monroe's statement, but didn't contradict him.

'No,' he replied. 'Hadn't come here before, didn't really think it was relevant to come back after.'

'How many days were you here?' Monroe asked as they walked out onto Cross Street, turning left past the roundabout and walking east, the ruin of Peveril Castle staring down at them.

'Only a couple in the end,' Declan said as they crossed a narrow stone bridge, the river underneath butting against the stone wall of the Castle Free House, following the road right. 'We turned up, settled into the Castle Tun, then went hunting. Found Harper the following morning. Ended up answering questions from the police, the MPs and whoever else was around at the time until the day after, when we were sent back to base.'

He chuckled.

'Paid for two nights, didn't sleep in the bedroom once,' he added. 'Maybe Eddie wanted to try out the bed finally.'

He stopped, crouching to tie his shoelace.

'Bloke, fifty yards behind us, black bomber jacket,' he muttered softly. 'What's he doing?'

Monroe stretched his arms, rotating his neck, looking around as he did so. They were currently between two pubs; on their right was The Castle Free House, while across the street was the stone-brick terrace of The Bull's Head, a building that ran all the way from a small open area and car park to the left, to the main entrance opposite them.

Back towards the roundabout, however, on the other side of the road and standing beside a patch of open grass, reading a National Trust sign stating it was the 'Town Ditch Field', whatever that was, Monroe could see the man Declan had spied. He was young, maybe thirties at best, although his thinning hair aged him a little. He had a leather bag over a shoulder, a phone in his hand and even though he appeared to be engrossed in the history of whatever land was next to them, he *wasn't* so engrossed that he'd miss them moving again.

Declan tested this by rising, leading Monroe down the road on the right.

'Spotted him in the car park,' he said. 'Moment we arrived, he was on his phone. Then, as we walked, he followed.'

'There's a hundred tourists here at least,' Monroe argued. 'One bloke with a phone—'

Declan stopped; they'd walked out of sight now, and after a couple of moments Declan turned and walked back out of the street, towards The Bull's Head.

The man was gone.

'See?' Monroe walked up behind Declan, looking around. 'Told you. Tourist. Now, can we get on with this?'

Reluctantly, and still convinced he'd been correct, Declan turned back up the side street, leading Monroe towards the Castle Tun Guesthouse.

If he'd watched for longer, he might have seen the young man in the black bomber jacket peer out from behind The Bull's Head's westerly wall, moving out from the car park and checking his phone.

On it was a photo of Declan.

Nodding to himself, the man carried on down Cross Street.

He didn't need to follow Declan anymore.

He knew exactly where Declan Walsh was going.

———

'THIS IS THE TESTING ROOM,' THE RESEARCHER THAT DOCTOR Cullen had tasked with continuing the tour explained as Anjli and De'Geer followed him into the basement. It was deep and wide, with pillars throughout, holding up the building above them. Anjli could see they had built it into three long rows, running the length of the building; the left row seemed to be filled with wire cages, holding metal shelves filled with plastic boxes, while the right one held plasterboard wall partitionings with doors and windows placed into them. Walking to the first, she opened it up, finding a makeshift medical office.

'Much need for this here?' she asked. The researcher shrugged. He was tall, almost as tall as De'Geer, but didn't carry any of the muscle, and Anjli was convinced that his messy blond hair gave him at least two inches of extra height advantage.

'I don't come down much,' he admitted. 'But we do test things down here, so maybe it's in case something explodes or shoots someone.'

'What's your name again?' Anjli was now walking down the middle row, a well-lit, slim area that gave the distinct impression of a firing range. At the back of the space, Anjli could see a lit concrete slab peppered with bullet holes.

'Peterson,' the researcher explained. 'I didn't know Lieutenant Colonel Falconer well, or his team.'

'He had a team?' asked De'Geer, noting this down. Peterson nodded.

'We're all given areas,' he said. 'I never worked on the laser kit, I'm on more bio-engineering, but Falconer took over this entire basement. Was here a lot, especially at night. Doctor Cullen worked with him, there was also another bloke who'd be in here, a rifleman, I think. He fired the weapons when they were testing. Lots of bangs, at least.'

'Falconer didn't do it?' Anjli was surprised. 'Looking at his office, I thought he'd jump at the chance.'

'Falconer liked guns, not rifles,' Peterson shook his head.

'Said they were clumsy and not very graceful. Personally, I think it was because he had rubbish firing range scores. But, when you run the place, you can get people to do whatever you want.'

He looked at his watch.

'Are we done?' he asked. 'I'm missing lunch.'

'Yeah, we're done,' Anjli took a photo of the room on her camera, but Peterson blocked her way from leaving. He wasn't more than a wisp of a man, but Anjli knew there was a problem here.

'Sorry, no photos,' he said. 'You'll have to delete that.'

'We've both signed the—'

'I know what you've signed, you wouldn't be in here if you hadn't, but the phone hasn't. And your picture could go to people who haven't, either.'

He stopped, sighing.

'Look, I just need you to delete the picture,' he pleaded. 'The gate guards shouldn't even have let you in with them.'

Anjli nodded, showing the image being deleted.

'And the trash bin,' Peterson insisted. 'I know it stays in there for thirty days.'

'Annoyed, Anjli deleted the other folder; she'd hoped Peterson wouldn't consider this, but obviously he was more competent than she thought.

'People died down here,' she said finally, looking around the basement, wondering exactly where it was that Patrick Harper had fallen all those years back.

'As long as it's not me, I don't care,' Peterson said, waving to the door. 'Now, can we please leave so I can go eat?'

Anjli stopped, looking at the floor of the basement.

'One moment,' she said, walking across to a table in the

middle row. Crouching down, she pulled out a swab from her pocket, wiping it on the floor.

'There's dried blood here,' she said, placing the swab, flecks of dried blood on it, into a clear bag. 'Any idea whose?'

Peterson shrugged.

'Probably Falconer's,' he replied. 'Silly bastard was always injuring himself down here. I was always refilling the medic's room.'

Anjli now walked into the room she'd seen earlier. In there was a gurney, a chair, a sink and several drawers in a white cabinet. It stank of antiseptic, more so than a room should.

'Someone was in here, being treated,' she muttered, mostly to herself. 'Who, though?'

'Probably just a spill,' Peterson protested, his stomach joining in by rumbling. 'Can we please move on?'

Anjli nodded. She needed to get the swab over to Doctor Marcos, anyway.

'Is the way we came in the only way out?' she asked.

'No idea,' Peterson had given up being helpful, already regretting his offer to help. With a wintry smile, Anjli walked over to him, pulling out her handcuffs.

'PC De'Geer, stick these on Mister Peterson, please?' she said pleasantly. 'I think we need to take him in.'

'Wait, whoa,' Peterson waved his arms in the air frantically. 'No need for that. Yes, there's an emergency hatch right at the end, in the room on the left. Only for emergencies, never seen it open.'

'Where does it go?'

'No idea. Whoa! No! Really!' Peterson backed away from De'Geer as he approached. 'But the plans are in the records office! They'll show you!'

'Good enough,' Anjli took the handcuffs back from De'Geer, looking up at the terrified Peterson. 'We really should go. You're missing lunch.'

'That's okay,' Peterson replied, his voice shaky as he spoke. 'I seem to have lost my appetite.'

COLIN DELANEY WAS SWEATING AS HE ENTERED THE *NORTHERN General Hospital's Accident and Emergency* department, three miles north of Sheffield city centre. In his thirties, he was muscular and broad-chested, the result of a very active, outside job as a window cleaner, while also an active member of the Sheffield Bailey Barracks Army Reserve, better known as the Territorial Army. Here he held the rank of *Gunner*, which was effectively a fancy way of saying Private.

Colin hadn't really cared about rank; he was there because he wanted to be a soldier, without actively *being* a soldier. He liked the idea of being one and knew people who'd left the army and stayed on as reserve soldiers. They always spoke highly of it. He also knew people who'd joined like he had, people who'd never been able to join when they wanted and make a difference, in the process working their way up the ranks while doing the twenty-seven days minimum service a year. And that was all fine for them, exactly what they agreed for.

Colin's dream was to be in a *war*. He knew reservists had fought before, and last year he'd been told that two reserve infantry battalions, 6 and 7 Rifles, had once provided the framework battalion for peacekeeping in Cyprus.

He could peace keep in Cyprus.

Maybe as part of an armoured reconnaissance as Britain's forward presence somewhere violent and dangerous.

But in the three years he'd been a reservist, the furthest he'd been was Catterick, which was definitely not the exciting world that the adverts on TV had given.

He'd got bored. He'd looked for outlets.

He'd found them.

And now, at lunchtime on a Thursday, Colin stumbled into the main waiting room of A&E, wiping his clammy hand on his hoodie as he used the other arm to wipe the flop-sweat from his forehead.

The receptionist at the counter saw him first, and could see immediately that there was no way the stumbling, sweating man was going to make it to her before collapsing. The poor man was leaning against a chair, holding his gut like it was about to fall through his fingers. Looking to the side of the reception, she called over a hospital porter, wheeling an old lady into it. She'd just had her nurse visit, and now she was being brought back into the reception waiting area until called again, but it meant there was someone who could help

'Pete, can you help that gentleman?' nodding at the sweating man who carefully made his way over to Colin, now taking deep breaths as he built up the strength to continue.

'You alright, mate?' Pete asked, moving closer, cautiously keeping his distance. There was every chance that the man in front of him was on some serious drugs, and this could be the start of some very nasty psychotic episode.

Pete stopped when he noticed the blood seeping through the hoodie, a nasty looking wound stemming from some-where near the intestinal area.

'Ah, bugger,' he muttered to himself, looking back at the

receptionist. 'Heather, call for a stretcher. I think he's about to—'

As if on cue, Colin slumped to his knees and coughed, the blood speckling his lips as his eyes rolled into his head and he tumbled to the floor. As the surrounding patients all jumped back in shock, terrified at catching whatever this interloper had, Pete nodded to some emergency nurses and paramedics, already running in with a stretcher, pulling Colin up and placing him on his back onto it.

'Stomach wound, possibly a stabbing,' one said as he pulled the hoodie up. 'Christ, it looks like he's got sepsis. Bloody idiot tried to treat it himself.'

If Colin could hear the insult, he didn't reply. Instead, part-time Gunner Delaney was wheeled out of the reception and into the A&E ward, as the blood trickled from his mouth and the paramedics tried to stem the flow of blood from his gut.

In a way, Colin had gained his combat experience.

He hadn't expected it to be at the potential cost of his life, though.

8

LOST PROPERTY

'I WONDERED WHEN YOU'D TURN UP,' MAUREEN WILLIAMS, THE landlady of the Castle Tun said as Declan and Monroe stood in her reception area. 'Been a bloody year since your buddy disappeared.'

'Sorry about that,' Declan replied. 'As you can understand, we only found the body last week—'

'What?' Maureen looked confused at the comment. Declan glanced from the landlady to Monroe and back again.

'I thought you knew?'

'He was the body in the cave?' Maureen was getting agitated now, and Declan couldn't work out whether it was because of anger or excitement. He really hoped it wasn't the latter. 'That was on the news! Dammit, we could have made a fortune selling the story to the press!'

Declan shifted his footing now; this wasn't the conversation he'd expected. When they'd arrived at the door to The Castle Tun, they'd found it open, as most guesthouses were. Maureen had appeared the moment they entered, saying *there were no vacancies,* but after Declan had showed his warrant card she'd calmed down, until the moment Declan had commented that he'd been here a decade ago with Eddie Moses.

From that point, she hadn't shut up.

'What story?' Monroe asked now, stepping forward. 'If there's a story to be sold here, maybe it's something we should know first?'

Maureen stopped, realising perhaps how her enthusiasm had placed her in the crosshairs of the police.

'Just that he was here, you know?' she forced a smile. 'Seemed strange.'

'Not so strange that you didn't call it in?'

Maureen shrugged.

'Not my place.'

'Do you know when he came, and when he disappeared?' Declan changed subject.

'Checked in on the twenty-ninth of June, it was a Monday,' Maureen considered this for a moment. 'Paid for two weeks, said he might need a couple of weeks more and that was okay, but we said we were booked up when the school holidays started, so he had to be gone by then. Last we saw him was Sunday the Twelfth.'

Two weeks. Eddie had been here for two whole weeks.

'And you're sure of that?' Monroe opened a notebook, writing this down.

'Oh yes. It was the anniversary of the *Battle of the Boyne*, and he came in early in the morning, during breakfast. He'd been out all night, and he was in a state.'

'What kind of state?' Declan asked. 'Drunk?'

'He'd had the tar beaten out of him, I reckon,' Maureen suggested softly, lowering her voice in case anyone heard her. 'Blood on his shirt, around the left shoulder area. Like he'd been stabbed. I remember Keith, that's my husband, commenting that he should go to the hospital, and Mister Moses saying he'd fallen and it was a graze that had seeped through. But he was wincing as he went upstairs, and Keith mentioned he looked like he was celebrating the Boyne by being in a battle. Hence why I remember the day.'

'Not many people celebrate the Battle of the Boyne,' Monroe frowned.

'I didn't say *we* celebrated it, I said we knew it was that day,' Maureen replied haughtily. 'Keith has family from County Louth. I know my history.'

Monroe raised his hands.

'I believe you,' he said. 'Did anything else seem strange that day?'

Maureen shook her head.

'Not really,' she replied. 'Just that he went up and never came down. That we saw, anyway.'

'How many exits do you have?' Declan looked around. Although he'd stayed here a decade earlier, he hadn't exactly *stayed* here. Maureen counted them off her fingers.

'Front door, but to get to it, you walk past the living room, and that's where we usually congregate. Back door, but you have to walk through the kitchen and there's always someone there. I suppose he could have jumped out of his window onto the coal shed—'

'You have a coal shed?' Monroe was surprised at this.

'Well, not anymore. We've got gas central heating and a wood fire in the main room, but back in the day there would have been coal. Building's still attached. We want to turn it into something, but the council keeps claiming that it's got to stay like it is for historical purposes; as if nothing else around here can cover that.'

She stopped, realising she was rambling.

'Anyway,' she said, returning to the original comment, 'he could have jumped onto that from his room, but I doubt it. Not with his injuries.'

'But somehow he disappeared,' Monroe asked. 'Did he take his items, at least?'

'What, his underpants and stuff?' Maureen shook her head. 'Nope. Did a runner and left everything, even the gun. In the end, we dumped them all in his kitbag and left it in the basement for him to pick up. He never did—'

Declan held up a hand at this.

'Hold up,' he said. 'Gun?'

At this, Maureen laughed.

'Yeah, we found a gun,' she said, shaking her head as if this was one of the funniest things she'd seen. 'Not a real one, but a replica. Cap gun.'

'Eddie Moses had a cap gun in his possessions?' Declan wrote this down. 'Like a cowboy one? Or a military, army one?'

'Cowboy one. Got tossed away in the end,' Maureen replied. 'Well, that is someone came and took it.'

'Okay, we need to step back for a moment,' Monroe shook his head. 'Eddie Moses stayed here, disappeared, and then someone came to pick up his plastic cowboy pistol?'

'Well, it wasn't no plastic thing, it was solid metal,' Maureen said defensively. 'Just wasn't a *gun* gun. Not even a starter's pistol.'

She leaned in conspiratorially.

'Keith, my husband? He showed it to some soldiers,' she explained. 'They said it was worthless, just a collector's thing. Barrel blocked up and no way to put a bullet in. *Cowboys and*

Indians and all that. Gave it to our boy to play with. Until they asked for it back.'

Declan couldn't understand why Eddie would have such a toy, but that said he didn't really know the man anymore.

'Okay, so someone came to take the gun—' he started.

'Toy gun. We never had no real guns here, thank you.'

'Sorry, yes. And you never went to the police?' Declan shook his head. 'Told them he'd been beaten, and then he disappeared?'

'Look, detective whatever your name is,' Maureen placed her hands on her hips, squaring up to Declan. 'He appeared out of nowhere, spent two weeks pissing people off in the town, stuck his nose into things that weren't his to look at, and then got a beating for it. The next day he's gone, we assumed he'd taken the hint and left. And, as he hadn't yet paid for the next week, we assumed he'd gone without checking out.'

'Leaving his things.'

'A spare uniform, a jacket, some undies and a toy gun aren't really a lot of priceless items,' Maureen protested. 'And as I said, we held them for him, which is more than a lot of folk would do around here.'

Declan sighed, nodding at this.

'Did anyone visit him while he was here?' he asked.

'Young lass, brunette,' Maureen nodded. 'I remember her because she was half his age, and I thought that wasn't right, yeah?'

'Did she give her name?'

'Yes, but I can't remember it.'

'Was it Carrie, by chance?' Monroe asked.

Maureen considered this and then smiled.

'Very likely,' she said. 'Miserable cow, she was. But then if you're dating someone that old—'

'They were definitely an item?' Declan pressed.

Maureen, realising again that her enthusiasm for gossip was possibly getting her into trouble, stopped.

'Well, I know that there was a soldier, claiming to be her brother, that was pissed she was talking to him,' she replied. 'Saw them outside Edmund's church, having a right old barney. Probably him that gave your Staff Sergeant Moses a beating. Keith told me to mind my business. Got a right old face over it, too. Says I always stick my nose in too much.'

Declan looked at Monroe. If the girl had been Carrie Harper, then this meant Devin Harper could be even more of a suspect than they first believed.

'There was another,' Maureen nodded to herself. 'You might want to have a chat with Old Ram. They seemed to be tight in the pub before he disappeared.'

'Old Ram?' Declan had a vision of, well, an old, well dressed humanoid ram. 'Does he have a name?'

'Of course,' Maureen sniffed. 'Ramesh Abbasi. Old Indian, big grey beard. You can't miss him.'

'And where might he be right now?' Monroe smiled winningly. Maureen looked up at a clock on the wall, considering this.

'Try the café in the Visitor Centre,' she suggested. 'He usually sits in there and nurses a hot tea just after lunch.'

'And you're sure of this?' Declan turned from the door to face Maureen now.

'Pretty much,' Maureen shrugged. 'Pubs only just opened, and he doesn't want to look too eager.'

'Thank you so much for this,' Declan smiled. 'Can we get the kitbag?'

'Do we get a holding fee?' Maureen enquired impishly. 'I say this because we *have* kept it for a year.'

'And you didn't bother telling anyone he was missing for a year, while he rotted in a body bag in a cave,' Declan snapped. 'Do you think you warrant one?'

'That's enough,' Monroe took Declan's arm, slowly moving him back. Declan hadn't even realised he'd moved towards the landlady. 'We'll take the bag and go, Ma'am. And I think you should be happy we don't investigate more.'

'So you say.'

'If we found the gun, would you be able to identify it?'

'Definitely,' Maureen was glaring still at Declan. 'The boy scratched his name into the handle. Right furious I was at that. But the man never noticed, so we kept quiet. Boy claimed he hadn't, and Keith believed him, but he's a lying little bleeder at the best of times.'

'What's his name?' Declan asked. 'So we know what he scratched?'

'Oh, he didn't do his name, just what he's known as. *Boy.*'

Declan didn't comment on this, simply jotting it down. Monroe moved closer, taking over the conversation.

'Thank you, Maureen,' he said, exuding warmth and trust as he spoke. Declan almost laughed at it. If she ever met Monroe when he was pissed off, Maureen wouldn't recognise him from the smiling man that stood before her. 'Anything you can give us on the man who came for the gun would also help.'

'Oh, that's easy,' Maureen smiled, grateful for an opportunity to redeem herself in front of Monroe. 'We know who picked the gun up. It was that Lieutenant Colonel from the other side of the hill. Comes in the Ramblers Rest a lot.'

She nodded, as if confirming to herself she was correct.

'Charlie Falconer.'

———————

BILLY LEANED BACK IN HIS CHAIR, IMMEDIATELY REGRETTING IT as the horizontal middle strip cut into his lumbar region. He missed the ergonomic gamer chair, currently empty and unloved in Temple Inn—unless someone was illegally using it in his absence—and they'd only just hit lunchtime.

Stretching his arms and yawning, Billy looked around the Portakabin briefing room. It was empty, with Doctor Marcos and DC Davey currently in the morgue and the others out visiting various people and places in the courses of their enquiries, and usually Billy was happy for this; he enjoyed being on his own, but that was when he had great network speed and a multiple monitor setup. In Temple Inn, he was God. Here, he had a laptop, a spare screen and whatever he'd thrown into the Mini before driving up here.

To be brutally honest, the problem Billy had was that right now there wasn't a great deal to investigate. He'd already checked into the kinetic watch that Staff Sergeant Moses had worn, and found that it could have stopped any time in the latter half of the year, which didn't help with dating the time of death whatsoever. He'd also learned that because nobody had raised Staff Sergeant Moses as missing, or absent without leave, he'd fallen through the cracks in the system. Billy didn't understand why Colonel Yates *wouldn't* have raised this, especially with Moses being under his remit for over a decade; all he could assume was Yates felt he was covering for Moses somehow. That perhaps he hoped his Staff Sergeant would return, like a Labrador after it ran away from home, and everything would go back to normal.

Which was quite refreshing for a change.

It was, however, completely against regulations, and that raised a few warning bells in Billy's head. He'd known several army types in his own family, such as it was, and he knew that every one of them would die for their men and women, but at the same time still nail them to a tree if they betrayed their trust, you know, by doing something like walking away without an explanation of any kind. He'd therefore put in a request for Moses' history, to see if there were any other periods when the Staff Sergeant had disappeared for a protracted amount of time.

The bigger question was, however, the one that nagged constantly at Billy right now.

Why did Staff Sergeant Moses return to Castleton, and alone?

Because of this, and while waiting for additional evidence to arrive for him to disseminate, Billy had gone through the Patrick Harper case files; it was the only reason he could see why Edward Moses would return to the Peak District, especially off the books, in the same manner he'd arrived a decade earlier. He'd contacted Portsmouth and talked to a Lance-Corporal in records; they hadn't really known Edward Moses, but they'd been the one who emptied his room a few months back, when they needed it for someone else—and, more likely, when it was obvious he was unlikely to be returning anytime soon.

They'd explained that the rest of his personal items were already being sent up, and apart from one cryptic message on a post-it note, saying the postman was due just before 7pm, whatever that meant, they honestly didn't believe there was anything outstanding to be gained from the items.

Even the mobile phone that Eddie had used, left behind when he came to Castleton was wiped of all data. Either that, or he'd never used it. But, after a little cajoling from Billy, they'd sent across scans of the original files, and within these Billy had found the notes that explained the aftermath of the shooting over a decade earlier.

Private Malik had explained that while walking back to base from Castleton, she'd been taken by someone from behind and drugged; she believed it was chloroform or something similar, as a cloth had been placed over her mouth, stopping her from screaming, and she'd quickly passed out. She hadn't seen a face, but when she awoke, she found herself in a basement, chained to a concrete pillar, a bloody wound on her temple and Lance-Corporal Moses and Corporal Walsh watching over her, as Harper burst in with a rifle. She couldn't remember much else, and had drifted in and out of consciousness until the ambulance took her to hospital, but she was adamant that without the two Red Caps arriving, she'd be dead like the others.

The *others* she mentioned were identified as two female bar staff from Sheffield, which from a quick search by Billy on his phone's map app looked to be one of the closest cities to Castleton, and approximately a thirty minutes car drive away. Both women had been chained up in the same way as Malik, but differed from her because at some point of their captivity they'd both been shot in the forehead, the bullet entering between the eyes and killing them instantly, but then forcibly removed with narrow pliers afterwards, as if making sure nobody could ballistics match it to a weapon.

And then there was Susan Jenkins, the victim found dead in a ditch outside the base. During the investigation into her death, a statement had appeared from a Private in another Unit, claiming they had seen her in a local pub with Harper; but this had been disputed and eventually dropped after evidence proved Harper was still in Germany at the time of this occurrence.

However, when Harper had been posthumously charged with the deaths of the others, Susan had been quietly added to the list by someone in the military. The fact he couldn't have physically done it was irrelevant. The Private's statement of Harper and Jenkins meeting, and with no defence bothering to contest it now was enough to class it as gospel, and it was pointed out that like Malik, Harper had some connection with Susan Jenkins, one that probably killed her.

Billy knew this was likely because the army had wanted this matter closed and claimed publicly it was an internal matter that would be looked into. From what he could see, however, it never was. In fact, the only paperwork submitted on this case was done so after the posthumous trial, when a Lieutenant Eaton-Jones, now Major, had claimed on the record that Sergeant Patrick Harper was a troubled man with a history of mental issues, ones that Harper had apparently kept from the army medics, but that he was never a serial killer.

Nobody doubted that Harper hadn't killed Private Tooley though, and Billy wondered for a moment what the information was she'd found in Hamburg, that eventually ended her life.

Declan had been investigating the case, right up to the moment it was closed; even when it was squashed by the army, Billy could see his Guv's hand at work in the notes, and could guess the investigational route he took here, a route that Billy had already seen.

Something was wrong with the dates.

During the trial, Declan, then a Corporal had written in memos to his superiors that Jo Tooley and Susan Jenkins had both been killed slowly, a serrated blade to the throat, and then dumped in ditches with no attempt to hide them, while Lena Khoury and Sandra Tyler, the two women found in the basement had been chained up and shot, hidden from the world. The two M.Os didn't mesh, and Declan had argued how he believed this meant there had to be others involved; especially if the flight dates for Harper's arrival didn't match.

And, checking into this now, Billy could see they didn't.

When he was kicked out of Hamburg, the German authorities had booked Patrick Harper on two separate flights, both a week apart; the chances were he'd had to delay a week, or maybe they'd brought him forward when a space freed up, but looking at the manifests of the flights, Billy could see it was marked down that Harper took the latter date, returning home on a flight which left the day after Tooley was known to have been killed.

Which fitted the narrative.

However, the manifests *also* had him flying home the week before. Likely an error, but it was one that allowed Harper to be at both places at the same time.

If he flew on the earlier journey, he would have arrived the same day that Susan Jenkins went missing, and could therefore be charged with her murder. But if he went on the later one, he was still in Hamburg the night Jo Tooley died. He couldn't have been at both murder sites though, unless he'd arrived and then returned to Hamburg the same week; and this was the one piece of evidence the entire case was based on. Two days after Susan's disappearance, and before the second flight back, Harper's name was on a manifest that flew from RAF Brize Norton in Oxfordshire back to Germany.

A flight that had no proof he was actually on it bar a

hand-written name on a list, and a manifest only found after the trial had started.

Convenient.

Billy stared at the scanned documents on the screen, scratching at the stubble on his skin as he considered this. If you removed the erroneous flight back to Germany, you were left with two flights.

The first one allowed Harper to be tied into the kidnap of Malik and the murder of Susan Jenkins, but barred him from being in Hamburg and killing Private Tooley, who was actively looking for him when she died.

The other allowed him to kill Tooley beside a Hamburg airstrip before leaving, but meant he couldn't have killed Susan Jenkins.

The question was, which one was correct? Or was the manifest return real, and Sergeant Harper had in fact gone to the UK, killed and then returned, only to kill again?

Billy could see why this had eaten up Declan. It was a conspiracy, a plan to use Harper as some kind of executioner, perhaps.

Billy stopped.

What if he was?

Susan Jenkins was a journalist, hanging out in Castleton and possibly speaking to Harper. Private Jo Tooley had been hunting Harper.

What if the others were connected too? And why were they killed in the basement?

It was a mystery. And Billy Fitzwarren bloody hated mysteries.

9

COFFEE TIME

RAMESH ABBASI WAS A TALL, SLIM MAN IN A *BARBOUR* COAT, sitting at a corner table in the Visitor Centre, sipping what looked to be either a tea or a coffee from a disposable cup as Declan and Monroe entered.

'Old Ram?' Declan asked as he walked over to the table, showing his warrant card. 'DI Walsh, DCI Monroe. Can we have a quick chat?'

Old Ram looked up slowly at Declan. Without replying, he pulled a pair of reading glasses out of his inside pocket and, after placing them on his nose, peered at the warrant card closely before replying.

'Says you're City of London police,' he leaned back, looking up at Declan. 'Last I heard, Peak District is a little off your patch.'

'Working with the SIB,' Declan nodded to the chairs opposite Old Ram. 'Mind if we?'

'Military Police,' Old Ram ran his tongue around his teeth as he considered this, waving to the chairs. 'You're here about Eddie Moses. Or is it Falconer?'

'Can't it be both?' Monroe sat down on one of the offered chairs. Old Ram raised an eyebrow at this.

'Interesting times,' he muttered as he leaned back in his chair. 'Am I under suspicion or something?'

Declan sat now, staring at the man in front of him. Old Ram was an honest nickname for Ramesh; he was easily in his mid-sixties, his beard more white than black. His skin was clear though, his hair cut well and his jacket was new. He looked like a man who was well off, but trying to hide it.

'Should you be?'

Old Ram sipped at his tea.

'I should be a lot of things, but the universe makes space for random opportunities,' he smiled. 'I knew them both, if that's what you wanted to know.'

'How?' Monroe asked. 'Was it personal or professional?'

Old Ram laughed at this.

'I've not been professional anything for a while, mate,' he said. 'Army pension. I knew them from the pubs in Castleton. But Moses, Carrie Harper introduced him to me.'

Declan glanced at Monroe as Old Ram returned to his drink.

'She knew him well?'

'Well enough to introduce him to me,' Old Ram shrugged. 'For all the good it did him.'

'What do you mean?'

'I mean, I couldn't answer his questions, like I can't answer yours,' Old Ram straightened as he spoke. 'I just gave him pointers, suggestions. You were his partner, weren't you? He spoke your name, I didn't click until just now. You were with him when he nailed the wife beater. Carrie's dad.'

Declan nodded.

'I was there,' he said, watching Old Ram. There was

something nagging at him, and it wasn't the expensive jacket he was wearing. Declan was sure they'd met before, but couldn't think where.

'You believe he did the right thing?' Old Ram continued, bringing Declan back to the present.

'Let's just say I'm having doubts.'

Old Ram snorted.

'That's what he said, too,' he replied.

'Were you local army?' Monroe asked, changing the subject.

'You mean, was I *Derbyshire Regiment?*' Old Ram shook his head. 'They decommissioned that name two decades ago. Only brought it back as lip service when they unified the *Bedfordshire Light Infantry*, the *Cardigan Regiment* and the *Cumberland Fusiliers,* around twelve years ago, maybe more.'

Declan noted the dates; it could only have been a year or so before Moses killed Harper that the regiments changed their names.

'Which were you?' he asked.

'Cardigans,' Old Ram replied. 'Although I left before they got eaten up and spat back out. Medical discharge after I lost my foot in a mortar attack.'

Declan resisted the urge to look under the table, to see what kind of prosthetic limb Old Ram now sported.

'Deployment?'

'Iraq War,' Old Ram shrugged. 'Accidental, but enough to give me an out.'

'You wanted an out?' Monroe was surprised.

Old Ram deliberated the question.

'You're ex-military,' he said to Declan. 'I don't know about your Scottish mate there. But you know *don't ask, don't tell,* right?'

Declan did; *don't ask, don't tell* was the term given to a United States policy during the Clinton administration, where openly gay, lesbian or bisexual personnel were barred from active service, while closeted ones could still serve. It was a US forces rule, but one that had repercussions across the entire globe's military. In fact, after the furore surrounding the law in the US, the Ministry of Defence had lifted the law stating it was illegal to be a British serviceman if you were homosexual, back in 2000.

'You're gay?'

'I'm gay and Muslim,' Old Ram replied softly. 'Two things that don't go well together in a British Army unit, it seems, especially when I look Middle Eastern and we're in a Middle Eastern war zone. I didn't shout it from the rooftops, kept it to myself, but you know how things get.'

'You were targeted for it,' Declan nodded. 'I saw this a lot when I was in the SIB.'

'No offence, mate, but before the repeal, it was you bastards in the SIB who mainly caused the problems with us, thanks to your witch-hunts,' Old Ram muttered. 'Luckily for me, nobody ever grassed me up when I was in.'

'And how long were you in?' Monroe asked.

Old Ram counted on his fingers.

'Joined when I was eighteen, so 1976,' he replied. 'Left in 2003, so do the math. Parents moved here from Damascus in the fifties, before I was born, I was first generation British, although that meant sod all because after all that time, I'd only reached Captain rank at the end.'

'Over twenty-five years to reach Captain,' Declan shook his head. 'Harsh.'

'I started as a Second Lieutenant, and made Captain in the first decade,' Old Ram explained. 'But back then, few of us *brown* soldiers got much higher up. And there were enough people in the Regiment that didn't like it. I'd hit my glass ceiling.'

He sipped at his drink.

'I'm not saying the Army was racist,' he added, almost as an afterthought. 'But there were people within it who were. People that, to them, a gay Muslim Captain was an abomination. Especially ones who translated what the enemy was saying.'

'Like who?' Monroe asked.

Old Ram leaned back, staring out of the Visitor Centre window for a long moment before replying.

'Yeah, I'm not saying anything else,' he muttered. 'Not worth it.'

Declan went to respond, but Ram rapped his knuckles on the table for a moment, as if coming to a decision.

'Look. All good clubs have *initiations*,' he blurted, as if deciding to confess something, rising from the chair and finishing his drink. 'And all good secret clubs get right royally pissed off when someone shouts those secrets out. Or when the wrong type of person gets into the room and thinks they're part of it. Sometimes, these two things combine. That's all I have.'

Before Declan could reply, Old Ram nodded, turned and walked out of the café.

'Did you understand what he meant?' Monroe asked, shaking his head. 'What secret society?'

'I can help you with that,' a voice spoke, and the balding young man with the black bomber jacket sat down at the table, taking Ram's recently vacated chair as he nodded to both detectives.

'Owen Russell, *Derby Telegraph*,' he said as an introduction. 'I know who you both are, so no need to tell me.'

'Bloody journalist,' Monroe muttered. 'I bloody knew we were being followed.'

'I seem to recall I was the one who told you?' Declan raised an eyebrow at Monroe's comment.

'Aye, you pointed the wee bastard out, but I just knew.'

Declan looked at Owen.

'So, why were you following us?'

'Wanted a chance to talk,' Owen replied calmly.

'You local?'

'God, no. I turn up now and then so I'm known by the village, as this is our paper's catchment area, but I came down this week because of the deaths.'

'Plural?' Monroe scratched at his beard. 'Or do you mean the discovery, too?'

'Yeah, sorry,' Owen shook his head. 'Moses and Falconer. Both dead. Both connected.'

'You're investigating them?' Declan leaned closer. 'Or is this something else? I've known many journos in my time, and I can tell when they're off the path, making their own way.'

'Takes one to know one,' Owen said, unintimidated by Declan. 'I hear you favour leaving that path you talk of on a regular basis.'

'Aye, the laddie has you pegged,' Monroe chuckled.

'I'm here because it's personal,' Owen continued. 'I'm on the news desk, right? Ten years ago, the woman who sat in my spot was Susan Jenkins.'

'Ah,' Declan understood now. 'You're not convinced the case was—'

'Are you?' Owen interrupted. 'I saw your statement back

then. I know you didn't believe in the convenience of the flight back.'

'Flight back?' Monroe looked confused.

'I'll explain in a minute,' Declan looked to the door. 'Old Ram left the moment you walked in, didn't he?'

'Ramesh Abbasi doesn't speak to me,' Owen shrugged. 'He lives here. It's too personal.'

'So you know his story?'

'I know enough,' Owen nodded. 'Small town, the stories get told.'

'Do you know about the secret society?' Monroe offered.

'Old man, everyone knows about that,' Owen replied. 'Well, everyone who matters, anyway. And they're not talking either.'

Monroe's face darkened.

'Call me old man again, and we'll be seeing just how fast you really are,' he hissed. 'You know information on our case, and you're obstructing it.'

'How so?' Owen wasn't as cocksure now.

'By being an insufferable twat,' Monroe hissed. 'Old Ram was going to tell us who the racists were that caused him to leave. Can you answer that?'

Owen nodded.

'Major Eaton-Jones for a start,' he replied.

Declan shook his head.

'Wait, you don't mean the Major—'

'No, not the son, the dad. Winston. He's now a Brigadier, works in Whitehall on top-secret shit. But back in the nineties, he was a Major. Made Ramesh's life hell.'

'And you're sure it was deliberate?' Declan asked. 'I'm not saying it didn't happen, I'm trying to work out why my friend and onetime partner died.'

'Because he met with Ramesh and asked the same questions,' Owen leaned back in the chair. 'Although I don't think he had a fancy warrant card like you. He was alone.'

'What did then-Major Eaton-Jones do to Old Ram?' Monroe asked now.

'You ever see *The Godfather?*' Owen asked, and for a moment Declan wondered if he was wildly changing the subject.

'Of course.'

'You know the scene with the horse's head in the bed?' Owen continued. 'Eaton-Jones and his buddies did that. Although it was a pig's head rather than a horse, I mean, why waste a horse on someone like Ramesh?'

He leaned in.

'And they left him a message, written on the sheets in blood.'

'What kind of message?' Declan leaned closer.

'You got a pen?' Owen asked.

'You don't?' Monroe was surprised. 'Bloody useless journalist.'

'All done digitally these days, granddad,' Owen replied. 'Sorry, DCI granddad.'

'We're arresting him, right?' Monroe moaned as Declan passed across his tactical pen. Taking a napkin, Owen quickly drew out a line of images.

'I hope you write better than you draw,' Monroe commented.

'This is what Ramesh showed me when I asked,' Owen replied, ignoring Monroe, passing both pen and napkin to Declan. 'Said they smeared it in shit and blood.'

Declan stared at the three images Owen had drawn.

'Is it a code?' he asked.

'I wondered that, and I had a couple of people we know look into it,' Owen answered. 'They came back saying the closest they could find were two Maltese Crosses and a Swastika.'

He opened up his phone, showing a saved image.

'Ramesh confirmed this, saying they were the symbols of what he called the *Templar Corps*. *Ordo Templo Pricko*, or whatever Latin you want to use.'

'The *what* now?' Monroe took the napkin now, staring at the images. 'Templars?'

'Wannabe ones, at least. Massive right-wing bag of bastards,' Owen replied. 'Eaton-Jones' little band of brown-shirt pricks.'

Declan took a photo of the image with his phone, sending it as a message to Billy as he considered the possibility of such a group. Small, off the books groups like this weren't rare, unfortunately. He'd dealt with similar in his time as an MP, and more recently at least fourteen investigations had been carried out in 2019 into serving armed forces personnel.

Eleven of these had stemmed from far-right concerns.

There'd even been a document leaked to the press back then, one that had been sent to officers to use as effectively a bingo sheet for hunting radicalised soldiers. These individuals were known as XRW ones, standing for *Extreme Right-Wing*, people that called themselves *patriots*, or who added *istan* to British cities with vibrant ethic cultures, terms like *Londonistan* becoming popular amongst them, claiming that these multi-cultural hubs were lost cities and towns.

The XRW suspects would also talk about race wars, refer to Judaism and Islam with whatever conspiracies and fake news fitted their narrative, and become increasingly angry at what they believed to be threats to 'national identity', whatever they believed that to be at the time. From Oswald Moseley's *British Union of Fascists* all the way to the more contemporary *Britain First* and *National Action,* there would always be people who believed in such things, and charismatic leaders to lie to them sweetly.

And, unfortunately, many of these fanatics would find solace in the military.

'What happened to them?' Declan asked.

'What do you think?' Owen laughed. 'They got promoted. Look at the world we live in. Fear and suspicion are rife. Eaton-Jones senior may have been promoted out of the area, but his bloody son carried on where daddy dropped off.'

'Henry Eaton-Jones is a member of the Templar Corps?' Monroe was writing this down now.

'Possibly,' Owen shrugged. 'His name gets linked in whispers, but then people conveniently forget they said things to me.'

'Things like what?'

'Like Winston Eaton-Jones and the Cardigans being cancelled for war crimes in 2008. And no, I don't mean the bloody pop band.'

Declan had guessed that, but let the comment slide.

'And Eaton-Jones, Henry that is, he was part of the Cardigan Regiment with his father?'

'Well, that's the problem,' Owen smiled slightly. 'You see, I've checked around and spoken to a few old soldiers, ones that reckon Eaton-Jones junior gained a commission in the Cardigan Regiment, but the moment the Cardigans got amalgamated into the Derbyshire Regiment, with possible inquests and court-martials looming for the upper ranks, suddenly the officers list disappears from public viewing, nobody's admitting they were in the Regiment anymore, and records show that Henry suddenly comes into the Derbyshires from the Cumberland Fusiliers instead. But Brigadier Eaton-Jones was definitely a Cardigan alumni, and he most likely made sure there weren't any black marks on his son's ledger, by changing his history.'

'You mentioned a couple of others,' Declan replied. 'Do you have names?'

'That's the problem,' Owen shook his head. 'Nobody wants to go further when I ask. All scared of ending up with a silver ball up their arse.'

'Wait,' Declan leaned over, grabbing Owen by the arm. 'A silver *musket* ball?'

'Calling it that makes you think of duelling pistols and gentlemen's agreements,' Owen pulled his wrist away from Declan's grip. 'This is more *Clint Eastwood*.'

'*Tell me what you know!*' Declan hissed. 'Eddie was found shot with a silver musket ball.'

'Call it what it is,' Owen lowered his voice. 'A silver *bullet*.'

The café was quiet for a moment as Owen rose now.

'Look,' he whispered. 'I'm sorry about your mate, Staff Sergeant Moses, I really am. But he was asking everyone for information on Brigadier Eaton-Jones, and more importantly, his son. By the time I heard about him, it's Maureen bloody Williams standing in the *Castle Tun* telling us he'd had the shit beaten out of him and was bleeding badly, right before he ran away like a coward.'

He sighed, leaning against the table as he continued.

'He went up against the Templar Corps and they didn't like it. And they *ended* him. Stuck him in a body bag and left him to rot. You know that, I know that. He was asking questions they hated. And I'm doing the same about Susan, so I'm not going to be sticking my head up around here much longer. You'll need to carry the torch.'

'Why stop?' Declan rose to face Owen. 'You're a journalist. It's your job.'

'I know you,' Owen replied sadly. 'And I know about Kendis Taylor. I know how she didn't let a story, one just like this, die. And it killed her. No thanks, mate, that's not for me. I came here to give you what I know, and move on. I'm not another Jenkins.'

'What's that mean?' Monroe asked, suspicious.

'Susan Jenkins was a local paper reporter with a global ambition,' Owen replied. 'I read her stuff. She was good. She found stories nobody else did. She was writing about the 2011 Arab Spring a whole year before it even happened. Connecting dots, linking Putin with al-Assad, all of that. She reckoned she'd found connections with the British Military and the SSNP, in a Sheffield TA centre, and that it connected here.'

'SSNP?'

'Syrian Social Nationalist Party,' Owen said as he reached into his bag, pulling out a USB drive. 'Fascist organisation, filled with Syrian Nationalists, definitely not friendly. Let's leave it at that.'

'How do Syrian Nationalists connect to our more home-grown ones?' Monroe asked.

'That's what she was looking into,' Owen replied, passing the USB over. 'Everything I have, and it's not much, is on that. I hope you do better than I did.'

'Wait, why did Carrie bring Moses to Old Ram?' Declan asked. 'I would have thought with his distrust of coppers, he'd not want to talk to her either?'

'She's MDP,' Owen was already walking out of the Visitor Centre now, looking back as he spoke. 'She might have wanted to be army once, but she burned her way out of that idea. Ramesh believed she had the right intentions. Now? I'm not so sure.'

Declan stared at the now empty door long after Owen had walked out, looking back to the USB drive in his hand.

'I bloody hate these things,' he muttered.

'Aye, but Billy gets a tingle in his dingle whenever he touches one,' Monroe smiled. 'So give it to him and let the well-dressed bairn do his thing.'

Declan didn't move, staring out of the window, watching Owen as he climbed into his car.

'You okay, laddie?' Monroe asked.

Declan slowly turned to look at his mentor.

'You know what, Guv?' he replied. 'I don't think I am. I don't think I'm okay *at all*.'

And, this stated, Declan walked out of the Visitor Centre in silent fury. Standing outside, taking a breath, he watched across the car park, towards the Main Street and the hill that led to the ruins of Peveril Castle.

Old Ram was standing by the bridge, watching him.

'What aren't you telling me?' Declan muttered to himself as he pulled out his phone, dialling a number. He'd promised himself he wouldn't, but he needed a little more of an inside edge than usual here.

'Didn't think I'd hear from you again,' the voice of Trix Preston came through the speaker. 'You find anything in St Davids?'

'Yeah, I'll email you,' Declan said, still watching Old Ram, who'd now bored with staring back at Declan and had walked off. 'I need a favour, though. Whatever you can find on the Cardigan Regiment, and in particular, an old officer named Captain Ramesh Abbasi. Served under Winston Eaton-Jones.'

'Oh, I've met the Brigadier. He's a prick. Term of service?'

'From late seventies until 2003,' Declan replied. 'Anything you can do would be appreciated.'

'And then you tell me about Francine's death, right?'

'Yeah. Although I don't think she's dead. Bye.'

Declan disconnected before Trix could reply, almost chuckling as he did so. Trix was a spook, and she'd left him enough cliffhangers over the last couple of months.

Turnaround was fair play.

Looking back to the road, Declan saw Old Ram was gone.

'What's the issue, laddie?' Monroe walked out of the café, now standing beside Declan.

'You get outed from your Regiment,' Declan said. 'You have pig's heads and blood and shit and all that stuff, like major trauma stuff, and then you decide, once out, that you're going to live in the same town as the Regiment, still? That doesn't fit right.'

Declan started walking towards the Audi.

'That doesn't fit right at all.'

10

POWDERKEG

IT HAD TAKEN ANJLI AND DE'GEER ANOTHER HOUR BEFORE they gained entry into Lieutenant Colonel Falconer's private dorm room.

It was small, even by military standards; a double bed with a tartan duvet was to the side of it, a wooden side table holding a lamp and phone charger on its top. There was a poster of a military plane to the right of the table; Anjli didn't recognise it, but assumed it was something important, perhaps a stealth plane from the looks of it, shaped like a dart.

Under this was a bookshelf with an old globe, a collection of academic novels and two battered cricket balls scattered on random shelves. The other side of the door was a window, the musty orange curtains pulled, a side cabinet with a small flat screen television on it, a selection of military genre DVDs beside it, and two footballs and a fencing mask discarded on the floor in front.

On the back wall was a wardrobe, half open. Anjli could make out military fatigues, a leather jacket and what could be a dress uniform beside a selection of coloured shirts, far more civilian than the surrounding clothing. Finally, on the pale magnolia walls were A4 prints; old framed sketches and engravings, and all showing various duels.

'Definitely had a thing about fighting,' De'Geer muttered as he examined one image, pulling on his blue latex gloves before touching anything.

'Possibly more the guns than the duels,' Anjli was looking at another print, an image of a clean-shaven man in a black morning coat, holding a gun to a moustached villain's head as she pulled on her own latex gloves. 'This is a Sidney Paget *Sherlock Holmes* print. It's from *The Adventure of the Beryl Coronet,* by Arthur Conan Doyle.'

'I forgot you were a Sherlockian, Ma'am,' De'Geer walked over and examined the picture. 'Weird, this. The others are more military, while this is a little more fantastical.'

'You think Sherlock Holmes is fantastical?'

'Well, he did fall off a waterfall and live,' De'Geer smiled. 'And Watson was hit in two locations with one bullet. But perhaps I mean fictional, then? Because the other prints on the walls look like etchings of factual moments, or real-world pistols.'

He pointed at one wall, where above each other were two black-framed images; both sketches, one was a duelling pistol, the other a six-shot revolver.

'That's a bit modern, isn't it?' Anjli nodded at it. 'Not quite the romantic weapon the others give.'

De'Geer smiled as he took photos of the prints on his camera.

'It says in the corner it's a Remington New Model Army 1858,' he replied. 'Over a hundred and sixty years old, so I'm not sure if it applies as modern.'

Anjli chuckled.

'More modern than the others, then,' she said as she knelt down, looking under the bed.

'Oho, what's this?' she asked, pulling out a wooden box.

It was pale plywood, almost an inch thick, and just over a foot in height. It was wider by about another half, and currently unlocked, the padlock left open. As Anjli opened it, she saw eight compartments inside, set in a four by two arrangement.

'It's a black powder storage box,' De'Geer now kneeled beside her. 'I've seen them before. Fully compliant with the *Health and Safety Commission HSC regulations* on storing powder, they vary in size depending on how many compartments you want.'

Reaching into the first compartment, he gently pulled out a clear plastic baggie, currently filled with musket balls.

'I'm not an expert, but these look the same as the one we saw earlier,' he said, holding it up to the light. 'Could Falconer have killed Moses?'

'I'm not sure, they look like lead,' Anjli took the bag from De'Geer, peering at it. 'The ball Doctor Marcos found in the body of Eddie Moses was silver. That said, given the amount of people who have musket balls easily to hand in the UK, it makes it a fair bet Falconer's probably involved somehow. Unless Castleton has a real thing for duels, or games of *crap marbles*.'

De'Geer reached into the box, pulling out a bag of small white, circular wads of padding.

'What do you reckon these are?' he asked, frowning. Anjli shrugged, still examining the small lead balls, so De'Geer placed them back in the box and instead pulled out a metal flask with a small capped tube on the end. Tipping it into his hand, he poured a tiny pile of black powder onto it.

'Gunpowder?' Anjli looked up, sniffing.

'I reckon it's *Henry Kranck Fine Black Powder*,' De'Geer stared at it.

'That's pretty specific,' Anjli was impressed, but De'Geer nodded at one of the other compartments in the plywood box where a white plastic tub, these words written on the side of it, rested.

'Wasn't that difficult,' he said with a smile, examining the flask. 'I've seen similar to these on TV. You hold your finger over the end, click a clasp, turn it upside down and gravity allows out the exact amount to place in a black powder pistol.'

'So what, you pour that in to a chamber, ram a musket ball in and fire?'

'Probably more to it, but I suppose so,' De'Geer pulled out a small circular tin from a compartment. 'These are percussion caps; I'm guessing they work like cap guns?'

'Strike the cap, ignite the powder, fire the gun,' Anjli placed the musket balls back into the box. 'Take this with us. We can see if DC Davey can work anything out from it.'

The box now forgotten, the two officers started to search for the gun that went with it; but no matter how hard they looked they couldn't find anything else, apart from a bag of pipe cleaners and tools, and a plastic case filled with small plastic test tubes, which Anjli assumed were connected because they had the same gunpowder smell as the black powder on them.

Eventually, standing by the door, Anjli took a last look around the room.

'We examined everywhere, right?' she asked, a little

dejected. She'd really hoped to find something here, and currently, she was drawing a blank. Falconer wasn't married, and didn't have any properties off base that they'd found so far; unless it was here or in his office, there was no weapon to be found, laser or otherwise. 'Maybe we need to have a better look in that basement.'

'You think the Ministry of Defence will let us?'

'Yeah, probably not,' Anjli admitted. 'At best, we'll have the whining Peterson telling us he's missing his mid-after-noon nap or something.'

De'Geer, however, was staring at the chunky wooden side table beside the bed.

'There's something wrong with that,' he muttered, walking back over to it, pulling out the drawer to its furthest catch, angling his head to look into the drawer's pan. 'Been bothering me since I looked inside it.'

'Like what?' Anjli moved closer, mimicking De'Geer as she leaned in.

'I dunno, the side seems off, you know?' Removing a pen out from the drawer and holding it up horizontally, De'Geer noted the depth inside the drawer before using the same pen on the outside. 'Look, it's a shallow drawer, but the sides of it are about two inches deeper.'

'So what, it's a secret drawer?' Anjli leaned over, exam-ining the sides. 'If it is, there'd be a catch somewhere, some-thing small and—'

There was a *clack* as De'Geer pulled at what felt like a nail in the base of the front piece of the drawer, and Anjli backed away as the now freed front piece clicked upwards about an inch, revealing a hidden cavity behind it.

'Good call,' she said as De'Geer pulled up on the frontage,

revealing more space within and, more importantly, a replica pistol nestled into the hiding place.

'I think this is Lieutenant Colonel Falconer's gun cabinet,' he said, pulling the gun out and looking at it. 'I think it's a Remington New Model Army, like the one on the print.'

Anjli looked from the gun in De'Geer's hand to the image of the same gun on the wall.

'Yeah, you might be right,' she said, reaching into her pocket and muttering. 'I don't have an evidence bag big enough for that.'

'I do,' De'Geer was already pulling a large, clear baggie out of his fluorescent vest, gently dropping the pistol into it. 'If this uses all the other pieces we found to work, then this could fire the musket balls. This could be the weapon that killed Edward Moses.'

He thought for a moment.

'It's not a musket, so if we find it *does* fire them, do we still call them musket balls?'

'Let's hope it doesn't,' Anjli muttered. 'Because if it was, it means that Falconer could have been the killer. And, going on the basis that he was murdered the day Eddie Moses' body was found, then we're back to square one.'

She stopped as she saw something else glinting in the cavity. Pulling this out, she saw it was Falconer's ID tags; the chain caught on something at the back of the drawer.

'Why wasn't he wearing these?' she asked, tugging at the tags to loosen the chain.

'Probably didn't have to in the lab,' De'Geer suggested as he sealed the gun into the clear bag. 'Maybe the metal was conductive or something?'

'Look,' Anjli showed the first of the two tags to De'Geer. 'Three stamps, probably made with the same Torx and

Phillips screwdriver, in the same cross-star-cross config-uration.'

De'Geer glanced down at the gun.

'I think this weapon might have shot more than just Staff Sergeant Moses,' he muttered.

Anjli was once more examining the drawer space, trying to work out what was keeping the chain secured to the back.

'There's something else in here,' she said, reaching in with a pen to dislodge it, freeing the chain. 'A box, wedged right at the—'

With a last push from the pen, a slim blue box slid out of the drawer and landed on the floor of the dorm room. Anjli picked it up, turning it in her hand.

'Looks like a medal case,' she said, opening it up to see what was inside. It flipped open along its length, and as Anjli stared down at the medal inside, her face darkened.

'Yeah, it's a medal, alright,' she snarled as she turned it to show De'Geer. 'A *Nazi* one.'

'I don't know Nazi medals, the only one I've heard of is the Iron Cross,' De'Geer placed the gun, now in a baggie into his vest before looking. 'People link it to war movies, but they were around since Napoleonic times, so there's a chance this might not be from the war, and more importantly Nazis. Especially as Falconer has a fixation with pistols from that time...'

He stopped as he finally turned to see the medal; a silver cross with swords behind it, a red, white and black ribbon looped through the top, and a swastika emblazoned on the front.

'No, thats a Nazi one,' he replied, closing the box and passing it back, done with both the medal and the box. 'Why would a research officer have Nazi memorabilia hidden in a drawer?'

'If that's the only question you have, then we have a long journey ahead of us,' Anjli said as she looked nervously around the room. Lieutenant Colonel Falconer had some kind of secret interest in the Nazis, was obsessed by duelling, fired black powder pistols, and had been killed by a classified laser weapon that technically couldn't exist.

And it wasn't even lunchtime yet.

AFTER LEAVING THE CAFÉ, DECLAN HAD SENT MONROE BACK to, well, the MDP classrooms they'd currently requisitioned with the kitbag Eddie Moses had left at the guesthouse; he knew Doctor Marcos would want to examine it immediately, although being left for a year in a mouldy basement probably didn't bode well for evidence gathering.

Declan meanwhile, not wanting to have another confrontation with either Carrie or Devin Harper just yet had decided to stretch his legs, walking in the glorious sunlight along the public rights of way that led towards the cave where Eddie's body had been found; although open again to the public, the pathways were now a morbid curiosity, with remnants of scene of crime tape being taken as gruesome keepsakes by some tourists and walkers that went past.

Although technically, with the cave being over a rise and away from the path, only visited by an old woman looking for her dog and the occasional lost sheep, they shouldn't have been there to collect the tape in the first place, he thought to himself with mild irritation.

Declan had picked up a walking guide in the Visitor

Centre, which indicated that an ascending mile and a half walk lay ahead of him to reach the cave, although walking onwards to the army base would be far shorter, across more fields.

The cave where Eddie had been found was over the rise and impossible to see from the path, and Declan could understand why it'd been used as a hiding place; the only way to find it was literally to be hunting it with knowledge of the location.

That or being a Terrier, anyway.

What confused Declan, however, was the lack of sheep. The reports had stated that the dog owner claimed her dog had run off after a flock of them before becoming trapped in the cave, and a sheep carcass had been found in there with it, a rotten chunk of dead meat, where the awful stench likely masked Eddie's own. It was probably this that drew the Terrier to the cave in the first place; Declan remembered a dog in Hurley he saw as a child. Bloody thing wanted nothing more than to roll on its back in cow shit.

All Declan could assume was the owner of the sheep had moved them away from the army when they were entering the cave, and might still be over the rise, waiting for Declan to bugger off.

To check, Declan walked up the hill, glad for his wellington boots, taken from the Audi before Monroe drove off, as he sloshed across the wet grass and muddy ground. It was well trodden; most likely because of the large amount of firemen and soldiers around here a week earlier, as the path he now walked along was well off the established track.

He chuckled to himself as he remembered his first cases with the Last Chance Saloon; Savernake Forest, and then Epping Forest, had both been incredibly muddy, and he'd tried to navigate around the mud with his best shoes on, in a strange, spot-to-spot hopping dance. It had been Billy, always dressed-on-point Billy, in his trendy *Hunters*—or were they *Barbours?* Declan couldn't remember now, it felt so long ago —that suggested he invest in a pair.

He was going to miss Billy's three-piece suits when he left.

Rising over the ridge and finally looking down at the cave in a sunken hollow below him, Declan could see it was nothing more than a slit in the side of a cliff, no higher than a foot and a half, and only about ten feet in width. There was a steep bank to get to it, and like the path he'd been on, the grass on it too was poached by multiple boot wearers, likely the people and machinery tasked with removing the body bag. Slipping and sliding as he did so, Declan struggled his way to the lip of the cave, cursing as he stumbled and rammed his knee into the mud.

Another suit ruined. Still, it wasn't as expensive as the ones Billy wore.

Declan pulled a torch out of his pocket, shining it into the sliver of darkness, lighting up the small cavern behind it. There wasn't much space, but there was enough for a man to stand in, and Declan sighed reluctantly as he decided he had to enter, to have a closer look, realising he was about to scuff up more than just the knee of his trousers as he dropped onto his stomach and shimmied his way horizontally through the gap, feeling the lip of the hole scrape against his back as he did so, exhaling out to gain an inch, wishing he'd spent more time surfing and less time eating carbs over the last couple of weeks.

Eventually he passed the narrowest point, slithering side-ways as his leg dangled over the lip, finding purchase on the floor of the cavern as he turned himself around, now standing with his chest half-trapped, moving slowly backwards away from the entrance and holding his nose in disgust. The smell of dead sheep was still strong here, and Declan could see the remains of the carcass to the side, as he shone his torch down at it.

Of course, the smell could also be the remnants of Eddie Moses, but Declan really didn't want to consider that right now. What was interesting however, was that the remains were still here; a police forensics team would have cleaned the whole place out while this seemed to have been left as was. Declan recalled his time in the MDP, and he knew they would never have left it like this.

This was deliberately left. As if they'd been told to get the body and then go. But why? Were they worried about a cave in?

Shining the torch around, Declan could see a ledge to the left; it was about chest height, and around seven feet in length, recessing into the wall about three feet, easily enough to position a body in a bag. Declan moved his torch's beam over the ledge; he worried it'd been picked clean by forensics, but the evident carcass behind made him wonder if there could still be clues left here; items left in the rush to remove the body, probably in case the whole damn thing fell on them.

'Sorry, mate,' Declan muttered, half to himself as he stared at the ledge. 'I should have been there for you. I wasn't. But I'll find your killer, I promise.'

He looked back to the gap in the wall where the sliver of outside light was still visible, and frowned. It was about five feet from gap to floor; *how had the Terrier not hurt himself when he fell in here?* Declan made a mental note to check on that when he returned. Turning around the cavern and searching the floor, Declan knew this was futile; everything had been examined and catalogued well before he—

Something flashed in the light; a dull glisten, but enough to catch his eye, and Declan spun the torch back to it, walking over to the glinting item, kneeling and brushing away the surrounding gravel.

Another silver ball, possibly a musket ball like the one found in Eddie's body. *Had he been shot twice? Had someone dropped it?*

Declan pulled a clear plastic bag out of his pocket, using the sides of the bag to pick up the ball, making sure he didn't touch it with his fingers.

It looked smaller than the other one, but then he wasn't an expert on how musket balls worked. He went to move on, but something else now caught his eye; at a lower angle, he could get a better view into the back corner of the cave, and he could see behind a wide outcropping of stone that reached up to the roof.

The wall looked the same as the rest, but at this angle, Declan could see there was a stone, a couple of feet square, placed against the wall, as if fallen—but there was no obvious place it could have fallen from. Something about it didn't feel right.

He couldn't explain it, he felt as if he was being drawn to the stone and, as he pulled at it, he struggled to dislodge it from the ground, wondering if he'd made a mistake here—

The stone eventually shifted, and shining his torch under it, Declan saw a small, man-made hole with something metallic glinting in the light. Declan pulled on his latex gloves, reached into the space behind the stone and carefully removed a tin box, no larger than a phone. It was a tobacco tin, and as Declan held it up to the light, he could see that someone had scrawled on the top with a black marker pen.

It was a design he'd seen before, earlier that very day in fact, but this one had more time spent on it than the sketch on a napkin that he'd taken a photo of.

The Templar Corps had been in the cave, it seemed. But had this been before or after Eddie Moses was dumped into a body bag and thrown onto a shelf in here?

Declan was about to open the box when there was a quiet, almost imperceptible sound outside the cave. From where he was positioned, the pillar to his left blocked a view out to the entranceway, so Declan slid the tin into the clear baggie, placing it into his jacket pocket and turned to back cautiously out of his nook. There was definitely someone out there, though; the footsteps were heavier than an animal, and had the regularity of two, rather than four feet.

'Hello?' Declan called out. 'Who's out there?'

There was no reply, and Declan eased towards the entrance, turning his torch off as he did so. The fact they hadn't answered made him think perhaps they might not be there with his best interests at heart—

There was a *plink*, a sound that Declan recognised with a chill of horror; the sound of a grenade pin being removed, and immediately after this, a small pineapple-shaped object rolled into the entranceway.

'Christ!' Declan yelled, immediately diving left, onto the ledge, into the stone recess, rolling away from the entranceway as the grenade exploded.

There was a crash of noise and a rumbling of sound, a deafening cacophony of stone collapsing, and it plunged the cavern into darkness.

Declan coughed, the dust all around him as he still lay in

a foetal position, held within the safety of the recess. But although it'd stopped the ceiling from collapsing on him, it hadn't really done much to help him...

Because the entranceway had been sealed up with collapsed stone, and Declan was trapped.

11

BATTLE SCARS

DOCTOR MARCOS HAD BEEN EXAMINING THE BODIES FOR A good hour by now, and already she was getting annoyed.

Not at the bodies; *you couldn't be angry at bodies, it wasn't their fault they were dead,* but at the people around her. The reports had suggested the autopsy had been well attended, but now she examined the bodies herself, she'd realised the forensic autopsy before her had basically extended as far as going 'yup, he's dead', and leaving it there.

Repeatedly.

She'd arrived early and examined Lieutenant Colonel Falconer first; after all, this was the murder that Whitehall had sent them up here to investigate, and to be honest, it was quite straightforward. His pacemaker hadn't exploded, but had definitely sustained intense heat damage; in the process melting vital parts of the ICD unit inside him, which would have most likely stopped his heart. It wouldn't have been instantaneous, but whatever was used on him had to have been done so with the knowledge this would be *fatal*.

Besides this, slightly above and to the left of the pacemaker's internal location, the external skin was reddened and burned, the chest hairs singed, as if scalded by a hot stove, or burned with a lighter. There was a small mark, no larger than a five pence piece on his upper chest, and Doctor Marcos guessed this might be from a focused laser, like the one Whitehall were having kittens about; an invisible beam of death that struck him, the energy passing through his epidermis and muscle, and eventually hitting the ICD, which then absorbed the rest of the energy as the muscles behind it weren't charred by the incredible heat.

Which, if he was standing at a pedestal for a long period, meant that someone fired it from above and straight ahead of him.

The problem for Doctor Marcos, however, were the *other* scars on Falconer's body.

She'd checked his records before starting; Falconer had been deployed into war zones over the years of his service, joining the Infantry as a Lieutenant around eighteen years earlier, following a master's degree in Oxford, but had never been in active combat. Even his time in Syria had been mainly spent in research. However, with only a cursory glance, Doctor Marcos could see this must be incorrect as there were definitely two very visible, potential bullet wounds; one on his lower right side and one on his left thigh. They'd been roughly patched up too, as if a combat medic had fixed Falconer's injuries rather than taking him to a field hospital. On examination of these, she'd also found traces of *sulpha* in the healed scars, which led her to believe that the wounds had, at some point, been treated with *Sulphonamide Powder* as an antibiotic.

Which hadn't been used since the Second World War.

Added to the fact that Staff Sergeant Moses had a silver

musket ball inside him—or at least in the bag, having fallen out of him, Doctor Marcos was wondering if time travel was involved here. Or maybe that Billy was right, and Moses was a werewolf.

Moving onto Staff Sergeant Moses now, Doctor Marcos had found this a far harder examination; a year in a body bag didn't help keep a body prepped for autopsy. However the body had dried in the last week since being exposed to air and Marcos could now see a visible hole in the skin around the left shoulder, where the musket had probably struck. Or, at least, where the *believed* ball had struck, she reminded herself, as there was no proof it'd even been in his body, the ball found in the bag by the time they'd removed it. There was also a darkening, a possible bruising in the chest region that didn't seem to be consistent with the decomposition of the body. In a way, it bore a strong resemblance to the marking on Falconer's chest.

Had Staff Sergeant Moses been hit with the same laser a year earlier?

There was another marking on the arm; a long brutal scar across the side, as if a bullet had grazed past at an earlier point. *Another musket ball, perhaps? Or had Moses had more combat action than his own record indicated?* Checking this, and examining the other wounds once more, Doctor Marcos tried to take in what she was looking at.

These bodies had died a good year from each other, but both had *Sulphonamide Powder* embedded in their wounds.

Doctor Marcos shook her head. Usually she liked a good mystery, but this was starting to take the piss a little right now.

Deciding to move away from the bodies, Doctor Marcos

examined the silver musket ball instead. *Surely there would be no more surprises there.*

She was wrong.

MONROE PULLED UP OUTSIDE THE MINISTRY OF DEFENCE POLICE offices and, climbing out of Declan's Audi, slung the kitbag over his shoulder as he made his way into the building, a fierce expression on his face. To be brutally honest, he'd hoped to find Carrie Harper back at her desk; after talking to Maureen and then both Old Ram and Owen, he had a few new questions he wanted answered. Primarily, why Carrie had told no one she'd visited Eddie Moses in his guest house room, which proved she knew where he'd been staying, and also why she'd put him in contact with several of the locals with axes to grind against the military, in particular her brother's Regiment. Unfortunately, Carrie wasn't there, and the Desk Sergeant claimed she'd been called out on a different matter in connection with the SIB.

What Monroe found, however, was Colonel Yates.

'Staying for the night?' Yates nodded at the kitbag. 'Thought someone like you'd have a more gentrified holdall. Maybe a cabin case on wheels. Tartan, of course.'

'These are the personal effects of Eddie Moses,' Monroe placed the kitbag onto the floor as he stopped. 'Declan worked out the note. It said he knew where Moses would stay, because it was where they stayed before.'

'Clever,' Yates nodded to himself. 'Backup note in case of the worst. Looks like I made the right decision bringing him on board. Did the Williams crew say anything?'

'The racing team?'

'It's what the locals call Maureen and Keith,' Yates smiled. 'Locals and their names.'

Monroe went to speak, but then stopped.

'I never mentioned Maureen Williams,' he replied.

'No, but I remember the report from a decade back, and Declan and Eddie stayed with her in Castleton,' Yates shrugged. 'Well, booked rooms at least. I don't think they even managed to lie on the beds. I'm a detective too, Monroe. Even if I wear a uniform. *Special Investigations Bureau*, remember? The clue's in the middle word.'

'Aye, all they remembered was Moses being in a fight,' Monroe accepted the explanation, but bristling at the patronising manner it was given. 'That and he had a toy gun.'

'A toy gun?' Yates shook his head. 'Surely they mean a real gun?'

'Apparently not. And Charles Falconer picked it up a few days after Eddie Moses disappeared.'

'Disappeared or checked out?'

'Disappeared,' Monroe insisted. 'He never checked out. That's why they had his kit.'

Monroe watched Yates for a moment before continuing.

'Can I ask a question?' he scratched at his beard, not waiting for a response before continuing. 'Why are you here?'

'What do you mean?' this confused Yates. 'One of my men turned up dead. Wouldn't you do the same?'

'I get that, and I know I would too, but I'm a DCI, while you're a Colonel,' Monroe replied. 'More importantly, you're a Colonel who's not heard from his soldier for a year and assumed he'd gone AWOL. You came here, learnt about the murder, then called in Declan. Which I get as well, as he's an excellent investigator, and you needed someone out of the box, non-compromised, if there was any compromising going on and all that. But this done, your job is over here, surely?'

'You think I'm too close to this?' Yates' face darkened. 'You think I'm emotionally involved, perhaps?'

'I think both of you are,' Monroe answered. 'There's no way you couldn't be. Especially with the ghost of Sergeant Harper everywhere.'

He looked out across the car park, looking back towards Castleton.

'Our boss? D Supt Bullman? She wanted to stay here, help, but she understood her role, and she's gone back to London. She trusts us to do our job. Trusts Declan. But you don't. Is it us, or is it something else?'

Yates went to argue this, but stopped, his face softening as he sighed.

'Look, Alexander. That's right, isn't it? You mind if I call you that? Talk off the record?'

'Sure, *Barry*.'

'This is my fault,' Yates replied, ignoring the comment. 'I had an argument with Moses a year back. He was on this born-again cleansing kick, and I told him he needed to get closure. I didn't think he'd come back here to find Harper's kids and apologise to them.'

'What did you think he'd do?'

'I don't know,' Yates shrugged now, as if finally relieving himself of a year's worth of guilt. 'Get bloody therapy, perhaps. Speak to a shrink. Meditate. Not bugger off. I thought he'd packed up and gone, like he had before.'

'Before?'

Yates nodded.

'Three years back, he disappeared for a few months. Found him in Aleppo, getting Syrian refugees out during the

North Western Syrian Offensive. He wasn't deployed there, he'd just gone over after having some kind of breakdown. Kept seeing Harper everywhere. We brought him back, got him therapy, found him a purpose. He seemed to be okay after that.'

'That wasn't in his file,' Monroe watched the Colonel.

'Of course not,' Yates shook his head. 'That sort of thing kills a career. I wasn't going to do that to him.'

'Is this why you didn't report him as missing for a year?' Monroe asked carefully.

'Pretty much. For the last few months, I've been reporting him as undercover and sending sporadic messages,' Yates admitted. 'Of course, the moment he turned up having been a year dead, that's thrown me under the bus a little.'

'Is *that* why you're not back in the office?'

Yates smiled.

'A little,' he replied. 'I'd rather return with an answer to the questions I'm going to get. And it's your team that'll hopefully get them for me, so I'm trusting you all. Of course, I didn't expect all of you. Just Declan and you. That's altered plans, somewhat.'

'How so?'

'Because it means that someone in Whitehall is burying bodies, hoping your investigation will light up something to do with Falconer. I'm not an idiot, Monroe. I know they're not here purely for Moses. For a start, your pretty Indian one has been in the R&D building for most of the day.'

'I think you mean my Detective Sergeant,' Monroe bristled.

'Is she pretty? Is she Indian?' Yates smiled. 'I'm military, Monroe. I state it as I see it.'

As Colonel Yates continued into the building, the conversation now over, Monroe pulled out his phone, pretending to read a message on it. He didn't want to walk in with Yates, because he now didn't trust the Colonel; Yates had shown surprise when Monroe had mentioned the gun, but hadn't batted an eyelid when Monroe had mentioned the gun being picked up by the other body in the morgue, Lieutenant Colonel Falconer.

Could this be because Yates already knew that Falconer and Moses knew each other?

Monroe suspected this was the case; he believed it with every fibre of his being, and his Glaswegian copper gut was *screaming.* And he might not have read the briefing notes as much as someone anal like Billy Fitzwarren may have, but he didn't recall the name of the guesthouse being mentioned in the reports that referred to Patrick Harper's death; just that Moses and Walsh had booked into a local one.

Which meant Yate's comment about *the Williams crew* came from other intelligence sources. Ones that weren't marked down anywhere. Ones that knew Anjli and De'Geer were in Falconer's offices.

And that felt *suss.*

Yates had more to lose here, Monroe was sure of it. He just didn't know *what* Yates had to lose, and how far Yates would go to keep whatever it was. And Monroe didn't know if Declan would even believe him if he told him this.

After all, Army was army. You could leave it, but it never left you.

Sighing, Monroe picked up the kitbag, slinging it back over his shoulder.

He already regretted agreeing to do this.

DECLAN DIDN'T KNOW WHETHER THE RINGING WAS INSIDE OR outside of his head, and that worried him as he opened his eyes.

There was no change in vision whatsoever. Open or closed, there was only blackness.

Christ, I'm blind.

Declan fumbled for a torch, still not moving from the position he was in, in case his movements dislodged more rocks. Carefully and slowly, he reached into his jacket and pulled out his flashlight, turning it on, wincing as the light hit his eyes. He covered his eyes for a moment, trying to minimise the brightness hitting his pupils, adjusting to the light, wincing as a band of white hot pain flashed through his skull.

Bringing his hand back from his head, he saw it was slick with blood.

That's not good.

He tried to turn, but felt the world spinning as he did so; he stopped, allowing himself to regulate his equilibrium. A touch-based examination indicated he was bleeding from the ears, the mouth and the nose, as well as from a rather painful gash near his temple. Looking at the alcove around him, he could see a sharp, jagged length of rock jutting out of the wall, one now with a smudge of blood on it. The chances were that the blast had slammed his head against this, and the jagged length had sliced his temple open.

It could have been worse.

Slowly, gingerly, Declan turned over to face the cavern, or rather, what was left of it. Now easily a third of the size it had been earlier, the route to the entranceway was completely blocked, and the shelf he'd dived onto must have been even more structurally secure than he'd realised, because as the cave collapsed around him, it'd kept him safe.

Of course, it also meant that Declan now had a good three metres of fallen stone to find a way through, before he could reach the now collapsed entranceway and survival.

And even then, whoever did this might still be there, waiting.

It was a well-known fact that going into these caves and fissures was always a bad idea, and warnings spoke of known occurrences when the roofs of the caves and caverns had collapsed on people; however, Declan hadn't expected someone to use *actual explosives* to make sure this happened.

So who did this?

Declan laid back on the shelf and considered the question. He brought obvious suspects to mind first; Carrie Harper, Devin Harper, Henry Eaton-Jones. All three weren't happy to see him there, but Declan couldn't believe they'd go so far as to kill him. This was too obvious a—

Was it?

Unless you were within earshot, you wouldn't know that the rockfall had been because of a grenade. It could have simply been the cave's time to collapse. It could have been several seismic events that caused it. Even Declan, clambering in himself, could have done it. And the casing of the grenade was now under a ton of rubble, never to be seen again. With Declan, the only witness to this cave-in now dead, nobody would ever know.

There'd be no Terrier discovering this dead body.

But here was the issue; Declan wasn't dead. And this, although a win with a very temporary shelf life, was still a win, as long as Declan could use it.

Declan reached into his jacket again, pulling out his phone. It lit up the cramped space like a lantern, and Declan saw with a sense of dread that there were no bars on the signal. He wouldn't be able to—

One bar.

No bars.

One bar.

It was fluctuating and barely there, nowhere near enough for a phone call, but there was a chance that a text could get through. With his torch placed beside him, Declan considered what to write. Perhaps—

DECLAN AWOKE.

The cave was still lit by the torch, but the phone was no longer on. Declan's head was still in pain, and he realised he must have passed out. *Did he have a concussion? If he did, what did that mean?* Declan wished he'd paid more attention when learning about them.

He opened the phone, noting that not only had fifteen minutes passed, but that his eyesight was blurrier now. Things were feeling swirly, swooshy even. It was as if he'd spun around in circles and then paused, his ears still spinning.

Get out Declan get out now

The air was thinning, and claustrophobia was edging in now as he typed out a message.

Help in cave roof collapsed can't get out

With a final tap of his finger, he sent it, lying back on the shelf, closing his eyes for a moment. He'd sent the message to all the Last Chance Saloon in a combined group chat; even if only one of them received it, they'd find a way to get to him, he was sure of it. He just had to stay alive long enough for them to do so.

He took a breath, but it didn't feel right. He was struggling to breathe a little, and for a moment he worried that he'd received internal chest injuries in the blast, maybe punctured a lung, but then he realised the air was rarified, thinner. It was like altitude sickness; there wasn't enough oxygen here for him.

He was running out of it.

He looked at the phone as it vibrated in his hand.

Your message could not be sent.

Tears welled up in Declan's eyes. *This wasn't how he was going to die. He wasn't going to let it finish him. Even if he had to dig his own way out, he would.*

There was a second, faint rumbling of stone, and Declan was sure he could hear movement outside. Was someone trying to get through? There was a lot of rock and stone between them, and Declan wasn't sure if he could even hear correctly, but even if this was the attempted murderer, the grenade thrower themselves, if ever there was a moment to jump from any frying pan into a fire, it was this one.

Slowly, carefully, forcing himself to push past the pain in his skull, Declan slid off the recessed ledge onto the ground and, with the torch in his right hand, he crawled on hands and feet towards the pile of rocks that blocked where the rest of the cavern had been, until the explosion.

'Help!' he cried out, wincing as the shout echoed around the tiny space. He coughed; there was more dust here than at the back, and the air was thinner.

Declan reached for a stone in the rubble, one around the size of a football and, with effort from his fading strength, rolled it back into the space behind him in an attempt to find a hole, some more air, light, anything. There was a new rumbling after this, though, and three similarly sized stones rolled into its place.

Declan couldn't help himself; he laughed. He'd actually made things *worse* by trying to escape.

Taking his phone out, he checked the screen. Another message had appeared.

Your message could not be sent.

Maybe if he was closer to the doorway?

Slowly, Declan clambered up the fallen stones, holding out the phone in front of him, watching for even a flicker of a signal.

There wasn't any.

And the air was thinning again as Declan coughed on more dislodged stone dust.

As Declan felt the world swirling around him once more, the phone lit up and mocked him again.

Your message could not be sent.

But Declan didn't see this message.

Because Declan had passed out.

12

BALLISTICS

ANJLI AND DE'GEER WERE IN THE OFFICE WITH BILLY WHEN Monroe arrived. As he placed the kitbag on a table, he noticed Anjli glance towards the door, as if looking for someone.

'He's gone to look at caves, lassie,' Monroe smiled. 'I'm sure he misses you, too.'

Anjli scowled at Monroe, but he noticed a slight reddening of her cheeks.

'Brought your dirty laundry?' she asked, changing the subject and nodding at the kitbag.

'Edward Moses' personal items,' Monroe was already opening it, coughing at the musty, old clothes smell. 'Been left in a guesthouse basement since he disappeared.'

'So you worked out where he was then?' Billy looked up from the laptop. 'Sorry, do I still call you Guv, now you're suspended? I don't know the protocols.'

'Even if I'm working in a supermarket, you call me Guv,' Monroe intoned solemnly. 'And yes, your scan of the paper gave Declan the clue to check a guest house in Castleton. Bit of a weird one, to be honest.'

'How so?' De'Geer asked, before adding a hasty 'Guv?'

'Well, this is apparently everything Moses owned, apart from a toy gun,' Monroe replied, waving at the bag. 'According to the landlady, that was picked up after he disappeared by our dead Lieutenant Colonel Falconer.'

He noticed a look of shock pass between Anjli and De'Geer.

'Okay, what have I missed?' he asked.

Anjli walked over to another table against the wall, where a plastic storage box was now resting.

'Did they describe the gun?' she rummaged in the box as she spoke.

'Just that it was a metal cap gun,' Monroe said, following her. 'Said they thought it was a real gun until they realised you couldn't put bullets into it.'

Anjli pulled out the gun she'd found in Falconer's room, still in the clear plastic bag, out of the box.

'Like this, maybe?' she asked.

Monroe took the gun, holding it up in his hands as he stared at it in a mixture of surprise and admiration.

'Bloody hell, lassie,' he muttered. 'Good work. Good work, the pair of you.'

'It's a Remington 1858 New Model Army,' De'Geer explained. 'Although Billy's just been telling us it's not actually from then, exactly, just that the patent was applied for back then.'

'And it's a replica, not an original,' Anjli added. 'we found it hidden in a secret drawer with a Nazi medal.'

Monroe raised his eyebrows at this.

'That's a turn of events,' he said, examining the base of

the gun. 'But I don't believe this is the gun Falconer took from Eddie Moses. The landlady said her son was playing with it before he arrived, and he'd scratched the word 'boy' into the handle.'

'Boy?'

'Apparently they're not that imaginative with nicknames around here,' Monroe rubbed the base of the grip with a fingernail, nodding to himself. 'As you can see, this one is spotless. Well looked after, in fact.'

'So we have two black powder guns out there,' Anjli mused, noting Monroe's confused expression. 'That's what these are. Replicas of guns that fire musket balls and use black powder to do so. We're waiting for information on them now.'

'So tell me about the Nazi medal,' Monroe passed the gun back to Anjli, who replaced it gingerly into the plastic tub, as if worried it'd go off. De'Geer picked up a blue box from beside Billy, passing it to the DCI.

'We thought it was an Iron Cross, but it isn't,' he explained as Monroe opened the box to stare at a silver medal.

'Well, that's definitely a Swastika,' he muttered.

'The Knight's Cross to the War Merit Cross, otherwise known as the *Ritterkreuz des Kriegsverdienstkeuzes*,' Billy explained. 'Created by the Nazis in 1940 and manufactured by *Deschler and Sohn* of München. Not as important as the better known Iron Cross, but given out more sparingly. Even prominent Nazis and buddies of Hitler didn't get this one. You had to be a super-Nazi to receive this, especially with the swords attached, which meant this one was only for combatants. Produced in genuine silver, ranging in grade from .800 to .935.'

'That's a lot of information about Nazis for such a well-spoken man,' Monroe smiled. 'Wikipedia?'

'Uncle Chivalry,' Billy admitted. 'He has an interest in such things.'

'Of course he does,' Monroe muttered. He'd met Chivalry Fitzwilliam, if that was even his real name, when they were working on a case involving ritual murders. 'Did he say anything else?'

'Only that there weren't that many given out, and that if this is actually a real one, then it's worth around five grand, if not more. He offered me four and a half for it. When the case is over, of course.'

'Five grand worth of medal hidden at the back of a secret drawer,' Anjli shook her head.

'Probably didn't want anyone to know he owned it,' Monroe replied, staring at the medal. 'I'm guessing the British Army aren't exactly fans of things like this. Can we find out if he had this legally?'

'Not really,' Billy pointed to a webpage where several medals were visible. 'Auctions will sell these for cash, and they're even on eBay. He could have collected it in many different ways—'

Walking over to the bag, Monroe waved at Billy, nodding to show he got the point as he started rummaging through it.

'What else do we know, then?' he asked.

'Which case?' Billy replied. 'Falconer or Moses?'

'I'm starting to think they're the same one, laddie,' Monroe pulled out a musty smelling shirt, examining it before placing it to the side. 'Something doesn't smell right, and it isn't this laundry, I'll tell you that for free.'

He looked up as a shadow passed the door.

'Hold that thought,' he said as he moved from the bag, exiting the room as quickly as he'd entered.

Anjli sighed, looking back at Billy.

'Never bloody changes,' she said.

─────────

'Detective Sergeant Harper!' Monroe called out as he walked into the corridor.

Carrie Harper, pausing by a door at the sound of her name, looked back at him.

'I'm busy,' she muttered. 'Schedule a time and—'

'I can do that,' Monroe walked closer, lowering his voice. 'I'll publicly note what it's about as well, if you want.'

Carrie frowned, unsure where this was going.

'That's probably best—'

'I mean, we're going to be talking about the Castle Tun, and how you visited Edward Moses there, something you didn't mention to—'

He stopped as Carrie nervously raised a hand.

'Let's talk outside,' she forced a smile. 'I need a cigarette and I'm sure whatever I have on can wait.'

'I thought that might be the case,' Monroe smiled back at her, his own as fake as hers had been. 'Lead the way, lassie. Lead the way.'

Reluctantly, Carrie led Monroe back outside, pulling out a cigarette as she did so and lighting it once they were in the open air.

'Why didn't you tell us?' Monroe asked carefully, watching the car park to make sure they were alone. 'That you were meeting Eddie Moses, introducing him to people?'

'There's more going on here than you know,' Carrie said,

refusing to catch Monroe's gaze. 'It's bigger than my dad. Bigger than—'

'Silver musket balls and Nazi medals?' Monroe interrupted. 'Because that's where we are right now.'

Carrie's expression gave a moment of shock before disappearing, placed by her usual cool indifference, and she took a long drag on the cigarette.

'Look, I can't talk to you, because I don't know you,' she replied calmly. 'I don't know Walsh, but at least I know he's ex-military. And then, at the same time, the fact that he *is* ex-military, and that he worked for Yates? It makes me trust him even less.'

'You don't trust Yates?' Monroe was surprised by this. 'Personal reasons, or inter-agency issues?'

'Bit of both, if you look at it,' Carrie shrugged. 'Yates was in command of the soldier that killed dad, and he didn't exactly push the case to hunt for any fresh revelations that might have exonerated dad. And, at the same time, there is always the SIB and MDP rivalry that occurs on bases.'

She held up a hand to stop Monroe from replying.

'I know we're *Mod Plod* to a lot of you, the place real coppers go to retire when they're sick of doing proper police work, we hear all the jokes. You know why we don't reply? Because we're too busy doing our bloody jobs, with a total budget that's less than you get for sodding coffee pods and plasma screens each year. We're stuck in this weird middle ground, laughed at by police and patronised by Red Caps.'

Monroe observed Carrie. He understood her anger, he'd seen it before, many times in various departments over the years. What he couldn't work out was whether this was genuine anger, or an attempt to distract from her surprise at Monroe's revelations.

'So why do it? Why not just join the Met, or sign up?' he asked, eventually.

'I've seen the military life, no thanks,' Carrie shook her head. 'And at the same time, it's all I've ever known. After dad died, mum lost it. The Regiment and Eaton-Jones ended up taking us in as mascots, I suppose. Like army units do with stray dogs when on deployment.'

'You think you were a stray dog?'

'Sometimes it felt like that,' Carrie smiled, and for the first time since he'd met her, it felt genuine to Monroe. 'Look, I told you Eddie came to me and apologised for shooting my dad. Offered to make any recompense I wanted. That's all true. The fact is, though, I didn't need anything back from him. But Devin was a different matter.'

'He apologised to Devin?'

'Of course he did,' Carrie looked amazed that Monroe would even consider the alternative. 'But whereas all I wanted to do was move forward, Devin was in the Regiment. He was all about tradition and the past. And he would only listen to Eddie if...'

'If what?' Monroe pressed.

Carrie rubbed at her forearm again, another unconscious gesture, and Monroe saw the three burn marks again.

'Did you do those?' he asked, knowing he was changing the subject, but needing to know the answer. Carrie looked down at the burns, as if realising for the first time in a while they were even there.

'Different time, different me,' she explained. 'Silly tattoos. It seemed easier than lasering them off.'

Monroe didn't comment on the term *lasering*. Carrie, not noticing his expression, carried on.

'Look, I knew he was at the guesthouse, and yeah, I visited him. I was offering to be his second.'

'A fight?'

'He'd got into a scrap, yeah,' Carrie was uncomfortable talking about this. 'But he knew what he was doing. Turned up the second time, ready to rumble. And then he disappeared, so I thought he'd run for Portsmouth. I didn't even realise he'd gone missing until they found the body.'

'Scrap,' Monroe nodded at this. 'Interesting term for a duel.'

Carrie paled at the word.

'I said nothing about duelling,' she muttered, glancing around. 'What makes you think—'

'Charlie Falconer picked up a gun from the guesthouse,' Monroe continued. 'We found a similar one in his dorm room, as well as a few, well, let's say less savoury items. So why don't you tell me about the medal, as you look like you knew all about it?'

'A few of us had heard about it, that it existed,' Carrie admitted. 'There's a couple of people on the base that are a little more right-wing than you'd think.'

'Anyone in particular?'

'I couldn't say.'

'Okay, then why did you put Eddie Moses in connection with Ramesh Abbasi?'

'Staff Sergeant Moses asked to speak to him,' Carrie replied carefully. 'Because of his time in the Cardigan Regiment.'

'The bullying?' Monroe asked. 'We heard about the pig's head.'

'Never happened, nothing but old wives' tales,' Carrie

shook her head. 'There's a long connection between him and Winston Eaton-Jones, though. Mostly antagonistic.'

'Why?' Monroe pressed.

'Because he beat him,' Carrie finally snapped. 'Because he was better than Eaton-Jones senior could ever be.'

'Owen Russell—'

'Owen Russell is a second-rate gossip and prints more unverified shit than the Mail Online,' Carrie laughed. 'Takes everything he hears as gospel. The pig story? Told to him for a laugh, see if he'd post it. Old Ram never verified or denounced it, because Old Ram won't give him the time of day.'

Before Monroe could ask what Carrie meant when she said Old Ram had beat Winston Eaton-Jones, he felt a buzzing in his jacket pocket. As he went to pull his phone out, motioning silently for Carrie to *hold that thought,* he noticed movement inside the building; the Last Chance Saloon were emerging as a group, all with their phones in their hands.

'Did you get this?' Anjli asked, brandishing her phone, her voice showing strains of increased urgency. Monroe stared down at the message on the screen.

'Oh Jesus,' he muttered, as Carrie, leaning in, also read Anjli's phone screen.

Help in cave roof collapsed can't get out

'What's the quickest way to the cavern?' Monroe demanded, already looking around for help.

'What cavern?' Carrie was confused. 'There're loads around here—'

'The one they found the body in!' Anjli snapped, already waving De'Geer off to get help. Carrie, as if realising what

Anjli finally meant, shook herself into action, running for the exit to the camp.

'The only way by car takes you through Castleton,' she shouted. 'The fire brigade will come from there. We can run across the fields, along the base of Mam Tor's hill far quicker.'

Anjli spun to face Billy.

'Call the fire brigade!' she shouted. *'Get help!'*

As Anjli started after Carrie, Billy turned to run back into the buildings, but stopped as a Land Rover pulled up beside him, Devin Harper clambering out, watching the detectives running off.

'Where's my sister going?' he enquired in confusion. 'I needed to speak to her.'

'There's been a cave in,' Billy was already dialling 999 on his phone. 'One of our detectives is trapped.'

'The place Moses was found? That's a bloody deathtrap,' Devin replied, rubbing at his chin as he already considered options. 'You'll need diggers. I'll get the Regiment over.'

With that, Devin now ran the other direction, towards the barracks, while Billy turned his attention back to the phone.

'I need the fire brigade,' he said as the operator answered. 'Police emergency.'

As he waited to be connected, he glanced back at the building.

Colonel Yates was staring out at him.

'Declan's been caught in a cave in!' Billy shouted, but Yates either couldn't hear him, or wasn't actually looking at him, because as the operator connected Billy, Colonel Yates had already walked off.

By the time Monroe and the others reached the cave, there were already a handful of soldiers there, led by Major Eaton-Jones, pulling at the dislodged stones, using whatever they had to hand to roll them away from the entrance.

'How did you get here so fast?' Carrie asked, and Monroe could have sworn there was a hint of suspicion in her voice.

'We were on manoeuvres down by the Odin Mine Crushing Wheel,' Eaton-Jones said, waving off to Mam Tor, rising behind them. 'We heard a small explosion, like a grenade going off. I thought it was one of my men playing silly buggers, or a mortar that'd gone off track, but when we got here, we found this.'

He nodded at the cave in.

'We assumed it was a caver, but I'm guessing it was one of yours?'

'It's DI Walsh,' Monroe replied.

Eaton-Jones' eyebrows rose as he did an almost cartoonish double-take.

'Bloody hell,' he breathed. 'Killed in the same damn place.'

'We don't know he's dead, yet,' Anjli replied, looking up the road as in the distance they could hear sirens.

'Sweetheart, if someone blew up the cave, the whole sodding thing went down,' Eaton-Jones shook his head. 'I've seen the results of accidents like this. You don't want to be here.'

'Accidents?' De'Geer turned angrily to the Major. 'Are you saying someone *accidentally* blew the place up?'

'Of course I'm saying that!' Eaton-Jones snapped back. 'Because the alternative is too horrible to consider! I don't even know if the explosion was from this! It could have been a natural occurrence! Or even your man in there hitting the walls with hammers or something until it crushed him.'

'He's alive,' Anjli showed Eaton-Jones the message. 'But how long for, we don't know.'

Monroe had left the conversation, already pulling at stones with the soldiers. He didn't want to consider the alternative, because the alternative was that someone deliberately tried to kill Declan.

Had killed Declan.

No, he wasn't accepting that. Not until they found a body. Declan had got through a lot worse than this. A bloody ceiling wasn't going to kill him.

They'd already made a hole in the entranceway, and one soldier was shining a torch into it.

'What can you see?' Monroe asked, trying to shift past the soldier, no older than a teenager, to get a look himself.

'It's a body, sir,' the soldier replied. 'It's pretty mangled. You don't want to look.'

'Why aren't we going in after him?' Monroe again went to move forward, but the soldier stopped him.

'Sir, with all respect, that roof's one falling stone from collapsing even more. And the poor bugger in there? They're dead. It completely caved the head in.'

Monroe heard a gasp and glanced behind to see Anjli standing there, hand to mouth. She'd heard the soldier's words, and quickly, Monroe walked over to her.

'He's twelve,' he muttered. 'He doesn't know anything.'

As Monroe pulled Anjli aside, more soldiers arrived now, led by Devin, and arriving in covered trucks. They started pulling out lengths of metal and scaffolding, and Monroe assumed they were engineers of some kind, finally bringing tools that could be used here.

Tools that were possibly too late to help.

'Secure the roof!' Devin Harper shouted, now being the Lieutenant his rank stated he was. 'We need to check for life!'

'I don't think that's likely, sir,' the young soldier replied sadly. 'With no head, I reckon they're done for.'

As Devin and the soldiers ran past, already strengthening the sides with poles, Monroe moved Anjli away from the cave, back towards the road and the waiting De'Geer.

'It's not him,' he whispered soothingly. 'It's not. It can't be.'

But even as he whispered it, he knew he was possibly lying. Declan had gone to the cave on his own. Nobody else had gone with him. And if they found a single dead body, it pretty much meant one thing.

Declan Walsh was dead.

13

LIFE AFTER DEATH

'I've missed you,' Declan said as he sat in the boat, staring out across the lake. 'I didn't think I'd see you again.'

'Well, not in that life, at least,' Kendis Taylor laughed, brushing her frizzy black hair from her face. 'Now we have all the time in the world together.'

Declan nodded, still watching out across the lake. He couldn't recall how he got here, or why he was even in a boat with his dead ex-girlfriend.

Something felt wrong.

He rubbed at his head; it was hurting, as if someone was squeezing it. As he pulled his hand away, he found it slick with blood.

'How—'

'You're *dead*, you bloody idiot,' DI Frost said, pulling off his rimless glasses to clean them with the end of his tie, doing nothing more than wiping the blood congealed on it onto the lenses. Declan looked around in confusion.

'Kendis?'

'She's gone,' Frost smiled, placing his bloodied glasses

back on. 'But let's be honest, you don't want her, do you? You don't love the dead anymore.'

'Great, still with the bloody riddles,' Declan grabbed at one oar, intending to use it to strike Frost, knock him out of the boat and into the water, but it was secured to the hull and just rattled around as he pulled at it futilely.

'Of course I'm giving you riddles,' Frost smiled. 'We have all the time in the world together. Why get to the point quickly when you have eons to play with?'

'No,' Declan was rising now, staring around the water, looking for a shore. 'I'm not staying on a boat with you.'

In the distance, through the fog, he could make out some trees, so that seemed to be the best direction to take. Sitting back down, he grabbed the oars and turned the boat around.

'It's no use,' Frost laughed. 'You can't cheat death.'

'You're just a dream,' Declan hissed, looking back to the shoreline, now appearing out of the mists behind him as he rowed towards it.

'Of course we're dreams,' two voices now spoke and, as Declan turned back to the boat, he saw Eddie Moses and Jo Tooley sitting together, watching him.

'You can't be dead, Declan,' Eddie said with conviction. 'You can't avenge our murders if you're dead.'

'I'm going to get you justice,' Declan pulled harder at the oars. 'I need to get off this boat first.'

'I don't want justice,' Tooley snapped, and as she looked upwards, Declan saw the gash across her neck, the blood gurgling out with little air bubbles as she spoke. 'I want bloody vengeance.'

'*You had it!*' Declan shouted out across the lake. '*Eddie killed Harper!*'

'You never believed Harper was the killer,' Eddie pursed his blue, cracked lips. 'Maybe it's time you work on that.'

'Who killed you, Jo?' Declan pleaded with Tooley now, still rowing, as he turned back to face her. 'Tell me who did it.'

'I can't tell you that, you muppet,' Tooley laughed. 'I'm just a figment of your imagination, your memory. Christ, Eddie, how did you work with him for so long?'

Declan went to reply to this, looking away to calm his temper, but stopped as he turned back and focused at the man now sitting in front of him, the hole in his chest still bleeding out into his uniform.

'High... all...' Patrick Harper gurgled as he watched Declan, raising his hand in some kind of salute. 'High... all...'

Declan stared at Harper, watching him as he kept reaching up towards Declan, the guttural sounds from his mouth forming words.

He wasn't grasping at the sky, as Declan had believed, over ten years earlier.

He was saluting.

'High... all...' Harper repeated, and finally, Declan knew what the Sergeant was saying.

It wasn't *high all.*

It was Heil.

Declan went to reply to this, but behind him the boat bumped against land. He quickly glanced behind, rising as the boat slid back into the lake, but as he looked back at the boat, there was nobody else in it.

Sergeant Harper, Jo Tooley, Eddie, the man with the rimless glasses who might or might not have been named DI Frost, even Kendis had all left him now.

He grabbed at his head, grimacing as it throbbed in pain—

'YOU GAVE US A BLOODY SCARE, LADDIE,' MONROE SAID AS Declan opened his eyes a second time, wincing as the light in the ceiling filled his vision. 'Thought you were for the grave.'

'Declan!' Anjli moved into view now, leaning over him. 'You bloody idiot. What the hell were you thinking?'

Declan looked around the room now; he was in a hospital bed, in what looked to be a single bed wardroom.

'Where am I?' he asked, his voice hoarse.

'*Northern General Hospital*, in Sheffield,' Monroe explained. 'It was this, or one half an hour in the other direction. I remembered you used to be a Sheffield Wednesday fan, so this won.'

Declan gingerly touched at his forehead and felt a bandage across it.

'I thought I was dead,' he whispered. 'There was no phone signal.'

'There was enough,' Anjli smiled. 'It must have got through, eventually. We all received the message.'

Declan shifted in the bed, trying to rise, and Monroe rose to stop him.

'Careful, laddie, you had a roof land on you,' he said. 'You need to rest.'

'I need to work out who did this,' Declan muttered.

'We know who did it,' Monroe replied, his voice cold. 'They were found in the rubble, also dead.'

Declan stopped moving, slowly looking back at Monroe.

'There was nobody else in the cave,' he croaked. 'The grenade came from outside.'

'Well, someone was in there with you, because we found their body in the rubble as well,' Anjli leaned back in now. 'The collapsing roof took out their skull.'

'It was a young man, white, slim, black bomber jacket,' Monroe interrupted. 'The head was bashed in, but it was Owen, Declan. The journalist. Your old boss, Yates, he thinks Owen could have been the one that caused the fall in, but then got caught in a second fall when he went to check on you.'

Declan stared at Monroe, trying to make sense of what he was hearing.

'Owen Russell wasn't there,' he said. 'And he sure as hell wouldn't have been the one lobbing grenades in. He came to us, remember?'

'That's why *I* think he wasn't the killer,' Monroe replied. 'I think he followed you, maybe still didn't trust you, even. Saw the cave collapse, went in to see if you were alive, got caught in a second collapse.'

'They pulled the body out,' Anjli added. 'Doctor Marcos is examining it now.'

Declan shut his eyes, the pain building behind the eyelids, as he felt anger and frustration rising.

'He wasn't in there before the explosion,' he repeated. 'The cave was too small for me not to see him. If he was pulled out? It's because someone placed him in there afterwards. They thought I was dead. They needed a simple murder that could be solved quickly. Nobody would ever know.'

'We were there within minutes of the text,' Monroe looked at Anjli. 'They wouldn't have had time to do that—'

'They had time,' Declan muttered. 'I passed out. Fifteen minutes, maybe. When I woke, the text hadn't gone through.'

He thought for a moment.

'I heard noises outside, like movement...'

He stopped.

'Owen must have seen the explosion, maybe seen who threw the grenade in. And they saw him,' he shook his head. 'How did you find me? I was deep in the rubble, too.'

'The Regiment arrived with machinery,' Monroe replied. 'They just kept removing stones until they broke into the back section where you were.'

'My items,' Declan looked around the room. 'Jacket...'

'You're not going anywhere,' Monroe patted him on the shoulder. 'You're under observation until—'

Jacket! Declan hissed, wincing as his head throbbed with a burst of pain. 'Box in forensics bag in pocket. Templar Corps logo on it.'

'Sorry, Dec, but if there was something in your jacket, it fell out during the rock fall,' Monroe replied. 'All you had in your pockets were your tactical pen, notebook, wallet and a silver musket ball. It's still in your jacket, on the chair to your right. I was going to take it to Doctor Marcos, but she's already got enough on her plate, what with Owen and all the other stuff.'

'No...' Declan leaned back onto the bed, distraught. The one thing he'd found was gone, left in the cavern. 'The box... it was important.'

'Forensics are going over the cave right now,' Monroe was already texting a message as he spoke. 'Davey and De'Geer are heading it. I'll tell them to look for anything box-shaped. Small enough to fit in your jacket, and in a forensics bag, right?'

Declan nodded gently, shutting his eyes. Someone had tried to kill him with a grenade. Either that, or had wanted him secured underground until he could be picked up. A box he'd found was now missing, and a crime scene that may have held other secrets, especially those of some secret far-right group, was now gone forever.

And Owen Russell, possibly the only other person who could answer his questions, was dead.

'I think I might need to stay here,' he mumbled, his eyes still closed.

'That's fine,' Anjli leaned closer. 'We'll be in Castleton, only a phone call away. You rest, we'll speak to you tomorrow.'

She didn't consider what she did; it came naturally as she leaned closer, kissing Declan's forehead.

Surprised, he opened his eyes.

'Did you just kiss me?' he asked.

'A peck,' Anjli backed away, mortified at what she'd done. 'You looked like you needed... consoling.'

'And kissing my forehead consoles me, does it?' Declan frowned.

'I'm sorry,' Anjli shook her head. 'I didn't—'

'No, it's fine,' Declan smiled weakly. 'It was consoling. It really was.'

'Oh,' Anjli was smiling now, a mixture of relief and delight. 'Okay then. Good. You go to sleep.'

Declan nodded again, his eyes shutting.

'I'll be okay in a bit,' he whispered. 'Just need... a break...'

Monroe tapped Anjli on the arm and, grabbing her jacket, she followed him out of the ward.

'Consoling,' he chuckled.

'So how are you and Doctor Marcos doing again?' Anjli snapped back, embarrassed.

'Low blow, DS Kapoor,' Monroe conceded the point. 'And you can call me *Guv*, when we're working.'

He grinned.

'Unless you want to console me too?' he closed his eyes and pursed his lips together, making a *kissy kissy* face. He opened an eye, watching Anjli.

'No?' he enquired.

Anjli, in reply, simply shook her head.

'And Doctor Marcos finds you attractive,' she muttered.

'She does?' Monroe mocked surprise at this.

'Look, it seemed like the right thing to do. You and Doctor Marcos are way better at it than anyone else,' frustrated, Anjli stormed out of the hallway, but Monroe grabbed her arm.

'Rosanna and me? It's complicated,' he whispered, now serious. 'You and Declan? You almost lost him today. Maybe you should talk to him about how you feel.'

Anjli stared at Monroe for a breath before replying, calming herself down.

'He's leaving,' she replied, pulling from his grip and walking to the stairs. 'Less than two months before he's out of the door. When he does, I'll end up moving out, because I won't be able to talk about work with him. I'll be a reminder of what he had to give up. I'll be *part* of what he had to give up.'

'You don't know that,' Monroe argued.

'I do,' Anjli was sad as she spoke. 'It was never full time, Guv. Never meant to last. Nothing ever does. Look at you and Doctor Marcos.'

With this last, depressing comment, Anjli turned and,

with no further resistance from Monroe, started down the stairs and towards the exit.

Monroe watched down the staircase after her.

'It might not last,' he whispered to himself, 'but if you don't try, you'll never know.'

Shaking himself back into action, he pulled out his phone, dialling Doctor Marcos' number.

Anjli was right. Not that things never lasted, but that he and Rosanna had been better at the relationship thing than anyone before.

And this was from the guy whose ex-wife wiped her entire identity from public records to get away.

No. Monroe had a lot to say to Rosanna, and he'd wasted a large amount of time not saying it. It was time to change that.

'It's me,' he said into the phone. 'We need to talk.'

DECLAN LAY ON THE HOSPITAL BED, STARING AT THE SILVER musket ball in his hand.

He'd found that as long as he moved slowly, his head didn't hurt. And, rising and walking to the window, now effectively a mirror to the room as the night pulled in, he could see that they'd strapped his head tight with a swath of bandages, but apart from that, he seemed unscathed. He'd remembered feeling blood from his ears, but there was no sign of that now; hopefully his eardrums hadn't ruptured, and it'd simply been blood from the head wound.

He chuckled, amused that he was hopeful that something was *just* a head wound. *Welcome to the new normal, Declan.*

Returning to the bed slowly and carefully, grabbing the

musket ball on the way, he now lay back on the covers, turning the ball in his fingers as he almost willed it to give him something, anything he could use. It felt smaller. He needed to find a ruler to verify that, though.

If the universe could hear him now, he could really use some kind of clue—

'That's the second of those I've seen today,' a voice spoke to the side, and Declan looked to the door where a young male nurse stood, nodding at the ball.

'A silver musket ball?' Declan sat up. 'How so?'

'I was in A&E earlier today,' the nurse came in, checking the board at the bottom of the bed, and then walking over to Declan. 'Lay back, I need to check your pulse.'

'You mentioned A&E?'

'Oh, yeah,' the nurse looked back at Declan, caught in the moment. 'Lad came into the hospital this morning with what looked like a stabbing wound, right here.'

He tapped at his stomach, just to the right-hand side as he looked down.

'We got him in to look at it, and we realised it was a gun shot. Hadn't gone through, still inside. We got him into theatre, and the surgeons pulled the bugger out, sewing him back up. Wouldn't have thought any more about it, until people started talking about the bullet, pointing out that it, well...'

'Didn't look like a bullet?' Declan nodded. 'Yeah, I get that. So what, he was shot today?'

'No, about a week back,' the nurse shook his head. 'Bloody idiot tried to superglue the wound together, used some old antiseptic powder soldiers used back in the day, you know, before proper medicine arrived, to clean it. Bandaged it up, laid in bed chewing down painkillers. But it got infected, mainly because he hadn't pulled the bullet out. Wasn't shiny like yours, more *lead* coloured. And a little bigger, although size isn't everything.'

He winked.

'Did he explain how he got shot?' Declan pushed himself painfully up in the bed.

'Cleaning a musket, he claimed,' the nurse shrugged. 'Apparently he was helping a friend and hadn't realised it was still loaded. We have some re-enactors around here, so there's a chance he was telling the truth. At least it wasn't up his bum.'

At Declan's confused expression, the nurse continued.

'You'd be surprised what people *accidentally fall on* when they're nude and alone,' he smiled.

'I'd rather live in ignorance,' Declan forced a smile, but in fact, was considering the story he'd been told. 'The lad, was he a soldier?'

'Can't say,' the nurse had pulled away now, looking suspiciously at Declan. 'Why the questions, anyway?'

Declan nodded back at his jacket.

'I'm a Detective Inspector, and I think he could be important to my case,' he explained. 'My warrant card is over there, but it might be a little dented.'

'No offence, mate, but you're not doing any cases today,' the nurse replied. 'You're going to sleep and get better.'

'At least answer me two things,' Declan smiled. 'What was his name and was he a soldier?'

'Delaney, and window cleaner,' the nurse's face darkened a little. 'Bit of a racist prick, to be honest. One of our nurses is black, and he made a fuss about her helping him. Even pushed her over, when telling her to piss off. Should have let the little scroat bleed out, I reckon. I think he's Territorial

Army, though, or whatever the playtime ones are. Looks the type. Probably plays airsoft, thinking he's Schwarzenegger in *Commando*. Kept saying he was *Gunner* Delaney when we called him Mister.'

Declan nodded.

'First name?'

'Colin.'

'Where is he now?'

'Why?' the nurse was suspicious at this. 'As I said, you're staying here and getting bed rest. Not buggering around playing Columbo, gipping all over the place.'

'Gipping?'

The nurse made a vomiting motion. Declan nodded, understanding.

'Okay, then what if I wanted to send him a message?'

'He's here in the Huntsman Building, just like you,' the nurse relented. 'Three doors down to the left. But neither of you are going anywhere, so grab some kip and I'll wheel you to him personally first thing in the morning.'

Declan nodded at this, shutting his eyes.

'Thanks,' he said, relaxing.

He didn't see the nurse leave, but he heard the door shut.

Opening his eye to confirm he was alone, Declan carefully moved to the edge of the bed, sliding his legs around and standing back up. He was wobbly, and the floor was cold on the bare soles of his feet, but he could stand. With the musket ball still in his hand, he inched his way carefully to the door, opening it and checking out into the corridor. It was wide, with doors on either side and a pine wood-topped nurses' station in the middle, but luckily for Declan, it was clear. Sliding gingerly out of the door, wincing at a mixture of stabbing headache and cold feet, Declan trudged the three doors down, checking through the entrance to the single-bed wardroom before entering.

There was one bed in there, and a small A4 sized white-board had C DELANEY written in black marker was set up to the right of it. A man, muscular and in his mid-to-late-thirties, was sitting up in the bed, watching a video playing on his phone as Declan entered. From the sound through the phone's tinny speakers, Declan recognised the music of *Platoon*.

'I think you might be in the wrong room, mate,' Colin said, frowning at the stranger's arrival.

'I don't think I am,' Declan smiled in response. He'd considered bringing his warrant card, asking some questions and leaving before he was discovered, but he also knew that standing in a disposable gown with his arse hanging out wasn't giving off any kind of professional vibe right now. 'Gunner Delaney?'

'Who wants to know?'

'Corporal Walsh, *Derbyshire*,' Declan lied. 'I hear we have something in common.'

'Yeah? What's that?' Colin rose in the bed, defensive now, and even though his gut was bandaged up, Declan knew that with his head still throbbing, the muscled window cleaner could still take him easily in a fight. Instead of replying, Declan walked over and dropped the silver musket ball onto the bed, so Colin could see it.

As Colin looked up in surprise, Declan tapped his head wound.

'Bugger got me here,' he said. 'I heard you were gut shot?'

'I never seen you before,' Colin was still suspicious. 'I don't know you.'

Declan decided to push the story, see how deep he could go.

'What, you think you've met everyone in the *you know what?*' he asked, hoping that a casual mention of the Templar Corps, or at least a suggested secret society, would work here. 'We're legion, mate.'

Declan was right. It did.

'My Colt Navy misfired,' Colin smiled, relaxing back as he placed his phone on his bed. 'I'd never used it before, borrowed it from one of the reservists.'

'Reservists?'

'Yeah, you know, like me, I suppose. Some bald ex-army Corporal offered me his to use. I didn't realise you had to use wax to crease the bullet.'

He picked up the ball, staring at it in awe.

'Same size as the Colt I used,' he said. 'I used lead though, as it wasn't an honour duel or anything. You must be hard-core though, not using vests.'

He rubbed at his gut.

'Not like they do much to help, that is,' he complained bitterly.

'Sounds like you made a rookie mistake with the wax,' Declan gratefully sat down next to Colin, unsure why a lack of wax would cause a misfire, and curious why honour duels would use silver bullets, but aware from Colin's sheepish expression that his wax-based mistake was likely to be a schoolboy error. 'We all did it, or something similar, when we were starting.'

He smiled warmly.

'You're TA though, right? I thought we weren't allowed to... you know...' Once more, Declan left the comment hanging, hoping Colin would carry on filling in the blanks.

'Oh, yeah,' Colin nodded eagerly, now in the presence of an actual Army soldier, an actual Templar Corps member. 'We don't usually. But there was a vacancy, and one of the originals needed practice. To be honest, the others weren't duelling him anymore, something about cheating in duels and there was talk about his membership being revoked, but the opportunity was too good to miss, and so I stepped up.'

'Falconer?' Declan raised his eyebrows, hoping he was correct.

'Yeah, it was Lieutenant Colonel Falconer that did this,' Colin patted the bandage, almost with pride. 'There was a special guest supposed to be coming up, another of the duelling club OGs. But he didn't make it. Falconer had everything set up so it became open mic night. Or, rather, open gun night.'

'OG? Who's that?' Declan thought asking wouldn't hurt.

Colin tapped his nose.

'The *Colonel*. He didn't make it though, something about a body in a cave.'

'Yeah, I heard about that,' Declan kept his face emotionless while working through what Colin had just said. If Colin had been shot by Falconer, and Falconer had died the same day as Eddie was found, then something was off with his dates if someone was looking at a body in a cave. Also, the only Colonel he knew was Yates. *Could he have been at the duel as well?*

'You ever see him duel?' Colin was excited as he spoke. 'Falconer? He never lost. Well, maybe a couple of times, but that's out of hundreds of duels. Mainly silver bullet level ones, too. Without armour or anything. Although he wore that cool flak jacket with the Robocop lights on when he did normal ones.'

Declan leaned back in the chair, watching Colin, caught in the bright-eyed hero-worship of a dead man.

'How long have you been involved?' he asked. 'I've only just moved up here, you see. Got back from—'

He paused, remembering Owen's conversation about extremists, adjusting a word in his head before continuing.

'—from *Londonistan* a week back. Desk job.'

'You don't look the type to ride a desk,' Colin frowned. 'Although you've got a bit of a paunch. Not been doing the course that much recently?'

'Yeah,' Declan took a minor offence at the line, but decided to make it work for him. 'Got stuck on office duty when I punched out some *locals*, if you get what I mean.'

Colin's face lit up.

'Yeah, man. I get that,' he said. 'Patriots.'

'Patriots,' Declan repeated with a plastered on smile. From the way he said it, Declan knew Colin used the word more as a call to action than description.

Colin frowned.

'You ever meet the Colonel?' he asked, and Declan worried he'd gone too far.

'No,' he replied cautiously. 'You?'

'Once,' Colin replied, leaning back on his pillows. 'That is, I saw him. Right confused me. Didn't expect him to be *a rag head*.'

Declan fought the urge to immediately question this. *Rag head was a derogatory term* used against Arabs, referring to the turban or keffiyeh they often *wore*.

The Colonel wasn't Yates.

'He's never been beaten,' Colin was almost hero worshipping the man he saw once. 'Well, he was once, but apparently the Lebanese bitch cheated.'

'How did you know that?'

'Because she never came back,' Colin replied. 'Was part of my unit too, Sheffield Bailey, many years back.'

Declan wasn't sure what Colin meant by this, but smiled as he mentally filed it away and tapped his forehead, changing the subject.

'So anyway, buddy, why don't you give me a primer on how the locals duel, maybe what I should do next time?' he asked. 'I don't want another of these.'

Colin shuffled in his bed, sitting up.

'Corporal? I'll tell you whatever you want to know,' he smiled. 'First off though, if they offer you it, wear the bloody *head gear.*'

14

BALLROOM BITS

BILLY SMILED HIS WARMEST SMILE AT MAUREEN WILLIAMS AS she stared across the reception desk at him.

'We don't usually take in single men from the street during tourist season,' she said, frowning. 'They bring in local girls and all sorts of troubles can stem from that.'

'I can honestly say, with my hand on my heart, that bringing girls back to my room is way down the list,' Billy shook his head. 'I just need a couple of days while I work on the Moses case.'

'Oh, you're one of *those*,' Maureen said, as she smiled for the first time since he arrived. Billy assumed, based on what Monroe had said earlier about her, that she was hoping Billy would become a source for gossip. 'I've had your colleagues come over already. You here to ask me more questions?'

'Only if the questions relate to whether you have a room spare.'

Maureen examined the booking list. 'Don't they give you a bed in the dorms?'

'Yeah, but it's a little basic,' Billy nodded. 'I wanted something a little more homely.'

'You'd have to pay,' Maureen tapped on a room number, deciding on it. 'We're not a police charity.'

Billy opened his wallet, revealing a selection of gold and platinum credit cards.

'You take cards, right?' he asked innocently, watching Maureen's eyes widen as she saw the potential in front of her.

'We do indeed,' she smiled. 'We also run a wonderfully cooked breakfast. I'll put you in room six, that's the furthest from the kitchen—'

'Actually, what was the room that Edward Moses stayed in?' Billy interrupted.

'Five,' Maureen replied cautiously. Looking down at the list in the book, Billy could see it, too, was empty.

'I'll take that one then,' he said, keeping his expression relaxed.

Maureen sniffed, shrugged, and spun the book around.

'Name, number and two nights in advance,' she said. 'Any dinner needed?'

'No, that's fine,' Billy started writing in the book. 'I'm meeting friends. Where's a good pub to eat?'

'They're all good,' Maureen shrugged back, taking the book from Billy and tapping on a card reader. 'If you decide to go to any though, tell them I sent you. '

She winked.

'Always good to keep the neighbours happy.'

'Of course,' Billy smiled. 'Can I get a wake up call, too?'

It was quiet in the bar by the time Anjli found Billy, sitting at the back of the Rambler's Retreat, at a table in a corner of the bar, and beside a radiator.

'You all settled comfy?' she mocked, sitting down. 'They tucked you in and everything?'

'The window was broken in the room at some point, and they've sealed it up,' Billy replied, passing her a drink, already ordered and waiting on the table. 'I only had a quick look around before coming here. How's the Guv?'

'Bloody stubborn and headstrong,' Anjli muttered, taking the offered glass and sipping from it, sighing slightly as she relaxed into the chair. 'God, I needed this.'

'Stubborn and headstrong,' Billy considered the words as he drank from his own glass of Merlot. 'So, just how you like him, then?'

'What's that supposed to mean?' Anjli snapped back, then holding up a hand before Billy could reply. 'Ignore that. I'm just in a bad mood. Monroe was taking the piss a little.'

'That's good,' Billy smiled. 'If he's taking the piss, it means he's getting better.'

'I'd rather it wasn't at my expense,' Anjli looked around the pub; it was old, but at the same time looked as if it'd been recently refurbished. Groups of walkers, fresh from their hikes, were huddled around tables in every corner.

'Why this pub?' she asked.

'Only one that didn't have any squaddies or MDP coppers in,' Billy shrugged. 'Kind of sick of seeing them today. Needed something normal.'

'And this is normal?' Anjli raised an eyebrow.

'My grandfather had a pub just like this on his estate,' Billy grinned. 'Never let the locals in, but it was almost identical.'

Anjli shook her head in mock disbelief. Because Billy had been cut off from his family, sometimes she forgot how wealthy the Fitzwarren clan he came from truly was.

'I thought you'd be reading Falconer's diary,' Billy said. 'Or at least flicking through it.'

'I was going to, but then...' Anjli left off the end. Billy knew where she was going.

'I'm glad he's okay,' Billy smiled. 'Bugger's too awkward for death to take him.'

Anjli nodded, shuddering as the thought of Declan no longer being around filled her with a surprising dread.

'Nobody else coming?' she asked, changing the subject.

'No idea about Monroe, and De'Geer and Davey are still at the cave,' Billy glanced at his watch. 'Although I'd expect them to be coming back soon.'

Anjli was distracted, staring at the bar.

'You okay?' Billy asked. Anjli, brought back to the moment, forced a smile.

'Sorry,' she apologised. 'I'm a little—'

'He'll be fine,' Billy replied, placing a hand on Anjli's. 'He's got through worse. Maybe this'll knock some sense into him?'

'You'd need a bigger cave to do that,' Anjli laughed. 'I—I *kissed* him.'

'You what?' Billy's hand snapped back as he half rose from the chair. 'Shut the front door! How? Come on, Anj, spill the tea!'

'It was a peck on the forehead,' Anjli glared at the now beaming Billy. 'So take that sodding smirk off your face! I was consoling him.'

'This is why Monroe took the piss, isn't it?' Billy sat back, folding his arms as he did so. 'He called you out on it.'

'So, did you find out anything while we were gone?' Anjli determinedly attempted to change the subject once more. Billy, deciding to let her off this one time, nodded.

'Few things, actually,' he replied. 'Monroe chatted to Colonel Yates before all hell broke loose, and Yates mentioned that Eddie Moses had disappeared before, back in early 2019. They found him in Syria, helping with refugees.'

'That's a hell of a breakdown. Who found him?' Anjli frowned. 'SIB?'

'From what I could find, a NATO logistics division was in the area sorting infrastructure issues,' Billy replied. 'A Lieutenant Colonel, seconded from the Derbyshires, was there in an advisory capability, and at some point found Moses. They spoke, and the Lieutenant Colonel realised who Moses was, contacted Yates to let him know.'

'And the Lieutenant Colonel's name was?'

'Charles Falconer.'

'Bloody hell. So Falconer knew Moses a few years back? How does that affect things?'

'I don't think it does, apart from showing a connection,' Billy shrugged. 'But it's something to add in the column with the other new things.'

'New things like what?'

Billy leaned in closer.

'Harper was convicted, after his death, of killing Susan Jenkins, a local journalist and Jo Tooley, the RMP Private. Both had the same MO, possibly even the same murder weapon. But they were a week apart from each other and in different countries. We have him flying to the UK the same day Jenkins went missing, but this means he wasn't around to kill Tooley. There's another flight though, a week later, that shows him on the manifest, and if he took that one, he could have killed Tooley—but not Jenkins.'

'So it's wrong?'

Billy leaned back, sighing.

'The only way Harper could have done this was to fly to the UK, kill Jenkins, fly back, and kill Tooley. There's a hand-written note saying he did fly back, but this is the army. They like their triplicate forms. Why isn't there anything else?'

He shook his head.

'The only other option is that there were two people involved, who both used similar weapons. Declan saw this and raised a report. Yates closed it down.'

'Yates didn't want the case continued?'

'Probably because he didn't want scrutiny on why two of his men were gunning down Sergeants in a warehouse,' Billy suggested. 'But that's not all I found. One of the two women found, Lena Khoury? The inquest pointed out she was a barmaid from Sheffield, not connected to anyone in Castle-ton. The body was discovered in the basement, and had been there for two months, based on forensics. Harper was in Hamburg then. But she knew someone else.'

'Let me guess,' Anjli replied. 'Falconer.'

'No,' Billy shook his head. 'Well, not that I've found yet. She was a member of the Territorial Army, was known for her rather controversial beliefs—'

'Racist?'

'Not from what I can see, more a *New World Order* style of woman. Anyway, she was in a training scheme run weekly by then-Lieutenant Eaton-Jones, who was in town at the time of her death.'

'Christ,' Anjli whispered. 'Was she part of the gang, or targeted?'

Billy looked around the bar.

'That's what I'm trying to work out,' he whispered. 'I've also asked the Boss in London to check if she can gain any information on the Cardigan Regiment, as there seems to be something there, too. Monroe and Declan spoke to someone who claimed several of our suspects could have been part of it.'

He looked at the door as De'Geer and Davey, both now in civilian clothing, walked into the bar, nodding at him as they approached.

'Marcos and Monroe are deep in discussion in the briefing room,' De'Geer said as he sat at one of the spaces around the table, his immense Viking frame almost dwarfing the chair he sat on. 'Nothing new found at the cave.'

'Apart from bits of head,' Davey muttered. 'How's the peaceful work going, rookie?'

Billy reddened.

'We're the same rank and we literally started the same day,' he replied. 'How am I the—'

He stopped as he realised everyone was laughing.

'Actually, I do have something you could help with,' he said, pulling out a piece of paper in a plastic bag. It was the receipt that Moses had in his wallet, the letters illegible, except for a faint JUL in the corner. 'I can't get anything from a scan. Any chemicals or something out there that could help?'

'Buy us both pints, and I'll show you how real forensics is done,' Davey took the receipt, examining it as Billy went to the bar and ordered two more drinks for Davey and De'Geer. Placing the pints of lager back onto the table, Billy sat down, watching Davey as she placed on latex gloves, pulling the paper out of the baggie.

'Who wants to see a magic trick?' she asked.

'Not really,' Anjli smiled, knowing it was the wrong answer.

'You have no joy in your heart, DS Kapoor,' Davey was reaching around the table, placing her hand on the radiator. 'Damn, it's not on.'

'It's July,' Anjli muttered, but Davey was already walking to the bar and speaking to the landlady. Billy saw her nod to the table and then show her warrant card. The landlady left, and Davey returned to the table with a smile.

'That the trick?' Anjli smiled. 'That wouldn't fool Penn and Teller.'

'Patience,' Davey sipped at her pint as, from the side door, the landlady emerged, a hairdryer in her hand.

'There's a plug just down there,' the landlady said as she placed it on the table. 'Let me have it back when you're done.'

Now alone again, Davey nodded to De'Geer to plug the hairdryer in.

'The till paper is thermal paper,' Davey explained as she held the small sheet up. 'My dad used to run a company that had a fax machine using the same stuff, but A4 sized. Thermal faxes don't need ink, because they use the *direct-thermal* method. The printhead converts electricity into usable heat—'

'Joule's first law,' De'Geer exclaimed excitedly, blushing as the others looked at him. 'It explains how heat is produced when you pass an electric current through a resistor.'

'Anyway,' Davey continued. 'The printhead applies heat in the right places, the chemicals in the paper react and cause the paper to darken as letters in those spots.'

She reached for the hairdryer.

'Problem is, after a while, the letters disappear. Thermal

paper is susceptible to heat and UV light, so extended exposure to these elements ultimately causes gradual fading. And when keeping documents for years, companies found that faxes with ink-based printers attached didn't lose the text. Thermal printers were phased out.'

'Let me guess,' Billy looked at the hairdryer. 'Receipts are made from the same paper?'

'Exactly,' Davey turned on the hairdryer, holding it a couple of feet away from the paper, letting the warm air hit the back of it as she moved the dryer from side to side. 'Always do this to the back, as the paper on the other side is treated. But, as it heats...'

On the receipt, Billy could see that the paper was darkening as the heat from the hairdryer affected the thermal paper. However, there were parts that were lighter, faded letters appearing like a negative image.

'... the parts that had already been heated, when the printheads wrote the letters don't darken again. And you get this.'

The receipt was now a chocolate brown in colour, as Billy stared at the visible words in DC Davey's hand.

'Second of July, last year,' he said, pulling his phone out and snapped a photo of the receipt, using an app on the phone to turn it into a more readable negative image. 'Looks like Eddie Moses bought himself a phone.'

'Didn't he have one already?' De'Geer asked. 'Being sent up from Portsmouth?'

'Yeah, but it was an SIB one, and was never really used,' Billy read the receipt. 'Eddie Moses was a bit of a Luddite, it seems. And if he used it, the phone was logged to his personal file, so any calls he made? Would have likely shown on official records. Not great if you want to be secre-

tive about something. This is a burner. One that nobody
knew.'

'Can you get the number?' Anjli asked.

Billy nodded.

'With the till receipt, we can narrow the day, time and
shop he bought from,' he replied, already typing an email on
his phone. 'We get the number? We can see who he texted,
phoned, everything in the days that led to his death.'

Anjli looked at Davey. 'Do you make balloon animals
too?'

'I learned that in clown school,' Davey replied, straight-
faced. 'I don't talk about it.'

Anjli stared at her colleague, unable to define whether or
not DC Davey was serious.

She decided she didn't want to press the issue.

'I'll let Monroe know,' she said, rising from the chair. 'I'll
drop DI Walsh one too, keep him up to date.'

'Remember to end it with X's,' Billy called out after her.
'He might not realise it's a love letter if you don't.'

ONCE OUTSIDE THE PUB, ANJLI LEANED AGAINST THE STONE
wall, letting out a frustrated sigh. She'd really intended to
contact Monroe, to tell him what Davey's magic trick had
revealed, but at the same time, she needed some space. As
much as Billy's mocking was annoying, it wasn't done out of
spite. What Billy didn't know though was even if Anjli had
thought that way about Declan, and to be honest even *she*
didn't think she did, watching both Monroe and Marcos and
De'Geer and Davey all swing for the fences and fail, relationship wise, didn't exactly fill her with optimism.

'You want me to believe in all this? Then send me a sign,' she muttered, half to herself as she stared upwards at the clear evening sky. The sun was still out; it wasn't past eight pm yet, and the light wasn't likely to drop for another couple of hours.

Relaxing, allowing the pent-up frustrations to ebb from her body, Anjli returned her attention to the phone in her hand. She didn't know whether to text Monroe or Declan first, although the logical thing to do would be to send it to both. More importantly, should she even send it to Declan? He was supposed to be sleeping, and she knew the moment he received the text, with knowledge of a mysterious burner phone out there, he'd be up and on the next bus back to Castleton.

She was about to type the message when she saw a moped turn into the street from the T-Junction at the end. Two helmeted figures were on it, one riding pillion, and Anjli's grasp on her phone unconsciously tightened. Moped thieves were commonplace in London these days; she wondered whether it'd reached out to here yet.

The moped, however, didn't speed up as it approached, a sure sign of something untoward about to happen; instead, it slowed, stopping on the street directly opposite her, facing left. The rear of the two helmeted riders looked at her.

'You need to piss off,' they said, the voice unmistakably male. 'Get your friends and leave before we make you.'

'Oh yeah?' Anjli reached into her jacket, pulling out the extendable baton she always carried. Flicking it out, she started walking towards them. 'And how you gonna do that exactly?'

'Same way as we did the others,' the helmeted man

replied, tossing a wallet down to the ground as he reached
into the leather jacket. 'Same way we'll do you, bitch.'

He pulled out his left hand, and in it was a pistol; a
familiar looking one, with a long, seven or even eight inch
barrel, forged in black steel. As he aimed it at his target, Anjli,
realising what was about to happen, dived to the side as the
wall beside her *spanged* with the smack of a bullet striking it,
as the sound of a gunshot echoed around the street.

'Hey!' A cry came out from the street, down to Anjli's right.
Glancing to the side, Anjli saw Devin Harper, his sister beside
him. They started running, but seeing this the moped quickly
sped off, the helmeted man returning the pistol into his
jacket.

On wobbly legs, Anjli rose, looking at the wall beside her.
A pocked hole revealed where the bullet had struck, and as
Devin and Carrie Harper reached her, Anjli saw the door to
the pub crash open as Billy, De'Geer and Davey ran through
it, almost as one unit.

'You okay?' Carrie asked, grabbing Anjli's arm. 'You see
who it was?'

'No,' Anjli could feel her heart beating, thumping so fast
that it wanted to burst out of her chest. She'd been so close
tonight. One more shot—

'They dropped something in the street,' she muttered,
pointing to the road. 'Tossed a wallet onto it.'

Davey was already there, still with her gloves on, as she
picked up the wallet from the road.

'Owen Russell,' she said, opening it and reading the credit
card visible within.

'The journalist?' Carrie was confused at this.

'The dead journalist,' Anjli replied, finding her legs giving way as she slumped onto an outside bench. 'He was the body in the cave. It wasn't an accident.'

'I found the bullet,' De'Geer held up a musket ball between two pencils, held like chopsticks as he rummaged in his pockets. 'Dammit, the bags are all in my uniform.'

Davey passed De'Geer a bag, making no kind of comment, and now in the clear wrapping, De'Geer stared at it.

'Looks smaller than the one in Staff Sergeant Moses,' he said. 'I don't think it's a Remington.'

'Bloody looked like one,' Anjli snapped, opening her eyes wide in an attempt to stop the urge to pass out.

'It's a .36 ball,' Devin said, staring at the bag. 'Lead based, fired from a Colt 1851 Navy black powder loading revolver.'

'That's pretty bloody specific,' Billy snarled, walking towards the Lieutenant, murder in his eyes.

'It's a pretty specific gunshot,' Carrie interjected, moving between Billy and Devin. 'We've both heard it a hundred times.'

'Oh yeah?' Billy now looked at Carrie. 'And how would you do that?'

'Because it was our father's gun,' Carrie admitted. 'The one he duelled with before Edward Moses killed him.'

15

CLEANING HOUSE

MONROE AND DOCTOR MARCOS ARRIVED AS DC DAVEY AND PC De'Geer finished up forensic duties; the bullet had been found, the wall examined, and the wallet placed in custody, so apart from that, there wasn't much else that could be done.

Billy had gone back into the pub to take witness accounts, but most of the customers hadn't even heard the gunshot over the background noise or else had believed it to be a car backfiring.

Nobody had expected an actual gun.

Picking up some pub sandwiches, Billy had then moved to a corner of the beer garden, laptop now on the table and open, eager to investigate the local road cameras, on the off chance he could find the moped. Or, at best, locate the shooter.

Grabbing one sandwich off his plate, mocking the fact that he'd brought his laptop to the pub while secretly grateful he had, Anjli returned to the pub's entrance with the others, standing beside the wall, mentally reenacting the moment time after time.

'I think the shooter had a beard,' she said. 'Bushy. Hipster. I just had a feeling of bulk around the neck, you know?'

'Maybe it was a buff, or a snood?' De'Geer looked up from the patio, where he was examining the ground beneath the bullet's impact point. 'I often wear those when riding, and you can place it over your face like a mask.'

'His voice was muffled,' Anjli admitted as, from the entrance, Doctor Marcos emerged, a glass of brandy in her hand. 'I just assumed it was the helmet.'

'Drink this,' she ordered, placing it in Anjli's hands. 'Doctor's orders.'

Anjli took the brandy and downed it in one swift gulp.

'Sipping's also good,' Doctor Marcos raised an eyebrow as she took the glass back.

'I'm fine,' Anjli protested. 'I've had worse.'

'Where's Tweedledum and Tweedledee?' Monroe looked around.

'I told them to come back tomorrow,' Anjli replied. 'Didn't really want to deal with them.'

'You think they have anything to do with this?' Monroe's voice was dark, suspicious as he spoke.

'I think they saved my life,' Anjli shook her head. 'Or at least stopped me from being shot.'

'That doesn't necessarily mean they weren't involved,' Monroe mused. 'Go home, lassie. You've had enough excitement for the day.'

'With all due respect, sir, home is a bunk in a dorm tonight,' Anjli straightened, tugging at her jacket to flatten it. 'I'd rather do something.'

'Good,' Monroe grinned. 'Then let's go do something, DS Kapoor.'

'Oh, did you get anything on the swab I passed you?' Anjli looked at Doctor Marcos, now examining the musket ball.

'They used a lead ball,' she muttered. 'Why not silver? That's their calling card.'

'Ma'am?'

'Oh, yes,' Doctor Marcos shook her head as she spoke. 'Nothing yet, definitely not connected to Falconer or Moses though. Some other poor bastard bled down there.'

'Got something,' Billy shouted out from his homemade cybercrime hub. 'Picture from that camera.' He pointed at the CCTV above him.

'Did we get the plate?' Monroe asked as he walked over. Billy nodded.

'Pub connected me to their admin network, so I can see their CCTV footage,' he said. 'Looking at this, the moped's plate is as clear as day.'

Monroe looked at the frozen CCTV image. On it, the moped passenger was aiming a revolver at Anjli. He shuddered.

'Chilling,' he muttered, glancing back as Anjli walked over.

'Hey, can I get a print of that?' she asked. 'Makes me look like an action hero.'

Monroe knew she was placing a brave face onto it; he remembered doing the same thing after almost dying at the hands of DI Frost earlier that year.

'It's okay to take a moment,' he whispered.

'I'll take a moment when this is all over,' she snarled, looking back at Billy. 'Do we have a name?'

Billy was typing on the laptop as he replied.

'In the database now,' he said. 'Looks like the moped's owner is a Laurence Graham.'

Billy tapped on the keys again, looking up in surprise.

'His house is next door to the *Castle Tun*.'

'Is it now, laddie?' Monroe's face darkened. 'We ought to have another chat with them after we speak to Mister Graham.'

'I'll go,' Anjli was already walking to the pub garden's exit.

'We'll go,' Monroe insisted, following her.

———

BULLMAN WAS SITTING IN HER OFFICE WHEN FRONT DESK buzzed up, stating that there was a very irate young woman downstairs who was demanding to see her.

Usually Bullman would have told them to take down some details and politely suggest the woman piss off, and considering the evening she was currently having, one where she'd learnt in quick succession that not only had one of her team almost died in a collapsed cave, possibly because of an explosive device being used, but also that her DS had been shot at outside a pub, she might not even have been polite about it, but when she heard the name of the woman waiting, she told the desk to buzz her up, and leaned back in her chair with a slight smile on her face.

A moment later, a young woman, barely in her twenties, slim in a navy blue suit and skirt, her long blonde hair pulled into a ponytail and a furious expression on her face stormed through the doors. As Bullman was currently the only one in at this time of the evening, she could have emerged from her office and met the woman halfway, but instead waited, allowing the new arrival to walk across the entire office before knocking on the glass door.

'Come in,' Bullman waved at the chair in front of her. 'Have a seat, Jennifer.'

Reluctantly, and visibly irritated at Bullman's use of her first name, Jennifer Farnham-Ewing walked to the chair and sat down, still managing in the process to give off the impression that this was all below her.

Which, a few weeks back, it probably would have been. Jennifer was, or rather *had been* the right-hand woman for Charles Baker, the obvious shoo-in for Prime Minister, until her overzealousness in stopping contact between Baker and DI Walsh resulted in the front gate barring Declan from entry to the Houses of Parliament as he sought to avert the mass poisoning of the entire Cabinet at a State Dinner.

Declan had wasted valuable minutes negotiating his way through; a delay that meant Declan and his (by then) congregated followers, including a BBC News crew, arrived moments after the desserts were eaten, and it was only the quick thinking of the Chef that had saved their lives.

Although Baker claimed credit, it soon became clear that his assistant had tried to derail the life-saving exercise, and it genuinely surprised Bullman that Jennifer Farnham-Ewing still had a job.

'I hear you're working with Rose,' Jennifer said by way of introduction. Bullman held up a hand.

'I think you mean 'Good evening, Detective Superintendent. I hear you're working with the new Prime Minister.''

Jennifer glared at Bullman for a long, silent moment before nodding.

'Apologies, *Detective Superintendent Bullman*, although I'd say *for* rather than with,' she replied. 'It's not been a great week.'

'Well, you're still employed, so that's good, yes?' Bullman

smiled. 'And Baker's still a Minister from what I see. Probably being kept close so he can't make mischief on the back benches, am I right?'

Jennifer squirmed in her seat.

'I wouldn't know,' she replied. 'I'm more in the pool now.'

'Oh, you're no longer his Right Hand Woman?' Bullman mocked surprise. 'What an utter shock. So sorry for your well deserved loss. Go on then, why are you here? I thought we'd become too poisonous for you?'

'Well, your man didn't exactly help my boss.'

'My *man*, as you so quaintly put it, isn't employed to help your boss. And, as I recall, he *would* have helped your boss if it wasn't for *your* heavy handedness,' Bullman emphasised the words like gunshots, watching each one hammer into Jennifer Farnham-Ewing.

Interestingly, the woman took them.

'And besides, my man is currently fighting for his life in hospital after an attempt on his life, so forgive me if I'm a little blunt,' Bullman ended. Jennifer swallowed a couple of times; she hadn't been informed of this as it wasn't public knowledge yet, and Bullman could tell that this was frustrating her.

Good.

'You're working for Michelle Rose, the new Prime Minister,' Jennifer eventually explained. 'Charles Baker wanted you to know all the facts.'

Bullman looked around.

'Awesome,' she said. 'Where is he?'

'As you can understand, it's not really that prudent for him to be here,' Jennifer explained.

'Didn't stop him in the past.'

'His every move wasn't being scrutinised in the past,' Jennifer retorted.

'Bullshit,' Bullman leaned back in the chair, amused. 'He was always being scrutinised. He knew, though, that being seen with Declan, especially after his life was saved by my team, and his career resuscitated more than once by us, was profitable for his election chances—right up to the moment they weren't.'

Jennifer Farnham-Ewing chose not to reply to this. Bullman sighed. It looked like she wasn't getting the fight she wanted tonight.

'Okay then, so you're his mouthpiece,' Bullman nodded. 'Personally, I'm stunned he didn't fire your stupid, opinionated arse, rather than dumping you down to *errand girl*.'

Jennifer opened her mouth, caught in mid-sentence by the rudeness of Bullman's words. Bullman followed up by standing, looking down at her.

'Your actions almost killed the Cabinet,' she hissed. 'Your ego almost killed the Queen!'

'She said she didn't poison the Queen,' Jennifer whispered, her eyes like saucers, filling with tears.

'Christ, are you about to *cry* now?' Bullman despaired. 'Does that work with the men you sit with? Because it sure as hell doesn't work with me. My *man*, as you called him, *resigned* because of your arrogance. He believed he failed when *you closed the door on him*.'

'I'm trying to make things right,' Jennifer's tears were gone, disappeared as quickly as they appeared, and Bullman wondered whether she'd gained a hold on herself, or whether they had been for effect. 'I'm here to talk about the Cardigan Regiment and their duelling club.'

At this, Bullman's eyebrow raised.

'Oh, now I'm all ears,' she said. 'Because the bloody Cardigan Regiment has been a nightmare to find anything on.'

'That'll be because of Brigadier Eaton-Jones,' Jennifer looked around the office. 'Any chance of a coffee? It's been a long day.'

'No,' Bullman replied icily. 'Tell me what Baker sent you to say.'

'So I don't repeat information you already have, can I ask what you know about them so far?' Jennifer appeared almost contrite as she spoke. Bullman leaned back in her chair as she thought through the question.

'The Cardigans? I know they were a victim of cutbacks,' she replied. 'Brought into the Derbyshire Regiment when it amalgamated the Bedfordshire Light Infantry, the Cardigan Regiment and the Cumberland Fusiliers.'

Jennifer nodded.

'I also know they weren't victims of cost cutting, and instead were quietly closed down because of war crime allegations,' Bullman continued. 'Although I've yet to hear what they were.'

'Insurgents being executed without a trial,' Jennifer replied, grateful for a question that she could reply to. 'Shot like dogs in the forehead.'

'And there wasn't an outcry?'

'By then Winston Eaton-Jones had moved on upwards, and could pressure people to look the other way,' Jennifer explained. 'Too many names on a list that knew it was happening. He wanted his son Henry removed from the lists too, so he didn't have a black mark on him. In the end, he saved around four of his officers and a couple of hangers on. There was a Colonel involved, no longer a part of them who was also advising him at the time, but he seems to have disappeared.'

'Henry Eaton-Jones was a member of the Cardigans,' Bullman nodded. This was already suspected. 'It's hard to find an accurate representation of who was actually there, you know.'

'Then-Sergeant Patrick Harper and then-Lieutenant Charles Falconer were also members of the Cardigans,' Jennifer replied. 'Although if you were to look, you'd see they were members of the Cumberland Fusiliers, instead of the Cardigan Regiment.'

'So there was a little bit of paperwork massaging,' Bullman watched Jennifer. 'You could have sent me this information by phone. Why the personal visit?'

'Mister Baker wants to help bring down the people behind this,' Jennifer stated, as if it was some kind of noble gesture.

Bullman laughed.

'So Michelle Rose is connected,' she said. 'And Baker thinks if he can nail her for something, or rather get us to nail her, she steps down and he steps in.'

Jennifer Farnham-Ewing simply sat there, unmoving.

'You might say that, but I couldn't possibly—'

'Don't you dare bloody quote *House of Cards* at me,' Bullman interrupted. 'You're no *Francis Urquhart*, and you never will be. Just get on with it. You said Duelling Club, too.'

Jennifer nodded, settling in her chair, like she was preparing to tell a story.

'What do you know about Olympic Duelling?'

'I know it's a load of bollocks,' Bullman replied candidly. 'Never took off, shown as an exhibition in 1908. Basically dick-measuring paintball with wax bullets.'

Jennifer stopped. She hadn't expected such a blunt response.

'Tell me I'm wrong,' Bullman smiled.

'In 1901, Doctor Paul Devillers, both a doctor and a keen duellist—'

'How the hell are you a *keen* duellist?' Bullman exclaimed. 'Someone wakes up and thinks 'You know what? I think I'll go down to the riverside at dawn, and shoot someone I don't like?' Today we'd call that pre-meditated murder and nick them.'

'—Designed a new, innovative wax bullet for duelling practice,' Jennifer continued, ignoring Bullman. 'He created it so that they were soft enough not to bruise the person who was the intended target.'

'How nice of him.'

'In 1903, Devillers persuaded the Parisian gun making firm of Piot-Lepage to make sets of special wax bullet duelling pistols for him, and he then created the 'Societie L'Assaut au Pistolet'.'

'The Gun Assault Society,' Bullman shook her head. 'Catchy.'

'It was like fencing, in that the combatants wore leather coats and face masks, although these were added with glass visors and sometimes gas masks,' Jennifer was in her stride now; that she wasn't reading from notes showed she'd either researched this thoroughly, or she was a long-time fan. 'It went global; there were even American societies. And then the First World War happened.'

'People found shooting wax balls a bit boring after that, I suppose.'

'Indeed,' Jennifer wrinkled her nose at the thought. 'Anyway, it stayed dead for a long time, but after the Second

World War, it returned, off the books, when someone started an Inter-Regiment contest in the seventies. Sporadic games with antique weapons which didn't work half the time. Again, it died off. And then, around twenty years ago, along came Major Eaton-Jones.'

'Guessing this is Senior?'

Jennifer nodded.

'The now-Brigadier one. Back at the turn of the millennium, he was in the Cardigan Regiment. He'd also started black powder shooting. At some point, he took the ideals of the Societie L'Assaut au Pistolet and made his own little group, mainly comprising officers in the Cardigans. They used the old leather face masks and blouses at the start, but then started creating their own when other sports, like airsoft, started creating better body armour. The problem was that they liked the danger; there weren't any wars around then, and so they upped the ante, removing the armour for specialist fights, making it more violent, dangerous.'

'Then we hit 2008?'

'Yes,' Jennifer nodded. 'And the Cardigan Regiment is thrown into disrepute with war crimes allegations. By this point Blair's gone, Brown's in power and people demand heads. When the 2010 election arrives, Winston Eaton-Jones, now a Colonel has moved himself from the firing line, but needs to save his son. And then along comes a young Junior Minister in the MOD. Michelle Rose, fresh from her first election victory and given a role so low down, you need potholing equipment to wave at her. She's ambitious, and Eaton-Jones is desperate.'

She shifted in her seat.

'And, with her help, he moves his son, and some of his more loyal officers, across to the Cumberland Fusiliers moments before they merged the now disgraced Cardigan Regiment with other units. The others in the Cardigans are dumped on the side, tainted by the record. But Falconer, Eaton-Jones Junior, even his pet Sergeant are saved.'

'Just those three?'

'That's the problem,' Jennifer admitted. 'We don't know. After the massaging, the records were lost in a data breach. Obviously the party kept this quiet, as *lists of serving officers abroad going missing* isn't a great headline for a recently elected government, struggling with an uneasy coalition with the Liberal Democrats. There are no records of the command structure *anywhere* anymore. We know Eaton-Jones Junior was a Second Lieutenant, Harper was a Sergeant and Falconer had been promoted to Lieutenant Colonel days earlier. There's a Major and another Lieutenant Colonel missing from the Cardigan Regiment books, although if Falconer had been promoted the second LC could have been promoted or transferred, and we have no idea who they are. All we hope is that if found, we could bring them in as witnesses.'

'Witnesses in what?' Declan asked.

'My boss wants to push for a War Trial,' Jennifer explained. 'They never paid for what they did.'

'And they did it under a Labour Government,' Bullman understood now. 'You're looking for things to distract from your own party's issues. And, if you can prove Michelle Rose deliberately moved officers to spare them back in 2010, then she'd have problems of her own. She might even have to resign.'

'The flag-shaggers might be zealots for all things Tory,' Jennifer replied with what looked to be a half-sneer. 'But if they hear we threw their own soldiers to wolves, or that enlisted men suffered while officers escaped, they'll bay for blood.'

'So why did Michelle Rose send us to look into Falconer's death?' Bullman rose now, pacing as she worked through the problem. 'Surely we'd find this out?'

'Charles Baker had been trying to gain a mole in the Derbyshires, someone who could answer his questions and tell him what was going on,' Jennifer looked uncomfortable now. 'He'd started moving on Lieutenant Colonel Falconer. We'd pretty much convinced him to come in, too, show us what we were missing, blow that whistle on the officers who escaped, who were creating a secret cabal, one that was diametrically opposed to Whitehall—'

'Secret Cabal,' Bullman realised with horror what Jennifer was getting at. 'You meant the Templar Corps, the alt-right organisation they created?'

Jennifer nodded.

'We know it exists, but not who runs it,' she explained. 'We could bring in Brigadier Eaton-Jones, or his son, and in the process make public the space laser they look to have stolen for their own use.'

'The laser that killed Falconer?' Bullman leaned forward. 'It exists?'

'Falconer told us he'd made a small one that could blind people in duels, connected to a flak jacket that held a variety of batteries around the torso. He'd also written that this could be built into a more powerful laser rifle which, if used properly, could take down any world leader with no one realising. He still wouldn't give us everything, promising to write it down. When he died, there was no rifle found, and we suspect it was because someone realised he was now a whistleblower, so took it and killed him.'

'So Falconer worked for you,' this threw Bullman. 'I had him as a loyal, career soldier.'

'He was,' Jennifer rose now, standing behind the chair. 'Before something made him reevaluate his life around a year ago and more susceptible to our advances. He had information that covered the last decade, and papers that proved that Michelle Rose had willingly broken the Geneva Convention. These, and the list he was going to give, would have ended both Rose and Eaton-Jones Senior, and probably killed his society.'

She looked at her watch.

'I need to go, I have a date waiting,' she said. 'We never had this conversation, and the Right Honorable gentleman didn't send me here. We understand this? Good. Check into the Cardigans, D Supt Bullman.'

'I will, Jennifer,' Bullman waved a lazy hand goodbye. 'Good luck in the trenches again with all the other ambitious sycophants.'

With a last nod, Jennifer left the office, and Bullman, standing alone now, scratching her head.

She'd hoped that with Charles Baker losing the Leadership election, she'd be out of all this cloak and dagger shit.

Now, though, it looked like the cloaks were made of kevlar and the daggers were pistols at dawn.

16

PAYING OVERTIME

IT WAS JUST BEFORE NINE IN THE EVENING BY THE TIME ANJLI and Monroe arrived at the house next to the Castle Tun.

That said, to call it *next door* was a bit of an oversight; The Castle Tun guesthouse actually took over three houses on the street, and the house beside it was more to the side and down a small cul-de-sac to the left, leaving a definite gap between the buildings.

'You sure you're okay to do this?' Monroe asked. 'You don't have to.'

Anjli looked along the side of the house; there was no moped visible, but that didn't mean it would have been outside.

'I'm good,' she said, walking up to the door and banging on it. 'Laurence Graham! Police! Get your arse out here now!'

Monroe stood back, allowing her this anger. He looked to the window; there was no sign of movement.

'They're not in, it seems,' he said.

'Probably out for a ride,' Anjli hissed, opening the letterbox and peering in. 'Mister Graham! Are you there?'

'He's in the hospital,' a voice shouted across from the other side of the open space and Anjli and Monroe turned to see a man, in his mid-to-late forties or maybe a good-for-his-fifties, his head shaved, the baldness framing his bushy red beard, wiping his hands on a tea towel as he walked out of the conservatory of the Castle Tun.

'What for?' Monroe turned and started walking towards him. 'And who are you, if I can ask?'

'I'm Keith Williams,' the man said, holding out his hand for Monroe to shake. 'You spoke to my wife earlier.'

'Ah, yes,' Monroe nodded. 'DCI Monroe, DS Kapoor.'

'Yeah, I know,' Keith looked at Anjli. 'Heard you got shot at. Pricks.'

'News travels fast.'

'Small village,' Keith nodded at the house. 'Larry broke his hip falling from a ladder, a couple of weeks back. He's a roofer. Nasty fall. Had to be air ambulanced and everything.'

'Painful,' Monroe replied. 'Wife or kids inside?'

'Girlfriend, doesn't live there, they broke up a few weeks back,' Keith carried on. 'Why?'

'Because the person who tried to shoot me was riding his moped,' Anjli snapped.

Keith frowned, tossing his tea towel back through the door and grabbing a ring of keys from the inside of the kitchen

'Impossible,' he said as he walked to the side gate, to the back of the house. 'I checked in on the house two days ago and it was in the shed.'

'Two days is a long time,' Monroe muttered as the gate was open and Keith entered the back garden.

'Heh, look at that,' he said, and Anjli was convinced there was no surprise whatsoever in his voice. 'It's gone.'

Monroe walked to where Keith was staring; on the floor was a bike lock, discarded to the side.

'How lucky,' he said, looking at it. 'They must have guessed the combination as well.'

'To be honest, mate, Larry loaned the bike out to anyone that needed it,' Keith walked back to the gate now, still relaxed. 'Half a dozen people know that code. I'll pop up the hospital tomorrow, tell him he needs to report it stolen.'

'Why not tonight?'

'Gone nine, visiting hours are over.'

Monroe, tired of this, stopped Keith, grabbing his arm.

'You need to get with the story here,' he snapped. 'Someone took this moped, drove to where my detective sergeant was and tried to shoot her!'

'I get that,' Keith replied, glancing at Anjli, giving her the once-over with his eyes. 'But you look okay, no harm done, probably kids pissing around.'

'Kids pissing around—' Monroe was fuming, but Anjli moved in, pushing Monroe out of the garden as she smiled at Keith.

'Thanks,' she said. 'It's appreciated. If you see anyone bringing it back, let us know, yeah? One of our team is staying in your guesthouse, so tell him if you think of anything.'

'I will do,' Keith nodded.

Anjli walked Monroe back to the road, glancing at her watch as she did so.

'You mentioned the gunman was bearded,' Monroe muttered. 'Could it have been him?'

'Not sure yet, but he can wait, boss. We need to go to the research building,' Anjli said urgently. 'There's definitely something familiar here with Mister Williams, though, and I think it was there.'

————

BILLY HADN'T WANTED TO RETURN TO THE MDP PORTAKABINS, and the evening was getting colder, so, taking his laptop, he made his way to the Castle Tun guesthouse and his bedroom.

Maureen Williams intercepted him before he could reach the stairs.

'Are you okay? Was it a gun? Was anyone hurt? Could it be terrorists?' the questions spilled out of her. Billy smiled, wearily.

'Yes, yes, no, no,' he replied. 'Still looking into it, and I can't tell you anything else.'

'They took Larry's moped,' Maureen added, as if believing that this was news for Billy to hear. 'My Keith spoke to the detectives. Someone stole it.'

'So I believe,' Billy replied, forcing himself to smile again. 'I'm sorry, I really need to do some work.'

'Did you at least have some dinner?' Maureen was following Billy up the stairs now.

'I had sandwiches.'

'Ach, that's not a dinner,' Mauren chided. 'Let me whip up a pie and—'

'Honestly, I'm fine,' Billy placed the room key in and twisted it. 'I'll call if I need anything. Goodnight, now.'

Before Maureen could say anything, Billy slid into the room, closing the door behind him. Taking a deep breath, he stood beside the door, allowing the moment to fade. Eventually, he straightened and, on a whim, glanced through the peephole to his door.

Maureen was still there.

However, she wasn't watching his door; she was texting. Billy almost had an irrational urge to burst outside and see who she was contacting, but there were privacy laws and, although she was annoying and gossip hungry, Maureen Williams wasn't yet a suspect.

Walking into the room, Billy tossed his messenger bag onto the bed before slumping into the chair, looking up at the room's ceiling. A year earlier, Eddie Moses would have sat in this exact same chair. *Did he know he was running out the clock? Did he know he was soon to die?*

Billy shuddered. That was something he didn't want to consider.

He stared around the room now; *what would he do if he was in such a position?*

Billy rose, staring out of the window. The only chance to escape was to clamber out, struggle across the coal shed and conservatory below, and land in the back garden. There was every opportunity here to be found, though, especially if he was as injured then as the body found suggested.

He must have known that.

Walking to the desk now, Billy picked up the headed notepad, pulling off and examining a sheet of it to the light. It looked the same shade of off-white that the torn note was from; the chances were Eddie Moses wrote his message to Declan on the same pad. Folding it, he placed it in his pocket.

Maybe Joanne Davey could work something out from it.

Billy stopped, looking at the bed in the room. Eddie Moses had placed a note in his wallet, one that said Declan would know where he was staying. He added a receipt, the only one that would show the details of the phone he'd bought.

These were deliberate. He was expecting to die.

There was no phone here; chances are it was taken when whoever stuck him in a body bag did that. His normal day-to-day one was in Portsmouth. He must have hoped the wallet would be overlooked. And nobody cared about till receipts.

Billy walked to the small table in his bedroom and pulled out his laptop from the messenger bag, opening it up as he sat down. The guesthouse had Wi-Fi, but now Billy felt a little nervous about using it; instead, he tethered his own phone's 4G network to his laptop, downloading his emails.

He paused as one of them loaded up on his screen; the phone network had come through with the last messages Eddie Moses made on the new burner phone before he died, spaced over three attached PDF sheets. Carefully, Billy scrolled through the messages.

Owen I need you

What happened are you ok did you do it

yes got shot but I can fix it up

So it's over?

No too many questions asked, they know I was probing.

I think they followed me.

I need to get out of here

Stay there am on way

There was a break of about fifteen minutes and then

Outside

Eddie I'm outside grab your things

Eddie it's been twenty minutes where the hell are you

I have to go they've seen me good luck

Billy leaned back in the chair, whistling. This had to be Owen Russell's phone Eddie was texting, but the fact he did this caused issues with Maureen Williams' witness testimony. She'd suggested to Declan and Monroe that Eddie Moses walked out, ran away from Castleton without anyone in the guesthouse noticing, but with a journalist camped on the doorstep, this would have been impossible.

Unless something else happened in the time Owen travelled to Eddie.

Billy swiped to the second sheet attached; another, unknown number Eddie had texted. Interestingly, these were all immediately after Owen had told Eddie to stay still.

How did it go

                                        Bad injured need to go

I can arrange that wait for my signal out back

Billy noted down the number, sending it off to be checked. He knew it'd take a while, but there wasn't much else he could do, except for dialling it.

On a whim, he picked up the phone and did just that.

It answered on the second ring.

'Hello?' he said, 'who is this?'

There was breathing down the other end of the line, but no words were spoken.

'I'm DC Fitzwarren, City police. You asked Edward Moses to wait for your signal, the day he—'

There was a click, and the line went dead.

Billy placed the phone down, trembling.

That was a stupid idea, Billy. Now whoever it is knows your name.

Trying to distract himself, Billy swiped once more, staring at the third page, and the last message Eddie ever sent, to another unknown number, immediately after the second number.

There was no reply to it.

> You bastard you set me up. I'm coming for you.

Billy jumped as his door rocked with a sudden banging. *How the hell had they found him so fast?*

'Yes?' he quavered, backing away from the door.

'Mister Fitzwarren? I made you some fish finger sandwiches,' he heard the voice of Maureen Williams through the door. 'It's no effort, I was making them anyway.'

Billy stared at the door, as if expecting it to burst open.

'Um, thanks!' he shouted. 'I was, um, in the shower.'

'I'll leave them right here,' Maureen's voice continued. Billy didn't move.

After a minute, he peered through the peephole, opened the door and brought the small plate of fish finger sandwiches in.

They smelled amazing.

It was just a shame that he was too paranoid now to even consider eating them.

———

By now the gate guard was getting used to seeing Anjli arrive, and with the dour Scottish DCI beside her, she was quickly waved through, while being told that most of the crew had gone home for the night. Anjli had replied this was fine, as she just needed to check a couple of small things.

Peterson was the researcher who walked out to meet them this time, his messy blond hair even wilder as he waved them into the building.

'Cullen's gone home for the night,' he muttered. 'I think, anyway. I've not seen her for ages.'

'How come you're still working?' Anjli asked. 'It's almost half-past nine.'

'How come *you're* still working?' Peterson tried to turn the question onto her.

'Because some prick tried to shoot me tonight and we're hunting him down.'

'Oh, right,' Peterson replied, followed by 'wait, really? Man, that's sick!' when his brain caught up to the conversation. 'You okay? We have that medical room in the basement.'

'I'm good, thanks,' Anjli said. 'I just need to see Doctor Cullen's office, and then the basement again.'

'Do I need to come with you?' Peterson asked, looking at his own office as they passed it. 'I'm on a deadline.'

'Just the first part, I need you to identify someone,' Anjli smiled. 'We can do the basement ourselves. No photos, I promise.'

Doctor Cullen's office was just as Anjli remembered, but as Monroe stared in awe at the machine in the middle of the room, Anjli walked over to Doctor Cullen's desk.

'Mister Peterson, can you tell me who these are?' she asked, showing him the photo of Second Lieutenant Cullen and two other soldiers, all in dress uniforms. She didn't need the name of one of them, though; she'd just met him.

'That's Keith, he runs the guesthouse in town,' Peterson tapped on the photo. 'He used to be in the Derbyshires, sharpshooter or something, but left about four years back.'

'He was in the army *and* ran a guesthouse?' Monroe asked.

'Course not,' Peterson smiled. 'His wife, Maureen, she ran it. But as it grew, and the tourist trade got busier, he demobbed and helped run it. I think she'd wanted him out for a while, to be honest.'

'And this one?' Anjli tapped on the other man in the image, embracing Cullen.

'That's Sergeant Graham,' Peterson nodded. 'No, he left the Derbyshires about a year back. Works as a builder or something. Been seeing Elaine—that's Doctor Cullen—for about seven years.'

'Still?' Monroe asked. 'We'd heard they'd split up.'

'They have?' Peterson's eyes lit up.

Anjli shook her head.

'We're done here, thanks,' she smiled. 'We'll call you if we need anything else.'

Peterson, grateful to escape and now with a piece of good news to consider, it seemed, didn't need convincing and before Monroe could add to this, he was gone, already hurrying to his office.

'Bloody workplace romances,' Anjli grinned.

'Nice catch, lassie,' Monroe took the photo frame, looking at it. 'So Graham, Williams and Cullen all knew each other.'

'And served in the Derbyshires with each other,' Anjli added. 'Likely with Falconer and the others.'

'And Graham left the Regiment around the time Eddie Moses died,' Monroe nodded. 'I think we need to find our Doctor Cullen and have a word with her.'

'Might have to wait until tomorrow, though,' Anjli was already leading Monroe out of the lab and down the corridor, towards the rear staircase and the downstairs rifle range, or whatever it was. Anjli still wasn't sure. And, when they entered the basement, the motion-detecting lights turning on automatically, Anjli saw nothing had changed since her visit earlier. Even the bloodstain on the floor was still there.

'Now that's a duelling range,' Monroe said, walking to the table that barred the open middle row of the basement. 'I can see them using this as some kind of duellist recreation room. And there's the gruesome addition that it used to have its own dead bodies.'

He shuddered.

'You want one of those ghost paranormal shows to come down here for the night. Call those kids we almost nicked in Greenwich, see if they want some.'

Anjli went to reply but stopped as the slightest scuff noise echoed around the basement.

'We're not alone,' she whispered, pulling out her extend-able baton for the second time that night, and raising her voice as she shouted out. 'Reveal yourself, whoever you are! You have to get past us to get out, so don't make it difficult.'

There was no response to this; no noise whatsoever.

'Maybe we missed something—' Monroe started, but stopped as at the back of the basement, at the other end of the open area of space, a black-clad figure suddenly made a run for the left of the middle row.

'There!' Anjli cried out. 'Shit, there's a back entrance! I remember Peterson mentioning it!'

By now, Monroe was already running for the other end of the basement, and Anjli started after him. She was younger, fitter and faster, and by the time they reached the end, she was already a good distance ahead as she ran into the wire mesh cage at the far left, noticing that there was a five feet by three feet square hatch open in the wall, built like the doors in a submarine.

'Don't wait for me! Get after them!' Monroe wheezed, and Anjli dived through the door, finding herself now in a narrow concrete tunnel that sloped upwards. There was the briefest of moments where she realised that running after a stranger with only a baton for defence was a bloody stupid thing to do, but the moment had passed for choosing a different route, and if someone shot at her again, she'd just have to accept that this was her new thing.

At the top of the tunnel was a grate, but someone had pulled this to the side, exposing the darkening sky. Cambering out of the hole, Anjli saw she was around fifty metres from the back of the compound, and interestingly, on the other side of the fence.

And, only ten feet away, was the black-clad figure.

'I need extraction!' The figure hissed, the voice female, hand to her ear, not realising Anjli had emerged into the tree line. 'I've been spotted! I—'

The hissing stopped as Anjli rugby tackled the black-clad female to the ground, catching her unawares as she pulled her left arm tight behind her back.

'You have the right to remain silent—' Anjli started.

'No! Wait! I'm on your side!' the woman whispered, pulling away her hoodie with her other arm to show Doctor Cullen, a bluetooth AirPod earbud in her right ear. 'I'm helping!'

'What the utter hell?' Anjli stepped back as Doctor Cullen, now released, turned to face her, one hand in the air as the other one pulled out her phone, connected to the earbud.

'Let me put this on speaker,' she whispered, crouching in the grass. 'And stay low so you're not seen.'

Anjli, utterly baffled, crouched beside her as, stumbling through the trees, panting as he did so, was Monroe.

'What the blazes—' he wheezed, but Anjli waved him silent for the moment.

'Crouch down,' she said.

'Gladly,' Monroe replied as he collapsed on the grass. 'Can someone tell me what the merry hell is going on?'

'I can,' a male voice spoke through the speaker on the phone. 'Who am I speaking to?'

'I know that voice,' Monroe muttered, moving closer with a dark smile now on his face. 'This is DCI Alex Monroe and DS Anjli Kapoor, Charlie boy.'

'Ah, bollocks,' the voice of Charles Baker muttered.

17

VISITING HOURS

DOCTOR CULLEN SAT IN THE BACK OF BILLY'S MINI, NOW parked outside the MDP Portakabins, holding the phone out in front of her so that Monroe and Anjli could hear Charles Baker.

'I spoke to your boss,' Charles explained. 'That is, my aide spoke to her. Tonight.'

'Aye, never the one to do the dirty work yourself, eh?' Monroe snarled. 'Why the hell are we even talking?'

'DS Kapoor,' Doctor Cullen explained. 'When she went off on a rant about Whitehall, I knew she couldn't possibly be working for the new Prime Minister. And by default, Brigadier Eaton-Jones.'

'Oh, you went off on a rant, did you?' Monroe smiled at the reddening Anjli. 'How unlike you.'

'We believed Lieutenant Colonel Falconer was passing us information,' Charles said down the line. 'That a top secret rifle, contradicting the Geneva Convention, wasn't only missing, but was possibly in the company of far-right extremists within the military. It was only today that we learned it was, in fact, his assistant, Doctor Cullen, using his log in ID.'

'I thought it'd hide me better,' Cullen admitted.

'You should think about hiding better,' Monroe muttered. 'Your ex-boyfriend's moped is being ridden by two pricks who tried to kill my DS here.'

'There's a reason we broke up,' Doctor Cullen admitted. 'That and I was sleeping with Charlie. Lieutenant Colonel Falconer, that is.'

'Nailed it,' Anjli muttered. 'Sorry, please carry on.'

'I'll leave you both to it,' Charles said, obviously desperate to leave the conversation. 'Feels good to be working on the same side again—'

'And you can shut it, too,' Monroe snapped. 'Michelle Rose may have skeletons, and she might not be the person to lead the country, but we've seen your closet too, Baker. Remember that. And we know that even though she apparently did some questionable things while in the Ministry of Defence, so did you. And we still have a folder marked *RATTLESTONE* to prove it.'

'I was told there were no copies,' Charles Baker's tone was icy.

'Aye, you were.'

There was a long pause. Eventually, tired of this, Monroe took the phone from Cullen.

'Rose sent us here to investigate Falconer's death. There's a very strong chance this happened because they believed him to be your mole. So both you and the Doctor here should consider that.'

And this said, Monroe disconnected the call.

'I killed him, didn't I?' Doctor Cullen asked. 'I used his ID, and I put crosshairs on him.'

'I won't sugarcoat it, but probably, aye,' Monroe admitted. 'But you can make things right, Elaine. You can tell us what you were passing to Baker, and we can see if we can find Falconer's killers in the process.'

'Where's the rifle?' Anjli asked.

'There isn't one!' Doctor Cullen protested. 'I said this before! I never saw one built here, just that stupid jacket for his little blinding laser thing.'

Monroe glanced at Anjli.

'So, if there was no laser, how was one used to melt his ICD unit?'

'I don't know,' Doctor Cullen sobbed now. 'That's why I was there tonight. I was trying to find the jacket, see if there was anything that gave away where the rifle was. It had to be there. But you turned up, and I got scared.'

'What happened with Graham?' Anjli asked.

'That's personal,' Doctor Cullen muttered, looking up at her from the back seat.

'I meant, why did he leave the army?'

Doctor Cullen nodded in realisation.

'Oh,' she said. 'He just decided he'd had enough one day. It was around a year ago, early July. He came home one night, said he couldn't do it anymore, put his papers in the next day.'

'Was he in Falconer's shooting club?' Monroe asked.

Doctor Cullen nodded.

'Did they shoot in the basement?' he continued.

Again, she nodded.

'Do you know who was in the Cardigan Regiment?' Anjli asked.

'Only the Eaton-Jones family, the Sergeant, Harper and

Charles Falconer,' she said. 'I wasn't bothered by all that. All I cared about was the research.'

Monroe looked around, noting that the car park was empty.

'Go on, piss off,' he muttered. 'We'll be coming to chat with you in the morning, yeah?'

Doctor Cullen nodded, and without another sound left the car after Anjli climbed out, pushing the seat forward to allow her to exit. Once the seat was back in place and Anjli had returned to the vehicle, she looked at Monroe.

'What if there isn't a rifle, sir?' she asked. 'What if there's a logical way to explain Falconer's apparent assassination that doesn't involve fatal death rays from invisible laser guns?'

'It'd be nice,' Monroe replied, leaning his head back against the seat. 'Unlikely, but nice.'

'Sir,' Anjli said slowly. 'You said we had a folder with Rattlestone on it. I didn't think we had any of those files.'

Monroe grinned.

'We don't,' he replied. 'I never mentioned files, I said folder. And give me a minute with a sharpie and we'll have the neatest Rattlestone ever written on one.'

He looked at his watch.

'Christ, I promised Rosanna we'd carry on the conversation, but it's now gone ten,' he muttered.

'Conversation?' Anjli raised an inquisitive eyebrow.

'Aye, conversation,' Monroe smiled. 'Baby steps. I'm growing as a person, apparently. You should try it.'

'What, growing as a person?' Anjli leaned back, unimpressed at the comment. 'That's harsh.'

'Nae, you bampot, the conversation part,' Monroe climbed out of the car. 'With Declan.'

Before Anjli could reply to this, Monroe shut the door

and walked off towards the Portakabins and MDP offices. Anjli chuckled, preparing to park up for the night too; she actually found herself jealous of Billy, having a nice en suite bedroom for the night—

She stopped, looking out of the windscreen into the night.

There, in the darkness, a man was watching her.

A figure, in the darkness, shadowed and beside the buildings, clearly facing her.

Anjli didn't move; instead, she flicked on the headlights, flooding the area with light. But, as she did so, the man turned and disappeared into the shadows behind the cabins.

'Balls to that,' she muttered, rising out of the car and slamming the door behind her. She was four steps along before she stopped.

What the hell are you doing?

Anjli leant over and retched, bringing up bile as she spat it to the floor. She trembled, the car park spinning.

Come on, you soppy bitch, what if Declan sees you?

'Boss? You okay?' It was De'Geer who asked, walking out of the building, his enormous frame being close instantly relaxing Anjli.

They can't kill you with him here. Bullets bounce off him.

'Man... over there...' she croaked, pointing. 'Got a stitch. With you in... a moment.'

De'Geer turned to where the Mini's headlights lit up the edge of the car park and, with a determined stride, walked over to the side of the cabins, pulling out his own torch as he did so.

'There's nothing here, Ma'am,' he said after a moment of rooting around in the undergrowth. 'But I think you should come and have a look at this.'

Gathering the courage to move, Anjli walked over to De'Geer, pausing as she saw what he was pointing at.

Behind where the man had been standing, there was a ditch, only three feet deep. And there, discarded, was an old, red moped.

Anjli looked up, scanning the area.

'Oh, I am sick of these sodding games,' she said. 'Write it up, PC De'Geer.'

'Yes Ma'am. And what will you be doing?'

'Me?' Anjli chuckled morosely. 'I'm going to bloody sleep.'

———

Declan couldn't sleep.

He'd tried, but there was too much noise outside; it was a hospital, after all, and he could hear people calling out for nurses, while the sounds of gurneys and wheelchairs rattled past his door regularly.

Eventually, he'd grabbed his phone, laying in bed and staring at it, as if willing it to beep, receive an email or a message, anything.

The phone beeped with a new message.

Bloody hell, Declan thought to himself. *If only I could do that with the Lottery numbers.*

It was from Jess.

Hey just checking in how's the Peak District? Is it pretty xx

Declan leaned back. He hadn't said anything about being in hospital, and he'd demanded that Liz, still his next of kin on his records, wasn't contacted.

They didn't know.

All good, call tomorrow xx

Busy?

A little.

On a case? Can I help?

Declan chuckled. Jessica Walsh was very much a chip off the old block.

Not unless you know about laser guns

They go pew pew pew and Han Solo shot first xx

Declan laughed out loud at this, wincing as his head throbbed at the motion.

Speak tomorrow x

Declan placed the phone on the side of the bed, but as he did so it lit up, ringing. He didn't check the number, simply connecting and placing the phone to his ear.

'Everyone knows Han shot first,' he said.

'Is this some kind of code?' the voice of Trix, perplexed, came through the other end. 'Do I need to know the movies?'

Declan straightened.

'Sorry, thought you were Jess.'

'Oh,' Trix replied, and Declan thought he could detect a smile as she continued. 'Does this mean I have to call you daddy now?'

'What do you have?'

'Questions, and I don't like that,' Trix's tone changed. She was back to being professional now. 'You wanted to know about Ramesh Abbasi. *Captain* Ramesh Abbasi.'

'Yes,' Declan said, confused at Trix's use of Old Ram's name twice.

'Christ Declan, you sound like shit. Where are you?'

'Hospital,' Declan winced as his head throbbed again. 'Cave fell on me.'

There was a moment of silence.

'Right,' Trix said, as if this was the most normal thing he could have said. 'Anyway. There's no Captain Ramesh Abbasi in the Cumberland Fusiliers, or the Cardigan Regiment.'

'You sure?'

'Do I tell you how to dress yourself in the dark? No,' Trix replied haughtily. 'I let you keep doing it because it seems to be what you know.'

'Harsh, but I get your point,' Declan conceded. 'So he wasn't a soldier?'

'No, he wasn't a Captain,' Trix's voice now held a hint of smugness. 'His entire record has been scrubbed. And that usually only happens—'

'When you're a spook,' Declan hissed. Emilia Wintergreen had done just that when she took over Section D many years earlier, in the process making it as if her marriage to Monroe had never existed.

'Yes, but he's not one of ours,' Trix replied. 'I checked with Wintergreen, and even she doesn't remember him, and she came over to the dark side in 2011.'

'So who is he? Who was he?'

'Well. I can answer that,' Trix's voice was even more smug, irritatingly so now. 'In 2003 there was a mortar explosion in Basra, and an officer lost his foot in the blast. The reports are all missing though, apart from one note made in a prosthetics lab when the replacement foot was being made. The name of the officer was Colonel Abbasi of the Cardigan Regiment.'

'*I lost my foot in a mortar attack. Iraq War. Accidental, but enough to give me an out.*'

'Christ,' Declan hissed. 'He wasn't being bullied by Winston Eaton-Jones. He was his bloody superior officer.'

'Not according to his military records,' Trix continued. 'In 2004, Colonel Abbasi simply disappeared. It looks like he went off grid, possibly working for the security services, and didn't return until 2010, when he moved to Castleton, buying his house outright. Since then, apart from a few trips abroad, he's lived there quite happily.'

'How soon after the closure of the Cardigans did he return?'

'A matter of months.'

Declan nodded to himself.

'Colin mentioned a Colonel,' he said. 'I thought it could be Yates, but Colin mentioned something that made me think the Colonel was Arabic. I think it could be Old Ram, as his parents were Syrian.'

'I'm guessing Old Ram's a cool, fun nickname for him?'

Declan nodded, but then remembered he was on the phone.

'Everything he does and says is to move away from the Colonel persona,' he muttered. 'Even led a journalist to local gossip, making him a bullied minority. Do you have anything on the Cardigans?'

'Still waiting,' Trix was typing as she spoke. 'When I get something, I'll send it to Savile Row.'

Declan knew she meant Billy by this and smiled.

'He'll appreciate it. And I owe you,' he said.

'You always do,' Trix replied. 'So how about you repay some of the favour and tell me what you found out in St Davids?'

Leaning back on the bed, Declan told Trix everything.

COLIN DELANEY WAS TIRED, BUT HE WASN'T GETTING ANY SLEEP tonight.

He was a nervous wreck; every time the door to his room opened, he jumped, usually to the amusement of whichever nurse was entering. In fact, Colin was convinced they were doing it deliberately now, every hour throughout the night, screwing about with his mental state. Probably heard about the scuffle in A&E when he came in, most likely. He'd seen the expressions when he pushed away the nurse; he'd been within his rights, the bloody woman probably couldn't even speak English. There were enough white staff around, and any of those could have dealt with his wounds. Less likely to infect him, too. Who knew what tropical viruses the nurse he'd pushed away had? He'd probably saved his own life by doing it.

Yeah. Exactly.

It wasn't his fault she overbalanced. God, the whining she made was shrill and annoying. He was the victim; he was the one with the gut wound.

And then he'd been talking to the Corporal about the club, and it felt good to talk to a proper Patriot, but something had felt off by the end and he'd said he was too tired to continue. It felt more of an interview than a back and forth, and Colin wasn't an idiot. He knew when he was being played. He'd probably given away more than he should before his survival instinct kicked in. It wasn't his fault. The black bitch had probably dosed him with something. A truth serum of some kind.

Yeah. That too.

The door opened again and Colin jumped, but this time someone new entered the room.

'You're in the wrong room, mate,' Colin hissed. ' but while you're here, get me a coffee, yeah? I ain't sleeping, so I might as well make the most of it.'

The man who'd entered walked over to Colin, hands behind his back checking the whiteboard beside him, as if he was some kind of medical expert and, in the light, Colin recognised him. He was wearing a *Barbour* jacket, so not a Doctor, but the beard was a dead giveaway, and the dark skin—

'I hear you've been talking to the police,' the man said calmly. 'About things you shouldn't be talking about.'

Colin paled.

'You're the Colonel,' he whispered. 'I heard about you.'

'What did you tell the police?'

'I ain't spoken to any police,' Colin insisted. 'I talked with another patient. He was a Patriot too.'

'Detective Inspector Declan Walsh,' the Colonel replied, his right hand appearing from behind his back, a phone in it. On the screen was an image; a man, standing outside a café. The same man that had been talking to Colin earlier that day, that had claimed a head wound from a duel.

Colin felt like he was about to be sick.

'I didn't know,' he said. 'The bitches, they put something in my drip. I swear.'

'It's all right, Gunner Delaney. We can fix this. Did you tell

Walsh anything from the night of your duel?' the Colonel asked as he glanced back at the door.

'Of course not!' Colin tried to puff out his chest, false bravado on his face. 'I don't shit where I—'

He didn't finish the statement, as the Colonel suddenly lunged across the bed, slamming Colin against the mattress with his right forearm while ramming a wet wash towel, held in his left hand against Colin's nose and mouth, sealing them, stopping him from breathing; as he opened his mouth to scream for help, he inhaled the water from the towel, causing him to cough and splutter as the man forced the cloth harder onto Colin's face, suffocating him.

This must be what it feels like to be waterboarded was the last thought that ran through Colin's mind before his eyes glazed over and he slumped against the pillow, dead.

The Colonel leaned back, wiping down Colin's damp chin and nose before folding the cloth and placing it in his outer jacket pocket.

And, after quickly checking for a pulse and nodding with approval at the lack of any sign of one, Retired Colonel Ramesh Abbasi left the now dead Colin in peace.

18

BRIEFED IN

MONROE CAME TO VISIT DECLAN AT EIGHT THE FOLLOWING morning, and was surprised to find him already up and dressed, sitting in the chair beside the bed with a smile on his face.

'Well, you're a ray of light,' Monroe smiled in return. 'Good night's sleep?'

'I think I've got a few new leads in the case,' Declan rose from the chair. 'First off, come with me.'

'Declan,' Monroe stopped him. 'I need to tell you something first.'

Declan paused beside the bed, watching Monroe.

'What?' he asked.

'Someone tried to shoot Anjli last night,' Monroe replied, his voice soft as he spoke. 'Some sort of black power pistol. Not the same as Falconer's, a smaller calibre—'

Declan started for the door again, anger in his eyes.

'She's fine!' Monroe continued as he followed. 'I think they did it to scare her. Apparently Carrie and Devin Harper were there, and they've said they'll explain everything.'

'Because of *course* they know about it,' Declan snapped, nodding to the quite surprised nurse who stopped as she was about to enter.

'I don't think you should be up and running,' she stated, frowning at Declan. 'You were in a very nasty accident.'

'And yet a night of bed rest has done me wonders,' Declan smiled. 'I'll just be a moment.'

Walking Monroe down the corridor, Declan stopped in front of a door.

'Why haven't you arrested them?' he asked, still staring at it rather than at Monroe.

'Because they didn't do anything,' Monroe replied, placing a hand on Declan's shoulder. 'Dammit, laddie, you need to calm down. They saved Anjli's life.'

At this, Declan sagged, as if the anger had suddenly dissipated from his body.

'I could have lost her,' he hissed. 'The whole bloody reason we're here is because I keep losing people.'

'No,' Monroe shook his head. 'It's because you won't *forgive yourself* when you do.'

Declan stared blankly at Monroe for a moment, before rapping his knuckles on one of the side doors.

'Now, why are we here exactly?' Monroe asked.

Declan smiled at him, opening the door.

'You decent, Colin?' he enquired jovially as he entered.

Monroe followed him to find a very confused young nurse, straightening an empty bed.

'Where's Colin Delaney?' Declan stopped, looking around the room, equally confused by the situation.

'And you are?' the nurse rose, hands on her hips. Deciding to speed things along, Monroe showed his warrant card.

'Not in the mood for any arguments,' he said, pointing at the bed. 'The man. Name that my colleague said. Where is he?'

'Poor bugger passed away last night,' the nurse explained, carrying on with the straightening as she spoke. 'Wounds were infected. It happens.'

'He was fine last night,' Declan hissed.

'As I said, it happens,' the nurse now walked past the two detectives, walking out into the ward, leaving them staring at an empty bed. 'Speak with the duty manager if you have any more questions, I'm sure there'll be an inquest, there always is in these cases. You're not the only ones not in the mood for any arguments.'

Declan stared at the now pristine bed.

'He was a TA in Sheffield Bailey Barracks,' he muttered. 'Duelled Falconer the day before Falconer died. Claimed he knew the mysterious *Colonel*, who I think is Ramesh Abbasi.'

'That's a bit of a jump,' Monroe exclaimed.

'Trix helped me,' Declan shrugged. 'Found some records that'd been missed. She's sending them to Billy. Looks like Abbasi scrubbed his identity, but he was a Colonel in the Cardigan Regiment back in 2003 when the blast in Iraq took his foot.'

'Looks like you have been busy,' Monroe nodded. 'Luckily, so have we. Come on, laddie. Let's get you out of here; the dead aren't going anywhere.'

———

BILLY SAT AT HIS COMPUTER, ALONE IN THE OFFICE, WORKING through databases on Owen Russell's USB drive, when Colonel Yates leaned in through the door.

'Terrible state of things last night, eh?' he said conversationally. 'DC Fitzwarren, right?'

'Yes, sir,' Billy looked up from his laptop, unsure whether he should stand, salute or just ignore the officer. 'But he's doing better.'

'Oh, yes, Walsh,' Yates considered this. 'I was talking about the Indian girl.'

'You mean DS Kapoor?' Billy's tone darkened. 'I don't think she'd appreciate being called that.'

'Apologies,' Yates raised a hand. 'Didn't mean to cause any problems, just wanted to see how the case was going.'

'Well, as an ongoing investigation—'

Yates walked into the room now, and immediately Billy felt the Colonel's imposing presence fill it.

'An ongoing investigation I brought you all in on,' Yates replied, his tone icy. 'How about you fill me in?'

'Well, we're still in the guesswork stage,' Billy said, trying to work out how to minimise the information that Yates would receive. 'Actually, could you help me with something?'

'Of course,' Yates smiled, but it never reached his eyes. 'Shoot.'

Ignoring the comment, Billy pulled up a sheet on his screen.

'I have Staff Sergeant Moses applying for an *acquire and keep* explosives certificate in late 2019,' he read from the screen. 'Did you know anything about that?'

'You mean, did I know he was keeping explosives? No, I don't think so,' Yates replied cagily.

'That's odd, sir, because we have you down as a reference,' Billy turned to face Yates. 'You're the reason he got it.'

'Is this for black powder?' Yates asked, changing his story

immediately. 'Yes, sorry, I don't really class that as explosives. It's a little bang, whereas I deal with items that create far more damage.'

'So you do remember this?'

'Of course,' the fake smile was back. 'He applied for it, I offered to assist him. He wanted to get involved with a military club we had down there.'

'The Templar Corps?' Billy asked.

Yates didn't reply, instead staring at Billy for a long, uncomfortable moment.

'Fitzwarren,' he said. 'You got military in the family? I seem to recall a Lieutenant Colonel Fitzwarren in the Yeoman Guard.'

'He's my second cousin.'

'Good man, I recall. Understands soldiering. I hear you turned down the dorms here?'

'Prefer my own company.'

'In the Castle Tun?'

Billy forced his expression to stay neutral while processing the fact that Colonel Yates seemed to know exactly where everyone was.

'Yes,' he replied.

'In the room Staff Sergeant Moses stayed in.'

'You know it?'

Yates shook his head.

'I never visited it,' he replied, almost wistfully, before turning back to the door. 'Well, I shouldn't keep you—'

'Did you not want the update?' Billy rose now.

Yates, now looking visibly shaken, shook his head.

'No, that's fine. I'll come back later.'

'Any messages for DI Walsh?' Billy asked.

'Where is Declan?' Yates looked back, suspicious. 'I heard he'd checked out?'

'Still in Sheffield, I believe,' Billy lied. He knew Declan was on his way back, as he'd just sent everyone an email about his chat with another patient there as Monroe drove him back to the office.

'Well, I hope he's okay, and not trying to interview Colin Delaney again,' Yates muttered. 'Gunner Delaney passed away last night. Complications, I hear.'

And before Billy could reply, Colonel Yates nodded to him and left the office, nodding absently to an MDP officer, standing half hidden by the door.

Billy stared after Yates; for a man who wanted an update on things, he seemed to know more than everyone else.

'Sorry, can I help you?' Billy eventually asked the officer.

'I hope so,' the officer replied. 'We have two boxes from Portsmouth for you. Staff Sergeant Moses' things.'

'Excellent,' Billy forced a smile. 'Pass them to DC Davey in forensics next door, please.'

As the officer left the doorway, Billy's attention was distracted by a *ping* on his laptop. It was an email from Trix.

Hey Savile Row, Declan asked me to send this to you if I found anything.

Cardigan Regiment - 2008, right before they were disbanded - no commanding officers named.

Cardigan Regiment - 2007, one year before they were disbanded:

Second Lieutenant Henry Arthur Eaton-Jones,

Major Charles Peter Falconer,

Major Barry Oswald Yates

Lieutenant Colonel Winston Lewis Eaton-Jones

Also

Colonel Ramesh Abbasi (Retired)

Billy stared at the message. They already knew Eaton-Jones had been a Colonel by the time he left, and that his son had joined as Second Lieutenant. They also knew that Falconer had only been made Lieutenant Colonel shortly before the disbanding, which matched this list, a year earlier.

Declan had primed them all in his email about Old Ram's true identity, but one name was a shock.

Colonel Yates of the Special Investigation Bureau had been in the Cardigan Regiment. He'd been the commanding officer of Eaton-Jones and Sergeant Patrick Harper, and the same rank as Falconer.

How did this affect the case, and what was Yates' connection to the murders?

———

DC DAVEY STARTED LAUGHING AS DECLAN WALKED THROUGH the doors to the classroom-turned-briefing-room, and current home of the Last Chance Saloon.

'Pay up,' she said to De'Geer, reluctantly reaching for his wallet. 'I told you he wouldn't stay in there.'

'Not only has he not stayed in there, so to speak, but he's also been questioning witnesses and going undercover,' Monroe replied, shaking his head at a surprised Anjli. 'Not my story to tell, lassie. I'm sure he'll be going over everything in the briefing.'

'We need to be brief in the briefing,' Declan said quickly, walking to the back of the room. 'We're on the back foot and need to move fast. Updates, then action. After I grab a brew, that is.'

As the others settled into places, Anjli walked over to Declan, now grabbing a mug of tea from a purloined kettle on a back table.

'How you feeling?' she asked.

'Better,' Declan replied, looking down at the mug. 'Headache lessened a lot once they loosened the bandage.'

'Well, they needed it on to keep your brain in,' Anjli said knowledgeably. 'They probably didn't realise there wasn't that much in there to save.'

Declan had been taking a mouthful of tea as she spoke, and now snorted it into the mug.

'Thanks,' he said, grabbing a tissue and wiping his face. 'Now I have mouth burns to add to the list.'

'More reasons we should tuck you up in bed.'

'Oh aye?' Declan raised an eyebrow impishly. 'You gonna be the one tucking me in, are you?'

Anjli paled.

'Oh, God, I—um, I mean to say I didn't—'

'I heard about the shooting,' Declan said, his face shadowing. 'You okay?'

'Yeah, it was just a scare,' Anjli tried to throw her nervousness off, but Declan could see she was still quite shaken by it. 'Led us to an interesting revelation.'

'Cullen?' Declan nodded gingerly, worried his head might fall off. 'Monroe caught me up in the car. That and the fact that Keith Williams and Laurence Graham might be part of this too.'

'Also, we think the rifle might not exist, either,' Anjli grinned. 'You disappear? We do way more work. You should consider making this permanent.'

She stopped, her eyes widening.

'I didn't—that is—God, I'm rubbish at talking today.'

'Don't worry, it's okay,' Declan looked back to the front of the room, nodding for someone to begin.

'Right then, let's get this started,' Doctor Marcos spoke up. 'As you're just getting on your feet, Deckers, you mind if I start?'

'Not at all,' ignoring the nickname, Declan leaned against the table as Doctor Marcos nodded to Billy.

'I can't put photos on the screen here,' he muttered in response.

'Yes, but I gave you blu-tac and some print outs, so you can go full analogue on us,' Doctor Marcos smiled winningly. 'Don't play with traditions, DC Fitzwarren. You heard the man. We're in a rush.'

Cursing under his breath, Billy stuck images onto the board as Doctor Marcos pointed at two already on there, those of Eddie Moses and Charles Falconer.

'So, we thought there were two separate cases here,' she said, looking back to the team; Declan and Anjli at the back table, De'Geer next to Davey, and Monroe beside the door. 'The body of Staff Sergeant Edward Moses, found a week back, but killed a year ago, and Lieutenant Colonel Charles Falconer, killed a week back, on the same day they found Moses. We now believe these deaths are connected.'

Doctor Marcos nodded to Declan as she continued.

'I don't know how much of this you already know, but when checking Falconer's dorm, DS Kapoor and PC De'Geer found some things,' she said, pointing at a plywood box and what looked to be a gun in a clear forensic bag.

'Is that the gun Falconer picked up from Moses' room?' Declan asked, leaning in to look closer.

'No,' Monroe shook his head. 'It's not marked. I checked.'

'It's a Remington New Army 1858 black powder pistol,' Doctor Marcos explained. 'That is, it's a replica. This one, judging from the patina on the side, is an *Uberti* replica from Italy, no more than a couple of years old.'

'And it fires silver musket balls?' Declan asked.

'In a way, yes,' Doctor Marcos pulled on a pair of latex gloves, opening the bag. 'We've checked it over, the only fingerprints on it are Falconer's.'

She held the gun up, showing it off to the class.

'It's the gun Clint Eastwood uses in his films where he plays *The Man With No Name*,' she said, pulling the hammer back. 'Released in 1863—'

'You said 1858,' Declan interrupted.

'I did, and well done for listening, Deckers,' Doctor Marcos replied with a hint of sarcasm. 'The patent was applied for in 1858, and the gun came out in 1863, just in time for the American Civil War to really get some use from it. As you can see, it's a single-action, six-shot percussion revolver in .44 calibre, with an eight-inch barrel length. The chambers, however, don't have traditional bullets inside; instead you pour in black powder, ram a greased wad in, put your bullet in by using a loading lever here—' she pulled a lever at the base of the barrel down, '—and once it's all wedged in, you place a percussion cap here, on a nipple at the back of the loaded cylinder.'

'*Cap gun*,' Declan nodded as he looked at Monroe. 'That's why Maureen Williams thought it was a toy.'

'It's far from a toy,' Doctor Marcos admonished. 'It's killed hundreds of people. Not this particular one, but the gun, over the centuries.'

'The bullet we found in Sergeant Moses was a .44,' Billy

pointed at an image he'd just put up. 'It matches the other balls found in Falconer's possession, which are a mixture of both lead and silver. He'd also been grazed on the arm with a bullet, and there was a darkening on his chest area which matched a possible burn or bruise, but the body was too far gone to accurately explain it.'

'Maybe the gun blew back on him?' Billy suggested. 'The black powder burning the skin?'

'Unlikely, as the chambers are blocked,' Doctor Marcos mused. 'And that's not the only thing, anyway. The grazed arm had remnants of *Sulphonamide Powder* inside, which hasn't been used since the war. And here's the fun part: I found the same powder in wounds on Falconer's body.'

'Falconer was apparently a top duellist, according to Colin Delaney,' Declan replied. He'd sent a message explaining who the Gunner was while Monroe had driven, and was grateful to see that everyone had read it, or at least was too embarrassed to ask who Colin was. 'He'd probably gained his share of injuries there.'

'He has at least two bullet holes, one in his thigh and one in his side, around here,' Doctor Marcos tapped her midsection, before pointing at a photo now stuck on the board behind her. It was a reddened and burned chest.

'As I said, Moses had a similar marking on his chest, but we know what *this* one is,' she explained. 'It looks like a scalding mark, and in a way, it was. It's above and to the left of the ICD unit that melted, and it looks as if someone was aiming down from that angle at him.'

'Falconer was giving a talk,' De'Geer read from his notes. 'Doctor Cullen, his research assistant stated the day that he died, he stood behind a lectern for forty minutes.'

'Easily enough time to aim and fire,' Anjli nodded. 'Although he would have felt the burning.'

'If the rifle even exists,' Declan muttered. 'I understand you have thoughts on that too?'

'Falconer created a portable laser that blinded his opponents,' Anjli read from her notes. 'He would fire it a second before his opponent fired, aiming at their face. They'd shoot wide, while he'd shoot true. Doctor Cullen was looking for it last night, but believed it was built into a specially made flak jacket.'

'I thought the club was supposed to be honourable?' Doctor Marcos asked.

'It is,' Monroe added. 'Cullen said he was likely to be kicked out because of it, but he'd started to slow as he got older, and he couldn't bear to be beaten. So he looked for ways to assist his shots.'

'By blinding the opponent. With that and the Nazi memorabilia, Falconer must have been great fun at parties,' Doctor Marcos muttered, her face scowling.

Declan nodded.

'Colin said similar,' he replied. 'Said Falconer looked like Robocop with flashing lights.'

'Sounds about right,' Monroe looked at Doctor Marcos. 'You have a theory?'

'Electromagnetic currents,' Doctor Marcos nodded. 'The jacket wasn't a major part of the laser, it was used to hold the batteries. A lot of them. All wired up to create the power for the millisecond blast he used to blind his opponent.'

'Doctor Cullen spoke to us about this,' Anjli flicked through her notebook, searching for something. 'She said anything that produces a strong electromagnetic field can affect a pacemaker, and that big laser batteries did this.'

'Exactly,' Doctor Marcos nodded. 'Falconer knew the risks of wearing the jacket in duels, because he'd worked with the magnetic fields for years while having a pacemaker attached. The duels were micro-bursts of energy, a millisecond of power, no more.'

She nodded to Billy, who placed another image on the whiteboard. This was of Falconer, on stage, behind a lectern.

He was wearing a flak jacket.

'The day Moses was found, Doctor Cullen believed that someone had learned she was whistleblowing on the Regiment and their actions, in particular the Templar Corps. But when I say she, I mean Falconer, because she was using his ID to keep anonymous.'

'So they thought Falconer was the grass,' Monroe added.

'Falconer heard this; people in the room stated he was tense throughout his talk, and, for some reason, wore his army flak jacket.'

'He feared being shot,' Anjli realised. 'But in the process, he wore the electromagnet battery for over half an hour. I think he didn't realise he'd turned it on.'

'And in doing so overloaded his IDC, melting components within which, a little while later, added to the intense heat from the battery and the stress he was under, forced his heart to give out.,' Doctor Marcos looked up at Declan. 'There's no sniper rifle. It was simply Falconer, paranoid, killing himself.'

'What about the burn on the skin?' Anjli asked. Doctor Marcos considered this.

'Find me the jacket,' she said. 'I reckon you'll find a burned out battery right here.'

She tapped her upper chest.

'Battery overheats and scalds the chest, Falconer probably

didn't even realise, with all the other stuff going on right then.'

'But nobody else realised this,' Declan leaned against the table, sipping his tea. 'God, they're hunting ghosts.'

'No, Declan, we're hunting ghosts,' Monroe smiled. 'And we've only just started.'

19

INTERVIEW WITH AN UMPIRE

'Okay then,' Declan continued. 'What else do we know?'

'Falconer knew Moses in passing, had met him in Syria three years ago and trusted him enough to lend him a gun, like the one Anjli and De'Geer found,' Monroe replied. 'Or at least take it back.'

'He also took part in some kind of inter-regimental war gaming,' De'Geer read from his notes. 'I'm guessing it was a little more up close and personal than dice and pewter figures, possibly the same as the ones mentioned between the Army and the Navy before World War Two.'

'I think we can pretty much confirm that,' Anjli nodded. 'So far, we have four guns; the Remington .44 we found in Falconer's room, the one Falconer picked up from Moses, which we're told had 'boy' scratched onto the base, and two Colt Navy .36 calibre pistols. One used by Colin, the other by the man who shot at me.'

'Maybe they were the same gun,' Declan replied. 'Colin said he borrowed his gun from some bald ex-army reservist.'

'Keith Williams is a reservist, and he's bald,' Monroe

muttered. 'And he knew where the moped was. And he'd have known how to get Moses out of his room a year back.'

'And the bullet fired at me was from that size,' Anjli nodded.

As if remembering something, Declan reached into his pocket, pulling out the silver musket ball.

'Prints!' Doctor Marcos hissed.

'It was found on the floor of the cave before it fell on me,' Declan replied. 'Any prints are long gone. What size is it?'

Doctor Marcos took the ball from Declan, checking it.

'Same as the one that fired at DS Kapoor, so a .36,' she said. 'Damaged, but not flattened like...'

She stopped.

'Hold that thought,' she said, leaving the room.

'How hard is it to get one of these guns?' Davey asked, watching her boss leave. 'Don't you need a licence?'

'You need an *acquire and keep* explosives certificate, which allows you to hold shooters powder,' De'Geer replied. 'Falconer had one.'

'So did Moses,' Billy looked up. 'I did some digging. He applied for one in Portsmouth. Colonel Yates signed off on his application.'

'You sure it was Yates?' Declan was surprised at this.

Billy nodded.

'That's not all. Trix Preston sent me a list of Cardigan officers, the year before it was disbanded,' he explained as he reached into his waistcoat pocket and pulled out his notebook, opening it up on the last page, reading from it. 'Names included Second Lieutenant Henry Eaton-Jones, Major Charles Falconer, as he gained his Lieutenant Colonel pips a year or so later, Lieutenant Colonel Winston Lewis Eaton-

Jones, Major Barry Oswald Yates and Colonel Ramesh Abbasi.'

'Postie's middle name was Oswald?' Declan shook his head. 'I don't know what the bigger revelation is there.'

'So now we have a list of the bastards, including the sneakiest one of all, Old Ram,' Monroe muttered. 'Another bugger to bring in.'

'Yates was here earlier,' Billy added. 'Although he left in a Land Rover before you arrived.'

'Tell me more about the licence,' Declan shook his head, returning to the problem at hand.

'Well, Eddie Moses must have known what he was getting into before he came up to the Peak District, if he was getting a licence—' Monroe mused, but stopped as he saw Billy shake his head. '—He didn't?'

'Guv, Eddie Moses came up here a year back. That we know. We also know he came up briefly before, to apologise to Carrie Harper. Before that though, he was deployed in Europe, was found in Syria after that... he applied for the licence *over two years* ago.'

Declan stared at Billy for a moment.

'Why else would you need one of these certificates?' he asked carefully. 'Is there a reason why Moses had this that *didn't* involve these guns?'

'Maybe if he was clay shooting, or something similar?' Anjli offered.

'Well, the *1997 Firearms Act* effectively banned all guns, except for things like muzzle-loading pistols and revolvers,' Billy read from a page on his screen. 'You also need a firearms certificate, and proof you're a part of a historical reenactment club or shooting club.'

'So as long as you're not a criminal or mad, you're probably okay here,' Anjli wrote this down. 'I'm guessing it's easier for serving military too?'

Declan leaned back, sighing.

'So we have some kind of duelling club, using American Civil War guns,' he worked through his thought process aloud. 'Members include Charles Falconer and Colin Delaney, as well as likely candidates Henry Eaton-Jones, Keith Williams, Devin Harper and probably Barry Yates. We'll come back to that in a minute. Tell me about the receipt.'

'Basic thermo-science,' Davey blushed.

'Eddie Moses bought a pay as you go phone in Sheffield the same day he arrived in Castleton,' Billy added. 'An *Alcatel 1* Android phone on the EE network.'

'Aye, we saw the texts,' Monroe nodded. 'Any ideas yet on the two numbers that weren't known?'

'Both burners, but I'm waiting to see if I can get anything more from the carriers,' Billy shook his head. 'I wouldn't hold your breath. I did, however, pick up a piece of guest-house stationary from the room and pass it to DC Davey.'

'It's a match for the paper he wrote the note to you on,' Davey nodded. 'He must have written it and tore it off the sheet the night he tried to run.'

'Or before he was taken,' Monroe's face darkened.

'Which brings us to the next elephant in the room,' Declan smiled. 'The Templar Corps.'

'Far-right racist dickheads,' Anjli muttered.

'Well, we think they're far-right and racist, but as yet we don't have conclusive proof,' Monroe replied. 'They're definitely dickheads though.'

'Either way, it looks like they're led by Eaton-Jones.'

'If not the son, then definitely the dad back in the day,'

Declan nodded. 'Who's now a Brigadier and in Whitehall. Can we check what he's up to these days, and how close he is to the new Prime Minister? Maybe Bullman got a hint when she spoke to Baker's lapdog?'

Billy walked to the whiteboard, pinning the image that Declan had sent him by phone.

'This is what Owen Russell drew,' he explained. 'Two Maltese Crosses and a Swastika. The symbol they used on Old Ram, according to what Owen was told.'

'Which is now likely a load of bollocks, deliberately designed to get Owen on his side,' Monroe muttered.

'Why?' Declan mused aloud. 'Why go to all this trouble? He leaves in 2003. Disappears, comes back in 2010. Colin called him The Colonel, talked about him like he was Jesus.'

'Maybe Ramesh Abbasi is the head of the Templar Corps,' Billy suggested.

'Of a racist Nazi group?' Davey's eyes widened. 'I don't think his type is usually allowed in those clubs.'

'Maybe it's not as Nazi as we think?' De'Geer suggested. 'I mean, I know we have the medals and all that, but something's definitely off here.'

'De'Geer may have something there. This is what the symbols would usually look like,' Billy reached back to his table and picked up another three sheets of paper. The first one was then stuck to the wall.

'That's what I saw on the tobacco box,' Declan nodded. 'Almost identical.'

'I think we've also seen it before in another way,' Billy pinned up another image; a close up of the screwdriver marks on Edward Moses' ID tag, the cross haired screwdriver marks either side of a star-shaped torq symbol. 'I think this is a way to say you're a member without showing symbols.'

'Christ,' Monroe leaned back. 'If you're right, laddie, then Falconer and Moses had these.'

'Not just them,' Billy reached back, placing another image on the wall. It was that of a woman, in her twenties, black hair hanging down over a coroner's table, her left, naked arm visible to the camera.

'This is an autopsy photo of Lena Khoury, one of the bodies found with Patrick Harper when he was killed, over ten years ago,' Billy explained. 'She was Sheffield bar staff, but she was also non-deployable TA infantry, just like Colin Delaney. Same Unit, just ten years' difference. Shot in the head, the bullet removed. But unknown to the killer, she had this tattoo.'

The image was similar to the one on the tobacco tin, but the Swastika had been replaced by a swirled image.

'She altered the middle circle,' Monroe mused. 'Maybe she didn't want her Swastika public?'

Anjli shook her head. 'No, wait. *Khoury*. That's Syrian, or Lebanon in name. Likewise Lena.'

'So?'

'So De'Geer's right. If you're a far-right racist, you're not letting a Lebanese woman into your order,' Anjli argued. 'And the chances are a Lebanese woman wouldn't want to be a Nazi.'

'You're both right,' Billy moved to his laptop. 'However, I found the same image in the USB files Owen Russell passed to us.'

On the screen, the image in Lena's tattoo was visible; now red, it was surrounded by a black circle.

'This is the symbol of the Syrian Social Nationalist Party, or SSNP,' Billy explained. 'They're—'

'A fascist organisation filled with Syrian Nationalists, definitely not friendly,' Declan intoned, reading from his notebook. 'Susan Jenkins was investigating them, maybe even Lena herself, given the closeness of their deaths.'

'They also work from Lebanon as well,' Billy added. 'Explains why Lena could have joined.'

'So, we need to work out what the Templar Corps was then,' Declan sighed. 'If it's more than a gun club, what was their plan? Are they led by one of the Eaton-Joneses, or Colonel Abbasi? Nazi or Syrian? It can't be a coincidence Eddie was there in 2019. And, more importantly, what caused him to be killed?'

'Billy mentioned in the bar last night that Khouri was a bit New World Order,' Anjli suggested. 'If she was SSNP, that definitely fits. Maybe that's more their line?'

Doctor Marcos walked back into the room now.

'Anything new?' Monroe asked. Doctor Marcos nodded at Declan.

'Your man, Moses, wasn't killed by the bullet we thought,' she said. 'The silver .44 was flattened as if it hit something hard. I assumed this was because the silver was softer than lead. However, the one you gave me? Looks more like the fired duelling bullets I'd been researching. The one we believed killed Moses? Matched the one that hit the wall beside DS Kapoor.'

'What are you saying?' Declan asked.

'I'm saying, and this is purely speculation, that the one you found is the ball that was in Eddie Moses, and a larger silver one, taken from another duel, perhaps one where it hit a wall and flattened slightly, was placed into the bag instead, the other discarded, possibly when the body was 'found' in the cave.'

Declan looked around the room.

'Colin gave me the impression the Colonel was with the body the night before Falconer died,' he said. 'If he swapped bullets, making the gun that killed Eddie a larger calibre, he was deliberately aiming it at Falconer.'

'He wanted Falconer discredited, maybe because he mistakenly believed he was informing on the Templar Corps,' Anjli nodded at this. 'And it means that whomever killed Eddie Moses was using a smaller bore gun.'

Declan sighed, rapping his fingers on the desk as he considered this. After a moment, he stopped.

'Guv, do me a favour and look into Major Eaton-Jones again. See what we missed, maybe press him on his dad. Look into the gun club too. DS Kapoor and I will have a chat with the Harpers. DC Davey, could you look at Falconer's diary?'

'Already on it,' Davey nodded. 'To be brutally honest, it's mainly just notes about his work, done with initials, probably to stop spies or something. We've worked out a few things, like EC being Elaine Cullen, his assistant, and CF being Charles Falconer. There's a RA that we can't—'

'RA?' Monroe looked up. 'Ramesh Abbasi?'

'Dammit, that makes sense, Guv,' Davey rolled her eyes. 'If the RA in the diary is part of the project, or at least involved in assisting Falconer, then he'd be given a pass to enter and leave the facility.'

Monroe went to reply, but stopped as he looked at the door to the room.

'Declan,' he breathed, and Declan looked around, seeing Devin Harper in the doorway.

'I think we need to talk,' he said. 'About everything.'

———

'Do we need this to be official?' Declan asked as he sat opposite Devin, Anjli to his side. Devin shrugged.

'Your call,' he said, cautiously. 'Although you might get more if this is off the record.'

Declan leaned back in the chair as he examined the man sitting in front of him.

'Where's your sister?'

'No idea,' Devin admitted. 'She was supposed to pick me up. I'm guessing she's running.'

'And you didn't?'

'I've nothing to hide.'

Declan gathered his papers together, reading a couple of hand-written notes before looking back up.

'Are you a member of the Templar Corps?' he asked.

'I thought you'd ask about the guns,' Devin replied, shaken.

'And I will,' Declan leaned back, placing his hands on the table. 'First, I want you to answer *that* question.'

Devin looked uncomfortable.

'I'm a member of the Templar Corps,' he admitted before looking back at Declan. 'But it's not what you think it is. It's a group based on order. About routine, planning. Standing still and facing adversity. It's why we use duelling; you stand still and face off against each other, honourably. There's no hiding—'

'And the *Nazi* part?' Declan interrupted, having had enough. 'Because from what I recall, they weren't that big on honourable things. The routines, planning, order, all that, *sure*. But they really weren't the people I'd have started a society emulating.'

'I didn't start it,' Devin snapped. 'I'm no Nazi. And I'm here to help.'

Declan stared at Devin.

'Where's the tattoo?' he asked coldly. 'I'm guessing you have it?'

'Dog tags, like the others,' he replied.

Declan nodded, writing this down.

'Carrie had the symbols tattooed on her arm, didn't she?' he asked. 'The Maltese Crosses and the Swastika? But what, she decided it was a bit much, and rather than laser them off she burned them away?'

Devin pursed his lips.

'My dad had them on his chest,' he said. 'Small tattoo, nothing major, stuck in the middle of a load of others. Henry —Major Eaton-Jones, that is, he told us about them, explained what they meant. We liked it. And as a teenager, she made her own.'

'I bet that made him proud,' Anjli muttered.

'It wasn't a Swastika then,' Devin protested. 'I mean, it was, but not the Nazi one. It's not the *hakenkreuz*. The symbol's been around for millennia—'

Anjli held her hand up.

'I know,' she said. 'I hear it all the time, how it was sanskrit, how *Coke* had it on their bottle at one point, *Carlsberg* too, even American military units during World War One used it. Doesn't make it right, doesn't stop what they did with it, what people still do with it.'

'No, it doesn't,' Devin agreed. 'Originally, it was used to represent the power of Thor. Thunder and lightning, matching the smoke and flame from a pistol. But over the years, it was changed. And, as the Templar Corps changed, so did the message. The middle symbol is personal to the member. Some have a Swastika, sure, but I had the original itineration, the symbol for Thor.'

'So is it Eaton-Jones senior or junior who runs it?' Declan asked. 'Or is it Ramesh Abbasi?'

'The Colonel,' Devin eventually replied. 'Abbasi. He created it with Eaton-Jones senior, but he disappeared for a few years. I think he was working undercover in Syria. When he came back, he took it over.'

'And Henry let him?'

'His dad was gone, and The Colonel—well, he was the next best thing. His time away changed him. Made him colder. The duelling club that was made to gain a little adrenaline rush became more, and Henry realised that even though they'd clashed in the past, Ramesh and he shared the same beliefs. Nationalism, all that.'

Declan noted this down. Ramesh Abbasi had sat in front

of him without a care in the world. An hour later, Declan had been buried in a landfall.

'Who threw the grenade?' he hissed.

'I don't know,' Devin replied. 'We were finishing manoeuvres. I went to find my sister.'

'So only Old Ram isn't counted for, and he was last seen walking in the same direction,' Declan mused. 'Carry on.'

'When did you join the Templar Corps?' Anjli asked.

'I started shooting when I was fourteen,' Devin replied calmly. 'Found my dad's revolver, and Charles Falconer helped teach me.'

Declan leaned back in his chair, considering what he'd heard.

'The .36?' he asked.

'Yes.'

'Ever shoot Eddie with it?'

Devin stayed quiet.

'Why did Eddie Moses come back?' Declan continued.

'He had issues with... with *me*,' Devin looked to the floor. 'He'd come back to apologise, some kind of apology tour. Part of the twelve steps and all that. He'd had a *come to Jesus* moment, and now he was making amends. He came to find us to apologise for killing our dad. Explained that he didn't know if he'd even done the right thing with it. Anyway, Carrie didn't really want to chat to him, said it was all fine and he could piss off, you know, but he goes looking for me. I'd just become Second Lieutenant, and I was just into the order, too.'

''So you challenged him.'

'Yeah. Bloody stupid of me, to be honest. I didn't know he'd been training down south with Yates.'

'Colonel Yates was a member too?' Declan considered this. 'He was ex-Cardigan Regiment. Of course he was a bloody member. And it explains why he signed off on Moses' application.'

'I thought it was an honourable duel,' Devin's voice was cracking a little as he spoke. 'Henry had brought me to the range—'

'The one under the research labs?'

'Yes, he took me there to second him on a contest duel with someone from Light Infantry, but when I heard Eddie Moses was in the area, I demanded satisfaction. Wanted a full on face off. As it was, it never happened. Until a year later.'

'When he came back,' Anjli was writing in her notebook.

'Henry was pissed that Yates stopped the duel and took it to the top,' Devin continued. 'Straight to daddy himself. Explained I'd been wronged, and Eddie Moses needed to follow the rules.'

'So he was pressured to come north?' Declan rubbed at his bandage; it was feeling tight again. 'Do you know who made him?'

'In the end, it was your old boss,' Devin continued. 'Didn't you ever wonder why Yates wanted the whole thing with my dad swept under the table? How you were pushed away from continuing with it? He's been involved since the bloody start.'

Declan looked at the door to the office, fighting the urge to rise, leave and find his ex-commanding officer right now.

'Your sister met with Moses before the duel, didn't she?' Anjli now enquired. 'She visited him at the guesthouse.'

'She did,' Devin straightened, as if expecting an argument. 'When you duel, you need a second. Staff Sergeant Moses had turned up without one. She'd accepted his apology, so offered to be it.'

'She introduced Moses to Colonel Abbasi in a pub, right?'

he asked. 'Moses had questions, needed pointers in what, how to duel?'

'He told her he'd only ever been in one other duel, and he'd been caught in the arm. Hurt like buggery, he said, and he didn't even touch the other fellow. They had all the gear on, stab vests and masks, with the arms and legs exposed.'

'Did you use stab vests?' Anjli asked. Devin shook his head.

'Not in honour duels,' he said. 'In those, you have full authenticity. Henry and Falconer even used silver bullets.'

'Made from what?'

Devin stayed silent once more. Declan considered this, making a horrifying revelation from it.

'Melted down Nazi medals?' he asked.

Devin nodded.

'Yeah,' he said. 'And he set the gun I used with them, too. I used dad's gun, and Falconer's silver bullets were bigger in calibre, so he forged me some special ones to fit the Colt Navy.'

'Well that's massively screwed up,' Anjli whispered, realising that the medal she found wasn't a keepsake; it was an ammo repository. 'What happened?'

Declan remembered what Doctor Marcos had only just realised; Edward Moses had been struck with a .36, not a .44 ball.

'Tell me how you shot him,' he whispered, his voice cold and emotionless.

'We duelled,' Devin replied honestly. 'It was all legitimate, or at least as much as you could with this. I caught him in the shoulder, he aimed away and shot into the ceiling. The whole Alexander Hamilton *aim at the sky* thing. It was like he *wanted* to be shot, like he thought he deserved it.'

'And what happened after that?' Declan stood now, the chair clattering away. 'Because at some point after that duel, Eddie Moses ended up *in a body bag in a cave!*'

'I know,' Devin whispered. 'But I wasn't part of that.'

'Yeah? Then who was?' Declan asked.

Devin told him.

20

MUSICAL CHAIRS

Declan walked back into the briefing room, Devin and Anjli walking out behind him. The others had all waited, almost as if they'd expected the whole investigation to change after this.

'I need to go,' Devin looked at his watch. 'They'll guess something's up if I stay around here.'

'You need to be arrested,' Monroe snapped from his desk.

'No, he's right,' Declan replied. 'He's helped on a few things, and we need to speak to his sister before we go any further.'

A grateful Devin Harper nodded to Declan as he almost ran from the office. Declan didn't envy him; there was every chance that by speaking to the police, he'd placed himself in the same crosshairs as Colin Delaney, whose only crime was that he spoke to Declan in a hospital ward.

Another one for the list.

'Let's go speak to the Williams crew,' Declan said. 'I need to stretch my legs.'

The legs, however, buckled as Declan slammed into a chair beside him, his head suddenly screaming with pain.

'You need to lie down,' Anjli muttered as she helped Declan back up. 'You're no good to me like this. *Us*. You're no good to *us* like this.'

Declan was so in pain, he didn't even mock her for the line.

'I just need a moment,' Declan smiled as he looked up at Billy, currently pacing in the room. 'Are you moving, or is my equilibrium screwed?'

'Sorry,' Billy stopped walking, instead grabbing a chair and sitting opposite Declan, 'I think I have something for you. I'm in the guesthouse, see? And I have the same room as Eddie Moses. Last night, I had a look around. There's one exit, out the front, or you can leave through the back, via the kitchen. However, if Staff Sergeant Moses wanted to escape the guesthouse, he'd need to find a different way.'

'Especially if Keith Williams was part of the gang,' Declan nodded gingerly. 'Go on.'

'The room's on the first floor, so looks out to the back garden, with the conservatory and coal shed below it,' Billy explained. 'The window is sealed up, but it looks like it used to open. I reckon Moses opened the window, climbed onto the coal shed and clambered down from there. After that, he's in the back garden and there are a dozen different ways to escape.'

'Or be taken,' Monroe considered. 'If he was running, he'd go for Owen out front.'

'We need to know who the unknown phone numbers are,' Declan leaned back, staring up at the ceiling as he willed his body to relax. 'And find Colonel Yates. I think there's a conversation we need to have too.'

'I found something else,' Billy rose and walked to the desk his laptop was still on, tapping a key to wake up the screen. 'You said Owen was following in Susan Jenkins's footsteps? It was literally that, it seems. He had all her notes; he'd scanned them and was working from them. When Patrick Harper met with her and then slit her throat, she was investigating the then-decommissioned Cardigan Regiment and alleged connections to Syrian Intelligence and the SSNP, but hadn't got any further. At the time, Owen's primary source on this was Ramesh.'

He looked back up at Declan.

'Who we now know was their old commanding officer, a man with Syrian ancestry, and possibly a member of the SSNP, giving him a reason to divert the story onto others, in particular Falconer, who was in Aleppo during the Syrian Civil War.'

Declan thought back to when Old Ram had left the Visitor Centre the previous day.

'He walked out the moment Owen turned up,' he said, realising. 'We thought he'd done this to allow Owen to talk, but what if he was finding a way to shut him up? Guv? Let's go find that son of a bitch.'

'Are you sure you're up to it, laddie?' Monroe was worried.

'Yeah, I'm feeling better already,' Declan lied, but then a thought stopped him.

'How did they know you were outside?' he asked Anjli.

'How do you mean?' Anjli looked perplexed at this.

'The two on the moped who came down the street,' Declan insisted. 'How long were you outside for before they arrived?'

'A matter of minutes,' Anjli thought back to the moment. 'I went out, took a breath—'

'Why?' Davey asked, mainly out of professional curiosity.

'Because I was stressed,' Anjli replied, looking at her. 'Declan was in the hospital, we weren't getting anywhere... Anyway, I went to call Monroe, or text him at least, I can't remember, and then the moped turned up. I remember gripping my phone because I thought it was moped thieves.'

'Castleton doesn't have moped thieves.'

'Considering that it seems to have dead duelling victims, Syrian spies and far-right extremists, that's not a saving grace,' Declan muttered. 'So what, maybe a minute? You can't tell me they were circling the pub, hoping you'd appear.'

'They don't,' Billy said. 'The footage the pub sent shows a half hour block. Fifteen minutes on either side, and the moped isn't visible for any of it.'

'So someone alerted them,' Declan nodded, instantly regretting it as more pain flashed through his head. 'Did the pub send the internal footage?'

'All of it.'

'Then show me the moment Anjli left the pub,' Declan waved at the laptop. 'Maybe we'll work something out.'

Billy nodded, tapping on the keys, bringing up a folder filled with video files. Picking four, he opened them up on the screen, one in each quarter.

'Here's the bar, the area we sat, the dining area and the door,' Billy said, scrolling through the feed. 'And here's where Anjli goes to make the call.'

On the bottom left screen, Anjli rose, flipping a finger at Billy as she went. Declan raised an eyebrow at this.

'Billy was being a dick,' Anjli explained, reddening.

'About what?' Declan asked.

Anjli wisely kept quiet as Billy paused the feeds.

'There,' he said, pointing at the screen on the top right.

'Bloke by the window on a date, picks up a phone and texts the moment she walks past.'

Declan leaned in, but it was Monroe who spoke first.

'Christ on a cross,' he whispered. 'That's Ramesh Abbasi.'

Declan stared at the bearded man on the screen; there was no doubt about it. Old Ram watched Anjli leave, typed a message on his phone and then watched out of the window. A moment later, people started looking at the door, and Billy and De'Geer rose to their feet.

'That's when the gunshot was heard,' Billy explained as, on the screen, all the members of the Last Chance Saloon ran for the door.

Old Ram and his date, however, simply sipped at his pint.

'The wee bastard's played us,' Monroe hissed. 'Who's the bird?'

'Betsy Darville,' Davey replied, nodding at her. 'I met her yesterday.'

'Why?' Anjli asked. Davey reddened at this.

'I asked her how her dog was,' she said. 'I knew Morten was worried.'

'Wait,' De'Geer rose from his seat. 'She's the Terrier's owner?'

'Okay, that's a major bloody coincidence,' Declan leaned back in the chair, fighting the oncoming headache. On the screen, as more people ran for the door, Old Ram could be seen finishing his drink, before rising and, with Mrs Darville beside him, leaving through the back entrance.

The bastards knew.

And Declan didn't know why he was even involved.

'Right,' he said. 'Find me Keith Williams and Ramesh Abbasi. Then—'

He sniffed, frowning.

'What's that musty smell?' he asked. Billy pointed at a couple of boxes under the table.

'Moses' things turned up today,' he said. 'They were supposed to pass them to Davey, but she wasn't there.'

'Snitch,' Davey replied. 'I looked through them, nothing major. Weird post-it note, nothing more.'

'Define weird?' Declan asked.

'The people in Portsmouth said it was a note about a postman delivering late, around 7pm, nothing more,' Davey said, opening the box up and pulling out a yellow, square post-it note. 'We just don't know what was delivered.'

Declan read the note.

POSTIE DELIVERING
1858 TODAY

'Christ,' he muttered. 'That's not what it says. Postie? That was Eddie's nickname for Yates.'

'1858,' Billy slapped his forehead. 'It's the bloody gun.'

'Yates delivering the Remington 1858 pistol today,' Declan intoned. 'He knew about the duel, and he provided the weapon—'

He waved to Billy.

'What was the last text Eddie sent again?'

Billy pulled it up on his screen,

'You bastard you set me up,' he read, looking back at Declan. 'I'm coming for you.'

'Yates did something to the gun,' Declan replied. 'And then made sure it couldn't be linked to the murder by getting Falconer to pick it up.'

'And Falconer would have known it was doctored, as he'd

have checked it as he picked it up,' Anjli muttered. 'Barry Oswald Yates. B-O-Y. They were his initials. And Keith Williams knew; that's why he believed his son when he claimed he didn't carve it himself.'

'But his wife didn't,' Billy shook his head. 'All she wanted was gossip, and she was the hub of the biggest secret going.'

'Why did Yates want Moses dead, though?' Monroe asked. 'I mean, Christ, laddie. I work with you and I'd want to kill you, but surely Moses was liked more?'

'Eddie was talking to a lot of people,' Declan remembered Maureen's words. 'He wasn't just here to duel. Maybe he was looking to close the Templar Corps as well? Maybe expose it?'

'That'd kill a lot of careers,' Monroe nodded. 'Enough to really hurt his life expectancy.'

'But why bring you here?' Anjli looked at Declan. 'Yates must have known you'd work it out?'

'He didn't realise I'd bring you all with me,' Declan thought back to the previous day when they'd all arrived. 'He was pretty furious you'd all turned up.'

'He wanted you here alone,' Monroe said, looking back at the tacked on printouts, walking over to them as he spoke. 'He knew you'd resigned, he thought you'd be without backup and easy to pick off, say, in a landslide or something.'

He pulled a printout off the whiteboard, showing it to the room.

DECLAN KNOWS

'He didn't know what you knew, but he was worried it could be enough to end him,' he said. 'What's better than bringing you in and removing you once you knew? Or, if you knew nothing, let you run out the clock, proving himself to be the good guy.'

'He didn't count on you surviving,' Anjli said. 'Although he needed your dead body as proof of accident.'

Declan pulled out his phone.

'Give me the number,' he hissed to Billy. 'The last one, the one where he says he's coming for them.'

Billy read out the number as Declan tapped it into his phone. After a couple of rings, someone answered it.

'Hello, Walsh,' Colonel Yates said through the speaker. 'How did you get this number?'

'You bastard,' Declan hissed. 'I'm gonna kill you.'

'I wouldn't be so sure,' Yates said, his voice relaxed, confident. 'Maybe you should speak to Carrie Harper first. Or is she missing?'

Declan looked up at the Last Chance Saloon, standing around him.

'Find her,' he mouthed. Anjli and De'Geer immediately left the room at speed.

'Take me off speaker, Corporal,' Yates said. 'And I'll know if you don't.'

Pressing the button to turn off audio, Declan held the phone to his ear.

'What have you done with Carrie Harper?' he asked.

'I haven't done anything,' Yates replied. 'Although she is somewhere dark and quiet with Colonel Abbasi right now. You remember being somewhere dark... and quiet... don't you?'

'Did you kill Eddie?' Declan hissed.

'Come on, with witnesses around you? Don't be silly,' Yates chuckled. 'I'm in the duelling range. I challenge you to a duel, Walsh. Traditional style. Alone. All of your little friends need to leave, or I shoot Carrie Harper. Or, I'll let the Colonel do it. He's great at headshots.'

'You think my team will stop hunting you?' Declan sneered.

'Oh, I know they will,' Yates said softly. 'Their authority here has been revoked. We've had some complaints of harassment. Keith Williams, Colin Delaney, Ramesh Abbasi, they've all said how your misfit toy box gang of friends has right royally torn up the town. Come on, Walsh, they had guns fired at them outside a family inn? Castleton's a tourist hub! Your people haven't made themselves welcome at all. And Whitehall doesn't like them either.'

Declan wanted to scream, to slam the phone down, but Yates continued.

'Brigadier Eaton-Jones wanted you gone, Walsh. The whole lot of you. Couldn't trust them to be loyal to the new Prime Minister, you see. But, if they piss off now, and you come here? We'll call it quits. Nobody will believe them, anyway. Keep to the clock, Corporal Walsh. You have until noon. That's a fitting time, wouldn't you say?'

'I don't know where you are!' Declan pleaded.

'Don't worry, I'll have someone pick you up,' Yates said.

The phone went dead, and Declan saw the time on his phone as the Lock Screen flashed up.

10:52am

'What's the plan, laddie?' Monroe asked.

'I don't know,' Declan replied. 'I haven't a bloody clue, but I have just over an hour to work one out.'

He was going to continue, to ask anyone if they had

another lead, or ideas on what could be done next, but there was a commotion outside and four armed soldiers from the Derbyshire Regiment stormed into the room, rifles at the ready.

'Get on the floor!' the lead soldier shouted, waving his rifle at them. 'Get down or we'll shoot!'

'What the hell?' Monroe complied, clambering to the floor. 'What's the crime?'

'Domestic terrorism,' Major Eaton-Jones said as he walked into the room. 'I know, I was shocked too. Who could have guessed?'

'So what, we're to be arrested?' Monroe replied angrily.

'Not at all, but Whitehall has revoked your remits to be here,' Eaton-Jones crouched beside Monroe, smiling. 'Well, theirs, that is. You came here with *him*.'

He nodded at Declan, and two soldiers pulled him to his feet.

'Head wound hurting?' he asked with mock concern. 'Don't worry. It won't for much longer. I'm here to take you to your duel.'

'Wait!' There was a scuffle outside the door, and Devin Harper pushed his way in. 'What's going on, sir?'

'None of your business,' Eaton-Jones replied.

'They took your sister,' Declan hissed. 'These are the people you stand beside.'

'Is this true?' Devin asked, shocked.

'She's safe,' Eaton-Jones shrugged. 'The Colonel has her.'

'And him?' Devin looked at Declan.

'Traditional duel,' Eaton-Jones was tiring of answering questions. 'So—'

'Who's his second?' Devin walked to Declan, standing

between him and the Major. 'If it's a trad duel, who's seconding him?'

'Now's not the—'

'I'll do it,' Devin replied, looking back at his commanding officer. 'I'll second Corporal Walsh.'

Henry Eaton-Jones went to argue this, but then stopped and smiled.

'Your funeral,' he said. 'Literally. Get them both out of here. The rest of you, keep these civilians safe until we decide what to do with them.'

And with Declan and Devin now held between them, the soldiers of the Derbyshire Regiment left the building.

———

As Declan was escorted to the Land Rovers waiting outside, Devin reluctantly led along beside him, they didn't notice Anjli and De'Geer watching from the shadows of the compound.

'Shite,' Anjli hissed. 'We were lucky there. What do we do?'

'Follow them?' De'Geer suggested.

'And how do we do that?' Anjli muttered. 'Billy's car keys and your bike keys are in the building, and I reckon the moment we go to get them, we'll be dumped with the others.'

'There is another way,' De'Geer smiled. 'I know where there's a discarded moped I can hot-wire.'

'Stellar idea, constable,' Anjli replied as slowly and silently they slipped back out of view.

———

21

HIGH NOON

'I LIKE WHAT YOU'VE DONE WITH THE PLACE,' DECLAN SAID AS he entered the basement of the Research and Development building. As he'd expected, the Land Rovers had been waved through, and as soon as they'd arrived at the doors to the building, Colonel Yates had walked out to meet them.

'Harper, surprised to see you here,' he said conversationally as the soldiers pulled Declan and Devin out of the back seats. 'Your sister is downstairs.'

'If you've hurt her, I'll kill you,' Devin hissed as they were led through the doors and into the building.

'Oh, she's fine. Catching up with old friends, in fact,' Yates said cryptically.

Declan hadn't been here before, but he'd read Anjli's report while driving back from the hospital, and he knew beneath him was a massive basement, built over a battered location of death, once upon a time.

'Must be really bringing back memories,' Yates said as they reached the stairs that led down. 'All those years ago, you and Eddie, making your way down here, oh, so carefully.'

'Were you part of this, then?' Declan asked. 'The murders?'

Yates didn't reply, opening the door for them to enter and following them as they walked down to the lower level.

'You know, Walsh, you always were a massive pain in the arse, but I respect you,' he said. 'If it wasn't for Eddie Moses mentioning you, I'd have left you well alone.'

He laughed.

'Christ, Declan, you wouldn't have realised!' he said. 'You weren't even aware he was dead all these months.'

He stopped, leaning in.

'In a way, your actions in Parliament helped, too,' he said. 'Although Baker would probably have been easier to deal with than Rose, we have enough on both of them. You would never beat us.'

'God, Barry, won't you ever shut up?' Declan sighed.

Yates backhanded him on the side of the head, sending Declan tumbling down the last four stairs, re-opening the wound in his temple.

'I'm *Colonel Yates,*' he hissed.

'Whatever, Bazza,' Declan smiled, wincing as he rose to his feet. 'Can we get this over with? It's almost noon, and I have a lunch date, arresting your arses.'

'Christ, you're a prick,' Yates moaned. 'I'd forgotten how happy I was the day you left for your life of married bliss. And how did that work out?'

'Not that great, thanks for asking,' Declan now walked out into the basement, seeing the three building length sections for the first time. 'How's your erectile dysfunction?'

Another backhand sent him tumbling again. Crouching on the floor, Declan retched, forcing himself to stand as the world continued spinning.

'Please stop that,' a familiar voice spoke, and Declan looked up, focusing on Old Ram as he walked over. This, however, wasn't the bearded man in the Barbour jacket he'd seen before; this was a man with a trimmed and neat beard, wearing the army uniform of a Colonel. 'I need Detective Inspector Walsh to not puke up his spleen before we shoot him.'

'Sorry, sir,' Yates said, standing at attention.

'Sorry, sir,' Declan mocked. 'God, Barry. When did you become so beta?'

'Please stop antagonising Colonel Yates, Declan,' Old Ram smiled. 'I'd hate to raise your threat level.'

'What happens if you do that?' Declan asked, curious.

'I break one of Carrie Harper's legs,' Old Ram replied, already turning and walking back to the long, shadowed duelling range. 'She has two, and we have time. I might even cut off a foot, so she's just like me.'

Declan swallowed and nodded.

'No need for that,' he said. 'I'll play nice.'

'Good man,' Old Ram said as he pulled out a chair, a folding metal one from the wide cages to the left. 'Now have a sit down and we'll get started.'

OUTSIDE THE COMPOUND, AND NOW CROUCHED BESIDE A MUD-splattered moped, Anjli and De'Geer watched the main entrance through the wire link fence.

'I don't think we're getting through there,' De'Geer muttered, his hand clenching and unclenching uncon-sciously.

'Luckily, there's another entrance,' Anjli whispered. 'Unfortunately, I'm not sure what the code is to get in.'

She looked around the path they were on; it was slightly above the compound and on the hillside to the east. It had been easier to push the moped up the rise than to ride it, especially as they didn't want the headlight—which seemed unable to turn off—to give them away, but at the same time they were staring directly into the noonday sun, which again could give up their exposed position at any moment.

'Damn, how did she get down there,' she muttered to herself. Doctor Cullen had to have known a route that got her back to the hatch into the basement, she'd literally guided Anjli and Monroe out of it the previous night. 'We should have kept her with us.'

'Kept who?' a voice said from the undergrowth to the side, and Anjli saw movement in the bushes as Doctor Cullen popped her head up, revealing herself. 'Sorry, saw loads of soldiers taking over the compound, thought they were after me, and I skedaddled. Did you say you actually wanted to go in?'

'Yeah, our Detective Inspector's in there,' Anjli replied. 'And Devin Harper, from the looks of things. We think his sister's in there too, as a hostage of Colonel Abbasi.'

'Old Ram's a Colonel?' Doctor Cullen mulled this over. 'Makes sense. And yeah, DS Harper's in there. But I think you might have the wrong idea of what's going on.'

She scrambled back into the bushes.

'Come on,' she said. 'I'll show you.'

Monroe sat on a chair in the briefing room and glared at the soldier currently staring at him.

'You a Private?' he asked.

'Gunner,' the young soldier replied.

'Almost met a Gunner this morning,' Monroe muttered, mainly to the room. 'He died last night.'

'Shame.'

'I don't think it was accidental, laddie,' Monroe continued. 'I think your lot killed him.'

'I think you're full of shit, old man,' one of the other soldiers, a Sergeant snapped. 'We don't kill our own.'

'Of course you do,' Doctor Marcos chuckled. 'You're Derbyshires, right? That's pretty much your motto. *We Kill Our Kin*.'

'Shut up!' the Sergeant snapped.

'Tell me, how much does Eaton-Jones tell you?' Monroe continued. 'I mean, did you dump the reporter in the cave, or was he there when you arrived? Did you drop the rock on his skull before or after you pretended to help?'

'Major Eaton-Jones is a valued officer!' the Sergeant snapped. 'He's a hero!'

'He's a goddamned killer,' Monroe snapped.

'Does he have an office here?' Doctor Marcos asked.

'Not in this building, but in the next,' the first soldier, the Gunner replied. 'Why?'

'Do me a favour,' Doctor Marcos smiled. 'We're stuck here until at least noon, so humour me. Go into his office and look for a dusty tobacco box with that logo on it.'

She pointed at the Templar Corps logo, pinned to the whiteboard. It was beside the one tattooed on the arm of Lena Khoury.

'What is that?' the Sergeant stared in horror at the image,

and Monroe assumed he hadn't seen the gruesome morgue side of the job before.

'That's one of your kin,' he said. 'Lena Khoury. Sheffield Bailey Barracks army reserve. Shot in the head by one of your superior officers, the bullet removed after death. And she's not the only one to die. Gunner Delaney died last night.'

'Bullshit.'

'I can check if you want,' Billy piped up now. 'I can show you the hospital ward CCTV. If nothing happens? Fine. If we see something though? You look for the box. Yeah?'

The Sergeant stared at his men, and Monroe could see he was wavering. This was a career soldier, realising his career could end rather quickly if he made the wrong choice.

'Go on then,' he muttered, lowering his rifle and walking to Billy. 'Just to prove you're wrong.'

Billy opened up a window on his laptop and started typing.

'I'd already asked for and been given access,' he said. 'The footage is here.'

It was a CCTV image of the entrance to the ward; it was well lit, and empty.

'Nothing's happening.'

'It's midnight,' Billy shrugged. 'What did you expect?'

There was a sudden flash of movement, and Billy stopped the feed.

'I was scrubbing through at twenty times speed,' he said, pressing the back button. 'Let's see what we missed.'

Another click, and Billy started the CCTV as the door opened and a man, hooded and sliding shiftily through the door, emerged into sight. He was making sure the nurses couldn't see him and keeping his head down to avoid the camera, but he was still pretty recognisable.

Old Ram.

Colonel Ramesh Abbasi.

'You know who that is,' Monroe rose now, walking to the Sergeant. 'And you know why he's there. To silence one of your own, just like he silenced Staff Sergeant Edward Moses of the RMP, among many others.'

The Sergeant stared at the image on the screen, watching Old Ram enter a side ward silently, closing the door behind him.

'Perkins, go check Eaton-Jones' office,' he ordered.' Look for a tobacco box, yeah?'

Monroe finally relaxed. There was a chance they could get out of this.

The problem was that Declan needed to do the same without their help.

———

'THIS IS THE PLAN,' RAMESH WALKED OVER TO DECLAN, PASSING him a holster and revolver. 'You're duelling today, but it's a game of fox hunt.'

'And what's that?' Declan asked, strapping the holster on and removing the gun, examining it carefully. It was as he expected; A Remington New Model Army 1858, with the carved initials B-O-Y on the base of the grip.

The gun Yates had given Edward Moses to use.

'You duel against three of us,' Eaton-Jones replied, examining his own gun. 'You take your shot, then we do. First death ends the game. Perhaps.'

'Sounds like a handicap match,' Declan said, walking over to Yates. 'What if I don't want to?'

'I don't think you have—' Yates started, pulling out his

own Remington 1858 revolver, but he was interrupted as Declan charged into him, slamming bodily into Yates' midsection, sending them both sprawling to the floor, the revolver slipping out of his hand as they tumbled across the concrete. Declan slammed a fist into Yate's jaw before clambering back up, picking up and placing his Remington back into the holster, jeering at Yates as he did so.

'That was for Eddie, you wanker,' he hissed.

'I get first shot,' Yates glowered at Declan as he wiped the blood from his busted lip.

'Screw that, I get first shot,' a female voice spoke now and Declan glanced around to see Carrie Harper walking out from one of the side rooms, her own revolver strapped to her thigh.

'You?' Declan asked, genuinely surprised by this.

'Damn right me,' Carrie replied, looking over at Devin, his mouth open. 'And what the hell are you doing, seconding this prick?'

'I thought you were in danger!' Devin shouted back. 'This was your plan?'

'You got to kill Moses, I get to kill Walsh,' Carrie pulled out the revolver. 'With dad's gun.'

'I didn't kill Moses, Carrie,' Devin pleaded. 'It was a wounding. Don't do this. He didn't shoot dad.'

'You as good as killed him,' Carrie wasn't being swayed by any of Devin's words right now, as she clicked the chambers around, locking the revolver into place, securing the percussion cap and sighting down the barrel. 'I just finished the job.'

'You killed Moses?' Declan paused, realising. 'You were the texts, the ones that said to wait for your signal.'

'Yeah, I guessed you had them,' Carrie looked at Declan, her face expressionless. 'Your DC called me last night.'

She looked at Eaton-Jones.

'Can we get this bloody well over with?' she growled. 'I need to sort my alibi out.'

Yates nodded to the other end of the basement.

'Walk down there, turn and stand,' he commanded.

'How far down there?' Declan asked as he looked down at the narrow space.

'Stop where you see the bloodstains,' Eaton-Jones smiled.

'So this is it? You three versus me?' Declan looked at Old Ram. 'Not you?'

'I've got no beef with you,' Old Ram shrugged. 'These three have, though.'

'Tell you what,' Yates said. 'You can have the first shot.'

Great, Declan thought to himself. *Even with one good shot, I still get two people shooting at me.*

Walking slowly down the range, Declan looked at Devin, walking beside him.

'Any words of wisdom?' he asked. Devin shook his head.

'I'm sorry,' he said. 'The gun they gave you is a dud.'

'What happened with Moses?' Declan glanced back as he spoke to Devin. 'You said he shot into the air.'

'He did, but his gun misfired,' Devin said. 'I caught him in the shoulder.'

'Misfired?'

'That's how I know it was tampered with,' Devin stopped, pointing to the ground. 'Bloodstains. Try to narrow your profile, face them side on. Less chance to hit a vital organ immediately.'

This advice given, Devin walked off, backing away to the cages beside the range.

Declan pulled the revolver out, turning the barrel, listening to it click, examining the percussion cap.

'Any time you're ready,' Yates smiled.

'I know what happened,' Declan looked up. 'I've worked it all out. Do you want to hear?'

'Not really,' Carrie replied honestly. 'Now shut the hell up and let us kill you.'

———

ANJLI HELD A HAND TO HER MOUTH AS SHE WATCHED DECLAN; they'd entered through the hatch, and now the three of them were in the very corner of the basement, watching the drama unfold.

'We need to stop it,' De'Geer whispered, only just audible to the women on either side of him.

'You'll die,' Doctor Cullen hissed. 'We need weapons.'

'Are there any here?' Anjli looked around; all she could see were torches and body armour. Which was good, as it meant she could protect herself.

At the same time, it was bad, as it meant Declan couldn't.

'No,' Doctor Cullen admitted. 'Shame, really.'

De'Geer had been staring at something to the side and, before anyone could stop him, he moved into the rear of the cage, pulling something from the wall. Sliding back to the front, he showed the flak jacket in his hands like a trophy.

It didn't look like the others; there was an LED display on the front that, when he touched it, lit up with a percentage value. And, on the end of a length of braided cordage, able to be strapped to a wrist, there was a glass lens.

'Robocop,' De'Geer smiled. 'It won't kill them, but we can at least blind someone.'

DECLAN STARED DOWN THE RANGE AT CARRIE, EATON-JONES and Yates.

'I get first shot?' he asked.

'Pinkie promise,' Yates smiled again, putting his revolver into his holster. 'Look, see? I'm not even going to try to shoot you.'

'What the hell are you doing?' Carrie snapped, but Eaton-Jones *shhh*ed her, placing a hand on her arm.

'Which of us are you going to shoot first?' he shouted out.

'Tough one,' Declan said, looking at each of his opponents. 'I think Carrie wants me dead most, but I can't kill her. I understand her anger. You're a prick, but you can't help genetics. But Barry there...'

Declan nodded to himself.

'I think I want to kill Barry,' he said, raising up the revolver.

He cocked the gun.

He pulled the trigger.

clack

Nothing happened.

The gun didn't fire. There was no smoke, no explosion, no bullet bursting out of the end; just a simple *clack* of metal hitting metal.

Declan hadn't thrown away his shot; the shot had simply not happened.

And it looked like Declan was now *screwed*.

'Good,' Carrie raised her revolver. 'My turn.'

22

THROW AWAY MY SHOT

DECLAN STARED AT THE REPLICA REMINGTON IN HIS HAND WITH what looked to be a mixture of shock and horror, as Carrie raised her own Colt, now aimed at him.

'Oh dear, you seem to have misfired,' Eaton-Jones said, looking over at Yates. 'Maybe he should have another shot?'

'Fine by me,' Yates leaned across and lowered Carrie's gun. 'Go on, Corporal, have another go.'

Carrie glared at Yates, annoyed at being stopped, but didn't go against him.

'No point,' Declan lowered his gun, sighing. 'You've fixed the gun, haven't you?'

'That wouldn't be sporting now, would it?' Eaton-Jones smiled. 'I do hope that wasn't what happened to your friend.'

'Bastards,' Declan laughed mournfully to himself. 'This is the same gun, isn't it?'

'There's a lot of New Model Army 1858s out there,' Yates shrugged. 'You'll never know.'

'Actually, I would,' Declan replied, looking over at his onetime superior officer. 'You see, when Eddie didn't come back to the guest house, Maureen Williams thought this was a cap gun. Let her kid play with it for a few days. Until someone arrived to pick it up, that is.'

He tapped the butt of the pistol.

'Right here, a little B-O-Y, carved into the handle. She thought it was scratched in by their son, but it wasn't, was it? It was your initials. And that's how you knew which gun was working, and which wasn't.'

Yates shifted his stance a little, and Declan knew this had thrown him.

'Just let me shoot the bastard,' Carrie growled.

'I get a last request, Carrie,' Declan snapped, looking back to his onetime commanding officer. 'After all, this is what gentlemen do, right? I'd at least like to confirm I got everything right.'

'You can't prove I gave that gun to Moses,' Yates replied, still staring at the Remington in Declan's hand.

'Eddie left a note. *Postie delivering 1858.* Portsmouth thought he meant he had a 7pm delivery, but I knew he meant you. *Postie* was our nickname for you, you see. You were giving him the gun to use; a gun that was set to fail. What was it, a blocked barrel? Must have really pissed you off, finding out that Eddie didn't die when he was supposed to.'

Yates pulled out his revolver, and Declan laughed loudly.

'Yeah, what I expected from an 'officer',' he spoke the last word as an insult, and Eaton-Jones raised his own arm, halting Yates from firing.

'Let's hear him out,' he said. 'He's right. We've got him dead to rights. The barrel's blocked, and he's got no way of surviving three of us. Give him his last words.'

'Go on then,' Yates muttered, turning away from Declan. 'Let's hear your amazing deduction.'

'It goes back to Patrick Harper,' Declan explained, looking at Carrie. 'Eddie didn't shoot your dad in self-defence, he shot him in anger. The rifle was fired by Harper as an automatic response. But that was the plan, wasn't it?'

The second part of the comment was now aimed at Old Ram, standing to the side.

'You're fishing, Walsh,' was all he replied.

'Not at all,' Declan shook his head. 'The *Duelling Club* was your idea, wasn't it? Back when you were a shiny Lieutenant Colonel in the *Cardigan Regiment,* back in 2000.'

He looked at Yates.

'You were a Captain in that Regiment before you joined the RMP, weren't you?'

Eaton-Jones and Yates glanced at each other, and Declan recognised the look.

Busted.

'You see, my boss in London learnt that the *Duelling Club* had been around for a while,' Declan looked down at the gun in his hand, feeling the weight. 'Pretty much since the 1908 Olympics. Apparently it was a favourite of officers in the Infantry, but only until the First World War came along. I suppose you didn't need to play at shooting when you had actual enemies to do it at.'

'It's a club, nothing more.'

'Ah, but that's where things go off the rail,' Declan smiled. 'You see, the wax duelling might have never become Olympic standard, but there was a strong inter-regimental mentality already there, and for years the Army, Navy and even what became the RAF had little contests, the equivalent of air-soft duels. And then the *Second* World War turned up, and it died off again. Until the Cardigan Regiment brought it back.'

Eaton-Jones looked at Old Ram for guidance. Old Ram simply shrugged.

'So?' he replied. 'That doesn't incriminate us. So we started a beloved tradition back up.'

'But you didn't,' Declan replied. 'You created a far more underground group than any other, with all of you and Henry's father at the top of the chain. I'm sure it was innocent to start with, but then the Iraq War hit. You found yourself in far more strenuous situations, so much though that shooting a little piece of wax became, well, tame.'

'Damn right it was tame,' Eaton-Jones snapped. 'We were facing life or death. A duel shouldn't be *sport*. We upped the ante.'

'You changed the guns to black powder firing ones, and added lead balls,' Declan nodded. 'But you changed that to silver for special duels. Why?'

'Because lead is for normal people,' Yates replied. 'Silver makes it *special*.'

'Well, it certainly was special,' Declan observed the three men as he continued. 'So special that you continued this, even after the Cardigan Regiment was disbanded in 2008 for war crimes.'

'Alleged,' Eaton-Jones snapped.

'True, they were never confirmed, but it still killed the regiment,' Declan accepted the comment. 'In fact, only three officers seemed to get out unscathed. Captain Eaton-Jones, Major Yates, and Major Falconer.'

There was a long moment of silence on the hill as Declan let that revelation sink in.

'Colonel Abbasi, by then, was long gone. In more than

just the name,' he continued. 'Were you a spook, or was it a rival power that used you for the next seven years? My money's on the Syrians.'

'You worked for the Syrians?' Devin looked at Old Ram before turning to Eaton-Jones. 'You let a foreign agent control our order?'

'It wasn't like that!' Old Ram snapped back. 'I lost a foot for my country, and they stuck me behind a desk! Syria understood my problem! My family came from Damascus! I met members of the Syrian Social Nationalist Party and they showed me the light! Showed me my path!'

'By destabilising the British Army,' Declan said icily. 'And the Derbyshire Regiment did everything they could to help you.'

He spat on the floor.

'Even when you killed Patrick Harper.'

'What?' Carrie's revolver lowered now as she looked around in confusion. 'What does he mean?'

'He's fishing,' Yates snapped. 'He's got nothing.'

'Maybe, maybe not,' Declan admitted. 'But Patrick Harper, poor, passionate Patrick, was always a pawn to be sacrificed, wasn't he? Never really *officer material.*'

There was a long, awkward, silent moment in the basement.

'I loved Paddy like a brother, but Christ, he was thick as a lump of wood,' Eaton-Jones eventually said. 'He was more a kind of doorman for us, making sure only the right people came in, and the wrong people were kept out.'

'By now, you were out of the picture,' Declan looked over at Yates. 'You'd moved to the SIB, and you were looking towards your own future. But Eaton-Jones there, he didn't know when to stop, and Old Ram, now recently returned from wherever he'd been—'

Declan stage-coughed, adding *Syria* into it, before continuing.

'—made sure the duels became more violent. Became games, like this *fox and hounds* bullshit you're playing now. And, more importantly, the body armour came off. You got shot in an 'honour' duel? You dealt with the injury. Or, the death.'

'We never had deaths,' Yates snapped.

'Bullshit,' Declan replied just as angrily. 'You just never admitted to them. And, as the club continued, you needed to find fresh blood, but not local stock. And so you brought in troops from the Territorial Army.'

'Army is army,' Old Ram sneered. 'We don't discriminate.'

'No, but you get really pissed off when you lose, don't you?' Declan said, his voice devoid of emotion. 'Staff Sergeant Lena Khoury, for example?'

'Khoury wasn't anything to do with this,' Yates argued. 'That was Harper—'

'Bloody hell, he never told you,' Declan was genuinely surprised by this. 'I assumed you knew. Lena Khoury was Sheffield bar staff, but she was also non-deployable TA infantry. The *Duelling Club* was the only way she could see action. She joined the Templar Corps, but she too was a follower of the SSNP. Had their symbol on her arm. We saw them in the autopsy photos.'

'Is this true?' Yates looked at Old Ram now. 'Why did you kill her?'

'Because she beat him in a duel,' Declan replied. 'Colin Delaney told me that. Was it you that killed him in his bed last night? Such a brave warrior.'

'Lebanese bitch cheated,' Old Ram hissed.

'Maybe, maybe not, but she recognised you too, right? Maybe met you at one of the super secret Syrian Fascist meetings? Being outed could really hurt your mission,' Declan snarled now, his hand unconsciously gripping the handle of the gun as he looked at Carrie. 'Your beloved Colonel there captured her, chained her into the underground shooting range he'd created down here and then shot her in the head.'

'It was a fair duel!' Old Ram exclaimed. 'She could have killed me too!'

'Not if she had a gun like this,' Declan waggled his Remington. 'Either way, she was dead. Things had gone too far. But before you could do anything, you learnt she had a friend who'd also been talking about this; Sandra Tyler. Suddenly, you were exposed, and you knew your Syrian masters wouldn't be happy. So, you did the same to her, leaving the bodies chained up in the hidden basement of the Quartermaster's Stores. And we all believed that Harper, the abusive, wife-beating maniac, had killed them. Just as we believed he'd killed Jo Tooley, Eddie Moses' girlfriend.'

He looked at Eaton-Jones.

'But he wasn't her only lover, was he, Major?'

Eaton-Jones stared furiously at Declan.

'No,' he eventually admitted. 'We were dating. I was using her mainly to see what Yates was doing. I didn't trust him, and I knew he was keeping tabs on me.'

'But it wasn't Yates who caused the problems, who caused Jo's death, was it?' Declan pressed.

'No,' Eaton-Jones repeated. 'I made a mistake. Pillow talk. I said how she didn't understand what it was like to take a life. Jo was an investigator. I forgot about that. She checked my records, saw I had no confirmed kills in actual combat. After that, she grew suspicious. I tried to aim her at Paddy, but by that point he was leaving Hamburg.'

'You tried to confuse the flights, didn't you?' Declan continued. Eaton-Jones nodded at Old Ram.

'I'd heard from the Colonel that there had been issues back at base,' he replied. 'I heard about the bodies from Harper when he returned there, and knew nobody would find them unless they really looked, but you and Moses were sniffing too close. So, I told Harper to make sure nobody found the bodies. But I meant get rid of them, not stand there like a bloody guard dog.'

'And Jo?'

'She confronted me,' Eaton-Jones looked at Yates now. 'You'd told her about me.'

'I may have suggested a direction for her to go,' Yates replied, shifting the grip on his gun as he turned to face Eaton-Jones. 'You gave her the ammo to fire.'

'That ammo killed her,' Declan said, regaining everyone's attention. 'Left her dead beside a Hamburg airstrip. This was something we couldn't work out, how Tooley and Jenkins could be killed by Harper at the same time, in different countries. You killed her, didn't you, Major?'

Carrie, confused, stared at Eaton-Jones.

'Dad didn't do it?' she whispered. 'You let people think he did?'

'I knew I had to fix this before anything else happened,' Eaton-Jones was almost pleading as he explained. 'I couldn't get back to Harper immediately, and the regiment was being used in an exercise. The plan was to get Tooley out of the way, come back and clean house.'

Declan shook his head. 'Poor Harper. All alone, doing his best.'

'He didn't do his best!' Yates screamed. 'He was an animal! He found Susan in the warehouse, and he killed her!'

'It's not murder when you put down a rabid dog,' Old Ram was strangely calm at this. Declan went to speak, recognising the line from a decade earlier, but stopped as Carrie now aimed her gun at the retired Colonel.

'All this time we thought dad was wired wrong, but all he was doing was following in your footsteps,' she hissed.

'He was killing random women,' Old Ram insisted.

'Susan Jenkins wasn't random,' Declan replied. 'She was a reporter following a lead, and right before she died, she was investigating a piece about Syrian Nationalists in the Territorial Army. Tell me, Ramesh, why did your loyal watchdog pick her in particular? Was it because you'd killed Lena and Sandra and she was about to find out? Was it because she was investigating your connection to Syrian agents? Did he know you were an *enemy spy?*'

Devin, moving from the cages, shook his head.

'You ordered my dad to murder?'

'I didn't need Harper to kill for me, I did it myself,' Old Ram snapped back. 'Yates was right. He was an animal. But he was useful. Jenkins was getting too close and had learned of Lena's connection to the Templar Corps. She'd become a threat, so I killed her. But then you bloody heroes turned up, so I had to sacrifice my pawn.'

'A pawn? That's all dad was to you?' Devin looked at Carrie. 'And you worship this man? I'm done with you.'

Carrie stared at Old Ram, conflicted.

'Why Malik?' she asked. 'She wasn't part of anything.'

'I honestly don't know,' Old Ram sighed. 'I didn't order that. Maybe Harper thought he was helping.'

'Jesus,' Yates muttered.

'You don't get to play the outraged victim here,' Declan turned his anger to Yates now. 'You covered the case up, agreed with Eddie Moses that it was self-defence—'

'I saved your career!'

'You saved your own!' Declan shouted now. 'You knew we'd look into Harper's connections, and the Cardigan Regiment would come up. The Duelling Club would appear. You sat down with Henry and Ramesh there and created the whole thing, making damn sure nobody else was blamed.'

'I spent years being bullied because of what you did,' Devin hissed. 'Years in therapy.'

'And look at you now,' Eaton-Jones mocked. 'Fine bloody example of a soldier.'

There was a long silence at this.

'As interesting as this all is,' Yates eventually cocked his pistol, aiming it back at Declan. 'I think it's time to put a stop to it.'

'I haven't explained about Eddie yet,' Declan smiled.

'There's nothing to say!' Yates spluttered. 'When you left, he lost his way! I brought him into the SIB, but he wasn't ready! His murder of Harper weighed on him until he ran away and died!'

'It wasn't as simple as that, though, was it?' Declan said darkly. 'He too learnt about the Duelling Club. He learnt about the Cardigans.'

'He was a bloody excellent investigator,' Yates sighed. 'He connected the dots when he met Falconer in Syria.'

'And then he comes to you,' Declan spat the words at Yates. 'Asks for you to help him gain an explosives licence.'

'He said he wanted to join the *Sealed Knot*.'

'And over the next year or so, he goes to some Duelling Club events,' Declan added, looking at Eaton-Jones now. 'Starts getting in close. He's on a revenge mission. You know why?'

'Because he knew I'd killed Jo?' Eaton-Jones muttered.

Declan smiled.

'Even better,' he said. 'Because Colonel Yates there *told* *him* you had.'

Suddenly Eaton-Jones and Yates were aiming their revolvers at each other.

'You wanker!' Eaton-Jones snapped. 'You threw your attack dog on me?'

'He needed closure!'

'You needed it, more like!'

'You were out of control! All of you!'

'Did he challenge you, or did you challenge him?' Declan asked, interrupting the argument for a moment.

'He arrived and challenged me,' Eaton-Jones replied. 'But Devin Harper had challenged him first. It was a blood feud, so took priority. I offered to duel afterwards, if he was still alive.'

'Carrie was his second, wasn't she?' Declan continued. 'She worked with him, showed him what to do. She didn't realise that Yates had already shown him.'

'I thought it was Eaton-Jones, not my brother at the start,' Carrie admitted. 'When I learned of the change, I put him in contact with the Colonel, hoping he'd be able to stop it. I had no issues with him by then.'

Declan shook his head.

'Old Ram didn't want to stop this. He wanted Moses dead. He knew Moses had been in Syria, and he didn't know if his cover was blown. And then you came along—' this last part was aimed at Yates, '—and offered your own gun. *This* gun.'

Yates nodded.

'I needed Eddie to lose to Devin, maybe get an injury, get the bloody closure he needed. I hoped he'd accept it, come home. And I thought Devin would bottle out.'

'But he didn't,' Declan replied, looking at Old Ram now. 'Eddie was shot in the shoulder by Devin, realised he'd been set up. Probably played dead while you argued on what to do with him, and snuck out before you could end him. Was it at the guest house where you confronted him, or after he left?'

'After he left,' Old Ram had given up on denial now. 'I confronted him. He knew all about me. I realised then he had to die. But in the arguments and confusion, he got out. Luckily the Castle Tun is owned by a member who alerted us he was back in his room. He texted for help—'

'He texted you for help,' Declan said, looking at Carrie.

'And I was going to offer it,' Carrie admitted. 'But by the time I got there, he was dead.'

'He was in a terrible state, Declan, the wound in the shoulder was bad,' Yates added. 'He just, well, died.'

'You want me to believe he ended just like that?' Declan's face reddened with anger.

'Believe what you want. It's the truth,' Eaton-Jones muttered. 'I was told by Keith Williams, called Yates, and told him what happened. He brought a body bag, and we hid the corpse in the cave.'

'But then bloody Falconer happened,' Yates fumed. 'Over the next year, he started getting cold feet. We learned from the Brigadier that Falconer was talking to Whitehall, about to whistle blow on everything. We were going to speak to him, convince him to stop. Eaton-Jones even went to the body, reopening it and swapping bullets, making it look like Falconer's bullet killed him—'

'Was that from a tobacco tin?' Declan asked.

'Yes,' Eaton-Jones admitted, nodding to a side room. 'Falconer had it in that room over there. After taking it, I snuck in, opened the bag, swapped them and left after leaving the tin under a stone, in case we needed to do more. We knew we could use this to shut Falconer up. But then the Colonel here went gung ho and melted his pacemaker, live on stage.'

'I didn't do it,' Old Ram moved into the light now, shaking his head. 'I thought you did it?'

Eaton-Jones, Yates and Old Ram glared at each other.

Declan started chuckling.

'Christ, what a bag of clowns you are,' he said, wincing as his head ached. 'Wanting to kill Falconer when it wasn't even him.'

'What?' Yates looked back at Declan.

'It was someone else, using Falconer's log in,' Declan was still laughing. 'They were the whistleblower. And Falconer was so paranoid you were about to off him, he pretty much did the job himself, wearing a massive electromagnet on his chest long enough to short his pacemaker out.'

There was a long, ominous silence.

'Crap,' Devin muttered from the side. 'He did it himself?'

'Bloody Cullen,' Carrie muttered. 'I knew she was trouble.'

'There,' Yates decided, raising the pistol at Declan again. 'Now you have everything, and yes, you were right. Well done. But you've got nothing to prove this, and I'm tired of listening to you.'

'Why did you bring me into the case?' Declan asked before Yates could pull the trigger.

'What?'

'You could have left me,' Declan replied. 'You could have carried on, I'd never have known. None of this would have happened.'

'I didn't know how deep you were involved,' Yates admitted.

'*Declan knows,*' Declan nodded. 'The message. You thought he'd spoken to me.'

'We did,' Yates nodded. 'I couldn't be sure how dangerous you were. Thought it was wise to bring you in. At best, we could lay the whole thing on Falconer. At worst—'

Before anyone could stop him, Yates fired his Remington replica at Declan.

Apart from a puff of smoke and a *clack of* sound, nothing happened.

'Misfire?' Declan smiled. 'Must be catching.'

'I don't get how—' Yates stared down at his pistol, examining it. 'I never—'

He stopped as he saw the faint *B-O-Y* etched on the butt. Etches that he himself had made years earlier.

'I swapped the guns when we scuffled,' Declan raised his own revolver back up now, aiming at Yates. 'I knew you'd given me a dud.'

'But it misfired,' Yates protested, confused.

'I took one of the percussion caps off, so it'd look that way,' Declan shrugged. 'Only one, though.'

And, with that, he pulled the trigger, and shot Colonel Yates with his own black powder pistol.

23

DOGFIGHT

As the bullet from Declan's pistol slammed into Colonel Yates' chest, spinning him around and sending him to the floor, Declan moved towards the closest office door to his left, firing blindly as Carrie Harper raised her pistol to fire—

And then screamed.

'I'm blind!' she cried out, clutching her eyes, falling to her knees, dropping the revolver. 'I can't see!'

'Drop your gun!' De'Geer now emerged from the cage at the back, Falconer's flak jacket on, arm outstretched like Iron Man. 'Or I'll melt your goddamn face off!'

'Bullshit!' Old Ram stepped forward. 'That's just his duelling jacket! The rifle isn't real! I've been trying to get it for ages!'

'For your Syrian buddies?' Anjli now moved out of the cage too, smiling as she approached. 'Yeah, we know. I also know you told the moped guys to come shoot me. I'm guessing it was Eaton-Jones and Keith in the leathers?'

'Maybe, maybe not,' Eaton-Jones smiled. I won't—'

He stopped as he saw the pinprick of light on his chest. Looking at Old Ram, he saw he had one too.

Lights that came from the cage.

'Falconer hadn't made the invisible laser gun, but he had prototypes,' Anjli explained. 'More visible and way more painful when they burn through skin. You can probably feel it heating right now. We have two of them trained on you. Gonna smell like a BBQ in about two minutes.'

Declan rose, gun aimed at Eaton-Jones.

'Drop it,' he said.

'Turn off the laser!' Eaton-Jones pleaded. 'I'll do anything!'

He dropped the revolver to the floor and Devin ran over, picking his Major's gun up, turning it onto him.

'You can turn the torches off now, Doctor Cullen,' Anjli smiled as, from the cages, and holding two thin penlight torches, Doctor Cullen emerged with a smile.

'You're bloody kidding me!' Eaton-Jones was beyond furious. 'I should—'

He didn't finish as Old Ram took this moment to dive forward, grabbing Carrie's discarded revolver and, blindly firing it at Declan, ran for the stairs, slamming bodily through the door.

'I'm after him!' De'Geer was already running for the door Old Ram had escaped through. Henry Eaton-Jones slumped, beaten.

'Yates needs medical help,' he muttered as beside him, the groaning Colonel clutched at his upper chest. Doctor Cullen walked over, examining him as Devin crouched beside his sister, checking on her.

Declan, however, moved toward Eaton-Jones.

'Why the badge?' he asked.

'What?'

'When you killed Jo Tooley, you took the badge from her beret,' he said. 'Also, you took Eddie's dog tag. Why?'

'Trophies,' Eaton-Jones admitted. 'I kept them in a box.'

Declan nodded.

'The box I found,' he said. 'Did you find it? When you dug me out?'

Eaton-Jones nodded.

'I didn't do that, though,' he said. 'Or kill Russell. That was the Colonel. He followed you. Threw in a grenade, but then Owen turned up; he'd been using you as bait, seeing who bit. Unfortunately, he caught a shark, and the Colonel smashed his head in with a rock. Threw the body into the rubble before we arrived.'

Declan winced as his headache grew.

'Colin Delaney?' he asked.

'Probably the Colonel too.'

'How much of this did your dad know?' Declan turned Eaton-Jones around as Anjli pulled out her handcuffs.

'My name is Henry Eaton-Jones,' Eaton-Jones smiled. 'My rank is Major.'

'Yeah, you can shut up,' Declan left the Major with Anjli as he now walked over to Carrie, being helped to her feet by Devin.

'I have to arrest you,' Declan said. Carrie looked blearily at him.

'I understand,' she said. 'But do me one thing.'

'What's that?'

'Exonerate my dad,' she said. 'I'll testify to what I heard.'

'I will,' Declan promised, looking back at Anjli. 'I should

check on De'Geer,' he said. 'He had a jacket on, but the bullets—'

'De'Geer's fine, trust me,' Anjli winked. 'The cavalry's arrived.'

———

OLD RAM SLAMMED OPEN THE FIRE EXIT ON THE SIDE OF THE building, panting with exhaustion as he looked around the open space. He was still within the compound, but it was a lot easier getting out than in. Once free, he'd need to find a car, get to a Syrian Embassy, claim asylum. From there, he could get to Aleppo, maybe—

'Ramesh! On the ground!' PC De'Geer, only twenty feet behind him, now burst out of the same door. Old Ram spun around, firing the gun, wincing as it echoed around the open space, De'Geer diving behind some pallets.

Shit. Now the soldiers will know something's up.

Old Ram tossed the gun aside; if they found him with it, he was even more screwed than before. That said, the Derbyshire were loyal; some of them would be Templar Corps. Even without Eaton-Jones there to order them, they would let him pass.

'Old Ram,' a familiar voice spoke loudly as Old Ram emerged into the car park, running for the gate. As he turned, he saw the uniforms of the Derbyshires, lined up, rifles aimed at him—

And, at the front, DCI Monroe, grinning like a bloody idiot.

'Or should I say Colonel Ramesh Abbasi of the Cardigan Regiment?' Monroe continued, walking towards him. 'Or whatever the bloody hell your rank is in Syrian Intelligence?'

Old Ram didn't reply to Monroe. Instead, he turned on the Sergeant standing beside him.

'Your Major told you to stand guard,' he hissed. 'Is this how you honour him?'

'My Major is a lying, racist bastard,' the Sergeant snapped back, tossing a metal tobacco tin to the floor. 'And you're a murdering spy. You killed one of our own last night.'

'Delaney? He was a bloody window cleaner!' Old Ram couldn't help himself. 'I did nothing more than shoot a lame horse!'

Monroe walked over to Old Ram, turning him around as he handcuffed him.

'Not too tight?' he asked.

'They're fine,' Old Ram hissed, already working through how to get out of this. He grimaced as Monroe tightened the cuffs a little more.

'How about now?' Monroe snarled into Old Ram's ear. 'You're bloody well buggered, mate.'

As Monroe walked off and soldiers of the Derbyshire Regiment walked up, Old Ram smiled. He knew he had loyal soldiers among them.

Whatever happened, he'd get out of this.

He just didn't know how.

———

MICHELLE ROSE WAS ABOUT TO HEAD TO PARLIAMENT WHEN her aide entered the office, obviously flustered.

'Charles Baker is here,' he said, wringing his hands. 'He has police officers with him.'

'What the hell?' Rose walked to the door, pulling it open, revealing a way-too-smug Charles Baker, standing beside

Chief Superintendent Bradbury, a handful of uniformed officers beside him.

'Ah, Michelle,' Charles nodded. 'Chief Superintendent Bradbury here is going to take you to Scotland Yard. We can do it through the front door, or we can make it a little more subtle.'

'Why exactly are we going there?' Michelle put on a false bravado as she spoke. 'I have duties I need to—'

'Your duties are cancelled, Mrs Rose,' Bradbury intoned ominously. 'We already have Brigadier Eaton-Jones in custody. We'd like to talk to you about a couple of things. Primarily, whether you were made aware that you were actively working with a Syrian agent on designing laser weapons forbidden by *Protocol IV* of the *Geneva Convention on Certain Conventional Weapons.*'

'This is insane!' Michelle Rose protested. 'I'm the Prime Minister!'

'Yes, you are,' Charles Baker looked at his watch. 'A Prime Minister who knowingly sent a police unit into a terrorist cell of far-right soldiers, placing them in danger while trying to cover her own back, at the same time ordering the murder of the whistleblower who could bring her down.'

He looked up at her.

'So, I'm thinking you're Prime Minister for about another half an hour. That should be long enough to write a superb resignation letter, right?'

DECLAN WALKED OUT OF THE COMPOUND BUILDING, ANJLI supporting him as they found Monroe and the Derbyshire Regiment placing Carrie Harper and Henry Eaton-Jones into separate Land Rovers. To the back of this, Declan could see Colonel Yates being placed into an ambulance.

'I hear you shot Yates and failed to kill him,' Monroe tutted. 'Thought you were a better shot than that.'

'I hit exactly where I intended to,' Declan smiled. 'The revolver pulled up a little, though. Where's Old Ram?'

'Military Intelligence,' Monroe nodded over at some black vans beside the entrance. 'Basically Section D on steroids. Billy called them in.'

'How did you get out?' Declan asked, confused. 'I get that Anjli and De'Geer were out of the building, but they had you dead to rights.'

'Not all soldiers are rotten apples,' Monroe shrugged. 'When they learnt their orders were corrupted, they freed us. And, once they found Eaton-Jones' box of trinkets, and realised he was killing their own, they happily offered to assist. I understand you solved the case?'

'We solved it,' Declan smiled as Doctor Marcos walked over, grabbing him, checking his bandage. 'I'm fine, honestly.'

'You're not taking credit,' Doctor Marcos kept examining. 'I think your head wound is worse than we thought.'

'Old Ram killed the girls, and Susan Jenkins,' Anjli added as Declan tried to pull from the Doctor. 'He admitted it. He also killed Owen Russell after trying to kill Declan.'

'Eddie Moses?'

'Apparently died from wounds gained in a duel with Devin,' Declan glanced over to the side where Devin Harper could be seen climbing into another Land Rover. 'Fell off a coal shed while trying to get to Carrie, smashed his sternum, couldn't breathe. They'll have to deal with that too. And Eaton-Jones killed Tooley.'

'Keith Williams has been picked up,' Monroe added.

'Davey found his prints on the bike you left up there. Looks like Maureen will be the subject of gossip for a change.'

'Don't be too harsh on her,' Declan replied. 'Her mention of the initials saved my life.'

Monroe chuckled at this. 'Finally, at Bullman's insistence, Bradbury is picking up Brigadier Eaton-Jones and Michelle Rose.'

'I bet Charles Baker is over the moon,' Declan sighed. 'He'll be bloody insufferable now.'

'I believe he was there as it happened,' Doctor Marcos stepped back. 'We need to get you into a hospital. You need to be properly examined.'

'Can we do it in London?' Declan half-pleaded. 'I really want to get out of here.'

'I'll drive him home,' Anjli offered to Doctor Marcos. 'Once we fill out our statements.'

'What about Cullen?' Declan nodded over at Doctor Cullen, alone in the car park, hugging herself while people passed her without a second glance.

'I think she'll be okay,' Monroe said, nodding at her with a smile. 'She has friends in high places. Possibly even higher right now than they were yesterday.'

Monroe patted Declan on the shoulder.

'Give your statements, get some food in you and go find a bloody hospital to get yourself looked at.'

'Orders, sir?' Anjli grinned. 'I thought you were suspended?'

Monroe shook his head.

'Not any more, lassie, I'm squeaky clean again,' he said. 'The deal Bullman made was once we located the rifle and identified the killer, all current investigations were dropped and removed from my permanent record. We did both, technically anyway, and therefore Bullman got it signed off by Bradbury before he went to Whitehall to arrest her.'

'I'm happy for you, sir,' Declan smiled.

'Are you?' Monroe frowned, leaning in. 'Because I'd be bloody worried. I wasn't around to tell you your resignation wasn't accepted before, but I am now, and as your superior, your resignation isn't bloody accepted.'

'Bullman already put it through,' Declan replied.

'It got lost,' Monroe smiled. 'Chief Superintendent Bradbury couldn't find it either.'

He motioned to Anjli, and she wisely moved away. Now alone, Monroe looked back at Declan.

'Do you remember what I said when I first invited you to Temple Inn?' he asked.

'Something about misfit toys?'

'If I could clap you around the skull, I would,' Monroe replied. 'I told you that sometimes, just sometimes, there are detectives of a higher calibre out there. Ones that are vital, useful even, the future of the police force, and to lose them would be a disgrace. To lose you would be a disgrace, Declan.'

He stepped back, nodding to himself.

'You can leave if you want to. But know you're the only person who thinks you failed. Go home, get rest. And then if you decide you do want a last chance at being a copper, come to Temple Inn when you're ready.'

'Not tomorrow at 9am?' Declan laughed, remembering the first time Monroe had said this.

'Christ, no,' Monroe shook his head, mock horror on his face. 'You're a mess, laddie. You look like shite. Worse than the day you joined. Go sort yourself out. We'll wait.'

And with that, Monroe walked off.

Anjli, having kept to the side, walked back.

'He's right, but it's your choice,' she said. 'We'll accept whatever you decide.'

Declan stared at Anjli.

'I thought I was dead, down there,' he muttered.

'Don't be silly,' Anjli lightly punched his arm. 'I was there.'

'Yes, you were,' Declan replied awkwardly. 'Look, I know things have been strange between us lately. I think we need to talk.'

'Yes,' Anjli reddened slightly. 'We need to write statements, and when we're done—'

'Screw statements,' Declan said, moving in and kissing Anjli lightly on the lips before she could reply.

After a moment, they parted.

'Sorry,' Declan muttered, embarrassed. 'That was inappropriate.'

'Damn right,' Anjli replied, flustered. 'You should have let me kiss you.'

Declan laughed at this, but winced as his head throbbed.

'You're concussed,' Anjli said, concerned. 'We need to get that looked at.'

'Probably,' Declan replied. 'Actually, I'm serious. We really should get to a hospital.'

'Can you do me a favour, though?' Anjli asked, sliding her hand into Declan's, grasping it, holding it tight.

'Of course,' Declan looked at the hand, confused why Anjli's hand was there. 'Anything.'

'Don't tell Billy we kissed,' Anjli smiled. 'He'll be insufferable.'

And, the kiss forgotten for a moment, Declan and Anjli

went to find the others in the Last Chance Saloon, and fill out some paperwork.

Declan knew right then he wasn't going to resign. He had too much to do.

And the Last Chance Saloon, beside Anjli Kapoor, was where he wanted to do it.

EPILOGUE

'I'm sorry I wasn't there for you.'

Declan stood in front of the small, unassuming grave-stone that had been placed within the boundaries of Aldershot Military Cemetery; behind him were chestnut trees placed as a small wooded grove, and along the path to his right was the Chapel, but here, at the base of a relaxed slope filled with military graves, was the final resting place of Staff Sergeant Edward Moses.

Declan hadn't been here for the funeral; Eddie had been buried quietly, with a minimum of fuss, and by the time Declan managed to find the right person to speak to about it, the burial had already occurred.

Declan looked around the graveyard as he fought to find something poignant to say. He'd expected to be doing this in Portsmouth, where Eddie had been stationed for much of his life, but he understood why the choice had been made.

He just hoped that someone would visit Eddie once in a while.

There was a rustle from behind him and, from the small

woodland to the side, Jess and Anjli appeared, keeping their distance but both nodding encouragingly at him. Declan had been happy to do this alone, but Jess wanted to tag along, and somehow, during the planning of the trip, Anjli was convinced to join them. They were talking, softly, so as not to distract Declan, and he smiled to himself as he looked away.

Jess knew about me and Anjli before we even did, he thought to himself.

Looking back to the gravestone, he composed himself.

'I avenged you,' he breathed softly, almost embarrassed to be seen talking to a block of stone. 'I found out who killed you. Christ, Eddie, you should have come to me with this. I could have helped you...'

He trailed off, realising he was starting to berate a gravestone now.

'Harper hadn't killed the women,' he said. 'But you probably know that. And I'm sorry you went to your grave likely realising you killed the wrong man, as I'm sure they told you at the end. But Henry Eaton-Jones is facing serious time, as is Carrie Harper. Devin has already plea-bargained, and he's telling the court everything.'

He sniffed, looking up at the sky.

'Falconer killed himself too, bloody idiot,' he muttered. 'And Yates is in a military hospital, about to have a whole ton of shit land on his head, and a shoulder wound that can predict bad weather.'

There was a crunch of gravel, and Declan glanced around to see Anjli and Jess walking over.

'Sorry,' Anjli said, reddening. 'We were trying to be quiet.'

'It's okay,' Declan smiled, looking upwards, at the clear July sky. 'He's not here, anyway. He never liked graveyards.'

'Any news about the Colonel?' Jess, annoyed she hadn't

been part of the case was still trying to glean information on it; she'd been constantly questioning her dad since he picked her up earlier that day.

'No,' he shook his head as, after one last nod to the gravestone he turned, walking over to them. 'Same as before. An hour after he was arrested, some men in suits arrived and took him away without a word being spoken. I talked to Trix, and although she said it wasn't Section D, it was likely one of Whitehall's covert agencies, looking to bring him in as an asset, perhaps against the Syrians.'

'He'll get a pass, won't he?' Anjli muttered as they started to walk back to the car, parked beside the Chapel. 'He'll get some kind of deal.'

'I don't know,' Declan shrugged. 'I got the impression that being a spy was one thing, but we still have several murders, including that of serving soldiers, to add. He'll not be getting his freedom any time soon. None of them will.'

The *none of them* was a nod to the others involved; Keith Williams had been picked up the same day, and was already giving a list of Templar Corps members throughout the British Military. And Brigadier Eaton-Jones had been swiftly removed, pretty much at the same time Charles Baker had quietly yet forcefully suggested to Michelle Rose she step down from her position.

Everyone involved in this was getting their just desserts, one way or another.

'So, are you still leaving the force?' Jess asked. 'I don't mind if you feel you have to, Bullman's already said she'd make sure I—'

'My boss is poaching you?' Declan raised his eyebrows as he growled in parental jealousy. 'Well, that's brilliant. And no,

I'm not leaving. Monroe would hunt me down if I did, anyway.'

'And this?' Jess grinned as she nodded her head, bobbing between Declan and Anjli.

'Slow at first,' Anjli said, her expression unreadable. 'We don't acknowledge anything at work, keep that purely professional, and at home, well—'

'We're keeping it slow,' Declan interrupted, bringing the subject to a close. 'Baby steps and all that. There's a lot of complications.'

'Like what?' Jess frowned.

'Like you, for a start,' Anjli deadpanned. 'I don't know how long I should give it before I start demanding you call me mum.'

'But I want gossip!' Jess whined. 'Come on, it's been two weeks already!'

'How are you and Prisha doing?' Declan replied with an impish grin. 'Been on a date yet? She seems a nice girl. How—'

'*Dad!*' Jess indignantly exclaimed. '*Boundaries!* You said you wouldn't pry—'

She stopped, as her brain caught up with her mouth.

'Boundaries,' she continued, smiling. 'Gotcha.'

Declan clicked the central-locking to the Audi, allowing Jess to clamber into the back as he hung behind, looking at Anjli.

'If we are going too fast, I can slow down,' he said.

'Do *you* think we're going to fast?' Anjli asked, raising an eyebrow.

'I'm not sure,' Declan replied honestly. 'I'm not the best at—'

Before he could continue, Anjli punched him on the shoulder.

'Well then you're a rubbish detective and I don't understand why Monroe keeps you on,' she said. 'I think it's probably just sympathy because a building fell on you.'

'It was a cave,' Declan muttered as he climbed into the driver's seat. 'Not the same.'

'Cavemen might dispute that,' Anjli said all-knowingly. 'And shame on you. Disparaging their homes like that.'

And, with the conversation on the correct architectural definition of the word *cave* continuing at length within, the Audi reversed out of its parking space and left the cemetery, including its military ghosts, to rest in peace once more.

DI Walsh and the team of the *Last Chance Saloon* will return in their next thriller

HEAVY IS THE CROWN

Released 24th April 2022

Order Now at Amazon:

http://mybook.to/heavyisthecrown

ACKNOWLEDGEMENTS

When you write a series of books, you find that there are a ton of people out there who help you, sometimes without even realising, and so I wanted to do a little acknowledgement to some of them.

There are people I need to thank, and they know who they are. People like Andy Briggs and Barry Hutchinson, who patiently gave advice back in 2020, the people on various Facebook groups who encouraged me, the designers who gave advice on cover design and on book formatting all the way to my friends and family, who saw what I was doing not as mad folly, but as something good, including my brother Chris Lee, who I truly believe could make a fortune as a post-retirement copy editor, if not a solid writing career of his own, and Jacqueline Beard MBE, who has copyedited all ten books so far (including the prequel), line by line for me, and deserves *way more* than our agreed fee.

Also, I couldn't have done this without my growing army of ARC readers who not only show me where I falter, but also raise awareness of me in the social media world, ensuring that other people learn of my books, including (but not limited to) Maureen Webb, Edwina Townsend and Maryam Paulsen.

But mainly, I tip my hat and thank you. *The reader*. Who, five books ago took a chance on an unknown author in a pile of

Kindle books, and thought you'd give them a go, and who has carried on this far with them.

I write Declan Walsh for you. He (and his team) solves crimes for you. And with luck, he'll keep on solving them for a very long time.

Jack Gatland / Tony Lee,
   London, January 2022

ABOUT THE AUTHOR

Jack Gatland is the pen name of *#1 New York Times Bestselling Author* Tony Lee, who has been writing in all media for thirty-five years, including comics, graphic novels, middle grade books, audio drama, TV and film for *DC Comics, Marvel, BBC, ITV, Random House, Penguin USA, Hachette* and a ton of other publishers and broadcasters.

These have included licenses such as *Doctor Who, Spider Man, X-Men, Star Trek, Battlestar Galactica, MacGyver,* BBC's *Doctors, Wallace and Gromit* and *Shrek*, as well as work created with musicians such as *Ozzy Osbourne, Joe Satriani* and *Megadeth.*

As Tony, he's toured the world talking to reluctant readers with his 'Change The Channel' school tours, and lectures on screenwriting and comic scripting for *Raindance* in London.

An introvert West Londoner by heart, he lives with his wife Tracy and dog Fosco, just outside London.

Locations / Items In The Book

The locations and items I use in my books are real, if altered slightly for dramatic intent. Here's some more information about a few of them...

The Derbyshire Regiment doesn't exist, and is in fact a Regiment used in the BBC TV show *Red Cap* in the 2000s. In addition the **Cardigan Regiment** was a military Regiment used in HG Wells' *The War Of The Worlds*, where they received a less than dignified end at the hand of the Martians.

Castleton is real, and is a thriving tourist village in the Peak District, under the watchful eyes of both Peveril Castle and Mam Tor, locally known as the 'Shivering Mountain'. The village was featured in episode 3 of *Most Haunted: Midsummer Murders* where the team "investigates" the 18th-century murder of an engaged couple. It also featured in national news reports in the early 1980s following the murder of Susan Renhard near the battlements of Peveril Castle.

There isn't a *real* military base anywhere near it, however; I needed a fictional location, and a particular series of locations which this fitted.

The Remington 1858 New Model Army is a real gun, and was integral in the US Civil War. It was also the gun used by 'Buffalo Bill' Cody in the 1860s. In June 2012, the pistol came up for sale at auction and sold for a reported sum of $239,000.

Olympic Pistol Duelling actually did happen, in a way. *Duelling Pistols* was a short-lived sport at the start of the 20th century, in which two heavily protected competitors faced off and shot wax bullets at each other. It is often stated that this was part of the Olympic Games in 1908, however, it wasn't even an official demonstration sport. The duelling competition was instead held at a similar time to the Olympics in 1908 by enthusiasts of the new sport, demonstrating the emerging French sport to the people of London.

However, at the 1906 unofficial Olympic Games two years earlier, there was another duelling pistol event, though in this format the shots were fired at plaster dummies dressed in frock coats from a distance of 20 or 30 metres.

The Duel After The Masquerade, or *Suite d'un bal masqué*, is a genuine painting, and is on display in the Musée Condé, in Chantilly, France. From Wikipedia:

The scene is set on a gray winter morning in the Bois de Boulogne, trees bare and snow covering the ground. A man dressed as a Pierrot has been mortally wounded in a duel and has collapsed into the arms of a Duc de Guise. A surgeon, dressed as a doge of Venice, tries to stop the flow of blood, while a Domino clutches his own head.

The survivor of the duel, dressed as an American Indian, walks away with his second, Harlequin, leaving behind his weapon and some feathers of his headdress, towards his carriage, shown waiting in the background.

It was characteristic of Gérôme to depict not a violent event itself, but the aftermath of such violence. The bizarreness of the scene in regard to the brightly coloured costumes turns to pathos at the sight of blood on the Pierrot.

Finally St Davids is a real city; it's the smallest city in the UK in fact, as it's a small town / village on the edge of the Pembrokeshire peninsular, and given city statement as, by being the birthplace of the Patron Saint of Wales, St David, it has a cathedral.

It also has amazing surfing at Whitesands bay; I learned to surf there twenty years ago!

If you're interested in seeing what the *real* locations look like, I post 'behind the scenes' location images on my Instagram feed. This will continue through all the books, and I suggest you follow it.

In fact, feel free to follow me on all my social media by clicking on the links below. Over time these can be places where we can engage, discuss Declan and put the world to rights.

www.jackgatland.com
www.hoodemanmedia.com

Subscribe to my Readers List: **www.subscribepage.com/ jackgatland**

www.facebook.com/jackgatlandbooks

www.twitter.com/jackgatlandbook
ww.instagram.com/jackgatland

Want more books by Jack Gatland? Turn the page...

THE THEFT OF A **PRICELESS** PAINTING...
A GANGSTER WITH A **CRIPPLING DEBT**...
A **BODY COUNT** RISING BY THE HOUR...

AND ELLIE RECKLESS IS CAUGHT IN THE MIDDLE.

JACK GATLAND

PAINT
— THE —
DEAD

A 'COP FOR CRIMINALS' ELLIE RECKLESS NOVEL

A NEW PROCEDURAL CRIME SERIES WITH
A TWIST - FROM THE CREATOR OF THE
BESTSELLING 'DI DECLAN WALSH' SERIES

AVAILABLE ON AMAZON / KINDLE UNLIMITED

EIGHT PEOPLE. EIGHT SECRETS.
ONE SNIPER.

THE
B⊕ARD
ROOM

HOW FAR WOULD YOU GO TO GAIN JUSTICE?

NEW YORK TIMES #1 BESTSELLER TONY LEE WRITING AS

JACK GATLAND

A NEW STANDALONE THRILLER WITH
A TWIST - FROM THE CREATOR OF THE
BESTSELLING 'DI DECLAN WALSH' SERIES

AVAILABLE ON AMAZON / KINDLE UNLIMITED

THEY TRIED TO KILL HIM...
NOW HE'S OUT FOR **REVENGE.**

NEW YORK TIMES #1 BESTSELLER **TONY LEE** WRITING AS

JACK GATLAND

THE MURDER OF AN **MI5 AGENT**...
A BURNED SPY **ON THE RUN** FROM HIS OWN PEOPLE...
AN ENEMY OUT TO **STOP HIM** AT ANY COST...
AND A **PRESIDENT** ABOUT TO BE **ASSASSINATED**...

SLEEPING SOLDIERS

A **TOM MARLOWE** THRILLER

BOOK 1 IN A NEW SERIES OF THRILLERS IN THE STYLE OF
JASON BOURNE, JOHN MILTON OR **BURN NOTICE,** AND
SPINNING OUT OF THE **DECLAN WALSH** SERIES OF BOOKS

AVAILABLE ON AMAZON / KINDLE UNLIMITED

JACK GATLAND

THE
LIONHEART
CURSE

HUNT THE GREATEST TREASURES
PAY THE GREATEST PRICE

BOOK 1 IN A NEW SERIES OF ADVENTURES
IN THE STYLE OF 'THE DA VINCI CODE'
FROM THE CREATOR OF DECLAN WALSH

AVAILABLE ON AMAZON / KINDLEUNLIMITED

Printed in Great Britain
by Amazon